THE SHROUDED WALLS
AND
THE DARK SHORE

The
Shrouded Walls

—— AND ——

The Dark Shore

by SUSAN HOWATCH

STEIN AND DAY/*Publishers*/NEW YORK

The Shrouded Walls

One

W<small>E</small> <small>WERE SEVENTEEN</small> when our parents died. Alexander was away at school in Harrow and I had just begun my last term at Miss Shearing's Academy for Young Ladies in Cheltenham, so neither of us was at home. My father had had an extravagant turn at the Races, drunk too much whisky and then had insisted on taking the reins himself from the coachman and had driven full-tilt across Epsom Downs before misjudging the bend of the road as it sloped to Tattenham Corner. My mother, who was with him, died instantly and my father himself only lived for seven hours afterwards. The tragedy was the talk of society, for our father was a prominent member of Parliament, a gentleman with a country seat in Lancashire and a considerable fortune invested in the cotton mills of Manchester, while our mother was an emigrée from the bloodbaths of the French Revolution, a daughter of an aristocrat whom Robespierre had sent to the guillotine.

Alexander and I did not at first realize we were destitute. It was Sir Charles Stowell, a friend of my father's who finally told us that my father's fortune and estates, including even the town house in London where we had lived all our lives with our mother, had reverted to my father's wife in Manchester. My father had been much too gay and carefree to bother to make a will to provide for his mistress and the twins she had borne him. I could almost hear him saying: "Wills? That's a damned sordid topic of conversation! Who wants to think about death anyway?" And he would have gone on just as before, never once stopping to think that although he himself did not care what happened after his death, there were other people who cared a great deal.

I certainly cared. I cared all the way up to London from Miss Shearing's Academy in Cheltenham, at the inns where we changed horses and stopped to eat, on the rough roads muddy beneath the rain of an English October. I cared when I reached my home, the elegant town house in Soho which my father had bought for my mother's comfort and luxury but never given to her, I cared when I saw the servants whom he had installed to attend our needs, I cared when I saw all the thousand and one other things which now belonged to the middle-aged widow secure in her country home in Lancashire. And most of all I cared when I went to Lincoln's Inn with Alexander to see Sir Charles Stowell and sat in his chambers where the walls were lined with legal books, and the lawns in New Square beyond the window were flaked with autumn leaves.

"But who is to pay for my school fees at Harrow?" said Alexander blankly to Sir Charles. "I have another year's study to complete there."

"My dear sir," said Sir Charles, who was the smoothest, the most charming and the most realistic of barristers-at-law. "I'm afraid you won't be returning to Harrow."

Alexander still could not grasp the full implications of his predicament. "But I wanted to study at Oxford," he exclaimed hotly. There was a fractious edge to his voice now which I knew and recognized. He had begun to be frightened. "What's to happen to my education?"

"I sympathize," said Sir Charles blandly, "but may I—since we are being so frank with each other—be so discourteous as to remind you that you are fortunate to have received any education at all? Your situation, sir, could be infinitely worse. Fortunately your sister has completed five years at that admirable establishment for young ladies in Cheltenham and will be qualified to seek a position as a governess. As a long-standing friend of your father's I will of course exert what influence I possess to help her obtain employment, but I trust you realize, miss," he added to me, "that your social position is not one which a good family will lightly overlook. However, there are wealthy merchant families who are anxious to employ young females brought up in a ladylike environment, and I dare say something suitable can be arranged. As for you, sir, I can only recommend that you enlist in the army, for you are far too young to be considered as a tutor and you are certainly not qualified to pursue any profession."

"I don't want to enlist in the army," said Alexander. He was white-faced now, very frightened indeed. "I don't want to be a soldier."

Sir Charles looked as if he might say 'Beggars can't be choosers,' but fortunately thought better of it. Instead he gave a regretful little smile, waved his hand in a vague gesture of sympathy and refrained from comment.

"May I ask you a question, Sir Charles?" I said.

"Certainly." He turned his advocate's eyes instantly in my direction. They were very dark and lustrous, and I noticed how his glance seemed to linger on my mouth and the line of my nose before he allowed his eyes to meet mine.

I could almost hear my mother say with contempt: "Men are interested in one thing and one thing only where women such as you or I are concerned. And the more well-bred and righteous the man, the more interested he will be. Let no one fool you."

"How much money do we have now?" I asked him courteously. "This moment, I mean."

"Twenty-five pounds was discovered among your mother's effects; then her jewelry will belong to both of you, and her clothes, and sundry other articles which may be established as gifts from your father to your mother. The house, of course, belongs to Mrs. Cavendish and the responsibility of dismissing and paying the servants will be hers whenever she decides to sell it."

"So in fact we have a little money."

"Enough," agreed Sir Charles, "to keep you until you have found positions for yourselves. That's true."

"Thank you," I said. "And how soon must we leave the house?"

"Mrs. Cavendish has requested that you leave it as soon as possible. Her eldest son—your father's heir—Mr. Michael Cavendish is at present en route to London from Manchester to settle your father's business affairs here. I understand he is to organize the sale of your mother's house."

"I see." My father had talked to us of Michael. "Dull as his mother," he had said, "and twice as pompous." Richard had been his favorite. Richard was the second son. Then there were the four daughters, but they were all older than us as my parents had not met one another until after Mrs. Cavendish's last child had been born. It was strange to think of our half-brothers and half-sisters whom we had never met and even stranger to think of my father having another home in addition to the town house in Soho. He had always seemed to belong to us so completely that the very knowledge that we had always shared him seemed unreal and absurd. Only once had I caught a glimpse of the reality that my mother never forgot, and that was long ago when I was a child and had tip-toed from my bedroom to see them leave the house for an evening at Vauxhall. They had quarreled in the hall in front of the footman. I could still recall the poor footman, his ears pink with embarrassment, as he had stood stiffly by the front door and pretended not to hear my mother cry: "Does it never occur to you that I may be tired of going to Vauxhall and hear all the aristocratic gossipmongers of London society whisper: 'There goes Mark Cavendish with his blue-blooded French whore?' Does it never occur to you that I might be tired of being ostracized from the circles where I was once accepted and recognized? You—you with your knowledge of London society—is it so impossible for you to visualize how it is to be not just a woman of standing engaged in an indiscreet affair but a man's kept mistress who has borne him two illegitimate children?"

My mother was always bitter. She could remember too clearly her life in the huge French chateau on the Loire and her brilliant match to the young Duc de Fleury just before the revolution. The London of the turn of the century in which she had found herself widowed and penniless some years later was very different from the world of the *ancien regime* from which she had come. "Emigrés were two a penny," she had told us once, "and if one could not pay the rent the English didn't care how much land one's father had once owned in France. Titles meant nothing at all. Nothing mattered except money, and we were all penniless. How can children like you ever understand? I had never handled money in my life! I was accustomed to ease and riches and luxury, and suddenly I was in a garret in Bloomsbury carrying pitchers of water up six flights of stairs and haggling with the butcher for a cheap portion of beef."

She had started sewing to try to earn money. She had first met Mark Cavendish when she had been altering an evening gown for his wife. Within two weeks she had escaped from the garret in Bloomsbury, the six flights of stairs, the cheap portions of beef. Her one great fear was always losing everything a second time to sink back into the hideousness of poverty, and during the twenty years she spent as my father's mistress she never lost this dreaded feeling of insecurity.

"Anything is better than poverty," she told us again and again. "Anything."

Even being called Mark Cavendish's whore.

"I understand your father," she had said. "I've no illusions about him—or about any other man. I have a pleasant house, sufficient servants, good clothes and my children are well-cared for. Why should I indulge in complaints and regrets? Mark is generous, gay, good-humored and good-looking. What more can a woman expect of a man?"

Kindness, I might have said. Compassion, Understanding. But I said nothing. It was hardly for me to point out that my father was as hard as diamonds, a man who drank hard, gambled hard, rode hard and worked hard. Hard people seldom think of others, not because they deliberately wish to be selfish, but because they are incapable of visualizing anyone else's feelings but their own. My mother might deceive herself because she preferred not to face the truth but I saw all too clearly that for him she was too often a mere convenience, a diversion whom he could always turn to whenever he was tired of his political intrigues at Westminster, his racing at Epsom or his gambling circles in Mayfair.

I never liked him.

Curiously enough I was always the one to whom he seemed the most attached. "Of all my children," he told me once, "I do believe you're the one who's most like me."

Which, considering my opinion of him, I could hardly regard as a compliment.

"Well now, Miss Fleury," said the lawyer, bringing me back abruptly to that book-lined room in Lincoln's Inn with the green lawns outside in the square. "If there are any further ways in which I can assist you, please be so good as to let me know. If you wish for any references while seeking a position as a governess—"

"Thank you, Sir Charles," I said, "but I have no intention of being a governess." I rose to my feet, and the men rose too, Alexander moving the chair so that it would not catch my dress and then assisting me to don my pelisse. "I'm most indebted to you for all your trouble, Sir Charles," I added to him with my most charming smile. "You've been more than kind."

"My pleasure, Miss Fleury. Please remember that if you should want any further assistance I am always at your disposal." He smiled back into my eyes, making his meaning explicitly clear.

"Thank you," I said. "Good-day."

"Thank you, sir," muttered Alexander, and hurried to open the door for me.

I swept through without a backward glance and outside in the office beyond the little clerk leaped off his stool to open the door which led out into the square.

It was a beautiful day. The sky was blue and cloudless and a light breeze danced through the trees. My mother, who hated

English weather, would have said it reminded her of France and the gardens of the chateau on the Loire.

"Oh God," said Alexander desolately.

"Be quiet," I snapped. I was too close to tears myself to stand any nonsense from him. The hired chaise was still waiting at the gates of Lincoln's Inn and presently we were on our way home to Soho.

"What are you going to do?" said Alexander at last.

"I don't know." I stared out of the window at the crowded dirty streets, saw the beggars rattling their almsbowls and the prostitutes already soliciting in the alleys.

"I don't want to go into the army," said Alexander.

I did not answer.

"Perhaps Michael would help us. After all, he is our half-brother."

I looked at him. He blushed. "I—it was just an idea . . ."

"A very bad one." I went on looking out of the window. "And totally unrealistic."

Presently he said: "You won't have to worry. You'll soon get married, and your problems will be solved. But what about me? How am I to earn a living and support myself? I don't know what to do."

"I should like to know who is going to marry the illegitimate child of an English gentleman and a French emigrée without dowry, portion or social standing," I said acidly. "Please try to talk sense, Alexander, or else don't talk at all."

We traveled the rest of the way home in silence. Soon after we arrived it was time for dinner, and we ate our way wordlessly through the plates of fish, fowl, mutton and beef in the paneled dining room. Above the fireplace our father's portrait smiled down at us, the ironical twist to his mouth seeming a shade more pronounced than usual.

"Perhaps Michael will be here tomorrow," said Alexander.

I was silent.

"Perhaps he will be quite a pleasant fellow."

A clock chimed the hour and was still.

"Perhaps I shall ask him if he can help us."

"If you say perhaps once more, Alexander—" I began and then stopped as the footman came in.

"Yes, what is it, John?"

"There is a gentleman here to see you, miss. He gave me a letter for you and his card, and I showed him into the library."

I took both card and letter from the salver.

"Michael?" said Alexander at once.

"No, it's not Michael." I stared at the card. The name was unfamiliar to me. "I have never heard of this gentleman, John."

"Perhaps the letter, miss—"

"Nor am I in the habit of entertaining strangers known only to me through a letter of introduction."

"Let me see him," said Alexander, standing up. "I'll find out what he wants. Perhaps he's a creditor."

"Pardon, sir," said the footman scandalized, "but he was most definitely a gentleman."

"Nonetheless—"

"Wait," I said. I had opened the letter. The address was New Square, Lincoln's Inn, and the signature at the foot of the page belonged to the lawyer, Sir Charles Stowell. "My dear Miss Fleury," Sir Charles had written. "I hope you will forgive me for taking the liberty to introduce to you by means of this letter an esteemed client of mine, Mr. Axel Brandson. Mr. Brandson, though resident in Vienna, has visited this country many times and as well as being well known to me personally was also slightly acquainted with your father whom he had met during a prior visit to London. On hearing of your bereavement, Mr. Brandson expressed anxiety to offer his condolences and as I was mindful of your present unfortunate predicament it occurred to me that it might perhaps be beneficial if an opportunity could be arranged for him to meet you. I offered to act as intermediary in this respect but Mr. Brandson is hard-pressed by business commitments and it was impossible for us to arrange a suitable time at an early date. Hence I hope that this letter will serve as sufficient introduction to his social position and personal integrity. I remain, etc . . ."

I looked up. The footman was still waiting. "Kindly inform Mr. Brandson, John," I said, "that I will see him shortly, if he would be so kind as to wait a few minutes."

"Yes, miss," said the footman, and withdrew.

"Who is it?" said Alexander immediately.

I gave him the letter.

"But what does he want?" he said mystified when he had finished reading. "I don't understand."

But I was remembering the expression in Sir Charles' dark eyes and the knowledge he had of my predicament and background, and thought I understood all too well. I rose to my feet, trying not to be angry. Sir Charles probably intended well enough. After all I had told him directly I had no intention of being a governess and he had no doubt assumed this declaration to be capable of only one possible interpretation. What else could a woman in my position do if she refused to be a governess? She could only marry, and as no man of any standing would want me for a wife, even that course was denied me.

"Are you sure you should see him alone?" Alexander was saying alarmed. "I'd better come with you. The man's a foreigner, after all."

"So was Mama," I reminded him, "and most of her friends. No, I'll see him alone."

"But do you think it's proper?"

"Probably not, but I don't think that matters so much now." I went out into the hall. In spite of myself I was angry and my pride burned within me like a flame no matter how hard I tried to subdue it by the cool persuasiveness of reason. In a moment of rage I wished the devil would swallow up Mr. Brandson, and Sir Charles Stowell too. I was determined not to make the same mistakes my mother had made no matter how many London garrets I had to spend my days in.

I crossed the hall with swift firm steps, turned the handle of the library door and walked into the room with my head held high, my cheeks burning and my fists clenched as if for a fight.

"Miss Fleury?" said the man, turning abruptly to face me. "How do you do."

He was not as I had expected him to be. I had instinctively visualized a blond giant as soon as I had read of his nordic names, but this man was dark. He had smooth dark unpowdered hair, and dark eyes which were as opaque as Sir Charles Stowell's dark eyes were clear and expressive; whatever thoughts this man had he kept to himself. He was dressed sombrely but with good taste in a dark blue coat and plain well-cut breeches; his carefully folded white cravat was starched to perfection and his Hessian boots would have satisfied the highest standards of elegance. He gave no obvious indication of being a foreigner for his English was flawless, and yet I was at once aware of some cosmopolitan nuance in his manner which was difficult to define. When he took my hand and bowed I noticed that his fingers were long and slim and cool against my hot palm.

"Pray be seated," I said graciously, withdrawing my hand rather too quickly. "May I offer you a cordial or some other refreshment?"

"Thank you, but no." His voice was cool too, I noticed. The lack of accent somehow seemed to take all hint of passion from his tone.

We sat down by the fireplace, opposite one another, and I waited for him to begin a conversation.

Presently he said: "You may well be wondering who I am and why I have effected this introduction to see you. I must apologize for trespassing on your privacy at such a distressing time. It was kind of you to see me."

I made a small gesture of acknowledgement.

"Permit me to offer my condolences to you on your bereavement."

"Thank you."

There was a silence. He crossed one leg over the other and leaned back in his chair with his hands tightly clasped in front of him. The light slanted upwards across his cheekbones and into his opaque eyes. "I consider myself Austrian, as I have lived in Austria most of my life, but in fact I am half-English by descent. My father is—was—an Englishman. He died ten months ago."

I wondered if I should comment. Before I could make up my mind he said: "My mother returned to Austria shortly before I was born and died five years afterwards, leaving me both property and income in Vienna. I was more than content to stay there, although I was educated in England and later often came here on account of my business interests; occasionally I would travel down to Sussex to see my father. He remarried soon after my mother's death and had other sons by this time."

He paused. I contrived to look intelligent and attempted to give the impression I knew exactly what he was trying to say.

"My father was a rich man," he said. "He had estates on the Romney Marsh and his ancestors were prominent citizens of the Cinque Ports. I assumed that when he died he would leave his house (which was not entailed) and his wealth to his eldest son by his second marriage, but I was wrong. He willed everything to me. My commitments in Vienna made it impossible for me to come to England earlier, but I am here now for the purpose of visiting the estate and seeing my English relations."

"I see," I said.

"I rather doubt whether you do," he said ironically, "since I haven't yet explained why I have come to see you. However, I appreciate your interest in what to you must seem a very puzzling narrative." His hands were clasped so tightly together that the knuckles gleamed white. He glanced into the fire for a moment and then looked back at me swiftly as if he had hoped to catch me off my guard. Something in his expression made me avert my eyes instinctively and make a great business of flicking a speck of dust from my cuff.

"Pray continue, sir," said my voice politely.

"I happened to visit my lawyer Sir Charles Stowell this morning," he said. "There were one or two matters relating to my father's will that I wanted to discuss with him, rather than with my father's lawyers in Rye. In the course of conversation Stowell mentioned your name and the—circumstances of your position both before and after your parents' death, as he considered it might be germane to my position."

"And pray, Mr. Brandson," I said so coolly that my manner was even cooler than his, "what is your position?"

"Why, merely this, Miss Fleury," he said, and to my annoyance I sensed that he was amused. "If I wish to inherit under the terms of my father's will, I must marry within one year of his death. Furthermore it's specifically stipulated that my wife must be English by birth. Unfortunately this condition is not nearly so easy to fulfill as it might have seemed to my father when he made his very insular stipulation. To begin with, the ladies of my acquaintance are all Viennese, not English; I know of no eligible young Englishwoman, and even if I did it's possible that her father would frown on my foreign blood and discourage the match. My father, as I am well aware, was not the only insular man in this extraordinarily arrogant country, and now when England is the richest, most powerful nation in the world she is more insular and arrogant than ever before. On the other hand, it was clear to me that I couldn't merely marry some serving-girl for the purpose of fulfilling the condition in the will. My wife must know how to conduct herself and be at ease among people of the class with whom I would be obliged to associate on accepting the inheritance. She must at any rate give the appearance of poise and breeding."

My coolness seemed to have turned to ice. I was unable to move or speak. All I was conscious of thinking was: He wishes me to masquerade as his wife. When he has his inheritance safely in his hands I shall be discarded and left penniless.

"I believe you are seventeen years of age, Miss Fleury," he said.

"I assume that by this time you will have considered the idea of marriage in general terms, if not in relation to any specific person."

"Yes," I heard myself say. "I have considered it."

"And?"

"And put the thought aside."

"May I ask why?"

"Because," I said, trying to erase all trace of anger from my voice, "I have no dowry, no portion and no social standing. The possibility of making a good match is out of the question."

"I think you underestimate your own attractions," he said. "Or else you overestimate the disadvantage of your background. I am sure you would have no difficulty in finding suitors."

"It's plain to see you're a foreigner, Mr. Brandson," I said, my tongue sharp in my desire to stab back at him for his casual reference to my illegitimacy. "If you knew this country better you would know that whatever proposals a woman such as I may receive, none of them would have anything to do with matrimony."

"But I have just proposed matrimony to you," he said undisturbed. "Am I to understand that my proposal was not worthy of your consideration? You at least cannot reject me as a foreigner, Miss Fleury! My father was as English as your father was, and your mother was as much a foreigner as mine. My reputation and standing both in London and Vienna are excellent—anyone will confirm that. I have no title, but my father's family fought with Harold at Hastings against the Conqueror and my father was one of the most respected of the landed gentry throughout the length and breadth of Sussex. If you married me you would find yourself the wife of a prosperous land-owner, mistress of a large and beautiful home with plenty of servants."

After a while I said: "You want to marry me?"

For the first time since I had met him he smiled. "I am only surprised that you should find it so hard to believe," was all he said.

"A legal binding marriage?"

"Certainly. An illegal fraud would be of little use to me in making any claim to the estate, and still less use to you."

My incredulity was succeeded by an exhilaration which in turn sharpened into panic. "I—we know nothing of each other—"

"What of that? The majority of marriages these days among people such as ourselves are preceded by a very brief acquaintance. Marriage is an institution of convenience which should confer benefits on both parties. The grand passion of a courtship culminating in married bliss is for operatic librettos and the novels of Mrs. Radclyffe."

"Well, of course," I said sharply, not wanting to be thought a romantic schoolgirl, "it was not my intention to imply otherwise. But—"

"Well?"

"I—I don't even know how old you are!" I cried out. "I know nothing of you!"

"I am thirty-four years old," he said easily. "I was married in my twenties, but my wife died in childbirth and the baby with her. I've never remarried." He stood up. "You will of course need to consider the matter. If you will permit me, I shall wait upon you tomorrow, and then if you wish to accept my proposal we will take a drive in the park and perhaps drink chocolate in Piccadilly while we discuss the plans further."

"Thank you," I said. "I assume you have no objections to my brother accompanying me? I would prefer to be chaperoned."

He hesitated slightly, and then shrugged his shoulders. "As you wish."

"Before you go," I said, for he was still standing, "I would like to clarify one or two matters in my mind."

"Certainly." He sat down again and crossed one leg over the other. His hands were no longer clasped tightly together, I noticed, but were limp and relaxed again upon his thighs.

"First," I said, "if I am to marry you, I would like to be sure that my brother is provided for. He has another year of studies at Harrow and then would like to go up to Oxford to complete his education."

"That could easily be arranged."

"And he could have a reasonable allowance and live under our roof whenever he wishes?"

"By all means."

"I see," I said. "Thank you."

"Was there some other matter you wished to clarify, Miss Fleury?"

"Yes," I said. "There was." My hands were the ones which were clasped tightly now. By an effort of will I held my head erect and looked him straight in the eyes. "There's one matter on which I'm anxious there should be no misunderstanding."

"And that is?"

"As the marriage is really purely for convenience, Mr. Brandson, am I to take it that the marriage will be in name only?"

There was a silence. It was impossible to know what he was thinking. Presently he smiled. "For a young girl educated in an exemplary seminary for young ladies," he said, "you seem to be remarkably well-informed, Miss Fleury."

I waited for him to speak further but he said nothing more. After a moment I was obliged to say: "You haven't answered my question, sir."

"Nor have you commented on my observation, madam."

"That's easily done," I said shortly. "My mother talked long and often of marriage and liaison and of the lot of women in general."

"In that case," he said, "you will be well aware that there are few marriages which begin in name only although the majority certainly end in that manner. However, if the matter is distasteful to you, there is no need for us to live together immediately. As you say, I am more interested in securing my inheritance and you are more interested in attaining your own security to be concerned with details such as those. We can discuss them later on."

My first thought was: He thinks I am as fearful as most young girls and might spoil his plans by refusing in panic at the last minute to marry him. My second thought: He has a mistress or he would not concede so much so carelessly.

And my relief was mingled with anger and irritation.

"Then I shall see you tomorrow?" he said, rising once more to his feet. "If I may, I would like to wait upon you at half-past ten tomorrow morning."

"Thank you," I said. "That would be convenient."

He took my hand again in his long cool fingers and raised it casually to his lips. I felt nothing at all. No shiver of excitement or anticipation or even revulsion. He merely seemed old to me, a stranger twice my age with whom I had nothing whatever in common, and it was at that time quite impossible for me to realize that within a month we would be sharing the same name.

"But we know nothing of him," said Alexander. "Nothing. We don't even know that he is as he says he it. He may be utterly disreputable."

"We shall go now and talk to Sir Charles Stowell. Tell John to have the chaise brought to the front door."

"But an Austrian! Viennese!"

"Austria is allied with us now against Bonaparte."

"But—"

"Listen Alexander. Please try to be practical and realistic. We're not in a position to be otherwise. Within a few days we shall be destitute—we have no money and soon we'll have no roof over our heads either. This man—if he is as he says he is, and I believe he was telling the truth—this man is going to provide us both with financial security and social respectability. It's a gift from the gods! I shall be an honorably married woman with a house and servants, and you will be able to complete your studies and then do whatever you wish. How can we turn down such an opportunity? What shall we do if we did turn it down? You would have to enlist in the army and I should have to be a governess, and while you may be content to spend the rest of your life marching and parading, *I* am not content to be consigned to some isolated country mansion to teach the stupid children of some provincial local squire! I want to marry and be a great lady in whatever county I may live in, not to be a spinster, an unwanted appendage to a noble household!"

"You would be content to marry this man?"

"You didn't see him!"

"I didn't care for your description of him."

"But Alexander," I said exasperated, "this is hardly the time to be particular and fussy about prospective brothers-in-law, or husbands. Mr. Brandson is not ill-looking, he is courteous and a gentleman, and he cannot help being old. It could be much worse."

"Well, I don't like it," said Alexander obtusely. "I don't like it at all. Who knows what this may lead to?"

"Who knows?" I agreed. "But I know very well what would happen if we ignored this offer. Suit yourself, Alexander, but which is the worse of two evils?"

"I wonder," said Alexander.

Mr. Brandson arrived punctually at half-past ten the following morning and I went to the library to greet him with my decision. I was wearing a dress of yellow muslin in the height of fashion, and my maid had arranged my hair in a most becoming Grecian style so that I considered myself exceptionally elegant. My self-confidence swept me across the floor towards him and only ebbed when I felt his cool fingers once more against my hand. There was some element in his manner which unnerved me. For the first time it occurred to me that he was sophisticated; he was probably amused at my attempt to present an adult poised facade to him, much as any mature man would be amused at the caprices of a precocious child.

With singular lack of finesse I managed to say gauchely that I had decided to accept his proposal.

It seemed that he had never once thought that I would do otherwise. He had all his plans carefully prepared. He had rented a suite of rooms near Leicester Square, he said. He understood the predicament in which my brother and I were placed, and suggested we might move to the rooms whenever it became necessary for us to do so. I might take my maid with me, if I wished. He and I could be married as soon as was convenient and could spend a few days in the country after the wedding while Alexander could return to Harrow.

I said that this would be eminently satisfactory.

News of my betrothal was soon circulated; my mother's French friends who eventually came forward to offer us assistance were all relieved to hear that I had been so fortunate although little was known of Mr. Brandson. However, one or two people had heard of his father Robert Brandson, the Sussex land-owner, and Sir Charles Stowell introduced me to a City banker who assured me of Mr. Axel Brandson's standing as a man of business in London and Vienna.

Mr. Brandson himself gave me a handsome sapphire ring and waited on me five out of the seven days of each week. Often he stayed no longer than quarter of an hour before making some excuse to be on his way, but occasionally we went for a drive in his phaeton, and once, shortly before the wedding he took me to Vauxhall.

I was unchaperoned. Now that I was officially betrothed and soon to be married it was no longer so important to be escorted by a third person, and besides Alexander had an assignation with some actress with whom he had become infatuated during frequent visits to the theater in the Haymarket, and I saw no reason to interrupt his schoolboy's idolization of some highly unsuitable female. The worst that could happen would be for her to be too indulgent towards him.

So I went to the pleasure gardens of Vauxhall with Axel Brandson and walked with him among the brilliantly-dressed crowds. I was just enjoying being seen in the company of my future husband by people I knew, and was just lagging a pace behind him to make sure that I had not mistaken some fashionable member of the aristocracy nearby when I heard a man's voice exclaim: "So you're back, Axel! And alone! What happened to the beautiful—"

I turned. The man saw me and stopped. There was a second's silence and then Mr. Brandson said without inflection: "Miss Fleury, allow me to present an acquaintance of mine . . ."

But I was not listening to him. The man's name was familiar to me. My father had spoken of him in vague amusement as "a dare-devil rake and a gambler soaked in his own debts." Since my father was a rake and a gambler I knew exactly the kind of man Mr. Brandson's friend was.

"You told me you had no friends in London," I said after we had left the gentleman behind.

"No close friends certainly."

"The gentleman seemed very well acquainted with you."

"Once perhaps fifteen years ago we were inseparable during my visits to England but that time is long since past." He seemed untroubled, but I thought I could detect a slight impatience in his manner as if he wished to be rid of the subject. "My personal friends are in Austria now. The people I knew in London are merely business acquaintances."

"And the beautiful lady he referred to? Is she also a mere business acquaintance?"

He gave me such a long cool look that in the end I was the first to look away.

"I have been a widower ten years, Miss Fleury," he said at last, and his voice was as cool as his expression. "As you are already so well acquainted with the ways of the world you will be well aware that once a man has become accustomed to female companionship he is loth to do without it later on. Shall we turn here and walk in another direction, or do you wish to go home yet?"

Tears pricked beneath my eyelids for some reason not easy to explain. I felt very young suddenly, and, what was worse, insecure and afraid. At that moment my betrothal seemed no longer a fortunate stroke of luck, a game which enabled me to parade among society at Vauxhall and display my future husband, but an exchange of freedom for restriction, of the familiar for the unknown.

It made no difference that I had already guessed he must have a mistress. The casual way he had not even bothered to deny the fact and his mockery of my desire to appear sophisticated were the aspects of his behavior which I found most hurtful. When I reached home at last I went straight to bed and tossed and turned with my tears till dawn.

The next morning he called with an enormous bouquet of flowers and was at his most courteous and charming. Even so I could not help wondering whether he had spent the night alone or whether he had visited his mistress instead.

We were married in the church of St. Mary-le-Strand less than a month after we had met and Alexander and Sir Charles Stowell acted as witnesses. It was a very quiet affair. My French godmother, an old friend of my mother's, attended, and two or three of my childhood friends. Afterwards there was a wedding breakfast at my husband's rented town house, and after it was over the carriage was waiting at the door to take us the twenty miles south into Surrey to the country house where it had been arranged that we should stay for a few days. The owner, an acquaintance of Axel's was at that time in Bath with his family, and had given instructions that we were to treat the house as if it were our own.

My traveling habit consisted of a fur-trimmed redingote of levantine worn over a classic white muslin dress, and accompanied by a matching fur muff and snug warm boots to combat the chill of November. Axel had given me plenty of money so that I could have the clothes I pleased for the wedding and afterwards, and although time had been short I now had an adequate wardrobe for the occasion.

"You look very fine," said Alexander almost shyly as he came forward to say goodbye to me. And then as he embraced me I could hear the anxiety in his voice as he said uncertainly: "You will write, won't you? You won't forget?"

"Of course I shan't forget!" There was a lump in my throat. Suddenly I couldn't bear to leave him, and hugged him fiercely to me with all my strength.

"I shall see you at Christmas," he said, "when I am able to leave school for the holidays."

"Yes."

"It won't be long. Just a few weeks."

"Yes." I disengaged myself and turned away before he could see how close I was to tears.

"You will be all right, won't you?" he whispered as I turned from him.

"Of course!" I said with dignity, recognizing his craving for re-assurance and not daring to acknowledge my own. "Why not?"

Axel was waiting a few paces away by the carriage. He had already said goodbye to Alexander. As I could sense they both disliked each other, I wasn't surprised that their parting from one another had been very brief and formal.

I reached the carriage.

"You're ready?" said Axel.

"Quite ready, thank you."

He assisted me into the carriage and then climbed in after me. It was not until we were well out of London that I was sufficiently in control of myself even to look at my husband, let alone speak to him. Finally as we passed through Wandsworth I was able to say: "How fortunate that the weather should be so fine."

"Yes," he said, "indeed."

I looked at him. His polite expression told me nothing, but I knew instinctively that he was well aware of my emotional battles and had carefully refrained from conversation to avoid giving me embarrassment. I suppose I should have been grateful to him for his perception and consideration, but I was not. I somehow resented the fact that he saw too much and understood too well, and I was angry.

We stopped at Epsom where we dined, and again at Leatherhead where we paused at the inn by the river to allow the grooms to attend to the horses. By the time we reached the village of Bookham and the mansion of Claybury Park it was dusk and I was feeling very tired.

The house seemed spacious and beautiful, even to my weary eyes, and the servants civil and attentive. Axel asked if I wanted

any refreshment and when I refused told one of the servants to
show me to my room.

A fire blazed in the grate and the lamp on the table illuminated
the gracious furniture of a room of elegance and style. After glancing around with interest, I locked the door into the corridor and
went over to examine another door on the far side of the room.
As I suspected it led into another bedroom where Axel's luggage
had already been placed by his valet. After glancing at the heavy
portmanteau, I closed the door and looked for the key to lock
that as well, but there was no key to be seen.

I decided not to summon my maid. She would be as tired as I
was, and I could manage well enough on my own. Undressing as
quickly as I was able, I loosened my hair, brushed it out and
dowsed the lamp. The flames still flickered in the grate and I lay
awake a long time watching them and listening for any hint of
Axel's arrival in the room beyond. Time passed. My eyelids grew
heavy and my thoughts became more detached. I thought fleet-
ingly and without distaste of my brief acquaintance with Axel
Brandson and the quiet unobtrusive wedding. I still could not entirely believe that I was a married woman and that Axel was my
husband. It was a pity he was so old and seemed to have so little
to say to me. It was true he was courteous and often charming but
I had always had the impression that he was making an effort to
appear so. I probably seemed a mere child to him, and he had
been bored.

I wondered what his mistress was like, and was suddenly determined to outshine her. "He shall not be bored by me!" I
thought furiously. "He shall not!" I hazily began to imagine pas-
sionate love scenes throbbing with romance and tenderness, a
state of ecstacy unrivaled by anything I had ever experienced
before. After all, as I reasoned, such a state must be enjoyable or
people would not spend so much time thinking of so little else.

My eyes closed. I was warm and luxuriously comfortable. I
was just about to drift into sleep when I thought of Alexander
and wondered if he was thinking of me.

The loneliness hit me in a hideous wave, driving away the com-

forting oblivion of sleep and making my throat ache with the longing to cry. I stared for a long time at the dying embers in the
grate, and then at last I heard movements from Axel's room and
I was conscious of an enormous relief. My pride alone restrained
me from running to him in my desire to shut out the loneliness
and seek comfort from the only person I could now turn to.

I waited. Gradually the sounds ceased and there was silence.
I went on waiting, my limbs stiff with tension, but he did not
come. I waited until the fire had died in the grate and then
I turned and buried my face in my pillow and wept myself to
sleep.

The next morning it was raining. My maid, Marie-Claire,
helped me dress and arranged my hair but I was disinclined to
talk and I could sense she was disappointed. When I was ready I
went downstairs, uncertain of my way around this strange mansion, and was directed by a footman to a small breakfast room
where I drank a cup of tea and ate a biscuit. Afterwards I wandered through the rooms listlessly and stared at the view from
the windows of the long gallery but the rain had brought mist to
the valley and it was difficult to see much. I wished that it could
have been fine for the grounds looked interesting and it might
have been pleasant to wander in them, but it was much too wet
to go out.

In the end I went to the library, found one of Jane Austen's
novels and tried to read, but the placid events which befell her
characters soon bored me and I turned instead to Fielding and
Defoe. There was even a copy of *Moll Flanders* which my mother
had never let me read, so the morning passed unexpectedly
quickly.

I saw nothing of Axel until dinner was served at three. I was
very cool towards him, but he seemed not to notice and was as
polite—and as remote—as ever. Afterwards I left him alone with
his port and went to the drawing room to write a letter to Alexander. I described the house in great detail and told him all about
Moll Flanders.

I felt better after that.

Presently it was time to go to bed and I took a great deal more trouble with my appearance and wore my best nightgown which weariness had made me ignore the night before. Once in bed I tried to stay awake for as long as possible but sleep claimed me before I was even aware of its approach and when I awoke the night was far advanced and I was still alone.

I think Marie-Claire was a little hurt that I should be so morose and silent for a second morning in succession, but I made no effort to talk to her and eventually she withdrew sulking while I went down to breakfast. Fortunately it was fine and I spent the morning wandering around the grounds, exploring the lawns and yew walks, the vegetable garden and orangery, the woods, the stream, and even the ruined temple which had been erected a generation earlier to ornament the grounds.

Axel spent the morning writing letters. I had gone into the library to return *Moll Flanders* to its shelf and he had already been seated at the desk with pen and ink. We had said good morning to each other and exchanged a few polite words. Later when I returned to the library before dinner to look for another book to read I found that he had gone but the letters lay on the desk where he had left them. I glanced at the addresses. Three were marked for Vienna, but one was addressed to "James Sherman Esquire, Sherman, Shepherd and Sherman, Solicitors, 12 Mermaid Street, Rye, Sussex", and the last to "Vere Brandson Esquire, Haraldsdyke, near Rye, Sussex." I stared at this last letter for some time. Haraldsdyke, I knew, was the name of the estate and house which Axel had inherited from his father, my future home where I would be mistress. Vere Brandson was the second son of Axel's father's second marriage. The eldest son, Rodric, Axel had told me, had died shortly after his father as the result of an accident. The youngest son, a boy of nineteen whom Axel had scarcely referred to at all, was called Edwin.

I was still thinking of Axel's English relations when I went down to dinner and was tempted to ask him more about them, but he seemed disinclined to conversation and apart from inquiring politely how I had spent my day and embarking on a discussion of landscape gardening, he appeared anxious to eat in silence. I was therefore a little surprised when he joined me in the drawing room later and suggested that I played for him on the spinet for a while.

I have never been fond of the spinet but I play passably well and sing better than I play. He seemed pleased at my ability, and as I naturally enjoyed his compliments I offered to play a piece on the harp. There is only one piece I can play well on the harp, and I played it. To my satisfaction he asked me to play more but I pretended to be too modest, and gracefully escaped the risk of spoiling the excellent impression I had created.

"I'm delighted I have such an accomplished wife," he said, and his smile was so charming that he seemed handsome to me for the first time. It was also the first reference he had made to our new legal relationship with one another. "I had no idea that you were so musical."

"There was no spinet in the rooms you rented for Alexander and myself," I said lightly. "I had no chance to play to you before."

"True." He smiled at me again. "You speak French, of course?"

"Yes."

"Perhaps you would read me some Molière if you were not too tired? There's nothing I like better than to hear French spoke with a perfect accent."

I was reminded again of his foreign background. No true Englishman enjoyed listening to the tongue of the great national enemy Bonaparte.

I read to him in French for half an hour. I was perfectly at ease in the language, as my mother and I had always spoken French to one another and I had had a French maid from an early age. Afterwards he again seemed pleased and we talked for a while of French literature and history.

We had a light supper by candlelight at last, and then he said that he was sure I was tired and that if I wished to retire to bed he would quite understand.

I could not decide whether he was being genuinely considerate or whether he merely wished to dismiss me. However, I went upstairs to my room, conscious of a feeling of disappointment, and sat for a long while before my mirror frowning at my reflection in despondency. Finally, trying to stave off my increasing loneliness I summoned Marie-Claire and made an elaborate toilette before preparing myself for the long hours of the night which lay ahead.

I had not been in bed more than ten minutes before I heard movements in Axel's room. There was the faint sound of voices as he dismissed his valet, and then later after more vague sounds there was silence. I was just straining my ears to decide whether or not he had gone to bed, when the communicating door opened and he came into the room.

I half-sat up in my surprise and at the same moment he turned to look at me. The flame flickered on the candlestick in his hand and was reflected in the darkness of his eyes so that their expression was again hidden from me.

I sank back upon the pillows.

For a moment I thought he was going to speak but he did not. He set the candlestick down on the table by the side of the bed and then gently snuffed it out so that we were in darkness. I heard rather than saw him discard his dressing gown; suddenly he was beside me between the sheets and I could feel his quick hot breath against my cheek.

I relaxed happily in the supreme bliss of my ignorance. I had thought myself so sophisticated in knowing all about the passion and ecstasy and fulfillment of the act of love. No one had ever told me that this same act could also be painful, embarrassing and repulsive.

Later after he had gone I curled myself up into a ball as if to ward off the horror of memory, and for the third night in succession I cried myself to sleep.

It was raining again the next morning and I was unable to walk in the grounds. After breakfast I took another of Miss Austen's books from the library and hid myself in the smallest morning room while I read it. Today Miss Austen's work was easy to read, her situations no longer mundane, her characters no longer boring but reassuring in their normality. I no longer wanted to read Gothic romances or any novel such as *Moll Flanders,* and Miss Austen's world of vicarage and village and social proprieties was soothing and comforting to my mind.

Axel found me at noon. He was wearing riding clothes, and I noticed for the first time then that although it was still gray outside the rain had stopped.

"I wondered where you were," he said. "I couldn't find you."

I knew not what to say. Presently he closed the door behimd him and crossed the floor slowly to my couch.

"I doubt whether there's much sense in delaying our departure for Haraldsdyke much longer," he said as I fingered the leather binding of the book in my hands. "Today is Saturday. Unless you object, I thought we might leave on Monday morning. If the roads are not too disgraceful we may reach Rye on Wednesday night."

"As you wish."

He was silent. Presently I felt his cool fingers against my cheek, but I did not look up; I was steeling myself against any reference he might make to the distasteful memory which lay between us, but in the end all he said was: "There's no need to look as if you think the company of the opposite sex is a sadly overrated commodity. Matters will improve in time." And then he was gone before I could attempt to reply, and I was alone once more with my book in the silent room.

I wondered when "in time" would be, but evidently it was not to be beneath the roof of Claybury Park. That night and the following night the door between our bedrooms remained closed, and on Monday we left the lonely peace of that beautiful house in Surrey for the mists of the Romney Marsh and the shrouded walls of Haraldsdyke.

Two

"Perhaps I should tell you more about my family," Axel said as we dined together on Monday night at Sevenoaks.

Outside it was dark, but where we sat in the private sitting room accorded to us by the innkeeper, a huge fire blazed on the hearth and the room was warm and comfortable. After the tediousness of the long hours of travel it was a relief to escape from the jolting post-chaise and the chill of the damp weather.

"Yes," I said uncertainly, "I would like to hear more about your family. You only described them so briefly before." I was uncertain because I was by no means sure that this was the answer he wanted. At the same time I was also annoyed that I should be so nervous with him that a single chance remark should throw me instantly into a state of confusion.

I began to examine a scrap of roast beef with meticulous care, but when he next spoke he seemed unaware of my embarrassment.

"My father died last Christmas Eve, as I've already told you," he said. "He was a man of strong personality, typical of many an English gentleman who belonged to the last century rather than to this one. He was a staunch Tory, a confirmed conservative, a believer in letting his land be farmed the way it had been farmed since the Conquest, violently anti-Bonaparte and anti-European. It always amazed me that he of all people could have brought himself to marry a foreigner, but maybe he was more liberal when he was younger. Or maybe his experiences with my mother contributed to his later prejudices against foreigners. They certainly weren't happily married. She left him even before I was born, but fortunately had the means to set up an establishment of her own in Vienna where I entered the world a few months afterwards. Following my birth she never fully regained her health and in fact died five years later. After that I was brought up by her elder brother, my uncle, who was later appointed to the Court of St. James's on some minor diplomatic mission in the days when the Emperor was still Holy Roman Emperor, and not merely Emperor of Austria as he is today. I went with him to London, and my uncle, who had always found me rather an intrusion on the privacy and freedom of his bachelor existence, arranged for me to meet my father in the hope that my father would perhaps relieve him of his responsibilities where I was concerned.

"My father came to London—probably more out of curiosity than anything else—to see what his half-foreign son was like. I remember very well when I first saw him. He was very tall, taller than I am now, and wore a wig which looked as if it had seen better days. He had an enormous paunch, massive shoulders and a voice which I believe would have frightened even Bonaparte himself. I could well understand how he managed to have such powerful influence in the town of Rye and the other Cinque Ports, he would dominate any gathering. England was, and is, the richest, most powerful country in the world, and he was to me then a personification of England—tough, arrogant, self-opinionated and rude—but generous to a fault with his money, compassionate when something touched his heart, and unwaveringly loyal to his friends, to his king and country and to those principles which he believed were right and just.

"'Ho!' he said, entering the room with steps which made the china tremble on the mantelpiece. 'You look just like your mother! Never mind, you can't help that. What's your name?'

"He nearly expired when I told him. His face went purple and his eyes were bright blue with rage. 'Damned foreign nonsense!'

he roared. 'I'll call you George. What's good enough for the king should be good enough for you. What's all that Frenchified nonsense around your throat and wrists?'

"It was the fashion in Vienna at the time for small boys to wear jackets with lace cuffs and a lace kerchief, but my English wasn't good enough to tell him so. 'Zounds!' he said (or something equally old-fashioned), 'the child can't even speak his native tongue! Never mind, my boy, we'll soon put that right.'

"So he promptly removed me from my uncle's care, much to my uncle's relief, took me to Haraldsdyke and hired a tutor to teach me English. He had married again by this time, but my half-brothers Rodric and Vere were little more than babies and Ned was yet to be born, so I was a solitary child. When I was twelve he sent me off to Westminster in the hope that boarding school would complete the process of turning me into a young English gentleman.

"I left there ignorant but tough at the age of eighteen and asked to go back to Vienna as I suspected my uncle of defrauding me and wanted to investigate how he was conducting his guardianship of my financial affairs. My father was very angry when he heard that I wanted to go back to Austria, but I remained firm and after he had roared and bellowed at me for an hour or more he realized I couldn't be dissuaded.

"So I went back to Austria—and became involved in the Austrian interests I had inherited from my mother. Eventually I married an Austrian girl of good family and—much to my father's disgust and disappointment—settled in Vienna.

"Yet my English education and my acquaintance with English people had left their mark. After my wife died I devoted myself more to my business interests and succeeded in establishing an outlet for my interests in London. After that I often journeyed to and fro between the two countries and occasionally managed to visit Haraldsdyke as well.

"But my father never entirely forgave me for returning to Austria. He had three other sons now by his second marriage, and I was always aware of being a stranger there, a foreigner trespassing on English soil."

He stopped. Flames from the enormous fire nearby roared up the chimney. Hardly liking to interrupt his first long conversation with me I waited for him to continue but when he did not I said puzzled: "And yet he left Haraldsdyke to you when he died."

"Yes," he said, "he left Haraldsdyke to me." He was watching the leaping flames, his face very still. "I knew towards the end that he was disappointed in his three sons by his second marriage, but I never imagined he would cut them out of his will. Yet they received merely nominal bequests when he died."

"Why was that? What had they done to disappoint him?"

He hesitated, fingering his tankard of ale, his eyes still watching the flames. "Ned the youngest was always a sullen, difficult child," he said at last. "No one took much notice of him. He was dark and ungainly and not in the least handsome. Vere, the second son, was too serious and staid, and he and my father could never agree on anything, least of all on how the lands should be farmed. Vere is keenly interested in agriculture and wanted to use new scientific methods which my father thought were a great deal of nonsense. The crowning disaster came when Vere secretly married a village girl, the daughter of the local witch. My father disowned him, then repented and forgave him later. I think in spite of himself my father was impressed by Alice, Vere's wife. She's clever enough not to try to be something she's not, and she's made no effort to adopt a refined speaking voice or wear clothes which are too grand and extravagant. She's quiet, very simple and unaffected in her dress and manner—and at least presentable. Also I believe she's an excellent mother. She's borne Vere five or six children, if my memory is correct. Not all of them have lived, of course, but I think three are surviving so far. However, in spite of the fact that the marriage was not unsuccessful, my father never fully forgave Vere for marrying beneath him."

"And the eldest son," I said. "Why was he a disappointment?"

"Rodric?" A sudden draught made the flames leap up the chimney with a roar again before subsiding beneath the glowing logs. The wind rattled fiercely at the shutters. "Rodric died. It was the day of my father's death. He rode off across the Marsh to Rye and the mists blew in from the sea to engulf him. I went after him but all I found was his horse wandering among the dykes and his hat floating among the rushes near a marshy tract of land. His horse must have missed its footing on the narrow path and thrown him into the boggy waters of the mere."

I shivered, picturing all too vividly the mists of the marshes I had never seen, the twisting path from Haraldsdyke to Rye. "Is there no road, then?" I said in a low voice. "Is there no road which links the house to the town?"

"Certainly, but Rodric didn't want to take the road. He was trying to escape, taking the old path across the road."

It was like that moment in many dreams when a familiar landscape is suddenly contorted without warning into a hideous vista. I had been listening so tranquilly to Axel's narrative that I did not grasp the drift of what he was saying until it met me face to face. The shock made the color drain from my face. I stared at him wordlessly.

"My father died as the result of a blow from the butt of a gun," said Axel quietly, "and it was Rodric who struck the blow."

The landlord came in then to inquire whether our meal was satisfactory and whether there was anything else we required. When he had gone I said: "Why didn't you tell me this before?"

Axel glanced aside. I sensed for a moment that I had come closer than I had ever come to disturbing the smooth veneer of his sophistication. Then he shrugged his shoulders. "The story is past history," he said. "It's over now, the affair closed. It's necessary that you should know of it as you will undoubtedly hear the story from other people, but it need not concern you."

But I felt that it already concerned me. "What brought Rodric to do such a terrible thing?" I said appalled. "I don't understand."

"No," he said. "You would not understand. You never knew Rodric."

"Tell me about him."

"He's dead," said Axel. "You need not concern yourself with his ghost."

"Yes, but—"

"He was as wild and turbulent as Vere was staid and predictable. He was like a child in his ceaseless search for some new adventure which would give him a bizarre sense of excitement. He was always in trouble from an early age, and the older he grew the more he resented his father's power. There was a clash of wills. However, my father tended to favor Rodric and in spite of all his rages did his best to extricate his son from each new scrape in which Rodric found himself. But the relationship deteriorated. In the end my father was threatening to inform the Watch at Rye of Rodric's current activities and swearing he would disinherit Rodric entirely."

"And was it then that Rodric killed him?"

"He was the last to see my father alive and it was known that they quarreled violently. Part of the conversation was overheard. Directly afterwards he rode off over the Marsh."

"And the gun—"

"It was his own gun. He had been out shooting and had just returned to the house when my father called out to him from the library. Rodric went in to see him, the gun in his hand. I know that to be true, for I had been out shooting with him and was in the hall when my father called out."

"Was it you, then, who found your father dead?"

"No, it was my step-mother who found him. Rodric had already left and Vere had been out all the afternoon on the estate. He didn't come back till later. Then the footman told us that Rodric had gone and I rode after him to try to bring him back. But I was too late."

"And the quarrel—part of it had been overheard, you said?"

"Yes, by Vere's wife Alice and by my father's ward and god-daughter Mary Moore, whom I don't believe I've mentioned to you before. They were in the saloon adjacent to the library and when my father raised his voice, he could easily be heard through the thickness of an inside wall. After a while they became embarrassed and retired to the drawing-room upstairs. Or at least, Mary did. Alice went off to the nursery to attend to the children."

"And your youngest half-brother Edwin, Ned, where was he? Didn't he hear or see anything?"

"He was in the hay with the second scullery maid," said Axel with a bluntness which startled me. I was reminded with a jolt of the relationship existing between us and the frankness that was now permitted in our conversation with each other. "The entire account of his adolescent escapade was duly revealed at the inquest."

"Inquest!"

"Well, naturally there had to be an inquest. The coroner's jury held that my father had been murdered and that Rodric had met his death by accident while trying to hasten as quickly as possible from the scene of the crime. They also recommended that no blame should be attached to the living for my father's death, so that although as a coroner's jury they were not allowed to judge whether Rodric committed the crime or not, their recommendation was sufficient to tell the world that in their opinion Rodric was guilty."

"I see." I was silent, picturing the inquest, the stuffy courtroom, the stolid jurors, the gaping gossiping crowd. "Was the inquest at Rye?"

"Yes, it was. Fortunately the coroner was a friend of my father's lawyer James Sherman and was anxious to spare us as much as he could, but the affair caused a tremendous amount of gossip and speculation throughout the Cinque Ports. There was even more gossip when the contents of my father's will became known and I discovered, to my acute embarrassment, that he had left everything to me. Everyone was stunned, of course. We all knew that he had threatened to cut Rodric out of his will, but no one had guessed that he had already actually done so. Furthermore, neither Vere nor Ned had had any idea that they too were disinherited. But according to James Sherman, the lawyer, my father had signed the new will on the day before he died."

"But if the inheritance was such an embarrassment to you," I said, "could you not have renounced it? Or assigned it to your brothers?"

"Yes, I could have done so and in fact I did consider it at first, but then I realized it would be a betrayal of my father's wishes and the trust he had placed in me. He had made this will in a sane rational frame of mind and no doubt had reasons for eliminating his other sons from any share of Haraldsdyke. I felt the least I could do to implement his wishes was to accept the inheritance nominally at least. However, I had my own affairs to manage and it was obvious to me that I could not stay long at Haraldsdyke. The estate was at any rate in the hands of trustees for a year—this was because my inheritance was contingent on my marrying an Englishwoman and was not mine outright until I had fulfilled this condition. I told the trustees, James Sherman and his brother Charles, that I wished Vere to be allowed the practical administration of the estate in my absence, and then I returned to Vienna to arrange my affairs so that I could return to England at the earliest opportunity and seek a suitable wife."

"But supposing you hadn't married," I said. "What would have happened to the estate then?"

"It was willed to Vere's son, Stephen, who is at present a child of three. Even now, if I die without issue, the estate is to pass to Stephen. If Stephen dies childless before the age of twenty-one, his younger brother will inherit—and so on . . . Every contingency is provided for."

"I see." I was silent. "Will you still have to go back to Vienna often?"

"About once a year. I've consolidated and delegated my business interests to enable me to spend most of the year in England."

"And Vere and Alice? What's to happen to them? How they must resent us coming to usurp them!"

"I see no reason why they should be usurped. I would welcome Vere's help in administering the estate for I know nothing of agriculture, and Alice will be able to show you how a country house should be run."

"But how old is Alice?" I said, feeling very insecure indeed. "Won't she be angry when I take her place?"

"You forget," said Axel. "Alice is a simple, plain country girl who has had experience of acting as housekeeper in a large mansion. You are a young woman of an education and background far above her. There won't be any conflict at all. It will be obvious from the beginning that you are the rightful mistress of the house. Alice won't mind in the least—it will give her more time to attend to her children. She's the most excellent mother."

"But the others, your step-mother . . ."

"Esther and I have always been on the best of terms," he interrupted. "She will be glad to see me again and anxious to see that you feel comfortable and at ease at Haraldsdyke. Who else is there? Only Mary, my father's ward, and she is a mere child of fourteen who will be far too busy trying to please her governess to be much concerned with you. You needn't worry about her in the least."

"And Ned," I said. "You've forgotten Ned again."

"Ned? Well, I hardly think he need concern you much either. I think I shall suggest to him that he enlists in the army. He must be nineteen now and it's high time he did something constructive with his life instead of idling it away in the taverns of the Cinque Ports or the haystacks of the Romney Marsh. He's not intelligent enough to go to a University. Any attempt at providing him with further education would be a waste of money." He drained his tankard of ale and took out his watch to glance at it. "I think we should retire soon," he said abruptly. "We have another long day ahead of us tomorrow and you should get plenty of rest to avoid becoming too tired."

"As you wish." I was recalled at once from my thoughts of the past by the dread of the night to come.

"The landlord fortunately has a private room for us both," he said. "So often in these English inns one has to share a communal bedroom even if not a communal bed."

I tried to look pleased.

"Perhaps you will have some wine with me before we retire?" he said. "It's such a damp chill night and the wine will warm us both."

I protested half-heartedly but then agreed readily enough. I would have seized on any excuse to postpone the moment when I would be alone with him in the bedroom.

The wine not only warmed my blood but made me feel drowsy and relaxed. I meant to ask him on the stairs what "activities" Rodric had pursued which would have offended the police at Rye, but my mind was hazy and I was unable to concentrate sufficiently to revive our earlier conversation. Marie-Claire was waiting for me in the bedroom, but I dismissed her at once to her own sleeping quarters for I could see she was greatly fatigued, and undressed as quickly as I could without her. I discovered that she had stretched my nightgown over the warming-pan in the bed, and I felt the luxurious warmth soothe my limbs as the silk touched my skin. A second later I was in bed and lying sleepily back on the pillows.

He had been correct in the assumptions he had made that morning at Claybury Park. Matters did improve; at least this time I was spared the shock of disillusionment. Afterwards he was asleep almost at once, but although I moved closer to him for warmth and even ventured to lay my head against his shoulder he did not stir, and I was conscious even then of his remoteness from me.

The next day we set off early from the inn at Sevenoaks and journeyed further south through the meadows of Kent until we reached the great spa of Tunbridge Wells which Charles II's queen, Henrietta Maria, had made famous over a century and a half before. It is not, of course, as celebrated as Bath, which is famed throughout Europe, but Axel found the town interesting enough to linger in and thought that a short journey that day would be less tiring for me. Accordingly we dined at an excellent tavern near the Pantiles and stayed the night at an inn not far from the Pump Room. Again we shared the same bedroom, but this time it was I who slept first and did not wake till it began to rain at seven the next morning.

We had not spoken again of his family, but as we set out on the last stage of our journey on Wednesday I began to think of them again. I was particularly anxious at the thought of meeting Alice. I hoped she would not be too much older than me so that my disadvantage would not be so great, but if she had had six children already it was probable that she was at least twenty-two or even older.

I began idly to count the months to my eighteenth birthday.

The journey that day seemed never-ending. We progressed along the borders of Kent and Sussex and the rain poured from leaden skies to make a mire of the road. At several inns we had to stop to allow the coachman to attend to the horses who quickly tired from the strain of pulling their burden through the mud, and then at last as we crossed the border into Sussex and left the rich farming land of Kent behind, the rain ceased and on peering from the carriage window I saw we were approaching a new land, a vast tract of green flatness broken only by the blue ribbon of the sea on the horizon.

"This is the Romney Marsh," said Axel.

It was not as I had imagined it to be. I think I had pictured a series of marshes and bogs which would remind me of descriptions I had heard of the Fen Country in East Anglia, but although there were probably marshes and bogs in plenty, they were not visible from the road. The grass of the endless meadows seemed very green, and occasionally I glimpsed the strips of farmland, and the huddle of stone buildings. There were no hedges or other enclosures, but often I could glimpse the gleam of water where a farmer had cut a dyke to drain his property.

"They plan to drain more of the Marsh," said Axel, after he had pointed out the dykes to me. "The soil is rich here if only it can be used. Vere has been experimenting with crops and growing turnips and other root vegetables instead of letting a third of the land lie fallow each year. There have been similar interesting experiments in crop rotation in East Anglia; I believe the late Lord Townshend was very successful in evolving the method, but my father held out against it for a long time and clung to the old ways. He distrusted all innovations on principle."

"And was all the Marsh a swamp once?"

"A great deal of it was below the sea at one time, but that was centuries ago. Up to the fourteenth century Rye and Winchelsea were the mightiest ports in all England, rivals even to London, and then the sea receded from their walls and the river silted up in Rye harbor so that now they're mere market towns with memories of medieval grandeur."

"And is Hastings nearby—where the Conqueror landed?"

"It's less than ten miles from Winchelsea. The ancestor of the Brandsons was reputedly a Dane called Brand who was in King Harold's entourage and fought with Harold against the Norman invaders."

"My mother's family was descended from Charlemagne," I said, thinking he was becoming too boastful and determined not to be outshone, but to my annoyance he merely laughed as if I had made a joke.

"My dear child," he said amused, "each one of us had an ancestor who was alive a thousand years ago. The only difference between us and, say, our coachman riding behind his horses is that we know the names of our ancestors and he doesn't."

This seemed to me to be a most peculiar observation and I found his amusement irritating in the extreme. I decided the most dignified course of action was to ignore his remark altogether, and accordingly I turned my attentions to the landscape outside once more.

The weather was improving steadily all the time, but now darkness was falling, and as I drew my redingote more tightly around myself I peered through the window to watch the shadows lengthening over the Marsh. The dykes now gleamed mysteriously, the flat ground gave curious illusions of distance and nearness. When I first saw the lights of Rye they seemed very close at hand, a cluster of illuminations dotting the dark rise of a hill, but it was another hour before we were finally below the walls of the town and the horses were toiling up the cobbled road to the great gate at the top of the rise.

"Vere said he would meet us at the Mermaid Inn," said Axel. "The carriage will stop there presently. Ah, here's the high street! You see the old grammar school? My father sent Ned there to learn his letters. Vere had a private tutor but it was hardly worth spending the money on such a luxury for Ned. . . . You can see how old the town is—I would think it probable that the streets and alleys you see now are little changed from the medieval days when they were built."

I stared fascinated out of the window. I had never seen any town like it before, for Cheltenham, where I had spent my schooldays, was now filled with the modern buildings of the eighteenth century, and the parts of London where I had lived were also relatively new. I was reminded of the city of London which lay east of Temple Bar, a section I had seldom visited, but even though there was a similarity between the city and this town, Rye still seemed unique to me as I saw it then for the first time.

The carriage reached the Mermaid Inn in Mermaid Street, the driver halted the horses in the courtyard, and presently I heard the shouts of the ostlers and the sounds of the baggage being unloaded.

My limbs were stiff. As Axel helped me down into the courtyard I slipped and fell against him, but before I could apologize

for my clumsiness he said abruptly: "There's Ned, but I see no
sign of Vere."

I turned.

There was a man in the doorway of the inn, and as he saw us
he stepped forward so that the light lay behind him and I could
not see his face. His movements seemed curiously reluctant.

"Where's Vere?" said Axel sharply to him as he drew nearer
to us. "He told me he'd be here to meet us."

"There was an accident." He had a deep voice with more than
a hint of a Sussex rural accent. The accent shocked me for I had
thought that all gentry, no matter where they lived in England,
spoke the King's English. He was not as tall as Axel, but was so
powerfully built that he in fact seemed the larger of the two. He
had narrow black eyes, a stubborn mouth and a shock of untidy
black hair which was cut very short in the manner of a yokel.
"The prize bull threw one of the farm hands and Vere rode himself to Winchelsea to get Doctor Salter. He asked me to meet
you instead and give you his apologies for not being here as he
promised."

"Couldn't he have sent you to fetch the doctor and come here
himself to meet us as we arranged?"

"He was too worried about the hand. They fear his back is
broken."

"I see." But he was clearly angry. I waited uneasily for him to
introduce me, for the man was looking at me openly now with
curious eyes.

"Where is the carriage?"

"Over there."

"Then let's waste no more time standing here, or my wife will
catch cold." He half-turned to me. "May I introduce my youngest
half-brother, Edwin . . . Ned, attend to our baggage, would you?
Is Simpson with the carriage? Get him to assist you."

But Ned had taken my hand in his and was bowing low with
unexpected ceremony. "Your servant, ma'am."

"How do you do," I said, responding to convention, and then

Axel's hand was on my arm and Axel's voice said coolly: "This way, my dear."

If Ned's Sussex accent had worried me about the gentility of the Brandsons, their carriage quickly restored my faith in their social position. It was polished and elaborate, well-sprung and comfortable, and clearly could only have been maintained by a gentleman.

"You were barely civil to Ned," I said in a low voice once I was seated. "Why was that?"

He had been stooping to examine the fastening of the carriage door, but once I spoke he swung around, seeming to tower above me in that small confined space. "He needs discipline," he said abruptly. "My father let him run wild and his mother cannot control him. He shows tendencies of becoming as wild as Rodric but with none of Rodric's charm and grace of manner." He sat down opposite me and the shaft of light from the porch shone directly across his face so that I saw for the first time the anger in his eyes. "And let me tell you this," he said. "I dislike the idea of reproving you so soon after our marriage, but I think I should clearly indicate from the start whenever I find your conduct unsatisfactory. If I was 'barely civil' to Ned, as you put it, that's my affair and has nothing to do with you. I did not ask for your comment, nor did I expect one. Just because you're my wife doesn't give you the liberty to criticize my manners whenever they may appear to your inexperienced eyes to be defective. Do you understand me?"

Tears stung my eyes. "Yes," I said.

"Then we shall say no more about it." He glanced at his watch and put it away again. "We should be at Haraldsdyke within half an hour."

I was silent.

I had expected Ned to join us in the carriage, but he evidently preferred to travel outside with the coachman and the servants, so Axel and I remained alone together. Within twenty minutes of our leaving the inn courtyard, Rye and Winchelsea were mere twin hills pinpricked with lights behind us, and the country on either side of the road was hidden by the darkness of the night. I felt very tired suddenly, and as always when my spirit was at a low ebb I thought of Alexander and longed for his companionship. Axel's anger seemed to have driven a wedge between us and made me feel isolated and alone again.

The darkness hid Haraldsdyke from my eyes. I had half-anticipated passing lodge gates and traveling up a long drive to the house, but there was no lodge, only tall iron gates set in a high weather-beaten wall, and then a sharp ascent to a level above the Marsh. I was to learn later that all the oldest houses on the Marsh were built on a slight elevation of the land above sea-level in order to escape the dangers of floods and spring tides. The carriage drew up before the house, Axel helped me to dismount, and then even before I could strain my eyes through the gloom to make out the shape of the gray walls, the front door was opened and a woman stood on the threshold with a lamp in her hand.

I knew instinctively that it was Alice. My nerves sharpened.

Ned and the coachman were attending to the baggage as Axel led me forward up the steps to the front door, but I had already forgotten them. My whole being was focused on the meeting which lay immediately ahead of me.

"Good evening, Alice," said Axel as we reached her. "May I present my wife?" And he turned to me and made the necessary counter-introduction.

Alice smiled. She was still plain even then, I noticed with relief. She had brown hair, soft and wispy, and a broad face with high cheekbones and green eyes. She had a heavy peasant's build with wide shoulders and an over-large bosom, and I would have thought her exceedingly fat if I had not realized suddenly that she was perhaps four months pregnant. The image of the meticulously efficient housekeeper and superbly conscientious mother receded a little and I was aware of an enormous relief.

She was, after all, merely an ordinary country woman and there was no reason why I should feel inferior to her in any way.

"Why, how pretty you be!" she exclaimed softly, and her accent was many shades thicker than Ned's. "Pray come in and feel welcome . . . Vere's coming, George," she added to Axel, and it gave me a shock to hear him called by the name his father had given him, even though he had warned me about it earlier. "He just returned from Winchelsea and went to change his clothes to receive you."

She led us across a long hall and up a curving staircase to the floor above. Within a moment we were in a large suite of rooms where fires burned in the grates and lamps cast a warm glow over oak furniture.

"I thought you should be having your father's rooms," she said to Axel. "They've not been used since his death, God rest his soul. Your step-mother still has her rooms in the west wing." She turned to me. "Let me know if there's anything more you need," she said. "George mentioned in his letter that you had a maid, and I've arranged for her to sleep in the room across the corridor for the time being. If you'd rather she slept in the servants' wing—"

"No," I said. "That will suit me very well."

"Then if there's nothing more I can do for you at present I'll leave you to refresh yourselves after your journey. The footmen will be up with the luggage in a minute, I dare say, and I've just had the maids bring up some hot water for you—see, over there in the ewers. . . . Would you like me to send any victuals up to you on a tray? Or some nice hot tea?"

I opened my mouth to accept, and then remembered Axel's presence and was silent.

He glanced at me, raising his eyebrows, and when I nodded my head, he said: "Some tea would be excellent, Alice. But please tell the rest of the family that we shall come down to the saloon as soon as possible."

The tea certainly revived me. Presently Marie-Claire arrived and helped me wash and change, and some time later when I was attired in a fresh gown and with my hair re-arranged, I began to take more notice of my surroundings. They were indeed beautiful rooms. It was true that they had not the light elegance of the London drawing-rooms, but each piece of oak furniture was a work of art of previous centuries, and the long velvet curtains at the windows and around the bed added impressiveness to the setting. I pulled aside one of the curtains to glance outside into the night, but it was too dark for me to see anything although I fancied I saw the lights of Rye and Winchelsea twinkling in the distance.

Axel came out of the dressing-room to meet me a few minutes later. His valet had shaved him for the second time that day, and he wore a gray coat with square tails, a striped waistcoat and long beige breeches cut in the French style which were slit at the sides above the ankle. He looked exceedingly elegant, yet curiously out of place in that quiet English country house. Perhaps, I thought alarmed, I also looked too elegant, even over-dressed, for the occasion. I glanced in the mirror hastily but before I could pass judgment on myself, he said: "Thank God you don't look like Alice!" and kissed the nape of my neck as he stood behind me.

He was evidently trying to make amends for his harshness at Rye. "Am I suitably dressed?" I said, still seeking reassurance. "I would not want to create a wrong impression."

"If you change your dress now I shall be very angry," he retorted. "You need not worry about creating wrong impressions when you look as well as you do now."

We went downstairs to the saloon.

Alice was knitting when we entered the room. I remember being surprised, because all the ladies I had been acquainted with in the past had spent their leisure hours sewing and I had never actually seen anyone knit before. There was a girl next to her on the couch, a lumpy girl with a pimpled face and an air of being near-sighted. This must evidently be Mary, Robert Brandson's ward, whom Axel had mentioned to me. My glance passed from the two plain women to the woman in the high-backed chair by the fireplace, and stayed there. For here was one of the most striking women I had ever seen, not perhaps as beautiful or as attractive as my mother, but a handsome, good-looking woman of about forty-five years of age with black hair tinged with silver at the temples and the wide-set slanting eyes I had noticed earlier when I had first met Ned.

She rose to her feet as we entered the room and crossed the floor towards us, every movement stressing her domination of the scene.

"Well, George," she said to Axel, "it took you ten months to find an English bride, but I must say the long delay obviously produced the best results! She looks quite charming." She drew me to her and kissed me on both cheeks with cool dry lips. "Welcome to your new home, child."

I disliked being called "child," but nonetheless contrived to curtsey and smile graciously while murmuring a word of thanks to her.

"How are you, Esther," Axel was saying to his step-mother, but he made no attempt to kiss her, and I realized then that he had shown no hint of affection to any member of his family. "You look much better than when I last saw you."

"Please, George, don't remind me of those dreadful days of the inquest . . . Mary, come over here—you're not chained to the couch, are you? That's better . . . my dear, this is Mary Moore, my husband's ward who lives here with us—ah, here's Vere at last! Where have you been, Vere? George and his wife have just come downstairs only a moment ago."

He was a slim pale man. He seemed to have inherited his mother's build, but otherwise he did not resemble her. He had fair hair and lashes, and his complexion was so light that it was almost feminine. In contrast his eyes were a deep vivid blue and were by far his most striking feature; I particularly noticed them because when he smiled it was with his mouth only and his eyes remained bright but without expression.

"Hello George," he said, and while I noticed that he spoke the King's English without trace of a country accent I also noticed that he spoke as he smiled, without expression. "We were beginning to think you weren't returning to Haraldsdyke."

He might have sounded disappointed, but he did not. However, neither did he sound pleased. The curious lack of inflection made me feel uneasy.

I was presented to him, but although he was courteous in his response I still did not feel at ease with him. We all conversed for perhaps ten minutes in that gracious, well-lit room, and then the butler announced that supper was served, and we crossed the hall to the dining room. I was hungry after the long journey, and was glad that they had a light meal waiting for us instead of the customary six o'clock tea. We had dined late that afternoon at an inn somewhere along the Sussex border, and dinner now seemed a long time ago.

There was a chandelier in the dining room and the silver glinted beneath its bright light. Axel went straight to the head of the table without hesitation, but I paused not knowing where I should place myself, anxious not to give offense.

I saw Axel frown and make a barely perceptible gesture to the other end of the table. Moving quickly I went to the chair which he had indicated, and sat down in haste.

There seemed to be a general hesitation which I did not understand. I began to wonder in panic what mistake I could have made, and then Vere, who was immediately on my right, murmured to me: "You do not intend to say grace?"

I was speechless.

"I think it unnecessary to say grace more than once a day," said Axel from the head of the table. "My wife is accustomed to saying grace only at dinner and not on any other occasion."

"Quite right too," said Esther from her place on Axel's right. "Times change. Nowadays I hear only the non-conformists say grace at every meal . . . Mary dear, do try and sit up straighter! What will happen to your figure if you tend to droop so?"

Not much that has not already happened, I thought dryly, and then felt sorry for the poor girl as she flushed in embarrassment and sat up as straight as a ramrod. It occurred to me that Esther had a sharp tongue behind her honeyed voice.

Supper began. We were halfway through the roast beef when the door opened and Ned came into the room. It was the first time I had seen him in a clear light and I was struck by the fact that his clothes were dirty and shabby, and that he obviously had not troubled to change or wash for the meal.

"I'm sorry to be so late," he said. "I was attending to the horses."

There was a slight pause. At the head of the table, Axel laid down his knife and leaned back in his chair.

"Whose job is it to look after the horses?"

Ned stopped, one hand on the back of his chair.

"Well?"

"The grooms."

"Have I employed you to be a groom?"

"No."

"Then in the future you will be punctual at meals and not tend the horses when you should be at the table."

Ned said nothing. I noticed that the tips of his ears were a dull red.

"And I'm afraid I can't allow you to sit down to a meal looking as unkempt and untidy as a farmhand. You'd better go and eat in the kitchens, and take care to mend your ways in the future, for next time you appear like this in the dining room you'll be thrashed."

The room was very still.

"Do you understand that?"

There was a heavy silence.

"Answer me!"

"Yes," said Ned, "you damned bloody foreigner." And he was

gone, the door banging behind him, his footsteps echoing as he crossed the hall towards the kitchens.

The silence was painful. The footmen tried to pretend they were mere statues incapable of sight or hearing; Esther looked horrified; the girl Mary's eyes were almost as round as the dinner-plates on the table before us. On my right, Vere was motionless, his knife still poised in his hand, and beyond him Alice seemed to be inspecting what appeared to be an imaginary spot on the tablecloth.

Axel shrugged his shoulders. "This food is excellent," he observed to no one in particular. "It would be a pity to let it grow cold any longer." And he leaned forward in his chair to resume his meal.

"George," said Esther in distress, "I really feel I must apologize for him—"

"No," said Axel strongly. "That's not necessary. I would not accept any apology which did not come from his own lips. There's no reason why you should assume responsibility for his insults."

"He gets more uncouth daily," was all she said. "I'm beyond knowing what should be done with him."

"He's trying so hard to be a second Rodric," said Vere, "that he has overreached himself and his attempts at emulation have merely resulted in a distorted parody."

"But he is nothing like Rodric!" Esther cried angrily. "Nothing at all!"

"No," said Mary, speaking for the first time. "He is so different from Rodric."

"Rodric had such charm, such wit, such . . ." Esther broke off, and to my discomfort turned to me. "It was the most dreadful tragedy," she said rapidly. "No doubt George has mentioned—"

"Yes," I said. "Axel told me."

"Now, ma'am," said Vere to his mother, "you mustn't upset yourself."

"No, I'm not upset, but it's just that now we're all gathered together again around this table I seem to see Rodric's ghost the whole time—"

"Ah come, Esther," Axel said unexpectedly. "Talking of Rodric's ghost will make you feel no better. We all miss Rodric to some degree, just as we all miss Papa, and certainly you are entitled to miss both of them more than any of us, but dwelling on your loss will only aggravate your grief. You must know that."

"I should like to know," said Vere, "—just out of interest, naturally—which of us had missed Papa."

His voice was extremely polite. While everyone looked at him he cut a slice of beef from the plate in front of him, speared it with his fork and ate it tranquilly.

"Well, of course," said Axel, equally courteous, "we all know there was little love lost between you and Papa, and still less between you and Rodric."

"One might say the same of you," said Vere. "We all know what you apparently thought of Rodric. It was clear from your silence at the inquest that in your opinion Rodric was a murderer."

"Are you suggesting that he wasn't?"

"Why no," said Vere, his blue eyes open wide. "If Rodric didn't kill Papa, then who did?"

There was a clash of a glass shivering into fragments. Alice rose abruptly in dismay, her dress stained with wine from the glass she had overturned. "Dear Lord, look what I've done—"

The diversion was immediate. One of the footmen darted forward with an ineffectual white napkin; the butler murmured "T-t-t-" in distress, and Esther said: "Oh Alice, your new gown!"

"So careless I was," said Alice. "So clumsy. Pray excuse me . . ."

The men rose as she left the table to try and repair the damage, and then seated themselves again.

"Such a pity," said Esther absently. "The stain will never come out." She turned to me without warning. "Well, my dear, tell us more about yourself. George said so little in his letter."

I began to talk, my voice answering her questions naturally, but my mind was confused by the glimpse of the emotions which I had seen unleashed during the earlier conversation, and I found concentration difficult. I was thankful when at last the meal was over and Mary and I retired to the drawing room while Vere and Axel remained in the dining room with their port. Esther had excused herself from us to see if Alice had been able to reduce the stain on her gown, and so Mary and I were alone together.

There was suddenly so little to say. Even though we were only three years apart in age the gulf between us seemed enormous. After five minutes of desperately difficult conversation I seized on the first topic which entered my head.

"If it will not affect you too much," I began cautiously, "please tell me a little about Rodric." That seemed somewhat bold, so I added, lying: "Axel told me he had a remarkable personality."

I could hardly have imagined the effect my words would have. All trace of nervousness seemed to leave the girl; her face was suddenly alive with animation. "George was right," she said. "Rodric was a most remarkable person."

I was prepared to relax now that I had discovered a topic on which we might both converse for a time, but I did not. Something in her manner was so unexpected that I felt my nerves sharpen more than ever in my effort to discern the truth.

"Mr. Brandson—my guardian—was most anxious that I—that Rodric and I . . ." She blushed, hesitated a little. "Of course, I was then too young for any formal mention of it to be made, but it was intended that Rodric and I . . ." She paused delicately.

I stared at her. "You mean Mr. Brandson wished you both to be betrothed when you were old enough?"

"Well, yes . . . yes, he wished, hoped . . ." Her hands worked nervously at her dress. "I am orphaned now, as you no doubt know, but my father was a baronet with an estate in Hampshire and I have a considerable portion which he willed to me . . . It would have been a suitable match." Her pale eyes misted slightly.

She turned her head aside with a sharp movement as if to hide her emotions.

"I see," I said, trying not to sound too amazed.

"Rodric was so noble," she said. "He was such a fine upright worthy person. Fond as I was of my guardian, I sometimes think that on many occasions he did not treat Rodric as he deserved."

"I heard," I said, "that they often didn't see eye to eye."

"My guardian was so blind, so prejudiced . . . Rodric is—was— unusually gifted."

"Gifted?"

"He wrote," said Mary. "He was never happier than when he had a pen between his fingers and an inkwell and paper on the table before him. He wrote mostly articles and political tracts— he concerned himself very much with politics and used to ride as far afield as Dover to speak for the Cause." Seeing that I looked blank she added: "The Whig Cause. It was a dreadful disappointment to my guardian who hoped Rodric would support the Tories and become a member of that party in Parliament. But my guardian didn't understand Rodric, didn't understand that Rodric couldn't acquiesce in accepting ideals he didn't believe in."

But I was more interested in Rodric's possible literary talent than in his possible noble soul. "Did he write any novels?"

"Only one—I read part of it and thought it excellent."

"What was it about? Where's the manuscript? May I read it?"

Her expression changed. "No," she said flatly. "Vere burned all the manuscripts after Rodric's . . . death."

In the pause that followed the door opened and Esther entered the room. Remembering her distress when the subject of Rodric had been introduced at dinner I knew that it would be impossible to continue the conversation with Mary. Apparently Mary had drawn the same conclusions, for she was already moving across the room in search of her sewing basket. "Alice managed to remove most of the stain from the dress," Esther said as she sat down by the fire. "She knows so many of these old wives' recipes! I believe she has a secret recipe for everything, from curing hay fever to making toadstool poison to feed the mice in the cellar. These village girls have an amazing knowledge of such things."

I was aware again of the honeyed tones which did not quite conceal the barbed sharpness of her tongue.

"She has just gone to the nursery to look in on the children," Esther was observing, and suddenly the slanting black eyes were turned in my direction. "Alice," she said, "is the most excellent mother."

I smiled politely, not fully understanding the sudden intentness of her gaze.

"Mary dear," said Esther, "just run down to the saloon and fetch my shawl, would you? I'm a little chilled."

The girl departed obediently.

"I did not quite gather, my dear," said Esther after a moment, "how long you and George have been married."

"Only a week."

"Ah." She picked up a copy of the "Spectator" idly and began to glance through the pages. "And have you known him long?"

"About a month."

"I see." She went on looking at the magazine. "So you don't know him well."

"Well enough," I said, "by this time."

She must have read some meaning into my words which I did not intend, for she glanced up sharply, her beautiful mouth curving in a smile, her unusual eyes sparkling with amusement. "Yes," she said, "I've no doubt you do. If George had anything in common with Rodric, it was his talent for making himself extremely well known to any woman he fancied in the shortest possible time."

If I had been less angry I might have thought how odd it was that Rodric's name was spoken so often in this house, but I was too incensed by the implications of her remark to notice this at the time. I sat facing her, she a poised woman well accustomed to the intricacies of drawing room conversation, I perhaps thirty years her junior but much too furious to be intimidated by her maturity and experience.

"All young men need to sow their wild oats," I said coolly, repeating a phrase my father had often used. "If Axel hadn't sown his in his youth I would have thought him strange indeed. I hardly think I need add that his behavior towards me has always been exemplary in every respect."

"Of course," said Esther. "Naturally." She smiled. "No doubt he now wishes to settle down and be a satisfactory husband. And father."

I did not answer.

"He is anxious for children, of course?"

I was certainly not going to tell her it was a subject we had never discussed.

"Yes," I said, "especially now that he owns Haraldsdyke."

The door opened. I glanced up, expecting to see Mary returning with the shawl, but it was Alice who stood on the threshold. She had changed her gown, and the style did not flatter her condition so that her pregnancy was very obvious.

I had a sudden, inexplicable longing to escape from that room and those women.

"Will you excuse me?" I said politely to Esther. "I am afraid the long journey has made me more than usually tired. I think it best if I retired to bed now."

They were both extremely solicitous. Of course I should rest and recover my strength. Was there anything either of them could do for me? Anything which could be sent up to my room from the kitchens? Could I find my way back to my room unaided?

"We so want you to feel at home here," said Alice. "We so want you to feel welcome."

I thanked her, assured them there was nothing further I needed, and escaped as courteously as possible with a candle in my hand to light the way down the long corridors.

I reached the door of our suite of rooms without difficulty and then paused as I heard the sound of voices raised in argument. The door of the sitting room, or boudoir, was ajar and a shaft of light slanted out across the dark passage before me.

I stopped.

"You think too much of Rodric," I heard Axel say, and his voice was harsh and cold. "It's time you stopped idolizing his memory and saw him as he really was. You're nineteen and yet you behave like a young schoolboy moonstruck by the current School Hero. Rodric wasn't the saint you imagine him to be, neither was he the crusader in shining armor, fighting for truth. He was a misfit who could not or would not conform."

"You were always jealous of him." Ned's voice was low and trembling. "You pretended to be friendly so that he was deceived, but you never liked him. You were Father's favorite until you went back to Vienna and then when you returned later on you found Rodric had taken your place. You resented him from the moment you saw he meant more to Father than you did—"

"What childish nonsense you talk!"

"And you hated Father for rejecting you because you chose to live in Vienna—you wanted to pay him back at all costs—and pay Rodric back for usurping you . . ."

"I'm beginning to think you want another thrashing. Be very careful, Ned. You forget I still have the whip in my hand."

"You can't frighten me! You can beat me and sneer at me and send me away into the army, but I'll still spit in your face, you bloody murderer . . ."

There was the stinging vibration of leather on flesh, a sharp cry of pain.

"You knew Father had altered his will in your favor so you killed him with Rodric's gun and then pushed Rodric in the Marsh before he could deny the charge!"

The whip struck again. I listened transfixed, unable to move. Then:

"You liar," said Axel between his teeth. "You . . ." And he used words I had once overheard my father use, syllables never used in civilized conversation.

Ned was half-sobbing, half-laughing. It froze me to hear him. "Deny it as much as you wish!" he shouted. "Curse as much as you please! But who inherited Haraldsdyke when Father died? Who inherited all the land and the money? Who had the best reason for wanting Father dead?"

"Get out! Get out, do you hear? Get out of my—"

"Not Rodric, George Brandson! And Rodric never killed him! Rodric wasn't a murderer!"

There was the sound of a scuffle, the impact of fist against flesh, a small spent sigh and then a jarring thud as if something very heavy had slumped to the floor.

Silence fell.

Very softly, almost unaware of my own actions I crept forward, snuffed my candle and hid behind the curtains that concealed the window at the far end of the corridor.

The silence seemed to go on and on without ending.

At last after an interval which seemed to endure as long as an eternity, the door opened and through a chink in the curtains I saw Axel walk away down the passage to the head of the stairs. His head was bent, his shoulders stooped and he moved slowly.

I went at once to the room. Ned was sprawled half-conscious on the carpet, the blood soiling his black hair as it oozed from a cut above his temple. As I knelt beside him and reached for his pulse he groaned and stirred feebly, so I poured him a glass of water from the pitcher in the bedroom and tried to help him to drink.

He opened his eyes and looked so ill that I thought he was going to vomit. Hastening into the bedroom again I seized the chamber pot, which was the first receptacle that I could think of, and brought it to him just in time.

Afterwards he started to tremble. He was chalk-white with the nervous reaction from the scene and as I helped him drink from the glass he seemed very young and defenseless, very frightened and alone. He seemed utterly different now to the enraged defiant accuser whom I had overheard earlier and I suspected he had only spoken in that manner out of bravado.

I was reminded of Alexander; my heart ached suddenly.

"I slipped," he said. "I was trying to hit George when I slipped, fell and hit my head." His voice was little more than a whisper and his eyes were dark with humiliation. Then: "What are you doing here? Leave me alone." He wrenched himself free, and as I stared at him with mute sympathy he stumbled towards the couch where his coat lay and dressed himself with shaking fingers.

"Why did you let Axel beat you?" I said at last. "You could have struggled and escaped."

"I did struggle," he said wryly, "and fell and cut my head." He sat down abruptly. I guessed that he was feeling dizzy again after his experience, and I went to him, as I would have gone to Alexander, and put my arm around his shoulders to comfort him.

He recoiled instantly. "Don't," he muttered.

"I only want to help you."

"I shall be well in a minute. Leave me alone." He looked at me suddenly. "George would be angry," he whispered. "He would be angry with you. Don't let him see you with me."

His eyes were bright with tears. I saw then that he was desperately afraid of Axel and terrified at the memory of the scene which had just passed. And as I stared at him in appalled silence there were voices far off in the distance and footsteps resounding in the corridor.

"Please go," he said. "Please."

"Certainly not," I said. "These are my rooms and I have a right to be here. I'm not afraid." But I moved away from him all the same, and my legs were strangely unsteady as I rose to my feet.

The door opened.

Vere came into the room followed by Axel. They both stopped short when they saw me.

I stood my ground, my head erect, my mouth dry, and looked Axel straight in the eyes.

"I came here a moment ago from the drawing room," I said. "Do you wish that I should return there until you have finished whatever business you have to discuss with Ned?"

After a moment, Axel said: "No, that won't be necessary. Vere has merely come to help Ned to his room."

Ned started to tremble again. For a moment I feared he might faint, but he seemed to recover a little. As I watched, Vere crossed the room to him.

"Have you nothing to say to George?"

There was a terrible silence. Ned's eyes were black coals in his white face.

"I've told Vere you are to leave at dawn," Axel said without expression. "I shall give you fifty guineas and then you can make your own way in the world. After all you've said to me I hardly think you would want to live beneath my roof a day longer."

There were tears streaking Ned's face suddenly, great silent tears, and then the harsh sobs tore at his throat and he sank down on the couch, his head in his hands, and wept as if his heart would break.

I could not bear it. He was Alexander to me then, even if he did not resemble Alexander physically. I ran across the room and pressed him close to me and begged him not to cry.

Axel called my name.

I stood up and went to him without hesitation. "Don't send him away," I said. "Please don't send him away. He didn't mean what he said to you, I'm sure. He was much too upset and unhappy to say meaningful things."

"Go into the other room," was all he said. "This is not a matter in which you need involve yourself."

"Please," I said, and I could feel the tears in my own eyes now. "My brother would often say stupid foolish things when he was in a rage, and afterwards he would regret them bitterly. My brother—"

"Your brother is at Harrow, ma'am, and Ned is a stranger whom you do not know. Now be so kind as to retire and leave us together."

But before I could move Ned spoke from the other side of the room. "It's as she says." His voice shook a little, but he was on his feet again without swaying, the tears wet on his cheeks. "I didn't mean what I said, George. It was all lies—all wickedness . . . suddenly I missed Rodric so much that I allowed my grief to cloud my mind and said terrible things which I knew were untrue. . . . Please forgive me and don't send me away. Tell me how I can apologize to you and make amends for what I said, for I swear before God in all truth that I'm sorry for everything I've done to offend you this evening and want only to act better in future."

There was a silence.

"Please, Axel, please don't send him away—"

"My dear," said Axel to me in a voice of ice. "I have asked you twice to leave the room. I trust I do not have to ask you a third time."

I curtsied wordlessly and went through into the bedroom where I immediately pressed my ear to the panel of the closed door. But the panels were thick, and although I could hear the murmur of voices I could not distinguish what was being said. Presently I sat down at my dressing table and began fidgeting idly with the silver brushes and combs, but my mind was numb and my thoughts became confused when I tried to think clearly. It occurred to me then how exhausted I was. Marie-Claire had laid out my night clothes so I undressed as quickly as possible and was just sitting before the mirror in my nightgown and brushing my hair when the murmur of voices ceased, a door closed far away and the next moment Axel himself came into the room.

I felt afraid suddenly. I could not look at him. But to my relief he went through to his dressing room without speaking, and I was left alone to brush out my hair and creep between the sheets of the huge double bed.

But still my nerves would not let me sleep. My limbs began to ache with tension and then at last he came back into the room and slid into bed beside me.

I had of course expected him to reprove me for my forward behavior in the sitting room when I had tried to comfort Ned; I had also half-expected some sort of explanation of the scene there, or at least a comment on what had happened. But he said nothing.

I waited rigid, scarcely daring to breathe, but he was silent beside me, so motionless that I felt I dared not move either. After a while the loneliness was even greater than my fear and muddled bewilderment. I whispered his name.

He turned sharply. "I thought you were asleep! What's the matter?"

"Oh Axel, I didn't mean to make you angry, I didn't mean it, I promise—" Exhaustion made me tearful; my voice broke a little and forced me to silence.

"My dear child," he said astonished. "Who spoke of me being angry with you? My anger was directed against other people and my mind was occupied with other things." And he drew me to him in an abrupt, not unkind way and kissed me on the forehead. "This has been a difficult evening for you," he said at last, "but I must insist that you don't worry about matters which concern me alone. The problem of Ned is entirely my responsibility and there is absolutely no need for you to share it."

"Is—is he to be sent away?"

"Not at present. He has apologized for his lies and his abuse and has promised to mend his ways. He is, after all, merely an overgrown schoolboy who has never been accustomed to any discipline at all from his family. Now, go to sleep and stop your worrying, and you'll see how much better everything will seem when you wake tomorrow morning."

But when I slept at last I dreamed turbulent nightmares, and saw Rodric drowning in the Marsh while Vere clapped his hands in glee and Alice whispered "We must make the toadstool poison to feed the mice in the cellar;" and suddenly Axel was standing smiling in the hall of Haraldsdyke and Esther was handing him a gun smeared with blood, and Mary was saying to me: "Rodric was such a wonderful murderer, you see." And the word *murderer* seemed to reverberate until its echo filled the hall, and all at once Ned was chasing me to my death in the marshes and calling after me in Alexander's voice: *Axel killed him! Axel's a murderer, a murderer, a murderer* . . .

But when I woke up gasping with the sweat moist on my forehead I found myself alone with the sun shining peacefully through the curtains and Axel's laugh ringing in my ears as he joked with his valet in the dressing room next door.

Three

FROM THE WINDOW I had my first view south across the Marsh in daylight, the flat expanse of green ending in the blue line of the sea not far away, the twin towns of Rye and Winchelsea seeming very near as they basked in the pale autumn sunshine. It was all so peaceful, so serene. I turned aside, feeling strangely reassured, and rang for Marie-Claire.

However presently I was aware that I was not as strong as I had anticipated and I slipped back to bed.

"Ask for a tray to be sent up to me," I told Marie-Claire in French. "I would like some coffee, very black, and a thin slice of burned toast."

She departed for the kitchens.

I was just lying back on the pillows and thinking that if all was well I would be sufficiently recovered by the afternoon to dress and go downstairs, when Axel returned to the room.

"How are you this morning?" He came over to the bed and stooped to kiss me on the lips. Some element in his expression when he looked at me seemed to suggest he found my appearance pleasing in the extreme, but although before I would have felt gratified I now felt an inexplicable desire to remain beyond his reach.

"I'm feeling a trifle delicate this morning," I replied truthfully. "I wondered if you might apologize to the rest of the family for me and say I shall come downstairs this afternoon."

"You're the mistress of the house," was all he said. "You need not excuse your absence to anyone except me. And I, of course, am merely sorry to hear you're indisposed. Perhaps I should send someone to Winchelsea to ask Dr. Salter to come and see you . . ."

"No, no—it's nothing really. I shall be quite recovered in two or three hours. I just feel somewhat tired and would prefer to remain in bed a little longer."

"I understand." He kissed me again and stood up. "I have business to do," he said abruptly. "Vere and I will be riding to Rye this morning to see my father's lawyer James Sherman. There's a possibility that we may be some time."

"I see. Will you be dining at Rye?"

"Possibly. It depends how long our business takes . . . I shall tell Alice you're indisposed and ask her to continue to supervise the household today."

"Oh yes . . . yes, thank you." I had forgotten I was supposed to be in charge of running the house now. After Axel had gone, I lay thinking about the difficulties of assuming a large responsibility about which I knew very little of practical value. I was just wondering if Alice would not perhaps like to continue to supervise the more mundane household details when there was a knock on the door, and Alice herself appeared.

"George told me you weren't well," she said anxiously. "We were all so sorry . . . if there's anything I can be doing for you—" She paused inquiringly.

I repeated the assurance that I had given Axel that I would soon be quite well, but Alice still seemed anxious.

"If you feel at all sick," she said, "I have an excellent herb recipe which I often take during the early months."

I saw she had misunderstood. "No, no," I said, feeling slightly embarrassed. "It's not a question of—" I stopped.

"You're sure? of course you haven't been married long, but sometimes . . . But if you're quite sure that there can be no question of such a thing—"

"Absolutely positive," I said so firmly that she evidently realized at last why I had decided to rest for a few hours further, and at that moment Marie-Claire entered the room with the coffee and burned toast.

I half-hoped Alice would leave then, but she must have thought I needed companionship for she sat down on the chair by the bed and began to talk of the menu she had planned for dinner that evening.

"I hear Vere and Axel may not be here for dinner," I said.

"There will still be ourselves, Vere's mother, Mary and Ned. Unless Ned stays away. He saddled a horse early this morning and rode off over the Marsh."

I was silent.

"Vere says," said Alice, "there was an unfortunate to-do last night between Ned and George."

"I believe everything is all settled now."

"Poor Ned," said Alice. "He does miss Rodric so." She gathered up her skirts and began to rise to her feet. "Well, I must go and see the children and let you rest—"

"No—please," I said suddenly. "Stay and talk for a while—if you can spare the time, of course . . . I am anxious to hear more about Rodric. Everyone seems to have been so fond of him."

Alice hesitated and then sat down again, rearranging her skirts carefully. "Yes," she said, "everyone was so fond of Rodric. Both his parents preferred him to Vere. Vere's mother doted on Rodric and wouldn't even hear a word against him."

"Not even when he got into trouble?" I remembered Axel's references to Rodric's wildness and the Watch at Rye.

Alice's green eyes widened. "You heard about that?"

"Axel mentioned it."

"Ah." She hesitated. Then: "There was nothing Rodric wouldn't dare do," she said. "He was bold. Nothing was sacred, nothing beyond his reach. He used to act the highwayman for his own amusement till rumor reached the ears of the Lord Warden of the Cinque Ports. But nothing was proved against him. At the end he was with the smugglers, working with Delancey the great

French smuggler, and in the night he would ride to Dungeness and dodge the Revenue Men on the watch there."

I was amazed. "This was common knowledge?"

"It—was revealed at the inquest . . . Rodric used to despise Vere because Vere would have none of his childish pranks. Highwaymen and smugglers indeed! Such play-acting! Vere was more of a man than he was. I always thought so from the beginning, even when they were boys."

"You knew him then?"

"Yes, I lived in the little village of Haraldsford a mile from here. My mother is a witch." She said it as prosaically as I might have said: "My mother was French." "Rodric and his big rough friends rode up to our cottage one morning and ducked my mother in the witch's ducking-stool over the village pond. They thought it a great joke. My mother put a curse on him afterwards and prayed he would die by water within ten years." She was very sedate, very undisturbed. "He died in the Marsh nine and a half years later," she said. "I wasn't altogether surprised." She straightened the coverlet absentmindedly. "Vere was quite different," she said. "He was always serious and eager to acquit himself well in whatever he undertook. He came to my mother when he was sixteen and asked for a spell which would make all the girls fall in love with him instead of with Rodric." She smiled suddenly, her broad face lightening with humor. "My mother said: 'Here is a girl who cares nothing for Rodric' and led him straight to me. We were very happy, right from the beginning."

"But how old were you then?"

"Thirteen. It was two years before we could be wed, and then Vere's father nearly killed him when he heard the news of our marriage. He wouldn't speak to Vere for two months and Vere worked on a neighbor's farm as a hired hand as his father wouldn't have him at Haraldsdyke. Then I was with child and the winter was cold and Vere sent word to his father asking if he wanted his first grandchild to die of starvation and cold, and so we returned to Haraldsdyke. But the baby died," she said, all trace of humor vanishing from her face. "Poor little thing. He only lived a few hours."

I murmured something sympathetic.

"It was hard for Vere at Haraldsdyke," she said after a while. "Nothing he ever did was right. His father would shout and roar at Rodric, but it was Rodric he loved the best. He never took any trouble to listen to Vere."

"How strange," I said, "that Rodric, whom everyone says was so delightful and charming, never married."

"Yes," she said dispassionately. "He was very handsome. He was tall and strong with a straight back and flat stomach, and his hair was dark as a crow's wing. But his complexion was fair. He had blue eyes, as blue as Vere's, and an easy smile and when he laughed, everyone laughed with him."

I was just deciding that after giving such an attractive description she must have been fonder of him than I had supposed when I saw the hate glitter unmistakably in her eyes.

My heart bumped unevenly with the shock, but she was already looking away. "Yet he never married," she was saying. "He was too busy trying to seduce other men's wives." And as I stared at her she shrugged and smiled again as if to make light of the entire conversation. "He was like that," she said. "It was no fun for him to get a woman who was easy. Everything had to be difficult so that the experience could be turned into a game, a sport, some new prank to amuse him. He was like that."

There was a silence. Then:

"Like the day he died, for instance," she said, and there was a distant expression in her eyes now and I guessed she was seeing other scenes of months ago. "It was Christmas Eve. George had arrived from Vienna three days earlier to spend Christmas with us, and this pleased Vere's father who had had an argument with Vere over the estate and discovered Rodric was up to some fresh nonsense; I think it was then old Mr. Brandson turned to George.

"I was in the parlor on the morning of Christmas Eve to prepare the menus for Christmas Day and Boxing Day. Rodric found me there. I saw at once that he was anxious for sport—any sport—which would relieve his boredom, but I was expecting Vere to join me and I knew he wouldn't be long. When Vere came minutes later he found me struggling with Rodric and crying for help.

"I have never seen Vere so angry. He would have tried to kill Rodric, I think, but George was with him and restrained him. Then George took Rodric out shooting over the Marsh and they were gone from the house till late afternoon.

"Vere went out afterwards; he had business to attend to on the estate and didn't return to the house till much later. That was a terrible day! I shall never forget when Vere returned to the house and I had to tell him his father was dead."

"I suppose Rodric had already gone by then?"

"Why, yes, Rodric had gone and George had gone too, to try to bring him back. Rodric left the house directly after he quarreled with his father—after his father was dead, we learned later. Esther, Vere's mother, found Mr. Brandson perhaps quarter of an hour after Rodric had gone to the stables and, according to Ned who was there at the time, saddled his horse in haste and rode off into the winter dusk. Poor woman! I heard her screams even though I was in the nursery with the children and I ran at once to the hall."

"It must have been a fearful shock for her."

"Indeed it was. Fortunately George was close at hand, for he and Mary reached Esther before I did. Mary had been in the drawing room while I had gone to the nursery. To begin with we were in the saloon downstairs by the library but then when Rodric began to quarrel with his father in the library we became embarrassed being as we could hear so clearly through the wall. Mr. Brandson's voice when he was roused was louder that the Town-Crier at Rye, and Rodric's not much quieter."

I longed to ask her what she had overheard but had no wish to appear too inquisitive.

"I suppose Mr. Brandson had challenged Rodric about his relationship with the smugglers," I said carelessly.

"There was rather more said than that," said Alice.

"Oh."

There was a pause. Alice rearranged herself comfortably in her chair. "Mr. Brandson swore he would disinherit Rodric without delay," she said. "He swore he would alter his will."

"But hadn't he already done so?"

"Yes, that was strange. I expect George told you that in fact Mr. Brandson had altered his will shortly before his death to disinherit all his sons save George himself. But no one knew that at the time of his death. When Rodric faced his father that afternoon he must still have thought himself due to inherit the money and property one day, and Mr. Brandson never told him he was already disinherited."

"Wasn't it considered strange that Mr. Brandson disinherited his other sons like that?"

Alice shrugged. "He never really favored George," was all she said. "I don't know what made him draw up a will such as the one he made before he died—the will where he left George everything. He and George were never close after George went against his wishes and returned to Vienna."

There was a knock at the door. I was so deeply engrossed in the conversation that I was unaware of the knock until Alice called out: "Who is it?"

"Mary. The rector's wife has called, Alice, and is downstairs in the morning room. Shall I tell her—"

"I shall see her." Alice stood up. "Our church is at Haraldsford," she said to me, "and the parish includes the villages of Haraldsmere and Conyhurst-in-the-Marsh. I expect we shall have several visits this morning from people who wish to call upon you and welcome you to Haraldsdyke. I'll explain that you're indisposed and ask them to call again later."

"If you would—thank you, Alice . . . and please give the rector's wife my apologies."

"Of course." She smiled reassuringly. "Don't you worry yourself about anything. I'll see to anything that needs attending to."

I relaxed in relief as she left the room, and settled down in bed to try and sleep a little more but the more I tried to sleep the more I thought of my conversation with her. Curiously enough, the part which remained most vividly in my mind was her description of Rodric. I could imagine him so clearly now, gay and careless, his zest for life equaled only by his zest for excitement, superbly free of all restrictive ties and the dreariness of responsibilities. The very picture of him stirred my blood. That was the kind of man I would have married if I had had the choice, I thought. Axel's cool sophistication and remoteness of manner was oppressive to me, and the great gulf of the years between us was stifling in the extreme. It occurred to me for the first time that I resented the discipline he already exercised where I was concerned, his bland assumption that I would do as he told me without question. It was true, I thought, that a woman must be submissive in some respects for in many matters the husband was sure to know best, but surely in this day and age she had a certain measure of freedom . . .

For when I was young the nineteenth century had barely begun, and I could not foresee then the great changes of the Victorian era and the dwindling of all women's independence.

Perhaps they had different ideas now in Europe, I thought. Perhaps Axel treated me in this way because he was a foreigner.

The morning passed slowly; I became restless and impatient, and finally at noon I summoned Marie-Claire and began to dress.

Some reason made me long to explore my new home on my own. I did not want Alice, or worse still Axel's step-mother Esther conducting me through each room in a formal tour of inspection. Accordingly when I was dressed I did not go down to the morning room or the saloon, but up the back stairs to the attics beneath the eaves, and when I paused at last it was at the top of the house before a small window which looked out due east across the Marsh. Someone had carved on the windowpane with a diamond.

Stooping so that I might see the inscription more clearly I read:
"God Save Englande and Ye Towne of Rye
"God Save Rodric Who Here Did Lye
"Imprisoned."

"JULY 1797"

It was the year of my birth. He would have been about ten or eleven years old, locked in the attic for a while perhaps as punishment for some childhood prank. I wondered where he had found the diamond, and then casting my eye around the little room I saw the huge boxes containing heaven knows how many disused clothes and other articles. Perhaps he had found some long-lost diamond by chance and seized upon it to amuse himself as he whiled away the long hours of imprisonment.

It seemed sad to think that he was dead. I traced the carving on the glass with my fingers, and suddenly he was so real to me that I would hardly have been surprised to turn and find him waiting at the door.

But when I turned there was no one there.

I shook myself impatiently and retraced my steps downstairs again, past the stairs leading to the servants' wing to the floor where Axel and I had our rooms. I stood on the landing, still undecided whether I should go down to the ground floor and risk meeting Alice or Esther, and then at length I turned down the corridor and began glancing inside the rooms which I passed. Several were empty. One I was about to enter and then I heard the murmur of voices so I hastily passed on again. One of the voices I seemed to recognize as the girl Mary's. Perhaps she was doing lessons with her governess.

Life perhaps would not be so unpleasant as a governess, I thought. No strange new relations to meet and satisfy, no mansion suddenly thrust into one's control, no husband whom one was nervous of displeasing. A governess could always leave her employment to seek a better position if she were unhappy. A wife could not leave her husband and home.

I reached the end of the corridor and paused to look back. I had a stifling feeling of being trapped then, a tremor of horror which swept over me in sickening waves. I would be here for the rest of my life at Haraldsdyke, and the future yawned before me, decade after decade of nothingness. I was only seventeen. I was still so young. Far too young to be trapped in an old house with a group of strangers who might or might not resent me, far too young to be shackled to a man I did not understand and certainly did not love.

It was not that I was afraid of him, I told myself. Merely that I was uneasy in his presence.

I was too frightened then to admit my fear and look it squarely in the face.

Reaching out blindly in an attempt to break my train of thought I opened the door at the end of the corridor and went into the room beyond.

There was a four-poster in one corner and by the window stood a huge oak desk massively carved. The room seemed quiet, unoccupied. I sat down on the chair by the window, my elbows on the desk, and stared out across the Marsh beyond.

It would be better when Alexander came down from Harrow. Perhaps we could even journey to London together for a few days. If Axel allowed it. If I managed to escape pregnancy.

The thought of pregnancy terrified me. I felt as if I were totally unready to face further unknown ordeals, and I had no desire to bear Axel's children.

I wished desperately then that I could talk to someone of my fears, but I knew as soon as the wish became a conscious thought that there was no one in whom I could confide. Even a parson would be horrified by my revulsion against pregnancy; I could almost hear the unknown rector of Haraldsford say shocked: "But marriage is for the procreation of children . . ."

But there were obviously ways of avoiding pregnancy, I thought. Otherwise my mother would have had other children besides Alexander and myself.

Perhaps a doctor . . . I almost laughed in contempt at myself for thinking of the idea. I pictured what the family doctor at Winchelsea would say if I were to ask him if there was a way in which I might avoid producing an heir for Haraldsdyke. He would go straight to Axel.

I was aware of fear then, the sharp prickle beneath my scalp, the sudden moistness of my palms. How absurd, I thought, trying to be angry with myself. I was never afraid of Axel until . . . Until I heard Ned accuse Axel of murder; until I realized later that Axel had the means, motive and opportunity to murder Robert Brandson last Christmas Eve at Haraldsdyke . . .

But Rodric had killed his father, Rodric who had apparently enjoyed life so much, yet had destroyed life in a fit of rage . . .

"I don't believe it," I said aloud to the silent walls of Haraldsdyke. "I don't believe Rodric killed his father. I don't believe it."

My heart was beating very fast. I sat frozen into immobility behind the great desk, my eyes seeing not the isolated sweep of the Marsh beyond the window, but the abyss which was opening before me, the ground which was crumbling beneath my feet. And as I sat there, my whole being locked in a paralysis of panic, the immense silence was broken by the sound of footsteps in the passage and the next moment the door was opening and someone was entering the room.

I whirled around as if the Devil himself had come in search of me, but it was only Robert Brandson's ward, the girl Mary Moore.

She was wearing a pink muslin gown and the color did not flatter her ungainly figure. Her hair was lank and was fast uncurling itself so that her ringlets were wispy and awry. I could not help wondering if she had been telling me the truth about an unofficial engagement to Rodric.

"Oh!" she exclaimed, much taken-aback, and stared at me in astonishment. "What are you doing here?"

She made it sound as if I were trespassing.

"What are *you* doing here?" I retorted lightly. "It isn't your room, is it?"

There was a pause. Then:

"It was Rodric's room," she said at last. "I come here sometimes."

I stared. And then suddenly I was looking at the room around me, the silent four-poster, the mute walls, the shelf of books which I had not even troubled to examine. I stood up, conscious of feeling uneasy sitting in the chair which he must often have used, my hands on the desk at which he must so often have written.

"I didn't know," I said, "that I was in Rodric's room."

She too seemed awkward and ill-at-ease. She had come to the room to sit for a while and remember him, and instead of meeting her memories she had discovered a stranger trespassing in a place she loved. I felt sorry for her.

"I must go," I said abruptly. "I was only exploring the house. I don't know why I stopped here."

She moved to let me pass, her cheeks flushed with her own embarrassment, her eyes averted from mine, and without reason I stopped, my hand on the door-knob.

"May I ask you something very personal?" I heard myself say suddenly.

She looked up startled. "What's that?"

"You were fond of Rodric. Do you honestly believe he killed his father?"

Her eyes widened. She was evidently stunned and appalled at my frankness and for a long moment she was incapable of speech.

"Come," I said, "tell me, for I'm curious to know. I find it hard to believe from what I've heard of him that Rodric could commit such a cold-blooded murder. Do you think he killed your guardian?"

She licked her pale lips, her eyes still wide and frightened. Then: "No," she whispered. "No, I never believed it. Never."

She was infatuated with him, I told myself. She idolized him. This was not an unexpected answer.

"Then who killed your guardian?" I said.

She looked at me as if I were some hideous monster. "I dare not say."

"Ah, come, Mary! Tell me!"

She shook her head.

"I won't tell anyone, I promise."

"No," she said, "no, I can't tell you. I have no proof, no way of knowing for certain. All I know is that Rodric never killed him. I never believed he did."

"Have you proof that Rodric didn't kill him?"

She shook her head.

"Well, then—" I said exasperated, and then controlled myself. I turned aside. She knew nothing and was of no use to me. "I must go," I said. "Pray excuse me."

I opened the door.

"Alice and I were in the saloon," she said suddenly, the words tumbling from her lips. "Rodric and Godfather were quarreling so loudly that Alice said we should withdraw upstairs."

"Yes, she told me." I opened the door a little wider.

"But she listened eagerly enough," said the girl, and the spite in her voice made me halt and look back at her. "Until Vere's name was mentioned. Then she suggested we should withdraw."

"What did Mr. Brandson say about Vere?"

"I suppose he was comparing Vere to Rodric. He said that although Vere had married beneath him and was a disappointment in many ways, Vere at least wasn't a constant source of embarrassment. Alice stood up as soon as she heard the phrase about her marriage—she was very angry," Mary added as an afterthought. "Not that she showed her anger greatly, but I knew how angry she was. She went very pale and her eyes glittered."

"And what did Rodric say to his father in reply?"

"There was a murmur which I couldn't hear well enough. Alice was talking of withdrawing from the room. Then I heard Godfather shout: 'I'll not tolerate that indeed! I'll disinherit any son of mine who works with that Frenchman Delancey! Why, we're still at war with France! It would be an act of treason and I would denounce any such traitor to the Watch at Rye, whether or not he were my son!'"

"Did you hear any more?"

"Only the merest fragment of conversation. Alice was virtually pulling me from the room. Godfather bellowed: 'The devil with scandal! There are some matters which cannot be condoned no matter how much scandal they may cause. To masquerade as a highwayman and play schoolboy pranks is one matter; to treat with one's enemies in time of war is high treason!' And Rodric began: 'Papa, please listen to me—' Then I heard nothing further for we were outside in the hall and Alice had closed the door."

"What happened then? You went to the drawing room, didn't you, until you heard Esther's screams when she found Mr. Brandson dead?"

But she was frightened now. She licked her lips again. "Alice went to the nursery," she said at last. "I—I was anxious to talk to Rodric . . . After a moment or two I went downstairs again to the hall."

"But didn't you tell anyone this before?"

"No, no, I—well it was not important . . . I only wanted to see him on a personal matter . . . I reached the hall, and Rodric came out of the library. He looked very agitated. I called but he didn't stop so I ran after him. He went to the stables. Ned was there. One of the scullery maids . . . was there too. They had been sitting in the straw, for I remember Ned dusting his breeches as he stood up. Rodric told him to saddle his horse. Ned said why should he, he wasn't a groom. Rodric suddenly lost his temper, and began to shout at him . . . It—it was rather distressing . . . I went back to the house without making any further attempt to speak to Rodric, and returned to the drawing room."

"But didn't Ned say afterwards that he had seen you at the stables?"

"He didn't see me. Rodric began quarreling with him while I was still outside, and I didn't venture past the door. Nobody knew that I had left the drawing room save Rodric, and Rodric—" She checked herself.

"What?"

"Nothing." She turned to me earnestly. "You won't tell anyone, will you? You won't say I left the drawing room and ran after Rodric to the stables?"

"Well, no," I said bewildered. "Of course not. But—"

"It was a personal matter," she rushed on awkwardly. "A matter purely concerning Rodric and myself. I didn't want anyone else to know I spent that afternoon trying to see Rodric alone." And an odd look of suppressed excitement flashed across her face for a moment to bewilder me still further.

"Oh," I said blankly.

There was a silence.

"What was Ned's relationship with his father?" I said suddenly. "Did Mr. Brandson never think of leaving the estate to Ned?"

"Oh no," she said at once. "There was no question of that."

"But why? I don't understand."

She flushed again and shifted from one foot to the other, the picture of embarrassment.

"I didn't understand either," she said, "for a long time. Then I overheard—" She stopped.

"Yes?"

"Ned wasn't Godfather's son," she said. "Godfather let him bear the name of Brandson only in order to avoid scandal, but Ned wasn't his son at all."

I went downstairs, my redingote draped around my shoulders, and the footman in the hall bowed and wished me good-day. When he saw I intended to leave the house by the front entrance, he opened the door for me and bowed again as I stepped out into the porch. Before me the ground sloped sharply to meet the level of the Marsh. Trees grew on the rise on which the house was built, but none grew on a high enough level to obscure the wide vistas visible on all sides, and to the south I could see the sun as it glinted on the roofs of Rye and Winchelsea and cast a brilliant sheen over the blue band of the sea; to the west was a glimpse of cultivated land; to the east stood the dots of grazing sheep white-gray against the green of the Marsh. Stepping down from the porch to the drive, I walked around the side of the house and found myself facing the stables. Between the stables and the house was a paved yard; a housemaid, engaged in hanging out the washing on a clothes' line, caught sight of me, dropped her basket of pegs and curtsied in confusion.

I smiled, bent my head slightly in acknowledgement and walked on. Perhaps after all it was not so oppressive to be the mistress of a large house.

I could hear the sound of voices from the stables as I approached, yet due to the way the building was constructed I could see no one within till I reached the doorway. Even then they did not notice me, and I saw at once how easy it would have been for Mary to have arrived on the threshold and withdrawn to eavesdrop without being seen.

I went forward into the stables.

They saw me then soon enough.

The two raw tousle-headed stable-lads fell silent and Ned picked himself up from the pile of straw which lay in one corner and flicked the dust from his breeches.

"Good afternoon," he said, looking a little surprised that I should venture into such a place. "I thought you were sick in bed."

"I thought you were out riding."

He laughed. "I've just come back."

"And I have just left my room."

We both laughed then. After a moment's hesitation he moved forward awkwardly and the stable-lads drew back and turned to attend their duties.

"I would offer to show you the garden," he said, "except we have very little garden to speak of. Behind the house, the land falls sheer to the Marsh. There's only a seat from where one can

gaze north and on a fine day perhaps glimpse the spires of Canterbury."

"Is it fine enough today?"

"We could find out, if you wish." He led the way outside even
before I could draw breath to assent, and I followed him into
the yard beyond.

In fact there was more of a garden behind the house than he
had led me to suppose. We passed an orangery and an artificial
pool and a walled kitchen garden, and at length reached the view
he had mentioned. It was indeed, a fine sight, for I could see to
the edge of the Marsh and, it seemed, far north into the more
diverse countryside of Kent.

We sat down on the wooden seat together while I surveyed
the view.

"I see no sign of Canterbury," I remarked presently.

"You never will," he said. "I only said that to coax you to come
here. I wanted to tell you how grateful I was to you for speaking
to George as you did last night. If I didn't seem grateful then it
was only because I was too upset to remember my manners."

"Please—"

"George and I don't get along as brothers should," he said. "We
never have and we never will. I don't want to lie to you about it
and feed you honeyed words, just because he's your husband. I
think he's a scheming foreigner and he thinks I'm a good-for-
nothing bastard, and there's no love lost between us."

I was entertained in spite of myself. "And is it true?" I said
amused. "Are you a good-for-nothing bastard?"

He looked at me askance with his slanting black eyes which
were so like his mother's. "Perhaps!" His glance became watchful.

"You're very enlightened," he said, "for a lady."

"In what way?"

"Most ladies seventeen years old could not bring themselves
to say a word like that. As like as not they wouldn't know the
meaning of it in the first place."

"I've heard it used often enough," I said.

We looked at one another. He was very still.

"Perhaps it's different in London," he said after a while. "Perhaps it's different there."

"I don't think so." And then I told him.

He was amazed. After a while he said: "Does anyone know?"

"Only Axel."

"He knew when he married you?"

"Certainly."

"But you're such a lady!" he said in wonderment. "No one would ever guess."

"Are all bastards supposed to walk around carrying a little plaque which announces their unfortunate birth to the world?"

He flung back his head and laughed. "I suppose not!" He was serious again. "But someone must have cared for you—spent money on your education . . ."

I told him about my parents. It was strangely comforting to talk to someone about them. I mentioned my education in Cheltenham, described our house in town, told him about Alexander. When I stopped at last I felt more peaceful than I had felt since my arrival at Haraldsdyke, or indeed since my wedding day a week ago.

"You were fortunate," he said when I had finished, and he didn't sound bitter. "You lived just as any legitimate child would have lived. Your mother and father loved each other and loved you enough to take care of you. You were never threatened by your illegitimacy until they died."

"I—suppose not."

"Nobody cared for me like that," he said. "And I never knew what was wrong. I used to think it was because I was ugly or stupid, or because I was the youngest and my mother hadn't wanted another pregnancy. I was brought up by a succession of nursemaids and then sent to the grammar school at Rye. Rodric and Vere had private tutors, but that was considered a wasted expense where I was concerned. My—father seldom troubled to speak to me and my mother never once came to the nursery to see me. It was unfair that no one ever told me why I was ignored so much; it would have been easier if I'd known."

"But when did you find out?"

"When?" He looked straight ahead across the Marsh to Kent and his body was tensed and still. Then: "Last year," he said. "On Christmas Eve. Rodric told me on the day he died that I was a bastard."

There were clouds gathering in the west. A scudding wind ruffled my hair and made me draw the folds of the redingote more closely around my body.

"You're cold?" said Ned. "Perhaps you would prefer to go indoors. It's late in the year to sit outside."

"No, I'm warm enough for the moment." I waited, half-hoping he would tell me more without my asking further questions, but when he was silent, I said tentatively: "Why did Rodric tell you then?"

He shrugged and then shivered suddenly as if in revulsion. "We were quarreling."

The breeze whispered again over the Marsh. Far away in the west I saw the landscape begin to blur beneath the dark clouds.

"I never quarreled with Rodric," he said. "I thought too highly of him. But that afternoon he was in an ugly temper, I'd never seen him so angry before. I was in the stables talking to one of the girls from the kitchens and he came in and shouted for me to saddle his horse. I said, half-joking: 'Who do you mistake me for—a stable-lad? Do it yourself!' And before I could even draw breath to laugh he turned around and shouted: 'You damned bastard, don't you ever do what anyone tells you? My God, as if I haven't had enough troubles today, with my father roaring and ranting like a madman and Alice tempting Vere to have a fight with me, and that wretched Mary running after me and pestering me to read her cursed love sonnets! And to crown a disastrous day, you have to practice your high-and-mighty bastard's bad manners at my expense!'

"I was so stupefied by this attack that I said the first thing that came into my head. 'You'd better not call me bastard again,' I shouted back at him, 'or I'll knock you off that fine horse of yours!' I was really hurt that he should speak to me like that. Rodric and I never quarreled. Never. He had never abused me before . . .

"He said without looking at me: 'Well, you're no more than a bastard, are you? Don't you even know who you are by this time?' And as I stared at him, he said: 'Why do you suppose Papa never troubled to give you a private education?'

"He had the saddle in his hands and was saddling the horse himself as he spoke. It was like some horrible dream. I went on staring at him, and then I turned to the scullery girl and said: 'You'd better get back to the kitchens. Cook will be looking for you.' I only knew that I wanted to be rid of her, that I didn't want her to hear any more.

"'I don't understand you,' I said to Rodric. 'I don't know what you mean.'

"'Then ask Papa to explain to you,' he said, 'for Lord knows I haven't the time. Or ask Mama who your father was—if she can remember.'

"He was leading the horse out of the stable. I was so numbed that I could hardly move. I managed to stammer: 'You've no right to say such a thing about Mama! You're her favorite—how dare you talk of her like that?'

"'Because I'm not afraid of the truth,' he said, mounting his horse without a backward glance. 'And I know too damned well that Papa hasn't spoken two dozen words to Mama in twenty years and has slept in a separate bedroom since before you were born. You're so busy consorting with stable-lads and scullery maids that you haven't seen enough of either Mama or Papa to realize they're married in name only. Why do you suppose Papa keeps a mistress at Hastings and Mama has discreet affairs with any man she can contrive to seduce?'

"Even speech was impossible now. I could only stand in the

doorway and lean against the post and watch the world crumble before my eyes.

"He was in the saddle. I remember that moment so well. The sun was shining down on him and his eyes were very blue. 'To hell with the lot of you,' he said, 'I'm going to ride until I'm too weary to care. To hell with you all.' And he rode off down the hill to the Marsh and the sun went in and I felt the rain sting my cheek. The mist blew in from the sea soon afterwards and the sun was gone."

There was a silence. To the west the Marsh was now indistinct and the clouds stretched to the blurred horizon. I was going to speak, but he spoke first, his eyes watching some distant point on the Marsh as if he were seeing other scenes long ago.

"I watched him go," he said. "I watched him until he was out of sight. Afterwards I thought how unfair it was that we parted in such anger, but at that moment I was aware of nothing at all, only a dreadful emptiness. Afterwards I went back into the stable and flung myself down on the straw again. I didn't even cry. That came later. After a time I thought: 'I must find Papa and ask him for the truth.' So I left the stables and went back into the house.

"There was no footman in the hall. I went to the library and knocked on the door but there was no reply, so I went upstairs to Papa's rooms. He wasn't there. Then I thought: 'I'll find Mama and speak to her.'

"At first I thought she wasn't in her rooms either. I went into the boudoir but that was empty and then when I was turning to leave I heard the murmur of voices from the bedroom beyond."

I turned my head sharply to look at him, but he was still staring out across the Marsh, his elbows on his knees, his fists clenched.

"I knew then it was all true," he said at last. "I didn't need to be convinced further. She was with some man. The very discovery seemed instantly to confirm everything Rodric had said."

I was perfectly still. "Who was the man with her?" said my voice with polite interest. "You're sure it wasn't your father?"

"Yes."

"How can you be sure?"

He did not answer directly. Then he bent down and began to tug up the grass at his feet as though some form of action however mild would excuse him from replying.

"Ned?" I was still very polite.

"I heard his steps crossing to open the door into the boudoir," he said in a muffled voice. "There wasn't time for me to escape so I hid behind the Chinese screen in one corner of the room. He came out a second later and she followed him."

"Who was he?"

"I'll not tell you."

I grabbed his wrist and jerked him as hard as I could so that he spun around to face me. I was trembling in every limb now no matter how hard I tried to conceal it.

"Was it Axel?"

"I'll not tell you."

"It must have been! There was no other man in the house who was not related to her."

"There were servants."

"Ned!"

"I'll not tell you," he said stubbornly. "I've never told anyone before and I'm not telling you."

"You didn't tell the coroner at the inquest?"

"No, why should I have done? He would have wanted to know why I went in search of my mother in the first place, and I had no intention of repeating to the coroner and half the population of Rye what Rodric had told me."

I stared at him.

"I wish I had never mentioned it," he said sullenly. "I don't know why I did. You made me forget to guard my tongue."

"Did they discover you in the boudoir?" I demanded, ignoring this. "Did they see you?"

"No, thank the Lord. It was lucky the screen was there, for there was nowhere else I could have hidden."

"What did they say to each other?"

"She said 'I must go and see if anything can be done.' And the man said: 'I'll come downstairs with you.' They went out of the room and I heard her say to him in the passage: 'What do you suppose he wanted?' And he said after a moment: 'Perhaps to ask you if you knew about the French contraband he found in the barn below the thirty-acre field. He told me two days ago he was watching the barn to catch whoever was in league with Delancey, but when I told him to go straight to the Revenue Men he wouldn't, too afraid it might be one of Rodric's foolish pranks again, I suppose.' Then they turned the corner to the landing, and I didn't hear any more."

"And the next moment you heard Esther's screams when she discovered Mr. Brandson dead?"

"No," he said. "It was about ten minutes later."

"Ten minutes! But it couldn't have taken her that long to reach the library!"

"Then maybe it took her ten minutes to draw breath to scream," he said, "for I didn't hear the screams till some time later. I left the boudoir as quickly as I could and went to my own room and lay on my bed thinking. I must have lain there at least ten minutes."

"How very curious."

"When I heard her screams I went to the head of the staircase. George and Mary were in the hall with my mother and Alice was descending the staircase ahead of me. I ran downstairs. One of the footmen was wandering around white as parchment and saying 'No one left the library save Mr. Rodric.' A great deal *he* knew about *that!* He hadn't even been there when I had knocked on the library door."

"What did you do?"

"I went into the library. The others were too busy soothing Mama's hysterics. Papa was sprawled across the floor and Rodric's gun lay beside him, the butt smeared with blood. Rodric had been out shooting with George that morning. I was stunned enough already and when I saw the scene in the library it made no impression on me at all at first. And then gradually I felt full of panic and a longing to escape so I ran back to my room, locked the door and broke down completely. I lay on my bed and sobbed till I had no strength to do anything except fall asleep. It was like being in a nightmare unable to wake."

"When did you hear of Rodric's death?"

"Later that evening when George returned. Mary came knocking at my door. Have you talked much to Mary? If you have, you'll realize she was infatuated with Rodric and used to imagine herself affianced to him and other such nonsense. Rodric tried to be patient with her out of kindness, but I fancy she irritated him more often than not. But, poor girl, she was beside herself with grief then and came to me because she knew how fond of him I was too. As soon as she told me I went downstairs.

"George was in the saloon with Vere, Alice and Mama. He was soaked to the skin and looked more shaken than I have ever seen him. I said: 'How did he die?' And George said: 'He must have fallen from his horse. There was a dyke, a tract of bog, and I found his hat nearby and his horse wandering further on. He must have drowned in the Marsh.' And Vere said: 'Perhaps he was overcome with remorse.' And Alice said: 'God forgive him.'

"That was what everyone said after the inquest. 'God forgive him,' everyone kept saying. 'God forgive him.' It was horrible! He was branded as a murderer without so much as a fair trial!"

Close at hand long fingers of white mist wreathed the landscape so that the Marsh seemed eerie, adrift in some strange twilight. I shivered.

"You're cold now," said Ned. "We'd better go in."

I stood up without argument, and we walked together in silence through the garden to the house. I felt so numbed that I hardly noticed that it was beginning to rain.

"Perhaps the greatest shock of all came when Mr. Sherman

read the will," Ned said. "We all thought that Haraldsdyke had been left to Rodric with a suitable bequest to Vere. We had no idea Papa had made the other will the day before he died."

"Yes," I said. "Axel told me it was a matter of embarrassment to him."

"Embarrassment!" scoffed Ned. "He wasn't embarrassed! I swore he knew all along about the new will! I was so angry that Vere, who's always worked so hard for Haraldsdyke, should have inherited nothing, that I lost my temper when I should have guarded my tongue. George was having a word with me in private before he departed for Vienna—he wanted to tell me he would arrange for me to have an income of thirty pounds a year, but he made it sound as if he were bestowing a great favor on me. And suddenly I thought how generous Rodric had always been with his money and that this man was now sitting in Rodric's place and dealing with money that should have belonged to Rodric himself.

"'I think I should have fifty pounds per annum,' I said. 'You can afford to be generous. You took Haraldsdyke from Papa after his death and you took his wife before his death—'" He stopped dead in his tracks.

It was raining steadily now. The mist was falling between us. Everywhere was very quiet.

"So it *was* Axel whom you found with Esther," I heard myself say calmly from a long way away.

He looked as if he could have bitten out his tongue. "Yes," he said at last, face flushed with embarrassment. "It was. But I never told him how I had seen him come out of Mama's bedroom that day. For God's sake never, never tell him that."

"Why? Are you so afraid of him?"

"I—" The words seemed to stick in his throat.

"You think Axel killed his father, don't you? That Rodric was innocent?"

"I—I've no proof . . . only that they went downstairs together to the library and that Mama didn't scream till fully ten minutes later. Perhaps Papa had found out they were deceiving him, perhaps there was yet another quarrel in the library after Rodric left . . ."

"But surely Mr. Brandson was already dead? You said that after lingering a while in the stables you returned to the hall, knocked on the library door, and received no reply—"

"There are a dozen other explanations for that. He may have stepped out on to the terrace for a moment—or next door into the saloon—or he may not have heard me—or he may even have been asleep. He did sleep there sometimes. I've no proof that he was dead then, just as I've no proof that he quarreled with George and that George killed him. But I think Rodric was innocent. I shall always think that. I'll never believe that Rodric killed Papa."

We reached a side-door which led into the saloon from the terrace, and he opened it for me. The saloon was empty. "What did Axel say," I said abruptly, "when you revealed to him that you knew about his relationship with Esther?"

"He asked me to explain myself. I merely shrugged and said: 'I saw you once with her.' I pretended to be very casual. Then I said as an afterthought: 'I wonder what the coroner would have thought at the inquest if he knew you had been having an affair with your step-mother besides having that will made in your favor?'"

I drew a deep breath. "What did he say?"

"He was very still. Then gradually he went white with rage. After a moment he said: 'If you so much as attempt to create a scandal for your mother after she has endured so much shock and suffering, I swear I'll break every bone in your body.' At least, he spoke in rougher language than those words, and called me a bastard—and other names as well. How I hated him at that moment! Presently I said: 'I've no intention of making a scandal, but I would like that fifty pounds a year which I mentioned just now.'"

"And what happened?" I said blankly. "Did he agree to the sum you wanted?"

"Oh yes," said Ned. "He agreed."

Four

AXEL AND VERE were not at Haraldsdyke for dinner. After the meal I was obliged to sit for a while in the drawing room with Esther and Mary while Alice went to the nursery, but at last I was able to make my excuses and escape. Dusk was already falling as I reached our sitting room upstairs; I lit two candles, carried them to the secretaire by the window and sat down. Pen and ink were quickly found, but there was no paper. I thought suddenly of the huge desk in Rodric's room. Surely there would be paper in one of the drawers . . .

I stood up, took one of the candles and went out into the passage. No one was about. I had some trouble finding Rodric's room again, but eventually I remembered my way and discovered a plentiful supply of the writing paper I needed. It was quite dark now. Back in my own rooms again, I sat down with a strange feeling of relief, picked up the pen and began to write to Alexander.

Time was short; at any moment Axel might return from Rye. My pen scratched rapidly across the paper, dropped a blob of ink and scratched on without pausing. The entire appearance of the letter would have horrified old Miss Shearing at my academy in Cheltenham. Miss Shearing and her environment all seemed very far away indeed.

"I hope you are well at school," I scribbled. "I wish it were the end of term, for I miss you even more than usual." I paused, mindful that I must take great care not to say too much. "Haraldsdyke is a most unusual house," I wrote quickly after a moment, "and the family have been most civil and kind. You would like it here because you could ride every day, if you wished, and there's plenty of game for shooting on the Marsh. Is it not possible that you could leave before term's end? Christmas is still several weeks away and it seems such a long time to wait till I see you again. I have so much to tell you, more than can ever be put in a mere letter . . ." Careful. I gnawed the end of the quill, absorbed in my task, oblivious to everything around me. I must, I thought, be a little more specific or the entire point of the letter would be lost. Alexander was not quick to grasp hints and allusions. "You will not credit this," I resumed presently, "but it turns out that Mr. Robert Brandson, Axel's father, did not die a natural death at all, as we were led to suppose, and was in fact the victim of a murderous attack last Christmas Eve. It was presumed by the Coroner's Jury that the perpetrator of the deed was Axel's half-brother, Mr. Rodric Brandson, but as he died but a few hours after his father as the result of an accident, he was never able to defend himself against such a charge of murder. Even though it is generally accepted that he was guilty, there are nonetheless some who say . . ."

There was a sound from behind me.

I spun around, and the pen spluttered on the paper beneath the convulsive start of my hand.

"You should have another candle," said Axel, "lest you strain your eyes in such a dim light."

I had never even heard him enter the room. Such was my paralysis of surprise that I could do nothing except stare at him and hope the light was dim enough to hide the pallor of my face and the expression in my eyes.

"Did I startle you?" he said. "I'm sorry." He was very close to me now, and as he stooped to kiss me he saw the letter and I instinctively turned it face downwards on the blotter.

"I had inkspots all over the paper," I said, speaking the first thought to enter my head. "If it were to anyone else but to Alexander I would write the letter afresh on a clean piece of paper, but he won't mind my untidiness."

"It was thoughtful of you to write so soon after your arrival." His fingers were against my cheek, the long cool fingers which I now knew so well. He was gently forcing me to look at him.

"How did you fare in Rye?" I said instantly, looking him straight in the eyes.

"Well enough. Aren't you going to give me a kiss?"

"Of course," I said, cool as spring water, and rose to my feet as I raised my face to his.

He slid his arms around my waist and kissed me on the mouth with an intimacy which was as unexpected as it was unwelcome.

"You have no idea how good it is," he said, "to ride home through the foggy dusk of a November evening and then find you here, looking as you look now . . . Are you feeling better?"

"Yes, thank you," I said, and then added, lest he should be harboring any ideas to the contrary, "but I shall be a trifle delicate for two or three days yet."

"You must take care of yourself." He released me and turned aside abruptly. I saw his glance rest again on the letter, and my heart began to bump uncomfortably once more. "I shall be riding to Rye again tomorrow," he said. "I'll take your letter with me. There's a mail-coach which leaves tomorrow at noon for Tunbridge Wells and London, and I can arrange with the coachman to see that the letter is safely sent from London to Harrow."

"Please, I wouldn't want it to inconvenience you."

"There would be no inconvenience. If you haven't yet finished the letter, perhaps you could add a sentence giving my regards to Alexander and saying that we look forward to seeing him at Christmas."

What else was there to say? I returned to my writing, and presently he rang for his valet and I heard him telling the man to arrange for a light meal to be served in our apartments.

"Will you sup with me?" he asked. "Or would you prefer to

eat with the others? I'm hungry and tired and have no wish to join them."

"I'm not hungry at present," I said. "It's not so long since I dined. I'll wait and then drink tea with the others, with your permission."

I re-wrote the letter to Alexander, carefully omitting any reference to the fact that Rodric's guilt was doubted in any way. From the subject of the murder, I then described Haraldsdyke in minute detail and mentioned each of the family by name. Finally I carefully added Axel's message and wrote below it: "Do come as soon as you can!" before signing my name.

By the time I laid down my pen, he was eating his supper at the table by the window.

"I would like to see more of Rye," I said on an impulse. "Would it be possible for me to travel with you tomorrow?"

"In your present state of health?"

"I—I wasn't thinking of riding, I thought perhaps the carriage."

"I think the journey would tire you all the same, and besides, I have business to conduct and wouldn't be able to attend to you. Another time, perhaps."

"Perhaps Ned would come with me if you were too busy."

He gave me a hard look. "Ned?"

"I—was talking to him today . . . I found him pleasant enough. I thought that perhaps . . ."

"You will not," said Axel distinctly, "travel to Rye with Ned."

"Very well. As you wish."

"You would be best advised to spend the day with Alice and learn more about your household. No doubt there will be callers too who wish to present themselves and you should be there to receive them."

"Yes," I said. I glanced at the clock on the mantelpiece above the fireplace. "Will you excuse me, Axel, if I leave you now? I think perhaps tea will be ready soon, and I'm hungrier now than I was earlier."

He gave his permission. Taking a candle I went out into the

corridor, and had just reached the landing when I remembered with horror that I had not destroyed my original letter to Alexander but had left it carelessly folded on the secretaire with my completed letter.

I turned at once and ran back down the passage. I was already in the room when I remembered I had not even paused to invent an excuse for my return.

Luckily I had no need of one; Axel had already gone into the bedroom beyond. Moving hastily across to the secretaire I snatched up the original letter and cast it into the midst of the fire. It was only as I stood watching it burn that it occurred to me to wonder if the folded notepaper had been exactly as I had left it on the secretaire . . .

The next morning was dull and tedious. Knowing that when Axel returned from Rye he would be sure to ask me how I had spent the day, I asked Alice to show me the kitchens and her household affairs. Then the rector's wife and sister called again, and I had to be civil and welcoming to them in an attempt to create a good impression. When they had gone, Alice took me to the nursery to show me her children, and again I had to be careful to say exactly the right words and choose appropriately admiring remarks. Stephen, the eldest, was a quiet shy child with fair hair and green eyes, but Clarissa, a year younger, was already as big as he was and much more boisterous. The youngest, Robert, had an aggressive chin which looked odd on so young a child, and a loud voice which he used with deafening effect.

"The little love," said Alice fondly, picking him up, and he was instantly quiet and well-behaved.

Seeing her with the children reminded me of my fear of pregnancy, and I was glad when I had the chance to escape to my rooms at last. But I could not stay in the rooms long; I was restless and had no wish at all to sit and think heaven knows what manner of thoughts, and soon I was donning my pelisse and some warm boots and slipping downstairs with the idea of walking in the garden. I had hardly taken a step outside when

Ned came around the corner of the house and nearly bumped into me.

We laughed; he apologized and I said it was nothing. Presently I asked him where he was going.

"To Haraldsford, the nearest village," he said. "I promised Alice I would take a ham and some pies to her mother. Why don't you come with me? It's not far—only a mile."

"Will we be back in time for dinner?"

"Why, yes—easily. We'll be gone less than an hour all told."

I was immensely curious to see Alice's mother, the witch.

"Very well, I'll come," I said, "only it must be a secret. I am supposed to spend all day at the house learning about the household affairs of Haraldsdyke."

He smiled, his teeth white and even, his black eyes sparkling. "Your secret's safe with me."

So we set off together for the village, and immediately the house was behind us I was conscious of relief and felt almost light-hearted.

We were soon there. The road was built up above the level of the land, which seemed curious to me, but around the village the level rose to meet the road. It was a very small place; there was a round Saxon church with a Norman tower attached, several cottages and an inn called "The Black Ram." Alice's mother lived in a tiny hovel apart from the others on the edge of the village; a nanny-goat grazed by the door and two hens peered out of the open doorway.

"She's a witch, I believe," I said casually to Ned as we drew nearer, but Ned only laughed.

"So they say—just because she knows a few old potions and a spell or two! I'll believe she's a witch the day I see her ride a broomstick, and not till then."

I was disappointed. I was even more disappointed when I saw that Alice's mother Dame Joan was not a hump-backed evil creature clad in black rags, but a broad strong country woman with an arrogant nose, a powerful voice and strange light eyes of no particular color but full of grays and greens and blue flecks.

"Good-day, Dame Joan," said Ned briskly. "Alice sent me with some gifts for you. I hope you're well and in good health."

She shot him a sharp look and then glanced at me. "You'll be the foreigner's wife," she said at once.

I suppose it was an obvious enough deduction, but I was childishly thrilled at the confident way she announced my identity.

"Yes indeed," said Ned, winking at me. "Mrs. George Brandson."

"I smiled at her and said "good-day" but she merely said: "You're an insolent rascal, boy. I saw you twist your face to mock me."

I was alarmed, thinking he had offended her, but he merely laughed. "Have you eyes in the back of your head, then, Dame Joan?" he said amused. "I was standing behind you—how could you see what I was doing?"

"I've ways," she said darkly. "You'd best be careful or next time you go changing the shapes of new scullery maids I'll not be so free and easy with my remedies."

But Ned refused to be either embarrassed or deflated. "Dame Joan is an authority on all manner of things connected with fertility," he said to me frankly with his careless smile. "If you're not pregnant and want to be so, she gives you a potion. If you're pregnant and don't want to be so she gives you another potion. If you're not pregnant and don't want to be so—"

"Young rascal," said Dame Joan. "Talking before a lady like that. The foreigner would beat you sore if he heard you."

There was something uncanny about her perception of Axel's attitude to Ned. Even Ned himself was caught unawares; I saw the smile vanish from his face for a moment and then he was laughing again, refusing to be perturbed.

"Dame Joan knows there's no love lost between me and George," he said lightly. "Well, we must be on our way home for dinner. Good-day to you, Dame Joan, and I hope you enjoy the ham and the pies."

But as we walked away from the village he said without look-ing at me: "I'm sorry if I spoke too bluntly. I had no wish to offend you."

"There was no offense," I said truthfully. "My father was always very frank in his conversation and didn't care a whit how out-spoken he was."

He smiled, obviously relieved. Presently he said: "I can't think how you'll settle at Haraldsdyke."

"Why do you say that?"

"Well! You're so—so alive, so . . ." He shrugged, at a loss for words. "You should be in a city," he said, "wearing beautiful clothes and jewelry and mingling with Society, not cut off here in the country with no one to impress save the local gentry and the merchants of the Cinque Ports! You'll be stifled, bored—"

"Nonsense!" I spoke all the more intensely because I was afraid there was an element of truth in what he said.

"But you're so alive!" he said. "So full of interest. So different from these country girls with their giggles and prudery and dreary conversation."

"You'd best stop this at once," I said, "or I shall become so vain that my head will be too swollen to permit me to walk through the doorway into Haraldsdyke." But I was pleased all the same.

Esther met us in the hall when we arrived back. I was half-afraid she had seen us walk up the drive together.

"Ah, there you are!" she said to me, and as I looked at her I thought instantly of her former relationship with Axel and had to repress my longing to rebuff her air of welcoming friendliness which I had never fully accepted as sincere. "We were wondering where you were, my dear," she said, and her dark eyes glanced from me to Ned and back to me again. "George is home from Rye, and asked to see you as soon as you returned."

Some instinct told me even before I entered the room that the interview which lay ahead of me would be unpleasant. Axel was in his dressing room; I heard him dismiss his valet as he heard me enter the apartments. The next moment he was entering the sitting room where I was waiting, and crossing the floor to greet me.

"Did you have a satisfactory day in Rye?" I asked, rather too quickly. "I'm glad you were able to be back for dinner today."

"I was surprised to find you absent on my arrival home," he said dryly, and gestured towards the hearth. "Let's sit down for a moment."

I settled myself on the edge of the high-backed fireside chair and folded my hands in my lap. My heart was bumping noisily; I tried to look cool and composed.

"Alice told me you spent some time with her this morning," he said. "I was glad to hear you'd taken my advice to heart."

I launched into a detailed account of the time I had spent with Alice. He listened intently. At last when I could think of nothing further to say he said: "After you left Alice I understand you went for a walk with Ned."

"Yes, to Haraldsford, to take some provisions to Alice's mother. But how did you—"

"Esther saw you leave."

There was a pause. I was suddenly very angry at the thought of Esther spying upon me, but I managed to control the impulse to put my thoughts into words.

"I see," I said.

"You remember that I had forbidden you to go to Rye in Ned's company."

"I remember."

"Surely you must have realized by now that I wish you to see as little of Ned as possible?"

"It had occurred to me."

"Yet you sought his company to walk to Haraldsford!"

"That was a mere chance." I explained what had happened. "I didn't think you would mind," I added, "or of course I wouldn't have gone."

"I mind very much you being seen alone in his company,"

Axel said sharply. "He has a bad reputation, particularly in regard to girls of your age, and he mixes with people with whom it would be ill-advised for you to associate yourself. You forget you're now mistress of Haraldsdyke, not a mere schoolgirl whose behavior can be overlooked or excused."

"I am perfectly well aware that I am mistress of Haraldsdyke," I said icily. "What you seem to forget is that Ned is your half-brother and by normal social standards would be considered a fitting escort for me on a short country walk."

I was furiously angry, of course, or I would never have dared to speak to him in that manner. For a moment he seemed taken aback at my audacity for I saw his eyes widen slightly, and then he was himself again, very cool and remote.

"He's no kin of mine."

"So I've been told," I said cuttingly, "but as this isn't generally known it would make no difference to the fact that in the eyes of the world he would still be considered a suitable escort." And I stood up and moved swiftly next door into the bedroom, the tears stinging my eyes.

He followed me instantly and closed the door. "Listen to me," he said. "Be that as it may, I still have reasons of my own for not wishing you to associate with Ned. I must insist that you heed what I say and see as little of him as possible."

My tears by this time made speech impossible. I was hopelessly upset, wishing with all my heart that I could run to my mother for comfort, and the wish only served to remind me that she was dead and lost to me forever. Tears scalded my cheeks; I stared out of the window, my back to the stranger behind me, my whole will concentrating on the task of concealing my lack of self-control.

"Are you listening to what I'm saying?" said Axel sharply.

I bent my head in acknowledgement.

"Then I would like your promise that you will do as I tell you."

I tried to speak but could not. Seconds passed.

"I'm waiting, my dear."

Sobs trembled in my throat. Suddenly my shoulders were shaking. I closed my eyes in wretchedness, and then his hand was touching my shoulder and his voice said with unexpected gentleness: "Forgive me. I see I've been too harsh."

To my shame I let him press me to him and hide my face against his breast; his fingers stroked my hair.

"But you were outwardly so proud and independent!" he said regretfully. "I did not realize—"

I turned aside from him, my tears under control. "There was no question of you being too harsh," I said stonily. "I was suddenly reminded of my parents' death and was overcome with grief for a moment. I'm sorry to have made such an exhibition of my feelings before you. And now, if you will excuse me, I shall change and dress for dinner."

He bowed silently and after a moment withdrew to his dressing room once more. I waited for him to call for his valet, but he did not and the silence remained like a pall over the room.

I was still by the window some minutes later when he came back to talk to me.

I gave a start of surprise.

"I quite forgot to tell you," he said. "I have asked the Shermans to dine with us tomorrow. James Sherman, as you may remember, was my father's lawyer."

"Very well," I said, perhaps sounding more dignified than I intended. "I'll see that the necessary arrangements are made to receive him. How many visitors will there be?"

"Five in all. Sherman himself, his wife and daughters, and his brother Charles."

"Five. Thank you."

A pause. The gulf yawned between us. Then:

"I have just one question to ask you about Ned," he said quietly, "and then we need make no further reference to the subject. Did he speak to you of Rodric?"

I stared. His face was watchful but I could not read the expression in his eyes.

"No," I said, and then realizing that this would seem unlikely I added: "At least, he merely mentioned him and said how fond of him he had been."

"I see."

"Why do you ask?" I said as he turned to go. "Is there some mystery about Rodric?"

"None that I know of," he said flatly, and withdrew without further comment to his dressing room.

Dinner was at four o'clock; outside dusk was falling and the rain came sweeping across the Marsh to dash itself against the window-panes. Axel and I entered the dining room to find Mary already seated in an unbecoming violet gown with puffed cap-sleeves which made her plump arms look even larger than they were. Ned came in a moment later; he was clean and tidy, and although Axel looked at him very hard it seemed he could find no fault with Ned's appearance tonight. Esther came in soon after Ned. She looked very handsome in black satin, the sombre shade of mourning suiting her much too well, the gown cut to compliment each line of her figure so that it was hard to believe she was old enough to be the mother of grown sons. She looked at me curiously, as if she were trying to perceive whether Axel had reprimanded me for walking to Haraldsford with Ned, and I was careful to smile with just the right degree of coldness so that she would realize I had survived her attempts at interference with ease and despised her for her prying into my personal affairs.

Vere and Alice came into the room to complete the gathering, I said grace as shortly as possible and we sat down to eat.

I soon noticed Vere's moroseness, but it took me till the second course to realize that he and Axel were not speaking to one another. In contrast Alice seemed untroubled and we talked together for a while of her mother. Mary as usual was too withdrawn to contribute much to the conversation and Ned seemed to have no other ambition than to eat his food as quickly and unobtrusively as possible. At the other end of the table, Axel and Esther maintained a formal conversation for a while, but in general it was a silent meal, and I was glad when it was over and it was time for the women to withdraw.

As we went upstairs to the drawing room I heard Esther say to Alice: "Has Vere quarreled with George?"

And Alice said: "There were difficulties today in Rye."

Further conversation on this topic was not possible between them as we reached the drawing room door a moment later.

After ten minutes I excused myself, saying I was tired after a long day, and in truth I did feel rather more weary than usual, probably on account of the strain of the morning spent with Alice while she had instructed me on household matters. In my rooms once more I summoned Marie-Claire, made an elaborate toilette and was between the sheets of the big double-bed by six o'clock.

At first I thought that sleep would come easily, but as sometimes happens, although my limbs soon became warm and relaxed my mind quickened and sharpened until in the end even the physical peace began to ebb and I tossed and turned restlessly. I was thinking of Axel's relationship with Esther still, examining the idea minutely until there was not a single aspect which had escaped my consideration. Esther was probably no more than twelve years Axel's senior, possibly even less; she was good-looking, worldly and shrewd, bored enough with her empty marriage to take lovers when the opportunity arose, sharp enough to see that her sophisticated step-son with his cosmopolitan city background could prove a welcome diversion.

And Axel, despite the respect he always claimed to bear towards his father, had allowed himself to be diverted. Her maturity would have appealed to him, no doubt; he would certainly belong to her generation more than to mine.

I pictured his arrival at Haraldsdyke the previous Christmas, the quick flare as the affair was set alight, the holocaust of discovery. I could almost hear Robert Brandson shout in the rich English voice I had never heard: "I made a new will leaving all to you, but I shall revoke it! I'll not leave you a penny of my my money, not a stone of Haraldsdyke!" And then afterwards Rodric would have been the perfect scapegoat, all the more perfect since he had not been alive to declare his innocence. Axel had ridden off after him into the mist and found only his horse and hat among the marshes.

Or so Axel said.

I sat up, sweat on my forehead, my limbs trembling and fumbled for the sulphur and the match jar to light the lamp.

Of course, the affair was all over now; it had ended in disaster and Axel would be sharp enough to see that any hint that such a situation had ever existed must be suppressed. He would hardly be foolish enough to continue the affair now.

Unless he loved her. It was obvious he did not love me. He was fond enough of me to make a display of affection effortless, but there was no question of love. Why should there be? I had not loved him. It had been a marriage of convenience and would remain so. Why not? Who married for love nowadays anyway? Only fools. Or paupers. Or those born to good luck and happiness.

I slipped out of bed, my throat tight and aching, and drew on a warm woolen robe to protect me from the damp chill of the November night. In the room next door the fire had burned low, but I stirred the embers with the poker and threw on another lump of coal with the fireside tongs. For a long time I sat on the hearth and watched the leaping flames and wondered if I would still imagine such terrible scenes involving Axel if he loved me and I loved him in return. Perhaps if I knew he loved me I would not mind whatever had happened in the past. Perhaps I would even be sorry for Esther, poor Esther whose youth was gone and who would soon lose much of the magnetism on which she relied to escape from the hideous boredom of widowhood in

the country. Nothing would matter so much if Axel loved me
a little, if I did not feel so lost and adrift and alone . . .

I stood up, went out into the corridor, moved to the head of
the stairs. Voices were still coming from the drawing room so I
assumed that no one else had yet retired, but there were no
sounds of masculine voices either, which seemed to indicate that
the men were still in the dining room.

I padded aimlessly downstairs to the deserted hall and wandered into the saloon next to the library in which Robert Brandson had met his death nearly a year ago. Candles were alight
on the table; a fire was burning in the grate and the room was
warm; when I heard the voices from the room next door a second
later, I paused, knowing I should not listen but aware only of
my curiosity. Finally the hesitation passed and the shame was
overcome; softly closing the door of the saloon behind me I tip-
toed over to the window and sat on the window-seat which lay
behind the long curtains and close to the communicating door
between the two rooms. The door, of course, was closed, but
evidently it fitted badly, for the conversation was audible and I
could understand then how easily Alice and Mary had heard
nearly every word of the quarrel between Rodric and his father
which had taken place last Christmas Eve.

"God damn you," said Vere in a soft distinct voice. "God damn
you, George Brandson."

"You may seek my damnation as often as you wish," said Axel,
cool as ice, the faint flavor of contempt lingering in each syllable.
"You may invoke the Deity from this hour to eternity, but it won't
alter my decision. When I left here after Papa's death it was
arranged with the trustees of his will that you were to have
enough power to administer Haraldsdyke and the estate for one
year or for such time as elapsed before I fulfilled the conditions
of my inheritance. You've been in control here for nearly a year.
And what's happened? You've incurred debts which you were
not legally entitled to incur, you've lost money hand over fist
and you've indulged in some agricultural experiments which I

think even the most enlightened agrarian would call hazardous in the extreme. The trustees, as we saw today, are seriously embarrassed and I don't blame them. I would be too if I were in their position and had to render accounts relating to the past financial year at Haraldsdyke. I had hoped to be able to rely on you heavily when it came to administering the estate, but now I see I shall have to revise my ideas. It's obvious you have no more grasp of finance than Rodric had, and Lord knows that was little enough."

"Don't you compare me with Rodric!" Vere's quiet voice rose in fury. "My God, I suffered enough from comparisons while he was alive to endure listening to more of them now he's dead! It was always the same, always—I was the only one who really cared for Haraldsdyke and wanted to improve the land, yet what chance did I ever have to prove myself when Papa was too pig-headed to permit any changes? He never listened to me! Nobody ever listened to me! Everything was Rodric, Rodric, Rodric—and what did Rodric ever do except squander his opportunities and spend money like water on his damnfool escapades? But Rodric was precious, Rodric was sacred! Papa listened to Rodric, even when he never had time to listen to me—condoned Rodric's affairs but wouldn't forgive me for my marriage—showered Rodric with money for his pleasures, but made me beg for any money to spend on Haraldsdyke."

"I'm not in the least interested," Axel interrupted acidly, "in your past grievances and grudges concerning Rodric. What I'm concerned about is the fact that over the past year you've lost a considerable amount of my money."

"It can be repaid. A great deal of it is merely a temporary loss which will be made good next year. I still maintain that my schemes are worthy of consideration."

"Then I'm afraid I am completely unable to agree with you."

"In God's name!" shouted Vere so loudly that I thought his cry must have resounded throughout the house. "Why do I always have to beg for what I want? I'm sick to death of begging! If I had any money of my own I swear I would wash my hands of you all and buy my own land and build my own farm!"

"I'm only sorry Papa did not provide for you in his will, but he evidently had his reasons . . ."

"I don't want your sympathy! The money would have come to me if Papa hadn't made the will in your favor without anyone knowing he was going to cut Rodric out of any share of the inheritance, the money was to come to me."

"Please," said Axel, "let's be realistic and not speculate about what might or might not have taken place if circumstances had been different. The money is mine and Haraldsdyke is mine, but I'm willing enough to share it with you to some extent and let you continue to administer the estate as you think best. However, obviously if my liberality is going to result in heavy financial loss—"

"You surely can't judge me on the results of a year's bad luck!"

"I think there's rather more than bad luck involved."

"And what do you know about the estate anyway? How can you tell? I've slaved and toiled and worked long hours for Haraldsdyke. I love it better than any place on earth! And now you come along and try to tell me I've deliberately misappropriated your money—"

"Nonsense. All I'm saying is that I'm not in favor of any further agricultural experimentation for at least three years and won't advance you large sums of money to apply to schemes which are as yet untried and dangerous."

"And who are you to judge? What do you know of agriculture anyway? Who are you to make decisions which may affect the whole future of Haraldsdyke?"

"My dear Vere," said Axel, half-amused, half-exasperated. "Haraldsdyke *is* mine! And it *is* my money! I think I'm entitled to some say in the matter."

"Yes!" cried Vere, "Haraldsdyke is yours and the money is yours because, luckily for you, Papa made a will in your favor in a fit of mental aberration and then conveniently died before he could change it!"

There was a short tingling silence. Then Axel said quietly: "Precisely what are you suggesting?"

"Why, nothing! Merely that it was fortunate for you that Papa died when he did—and that Rodric died before he could answer his accusers!"

"Are you by any conceivable chance trying to imply that . . ."

"I mean what I say, not a word more and not a word less!"

"Then you'd best be extraordinarily careful, hadn't you, Vere, because like any other gentleman I'm exceedingly averse to being slandered and am—fortunately—in a position to retaliate very seriously indeed."

The silence flared, lengthened, became unbearable. Then:

"Just remember, won't you," said Axel, the door to the hall clicking as he opened it, "that you and your family live here for as long as I wish—and not a second longer."

The door snapped shut; his footsteps crossed the hall to the stairs and were soon inaudible. In the heavy silence that followed I was just about to push back the curtains and leave the window-seat when the communicating door from the library burst open and Vere came into the room.

He could not see me; the long curtains before the window hid me from view, and as he slammed the door shut behind him the curtains trembled in the draft of air. I found a chink in the curtains, and not daring to move or display myself I remained where I was, frozen into immobility as I watched him.

He had taken the wine decanter and was pouring himself a drink. A minute later, the glass empty, he poured himself a second measure and then slumped into a hearthside chair and put his head in his hands. I waited, scarcely daring to breathe, hoping he would go, but he remained motionless by the fire. I began to worry; how long would he stay there? If Axel had gone to our rooms he would discover I was missing and wonder why I had not returned.

He had just finished his second glass of wine and was to my despair pouring himself a third when there was an interruption. The door opened and through the chink in the curtains I saw Alice enter the room.

"What happened?" she demanded, and her soft country voice was indefinably harder and more resolute. "What did he say?"

Vere sat down in the chair again, seeming to crumple into the cushions. In a sudden flash of insight I saw then as clearly as I saw them both before me that Alice was the stronger of the two.

"It was no good." Vere was drinking again as she sat on the arm of his chair and put an arm around his shouders. "He'll pay the debts but he won't advance me any more than the bare necessities. I'm reduced to the role of bailiff, it seems."

Alice's face was very set. "Tell me exactly what was said."

He told her, omitting nothing. When he had finished he half-rose with a glance at the decanter on the sideboard but she took the glass from him and poured the wine herself. I noticed that while he had his back to her she diluted the wine with water from the jug on the sideboard.

"Well, at least," she said as she brought the glass back to him, "we still have a roof over our heads."

"Temporarily." The wine was making him morose and apathetic. He seemed a mere pale shadow as he sat huddled in the vast armchair.

"It was a pity," said Alice, "that you had to go losing your temper and accusing him of murder."

"I didn't! All I said was—"

"He took it as an accusation, didn't he?"

"Well . . ."

"You really should be careful, dear," said Alice. "You really should. Let sleeping dogs lie. They decided Rodric killed your father, so leave it at that. Resurrecting old grudges and angers can only be dangerous to us, and if you offend George again—"

"He was having an affair with Mama, I swear it. I know when

she looks at a man as she looked at him last year . . . Supposing Papa found out, threatened—"

"You really should let it be, dear. Just because your mother may have wished to have George as a lover, you've no proof that he did as she wanted, and you've no proof that he killed your father, nor will you ever have. Let it be, dearest! If you start resurrecting the past, who knows what might happen? Supposing someone found out that you came back earlier to Haraldsdyke that afternoon than you said you did? You told me you went straight to our room and lay down for a while as you weren't well, but I never saw you, did I, dear, and no one else saw you either. Supposing someone saw you slip into the house before your father was killed that afternoon and supposing they spoke up and said so if you went accusing George of murder—"

"Who could have seen me?" He was nervous; the wine spilled from his glass and stained the carpet. "No one saw me!"

"Mary might have done."

"She would have said so before now."

"Perhaps."

"Besides," he laughed uneasily, "I had no reason for killing Papa."

"No, dear? People might think you did, though. He knew it was you, you know, and not Rodric who was involved with the Frenchies in the smuggling."

The glass jerked right out of Vere's hand and smashed to a hundred pieces. Vere's face went from a dull white to the color of ashes.

"He never knew that!"

"Rodric told him. Your father discovered the contraband hidden in the Thirty-Acre barn—"

"I know that, but he suspected Rodric! He never suspected me! He thought it was another of Rodric's escapades—he never suspected that his meanness over money had driven me to smuggling to help raise money for my plans."

"Yes, dear," said Alice, "he suspected Rodric, but Rodric denied it, why else do you suppose they had such a violent quarrel? In the end your father half-believed him, but not entirely. He shouted out: 'Neither of you will inherit anything under my new will! I'm finished with both of you!' he shouts. 'To hell with you,' said Rodric, shouting back, 'alter your will as you like—I no longer care!' But of course he didn't know that your father had already altered the will and made a new one the day before, leaving everything to George. I suppose he'd had his suspicions ever since he discovered the contraband two days earlier in the barn."

"But my God!" cried Vere, his voice trembling. "Why didn't you tell me before that you knew this?"

"I didn't want to worry you, dear. I saw no point in worrying you. And the less it was talked of the better. I didn't want anyone getting ideas and suspecting you of Lord knows what terrible things when it's quite plain Rodric was guilty."

"You really believe he was guilty?"

"He must have been, dear. He had the cause and he was there with your father in the library and both of them in towering rages."

"I suppose so. Lord knows I had no love for Rodric, but I hardly thought he'd be fool enough to kill the source of all his income."

"He didn't know your father had already altered his will to leave everything to George. He thought he would inherit money."

"True . . . But supposing George knew the will had been changed in his favor? He was the only one of us who really benefited from Papa's death."

"You benefited too, dear. If he had lived he would have told the Watch at Rye that you were in league with the Frenchies."

"But my God—"

"Let it be, dear. Do as I say and let it be. Whatever happened in the past doesn't alter the present situation—it doesn't change the fact that we live here on George's charity only and if we offend George we'll find ourselves with no roof over our heads."

"Oh Alice, Alice . . ." He turned to her in despair and I saw her broad arms gather him to her as if he were a little child and stroke his hair as he buried his face against her breast.

"There, there, dear," she said, much as she had spoken to her own children in the nursery that day. "There, there, my love . . ."

"I feel so helpless, so inadequate."

"Hush, don't say such things . . ."

They were silent, he clinging to her, she still clasping him in the comfort of her embrace, but presently he lifted his face to hers and kissed her on the lips. The atmosphere changed; there was passion in their embrace now, and such fervor in their gestures as I had never seen before between husband and wife. I glanced away, feeling that I was trespassing, and at the same time I was conscious of desolation as I saw the emptiness of my own marriage in a sickening moment of revelation. I was just wishing with all my heart that I could escape when Vere said suddenly: "I can't bear the insecurity of my position! What's to happen to our children? Even if we stay here, you nothing but an unpaid housekeeper and I nothing but a mere bailiff, there's no future for the children. George's children will inherit Haraldsdyke."

"If George has children," said Alice. "If he doesn't, our children will inherit."

"Why shouldn't George have children? He's fit and vigorous and the girl is young and healthy. She may already be pregnant, for all we know."

"I think not," said Alice. "Not at present."

"She will be before long." He buried his face in his hands again. "I don't know what to do," he said, his voice muffled, and then he raised his head in anger. "Why did George have to take up his inheritance? He had money in Vienna—and property too! What interest has he ever shown in Haraldsdyke? If he hadn't troubled to fulfill the conditions of the will by marrying an English girl within the year, the estate would have passed straight to Stephen, and I would have been trustee in my son's name till he came of age."

"It's no use saying that now, dear, not now that George has successfully claimed his inheritance and fulfilled the conditions of the will."

"And if the girl gets pregnant, it's the end of all our hopes! The devil take George Brandson! I wish—"

"Don't despair so, dear! You despair so easily. Why, a multitude of things may happen yet. Even if she does get pregnant, the child may be sickly and die. Or she may have a miscarriage. Or she may be barren. Or she may herself die."

A chill seemed to strike through that warm room. My blood seemed to run to ice and my mouth was dry.

"You're always so calm," Vere was saying, and to me at that moment it seemed as if he were speaking from a long way away, "so sensible . . . I don't know what I would ever do without you, Alice. Truthfully, I don't know what I would ever do if I didn't have you beside me at times such as these . . ."

They kissed. There was silence for a while. I glanced out of the window and saw my reflection in the glass pane, my eyes wide and dark in my white face.

"Come upstairs, my love," said Alice. "Come to bed. Don't sit here any more."

He rose obediently. The light caught his face and made him look haggard and drawn, and then he turned aside into the shadows and I could only see the gleam of his bright hair as he walked with Alice to the door.

They were gone; I was alone at last.

I was so stiff with tension, so unnerved by all I had overheard that I had to sit down and drink some of the wine from the decanter. Even after that I had difficulty in controlling my trembling limbs. However, finally I felt sufficiently recovered to return upstairs, and moving cautiously I stole outside and across the hall to the staircase.

The corridor above was in darkness and I stumbled unsteadily towards our rooms. When I reached the door of our sitting room at last I was so relieved I nearly fell across the threshold, but as I opened the door, I froze immediately in my tracks. For Esther was with Axel before the fireplace and it was obvious even to me in my confused state that she was very angry.

". . . chit of a girl," Esther was saying as I opened the door and halted abruptly on the threshold.

They both swung around to face me.

We all looked at one another in silence. Then:

"So there you are, my dear," said Axel, moving towards me. "I was wondering what had happened to you." And he drew me across the threshold and kissed me lightly on the forehead.

Over his shoulder I saw Esther bite her lip. "I must go," she said sharply. "Pray excuse me. Goodnight to you both."

"Goodnight, Esther," Axel said courteously and held the door open for her.

I said goodnight faintly as she swept past us out into the corridor without another word.

Axel closed the door again and we were alone together.

"Are you all right?" he said at once, and no doubt he was wondering why I had chosen to go wandering about the house in a robe with my hair trailing loose upon my shoulders. "You look a little pale."

"I—couldn't sleep." I went past him into the bedroom. "In the end I went downstairs for a glass of wine in the hope that it would make me sleepy."

"Did you find the wine?"

"There was a decanter in the dining room."

"Ah yes, of course, so there is. There's also a decanter kept in the saloon in case you should ever need it. The saloon is nearer than the dining room." He followed me into the bedroom. "I'm glad you arrived back when you did. I was having a rather difficult time with Esther."

I could not look at him for fear I might betray my knowledge of his past relationship with her. Taking off my robe and laying it aside, I slipped into bed once more and closed my eyes.

"What did she want?" I managed to say.

"She seemed to have some idea that she was no longer wanted here and would prefer to take a house in Rye. Naturally I had to assure her that she was mistaken."

I knew instinctively that he was lying. I thought I knew all too well why Esther had chosen to come to his apartments to talk to him and why she had left immediately I had arrived on the scene. If she was angry, it was not because she felt she was now unwanted at Haraldsdyke; she was angry because she felt she was now unwanted in his bedroom. Only a fool would have chosen such a time to fan the flames of an old love affair, and certainly whatever else he might be, Axel was no fool.

"I think she'd bored with country life," he was saying. "Vere has entertained very little during the past year, and Esther lived for her dinner parties and social occasions. To be honest, I think she wishes to take a house in Rye less because she feels unwanted here than because she is anxious to escape from this way of life now that she's free to do so."

"Why should she feel unwanted here?" I watched him through my lashes. He was undressing slowly, examining the fine linen of his shirt for any soiled marks.

"She was the mistress here for more than twenty-five years. Some women under such circumstances are reluctant to give way to a younger woman."

It was a clever excuse. It explained Esther's anger and her withdrawal as soon as I appeared.

"But why did she come to our apartments? She knew I had retired to bed."

"I had found you weren't in bed and as I went to the landing to look for you she came out of the drawing room and I asked her where you were. She said she had something to discuss with me in private and I suggested she come here." He took off his shirt and went into his adjoining dressing room.

I lay very still, my eyes half-closed, my limbs slowly becoming tense and aching again. I was appalled how smoothly he could invent plausible lies.

At length he came out of the dressing room, snuffed the candles and slid into bed beside me. His limbs brushed mine.

"How cold you are," he said, drawing me closer to the warmth of his body. "I hope you haven't caught a chill."

"No . . ." I longed to press myself even closer to him and feel secure, but I was only conscious of nervousness and panic. "Axel—"

"Yes," he said. "Your state of health is delicate just now. I remember."

He did not sound altogether pleased. I sensed rather than felt his withdrawal from me.

"I—I'm sorry," I was stammering, feeling a mere ineffectual child cowed by a maze of subtle nightmares which surrounded me on all sides. "I'm so sorry, Axel—"

"Why should you be sorry?" he said. "You've done nothing wrong. Goodnight, my dear, and I hope you sleep well."

"Thank you," I whispered wretchedly. "Goodnight."

But sleep was impossible. I lay in that great bed, my limbs chilled and my feet feeling as ice, but my mind was not as numbed as my body and the longer I lay quietly in the darkness the more vivid my thoughts became. I began to toss and turn and when I finally crept closer to Axel for warmth, he turned abruptly, startling me for I thought he had been asleep.

"What's the matter?"

"Nothing. I'm a little cold."

"Cold! You're frozen! Come here."

I felt better lying in his arms. I even managed to drift off to sleep but awoke soon in panic after Vere, Alice and Esther had all turned to me in a dream and said: "You'll really have to die, you know."

"My dear child," said Axel astonished as I sat up gasping in fright. "What on earth's possessed you tonight?" And he fired a match, lit the candle and drew me to him in consternation.

Such was my state of nerves that I could endure my silence no longer.

"I—I overheard a conversation between Vere and Alice when I was downstairs," I whispered desperately. "They don't want me to become pregnant—they want you to die childless so that their children can inherit—they want me to die . . ."

"Wait, wait, wait! I've never heard such a confused tale! My dear, Vere and Alice may, understandably, wish their children to inherit Haraldsdyke, but I can assure you that your death wouldn't help them at all, since there's no guarantee I wouldn't marry again—and again, if need be, though God forbid it . . . if they feel murderously inclined, which I doubt, then I'm the one they should dispose of, since I'm the only one who stands in their way at present."

He sounded so sane and balanced that I felt ashamed of my ridiculous panic.

"But they don't want me to have children, Axel—"

"No," he said, "I don't suppose they do. Neither would I, if I were in their situation. However, if you become pregnant there's nothing whatsoever they could do about it apart from cursing their misfortune anew."

"But—"

"Yes? What's troubling you now?"

"Perhaps—would it be possible . . . I mean, is it necessary that I have children now? Can I not wait a little and have them later?"

There was a silence. I saw the tolerant amusement die from his face and the old opaque expression descend like a veil over his eyes. At length he said dryly: "And how would you propose to arrange that, may I ask?"

"I—" My face was hot with embarrassment. "Surely—there are ways—"

"For whores," he said. "Not for ladies in your position."

I was without words. I could only lie there in a paralysis of shame and wish I had never spoken.

"You're not seriously alarmed by these chance remarks you overheard, are you?"

I shook my head in misery.

"Then why are you unanxious for children at present? I would of course see that you had the best medical care and attention throughout your confinement."

Speech was impossible. I could only stare at the sheet.

"I am most anxious for children," he said, "and not merely in order to establish myself at Haraldsdyke."

Hot tears scalded my eyes. It needed all my will-power and concentration to hold them in check. At last I managed to say in a very cold formal voice: "Please forgive me. I suddenly felt inadequate and too young for such a thing, but now I see I was being childish and stupid. I wish I hadn't mentioned it to you."

"Far from being inadequate and too young, I would say just the opposite. You will soon be eighteen, you're intelligent, capable and surprisingly mature in many ways. I'm sure you would be an excellent mother, and besides I think motherhood would probably be the best thing for you. You must have felt very alone in the world these last few weeks, and a child would alleviate your loneliness to some degree."

I was silent.

He kissed me lightly. "So no more talk about inadequacies and youth."

I did not reply.

He snuffed the candle so that we were in darkness once more and attempted to take me in his arms again, but presently I turned away from him and he made no attempt to stop me. My last conscious thought before I fell asleep was that if I asked Dame Joan the witch for a potion she would be sure to tell her daughter later, and then Alice and Vere would know with certainty that there was no threat to their children's inheritance for a while.

And once they knew that, I should be safe.

Five

I HAD PLANNED to steal away into the village some time during the next day, but this proved to be impossible. I had forgotten that Axel had invited the Shermans to dinner, and my morning was in fact spent with Alice preparing the menu, talking to the cook and supervising the dusting of the furniture and the cleaning of the silver. The strain of conducting the tasks was considerable even though Alice was at my elbow to advise and instruct me; I retired to my room soon after noon feeling exhausted and glad to be alone for a while before it was time to dress for dinner.

The guests were punctual; I was introduced to Mr. James Sherman, the Brandsons' lawyer, who was a portly gentleman in his forties, to his wife, Mrs. James, and to their two daughters, Evelina and Annabella, both of whom looked at me with frank jealousy, presumably because I had married the master of Haraldsdyke and they had not. On meeting them I was not surprised that Axel had looked elsewhere, and I turned with relief to greet Mr. Charles Sherman, Mr. James' younger brother, who was about the same age as Axel himself. Vere and Alice soon appeared upon the scene, Vere making an effort to appear relaxed and at ease, Alice seeming quietly self-effacing. Mary sat in a corner and fidgeted, unnoticed. Ned slunk in silently in the hope that no one would see him and presently vanished as unobtrusively as he had arrived. It was left to Esther to make the grand entrance, and she did so superbly, gliding into the room in a swirl of black lace and diamonds, and moving forward to greet each of the guests effusively.

All the men rose, young Mr. Charles Sherman preening himself like a peacock and dancing across at once to escort her to a couch where he could seat himself by her side.

"Dear Esther," said Mrs. James sweetly, each word barbed as a razor, "how well you look, even though the tragedy was less than a year ago. Mourning does so become you."

"Dark colors have always suited me," said Esther with a brilliant smile. "Besides only a young woman can look well in pastel shades, don't you think?"

Mrs. James' gown was pale yellow.

"Pray tell us, Mrs. Brandson," said Miss Annabella from beside me, "had you known your husband long before your marriage?"

I tried to concentrate on the conventional exchanges of formal conversation.

With a remorseless inevitability, the evening crept along its tedious path. In comparison with the small dinner parties which my mother had been accustomed to give from time to time, I found the visitors boring, their outlook provincial and their conversation devoid of any subject which might have interested me. The prospect of the remainder of my life being filled with such gestures in the name of hospitality and entertainment depressed me beyond words.

At long last when they were gone and their carriage was rattling off down the drive to the Marsh road below, I retreated to my room as rapidly as possible, kicked off my dainty high-heeled satin slippers and shouted irritably for Marie-Claire to set me free from the agonies of my tight laced corset. I had already dismissed her and was moodily brushing my hair when Axel came into the room.

I tried to smile. "I hope the evening passed satisfactorily to you, Axel."

"Yes indeed," he said with a spontaneity I had not expected. "You were splendid and the Shermans were very impressed with you. I was exceedingly pleased."

"I'm—very glad." And indeed I was relieved that my boredom had not been apparent. But later when he emerged from his dressing room he said casually: "No doubt it must have been very dull for you after the sparkling dinner parties of London."

I felt myself blush. "Different, certainly," I said, "but not altogether dull."

"It was dull for me," he said, "but then I'm accustomed to Vienna and even London would be dull to me in comparison." He paused to look at me, he standing by the bed, I leaning back upon the pillows, and as our glances met it seemed for one brief instant that a flash of understanding passed between us, a moment of being "en rapport" with one another.

He smiled. I smiled too, hesitantly. For a second I thought he was going to make some complimentary or even affectionate remark, but all he said in the end was simply: "You would like Vienna. I think I shall have to take you there one day."

Perhaps it was the relief of escaping at last from the tedium of the evening or perhaps it was because of that strange moment when we had exchanged glances and smiled, but for the first time I longed for him, for a release from loneliness, for a glimpse of what marriage might have been. The dinner party, as so often happens when the familiar is placed side by side with the horror of nightmare, had made my frightened thoughts recede into dim shadows from which I had no wish for them to emerge, and in the effort to seek a final oblivion for my unhappiness I turned to him absolutely and sought his embraces with a passion which must have taken him unawares. Passion sparked passion; flame ignited flame. I knew instinctively, as one knows such things, that after his initial astonishment he was conscious of nothing save the burning of our emotions and the whirling painful spiral of desire.

The night passed; sleep when it came was deep and untroubled, and then towards dawn the fears and doubts and anxieties in my mind began to clamor for recognition after the long hours of being forcibly suppressed. I awoke at seven in the agonized grip of a nightmare and lay trembling between the sheets for some time. And as I lay waiting for the day to break, the mist rolled in across the Marsh from the sea and thickened in icy shrouds around the walls of Haraldsdyke.

It was Sunday. I learned that the Brandsons customarily attended matins at Haraldsford Church every week, and accordingly after Axel and I had breakfasted together in our rooms I dressed formally in my dark blue woolen traveling habit in preparation for braving the chill of the mist later on.

The weather was not inviting. From our windows it was barely possible to see to the end of the short drive, and beyond the walls surrounding the grounds the dank whiteness blotted out all trace of the view south over the Marsh to Rye and the sea.

"A true November day," said Axel wryly as he sat down to breakfast with a glance at the scene beyond the window pane.

I felt ill-at-ease with him that morning for reasons I did not fully understand; the nightmare had wakened me with all my fears revived and my sense of being in any way in accord with Axel had vanished, just as my memory of the normality of the dinner party had receded. I now felt curiously ashamed of my demonstrative emotions of the previous night, and my shame manifested itself in an instinctive withdrawal from him. He rose more cheerful and good-humored than I had ever seen him before, but I made no effort at conversation and while not ignoring his attentiveness, I found myself unable to respond to it.

Presently he sensed my mood and fell silent.

"Are you feeling well?" he said at last. "I had forgotten your health had been delicate recently."

"Thank you," I said, "but I'm quite recovered."

He said nothing further but I sensed him watching me carefully and at last, almost in irritation, I raised my glance to meet his. He smiled but I looked away and when I looked at him again the animation was gone from his face and his eyes were opaque and without expression once more.

When he had finished his breakfast he went downstairs, for he was already dressed, and I summoned Marie-Claire. Some time later I followed him downstairs, my muff, bonnet and redingote in my hands so that I would not be obliged to return to my rooms before going to church, and wandered into the saloon to see what time it was according to the grandfather clock there.

The fire was alight in the grate but the room was still damp and cold. At first I thought it was also empty and then I saw Mary huddled in one of the tall armchairs near the hearth. Her hands were outstretched towards the flames and I could see the chilblains on her fingers as I drew closer. She smiled nervously at me, and muttered some half-intelligible greeting.

"It's a most unpleasant morning, is it not?" I said absently, sitting down opposite her. "Where is everyone? Isn't it time to leave for church yet?"

"I suppose we're the first to be ready," she said, stating the obvious. "Perhaps we're a trifle early."

We sat in silence for a while, both feeling awkward in each other's presence. In the distance I could hear Alice talking and Vere's indistinct response and then Axel called from somewhere close at hand: "Did you order the carriage to the door, Vere?"

"I sent Ned to the stables with the message."

There was more conversation. I heard Esther's voice then and Axel saying "Good morning" to her. Footsteps echoed in the hall.

"Everyone seems to be assembling now," I murmured to Mary, and then saw to my astonishment that there were tears in her eyes. As she saw that I had noticed them she blushed and made an awkward gesture with her hands.

"Sunday mornings always remind me of Rodric," she said shame-faced. "I so much used to enjoy traveling with him to church. He is not—was not—very reverent towards the rector but he used to make me laugh no matter how much I disapproved of his jokes on principle."

I stared at her curiously. It was not the first time, I suddenly realized, that she had referred to Rodric in the present tense. To do so once was a natural enough mistake; twice was still excusable, but I was sure she had made the error on more than two occasions. Wondering whether it was simply an affectation assumed to underline her grief or whether it had any other possible significance, I said off-handedly: "Why do you so often talk about Rodric as if he's not dead at all? You're constantly forgetting to talk of him in the past tense! Is it because you think he may be still alive?"

She stared at me round-eyed. Her mouth was open in surprise and I could see that one of her teeth was discolored with decay. And then as I watched her in mounting fascination she turned bright red, licked her lips and glanced wildly around the room to see if anyone had slipped in to eavesdrop while her back had been turned. I glanced around too, but of course there was no one there. The door was slightly open, just as I had left it, and from the hall came the vague sounds of footsteps and snatches of conversation.

"—my best fur," Esther was saying far away. "Quite ravaged by moth . . . Vere, you're not taking the child to church, are you?"

"Stephen behaves very well in church," said Alice, "and I shall take him to see my mother afterwards. Let me take him, Vere. Here, precious, come to Mama . . ."

"Where's your wife, George?"

"And Mary!" said Esther, faintly exasperated. "Where's Mary? That child is always late . . ."

"Mary?" I said in a low voice.

But she was shifting uneasily in her chair. "He's dead," she mumbled. I had never heard a lie told so badly. "Dead." She stood up, fumbling with her gloves, not looking at me.

"I don't believe you," I said, curiosity making my voice sharp and hard. "You're lying. Tell me the truth."

The poor girl was so nervous of me that she dropped both her gloves on the floor and started to grovel for them helplessly, but I was ruthless. "So he's alive," I said, pitting my will against hers and watching her defenses crumble beneath the pressure. "How do you know? Answer me! How do you know he didn't drown in the Marsh that day?"

My voice had risen in my determination to extract the truth. I saw her put her finger to her lips in an agony of worry lest someone should hear us.

"Shhh . . . oh please—"

"How do you know he didn't—"

"I saw him." She was half-whispering, still motioning me to speak more softly. "I saw him come back to the house after George had told us he had found Rodric's horse and hat by a bog in the Marsh."

I stared at her.

"I—I was so upset when I heard the news of his death," she said, "that I went to see Ned first, but Ned was too upset himself to comfort me. Then I went to Rodric's room to sit for a while with his possessions around me, I couldn't believe he was dead . . ."

"And he came back."

"Yes, I heard footsteps and hid behind a curtain because I didn't want to be found there. I didn't want to talk to anyone. And then—and then . . . he came in. At first I thought it was a ghost—I—I nearly fainted . . . He came into the room, took some money out of a drawer, glanced at his watch and then went out again. He wasn't in the room for more than a few seconds."

"And you didn't speak to him? You didn't call out?"

"I was too stunned—I was nearly fainting with the shock."

"Quite. What did you do then?"

"I waited for him to come back."

"And didn't he?"

"No, that was what was so strange. I waited and waited and waited but he never came. I never saw him again."

"But didn't you tell anyone what you'd seen? Didn't you—"

"Only George."

"Axel!" I felt a sudden weakness in my knees. "Why Axel?"

"Well, I thought and thought about what I should do and then since George was the one who broke the news about Rodric's death I decided to tell him what had happened. But he didn't believe me. He said it was a—a hallucination born of shock and he advised me not to tell anyone or people would think my reason had been affected . . . So I said nothing more. But I have gone on hoping. Every day I go to wait in his room in case—"

"But you did see him," I said slowly, "didn't you. It wasn't your imagination. You really did see him."

My belief in her story gave her confidence. "Yes," she said. "Yes, I swear I did. I did see him. I know Rodric was alive after George told me he was dead."

There was a draft from the threshold as the door swung wider on its hinges. Esther's voice said harshly: "What nonsense! What a despicable tale to tell, Mary Moore! You should be ashamed of yourself!" As I whirled around with a start I saw she was trembling in every limb. "Rodric's dead," she said, and her voice too was trembling now. "I loved him but he's dead and I accepted his death, but you—you stupid foolish child—have to invent fantastic stories of him being alive just to please your sense of the dramatic!" She was crying; tears welled in her eyes and she pressed her hands against her cheeks. "How *dare* you upset me like this—"

Vere was behind her suddenly, and Alice. Vere said: "Mama, what is it? What's the matter?" and beyond Alice I heard Axel's voice say sharply: "Esther?"

But Esther did not hear him. Fortified by Vere's arms around her she was weeping beautifully into a delicate lace handkerchief while poor Mary, also smitten with tears, howled that she hadn't meant what she said, Rodric was dead, she had never seen him return to his room late last Christmas Eve, she was merely indulging in wishful thinking. . . .

"Stop!" Axel exclaimed sternly in his most incisive voice, and there was an abrupt silence broken only by Mary's snuffles. "Mary, you should surely know by now that you must not try to impose your own dream world on other people. Haven't I warned you about that before? Day-dreaming is selfish at the best of times, a dangerous self-indulgence. . . . Come, Esther, the child didn't mean to upset you. Forgive her—it wasn't done maliciously. Now, are we all ready to leave? We shall be very late if we delay here much longer."

We were all ready. Within two minutes we were on our way to the church at Haraldsford, and throughout the service that followed I tried to make up my mind whether Mary had been telling the truth or not. In the end I came to the conclusion, as Axel had done, that her "vision" of Rodric must have been a hallucination born of shock. After all, I reasoned, if Rodric really had arranged a faked death for himself in the Marsh, why had he then risked discovery by returning to the house? And if he had indeed returned to the house, how had he managed to vanish into thin air after Mary had seen him? And finally if he were alive today, where was he? Despite my romantic inclination to believe him alive, my common sense would not wholly allow me to do so. He must be dead, I told myself. If he were alive, the situation would make no sense.

And yet for some hours to come I found myself wondering.

My mother had been a Roman Catholic once long ago before her flight from France and her struggles for existence in England, but her faith had ebbed with her fortunes and she had made no protest when a succession of nannies, governesses and finally schools had firmly imprinted Alexander and myself with the stamp of the Church of England. This was probably for the best; at that time there was still a large amount of prejudice against Catholics and besides, my father, although amoral and irreligious, was always quick to champion the Church of England against what he called "damned Papist nonsense."

The little church at Haraldsford was, of course, as are all Parish churches in this country, Protestant, the rector firmly adhering to the principles of the Church of England. As we entered the ancient porch that morning and stepped into the nave I saw a host of curious eyes feast upon us in welcome and realized that the villagers had flocked to church en masse for a glimpse of the new master of Haraldsdyke and his wife. Axel led the way to the Brandson pew without looking to right or to left but I glanced quickly over the gaping faces and wondered what they were thinking. It was, after all, less than a year since Robert Brandson and Rodric had come to this church. I sat down beside Axel, imagining more clearly than ever now the scandal that must have thrived at the time of their deaths, the gossip and speculation, the endless rumors whispering and reverberating through the community.

Throughout the service it seemed to me that I could almost feel the gaze of several dozen pairs of eyes boring remorselessly into my back, but of course that was a mere fantasy, and when I stole a glance over my shoulder during the prayers I saw that no one was watching me.

The sermon began. The child Stephen began to shift restlessly between his parents, and then Alice pulled him on to her lap and he was content for a while. I remembered that Alice was taking him to see her mother after the service was over, and I began to wonder how I could also manage to see Dame Joan that morning. Perhaps this afternoon I would be able to slip away from the house and walk back to the village. It was a mere mile, after all. It wouldn't take long. But supposing someone saw me leave, asked questions when I came back . . . I should have to have an excuse for returning to the village on such a chill misty afternoon.

During the final prayers and blessing I managed to roll my muff surreptitiously under the pew. No one noticed.

After the service was over, we paused to exchange greetings

with the rector and then returned to the carriage while Alice took the child down the road to her mother's house and Ned disappeared silently in the direction of the "Black Ram" for a tankard of ale. Within ten minutes we were back at Haraldsdyke. I managed to hide my bare hands in my wide sleeves so that no one should notice my muff was missing, and hastened to my rooms to change into a fresh gown.

Dinner was served earlier that day, I discovered, partly to revive everyone after the visit to church and partly to help the servants have a more restful evening than usual. With the exception of Alice, who had evidently decided to spend some time with her mother, we all sat down in the dining room soon after two o'clock.

Ned slunk in a moment later. I thought Axel was going to censure him but he took no notice and after Ned had muttered a word of apology nothing further was said to him. I noticed, not for the first time, how his mother always ignored him entirely. During the meal she conversed with Vere and managed to draw Axel into the conversation while also taking pains to address a remark to me now and again. I was careful to smile and reply sweetly, suppressing any trace of the dislike I felt for her, but by the end of the meal I was wondering if there really was any chance of her taking a house in Rye. Perhaps now that she was at last free and her year of mourning was nearly over, she would find herself a suitable husband and remarry.

I watched her, remembering what Ned had told me, remembering that she had been estranged from her husband for the twenty years before his death even though they had continued to live under the same roof. She must have hated him. What a relief it must have been for her, I thought, to have found herself a widow . . .

Alice came back just as we were finishing dinner, and said she would eat in the nursery with Stephen and the other children. Presently, Esther, Mary and I withdrew to the drawing room and within ten minutes I excused myself from them on the pretense that I wanted to rest for an hour or so. Once I was safely in my apartments I changed from the gown I had worn for dinner, donned my thick traveling habit once more and tip-toed out of the house by the back stairs.

No one saw me.

Outside the fog was thickening and I was soon out of sight of the house. It was unnaturally quiet, the fog muffling all sound, and soon the stillness, the gathering gloom and the eerie loneliness of the Marsh road began to prey upon my imagination. I continually thought I heard footsteps behind me, but when I stopped to listen there was nothing, just the thick heavy silence, and I came to the conclusion that the noise of my footsteps must in some strange way be re-echoing against the wall of mist to create an illusion of sound.

I was never more relieved when after several minutes of very brisk walking I saw the first cottages on the outskirts of the village and then the tower of Haraldsford church looming mysteriously out of the mist like some ghostly castle in a fairytale. I hurried past it. The village street was empty and deserted, chinks of light showing through the shuttered windows of the cottages, a lamp burning by the doorway of the "Black Ram." Everyone seemed to be indoors to escape the weather. Two minutes later I was by the door of Dame Joan's cottage on the other side of the village and tapping nervously on the ancient weatherbeaten wood.

There was no answer. I tapped again, the unreasoning panic rising within me, and then suddenly the door was opening and she was before me, broad and massive-boned, her curious eyes interested but not in the least astonished; behind her I could see a black cat washing his paws before a smoldering peat fire.

"Come in, Mrs. George." She sounded strangely business-like, as if there was nothing strange about the mistress of Haraldsdyke paying a social call on her at four o'clock on a dark November afternoon. It occurred to me in a moment of macabre fantasy that she seemed almost to have been expecting me, and then I put the thought aside as ridiculous.

"Thank you," I said, crossing the threshold. "I hope I'm not disturbing you."

"No indeed." She drew a wooden chair close to the fire for me and pushed the cat out of the way. I half-expected the cat to hiss and spit at this casual dismissal from the fireside but far from being incensed it rubbed itself against her skirts and purred lovingly. When she sat down opposite me a moment later it jumped up into her lap and she began to stroke it with her broad flat fingers.

"Some herb tea, Mrs. George? Warm you after your walk."

"No—no, thank you very much."

She smiled. I suddenly noticed that the pupils of her strange eyes were no more than black dots. They were very odd eyes indeed.

I felt unnerved suddenly, overcome by a gust of fright, and wished I had not come. I was just wondering how I could retreat without it seeming as if I were running away when she said: "Alice was here a little while past with my grandson. A beautiful child."

"Yes," I said. "Yes, indeed."

"You'll be having children of your own soon, I've no doubt."

"I—" Words stuck in my throat.

She nodded secretly and waited.

My hands clutched the material of my habit in a hot moist grip. "I was very ill this summer," I invented, and somehow I had the unpleasant suspicion that she would know I was lying. "My health is still delicate, and the doctors all said I should be careful. I am anxious to avoid pregnancy for a little while yet."

She nodded again. The firelight glinted in her eyes and gave them a strange reddish cast. Her lips were curved in a smile still and her teeth seemed sharp and predatory. I was by now quite speechless. For a moment there was a silence broken only by the purring of the cat in her lap. Then:

"There's an herb," said the witch. "Very helpful, it is, if taken properly. I've made many a potion with pennyroyal."

"A potion?"

"I have a jar now ready for Mary Oaks out at Tansedge Farm. Fourteen children in sixteen years and couldn't take no more. I've been making the potion for her for three years now."

"And she hasn't—during that time—"

"Not even the ghost of a child, Mrs. George. For three years."

"I—see . . ."

"Let me give you the jar I have ready for Mary Oaks and then I can make another potion for her tomorrow."

"If—if that's possible . . . I—have a sovereign here . . ."

"Lord love you, Mrs. George, what would I be doing with gold sovereigns? Alice sees I don't want for anything, and besides I never go to Rye to spend coin. Bring me a gift some time, if you like, but no sovereigns."

So in the end it was all extraordinarily easy. After she had given me the potion I forced myself to stay a few minutes longer for politeness' sake, and then I escaped as courteously as possible. As I stepped outside the relief seemed to strike me with an almost physical intensity. My legs were shaking and the palms of my hands were still moist with sweat.

The guilt began to assail me as soon as I walked away from the cottage through the village to the church. I began to feel ashamed of myself, horror-stricken at what I had done. I had reduced myself to the level of a loose woman, sought medication which was undoubtedly sinful and wicked in the eyes of the church. If Axel were ever to find out . . .

When I reached the church I was trembling in a wave of nervous reaction and remorse. I eased open the heavy oak door and slipped into the dark nave, my eyes blurred with tears, and stumbled to the Brandson pew where I retrieved my muff and sat down for a moment to think. I prayed for forgiveness for my wickedness and in a wave of emotional fervor which was entirely foreign to my usual passive acceptance of religion, I begged God to understand why I had acted so shamefully and promised to have children later in life when I was not so frightened or uncertain of myself and my husband.

At last, my guilt assuaged to a degree where I could dry my eyes and pull myself together, I stood up, walked briskly down the nave and wrenched open the heavy door with a quick tug of the wrist.

The shock I received then was like a dagger thrust beneath my ribs.

For there, waiting for me in the shelter of the porch, was none other than my husband, Axel Brandson.

My muff concealed the jar containing Dame Joan's potion but I could feel the hot color rushing to my face to proclaim my guilty conscience. I gave a loud exclamation and then hastily exaggerated my reaction of surprise to conceal any trace of guilt.

"How you startled me!" I gasped, leaning faintly against the doorpost. "Did you follow me here?"

His face was very still; he was watching me closely. "I saw you go into the church. I had come from the house to look for you."

"Oh . . . But how did you know I'd left the house?"

"Esther said you'd gone to your room, but when I went to look for you I only found your maid looking mystified since you appeared to have changed into your outdoor habit again."

"My muff was missing," I said. "I realized I must have left it in church this morning."

"Why didn't you send one of the servants to collect it? To venture beyond the walls of Haraldsdyke on an afternoon such as this was very foolish, not merely from the point of view of exposing yourself to such a chill, unhealthy mist, but also on account of the risk of meeting a stray peddler on the road."

"I—didn't think of it."

"I was extremely worried."

"I'm sorry," I said subdued. "I'm very sorry, Axel."

"Well, we'll say no more about it but I trust you'll be more sensible in future."

He made me feel like a child of six. However, so relieved was I that he had not seen me leave Dame Joan's cottage that I was quite prepared to tolerate any reproof without complaint. Accordingly I stood before him meekly with downcast eyes and said that yes, I would be more sensible in the future, and presently we left the church and set off back through the heavy mist to Haraldsdyke.

He scarcely spoke half a dozen words to me on the way home, and I knew he was still angry. I also had an unpleasant intuition that he was suspicious, although he gave no indication that he had disbelieved my story. We walked along the road as quickly as I could manage, and even while we walked the darkness was blurring the mist before us and making the gloom twice as obscure. By the time we reached the walls of Haraldsdyke it was scarcely possible to see anything which was not within a few feet of our eyes. The front door was unlocked. Axel opened it and we stepped into the hall.

The house was curiously still. I was just about to remark on the unnatural silence which prevailed everywhere when there was the slam of a door from upstairs and the next moment Vere appeared on the landing and came swiftly down the stairs towards us. He was wearing his riding habit and his face was a shade more pale than usual.

"Mary had just been taken ill," he said. "I'm riding to Winchelsea for Dr. Salter."

Alice was very distressed. "I left the nursery where I had had dinner with the children," she said to me, "and went to the drawing room. You'd just left to go to your room. Mary was huddled around the fireplace and it was damp in the room despite the fire so I suggested we had some tea to warm us all. I went down to the kitchens to give the order myself—I always like to spare

the servants as much as possible on Sundays. Presently George
and Vere came up from the dining room where they had been
sitting with their port, and Vere had the tray of tea with him—
he'd met the maid in the hall and said he would take the tray up
for her. George lingered for a while, handing around the tea as
I poured it out, but after a few minutes he said he was going to
look for you; however, everyone else, except Ned who had disappeared somewhere as usual, stayed and drank tea for a while."

We were outside the door of Mary's room in the dark passage,
I still wearing my traveling habit, Alice carrying a flickering
candle, her hand on the latch of the door. Axel had gone out to
the stables with Vere in an effort to dissuade him from attempting
the ride to Winchelsea in the thick mist.

"And when did Mary become ill?" I said uneasily.

"Perhaps half an hour later. The maid had collected the tea-
tray and taken it downstairs, and as the maid went out Mary
suddenly said she felt very sick and was going to vomit."

"And—"

"And she did, poor girl. All over the new rug. Esther—Vere's
mother—was most upset. About the rug, I mean. Then she saw
Mary was really ill and became alarmed. We got Mary to bed
and she was still ill and complaining of pains so Vere said he
would ride at once to Winchelsea for Dr. Salter."

"The mist is very thick," I said uncertainly. "And now that night
has come it's almost impossible to see anything."

"I know—I wish he wouldn't go, but I suppose he must. The
poor girl's so ill."

"Do you think it's anything infectious?" I had had a morbid
dread of illness since a childhood friend had died of cholera.

"No, she often suffers from her stomach. No doubt she's eaten
something disagreeable to her."

I shivered a little. I could remember stories of people dying in
twenty-four hours after being struck down with a violent sickness and a pain in the right side.

"You're cold," said Alice, mistaking the cause of my shivering.

"You shouldn't be lingering here. Hurry to your room and change into something warm before you catch a chill."

I took her advice and knelt on the hearth of the sitting room for several minutes while I stretched out my hands towards the fire. Some time later when I had changed my clothes and had returned to sit by the fireside, Axel came into the room.

"Vere insisted on going to Winchelsea," he said abruptly. "I wish he hadn't but I suppose it was the right thing to do. He should be all right if he keeps to the road, and the Marsh road at least is hard to wander from since it's raised above the level of the surrounding land. It's not as if he intended to cut across the Marsh as Rodric did."

There was a shadow in my mind suddenly, a strange shaft of uneasiness. Perhaps it was the recollection of how Rodric had died, or perhaps it was merely the mention of his name. It was as if Rodric was the center of an invisible whirlpool of dissonance, the unseen cause of all the trouble existing beneath the roof of Haraldsdyke. It was as if everything began and ended with Rodric. I thought of him then, as I had so often thought of him during the past week, and suddenly it seemed that his vivid personality had never been more real to me and that I knew every nuance of his turbulent personality, each new facet of his charm.

"Mary was always so fond of Rodric," I said aloud, but speaking more to myself.

"Yes, she idolized him," said Axel absently. "It's quite a normal phase for a girl her age to go through, I believe."

And then suddenly I saw it all, saw Mary saying "I did see him—I know Rodric was alive after George told us he was dead," saw everyone listening to her in the doorway, saw Axel's impatient expression as he dismissed her memories as a past hallucination of no importance. "I swear I saw him," Mary had said, and no one, not even I, had believed her—no one except perhaps one person who had at once realized Mary was in possession of a dangerous truth . . .

I stood up.

Axel glanced at me in surprise. "What's the matter?"

"Nothing . . . I'm a little restless." I went over to the window. My mouth was quite dry.

Presently I said: "I wonder how Mary is." My voice sounded as if my throat were parched.

"Perhaps we should go and find out." He was already moving to the door as if glad of the chance to accomplish something positive.

I followed him, my heart bumping against my ribs.

Esther came out of Mary's room just as we were approaching it. She looked strangely uncomposed and worried.

"George," she said, ignoring me, "I think I'm going to give her some of my laudanum—Doctor Salter gave me a little, you know, to help me sleep after Robert's death. Do you think that's wise? Normally I would be reluctant to give laudanum to a child, but she's in pain and Alice suggested we should use it to relieve the suffering . . ."

"Let me see the laudanum." He went with her into the bedroom and to my great relief turned to me on the threshold and said: "You'd better go back to our rooms, my dear. I'll let you know if there's anything you can do."

I went mutely back to our sitting room, but found myself unable to sit down for any length of time. I kept thinking of everyone drinking tea in the drawing room. Everyone had been there except Ned. Vere had brought the tray of tea upstairs. And Axel had handed around the cups . . .

I began to pace restlessly about the room. I was being absurd, hysterical, over-imaginative. Mary had a weak digestion. Something had disagreed with her.

Alice made toadstool poison for the mice in the cellar. Perhaps it was kept in jars in the pantry. Perhaps anyone could go there and remove as much as was required. Perhaps . . .

I went out into the corridor but the house was quiet and still, silent as a tomb, so I went back into the room again.

If only my nerves were not already so over wrought, then perhaps melodramatic thoughts would be easier to avoid. As it was, my mind refused to be reasonable, even though I tried to tell myself that Vere would eventually arrive with the doctor, that the doctor would prescribe something to soothe the digestion, that tomorrow Mary would be weak but at least partially recovered.

The evening dragged on.

At length, unable to bear the suspense, I went to Mary's room but there was no news, except that she was still very ill. Esther was sitting with her. I did not venture into the room itself. When I knocked on the door Alice came out of the room into the passage to talk to me again in a low voice.

"George went downstairs to wait for Vere," she said. "Pray God the doctor arrives soon."

But it was another hour before the doctor arrived, and even when he finally came he was too late.

Mary died at one o'clock the following morning.

Six

FOR SEVERAL HOURS I was too appalled to do anything. As if in a daze I heard the doctor cautiously diagnose the sickness of which I had heard before, the illness manifested by vomiting and a pain in the right side. I heard Esther talking of notifying Mary's distant relatives, of making arrangements for the funeral. I heard Axel arranging for the doctor to stay the night so that he did not have to travel back to Winchelsea until the fog had cleared. I heard the clocks chime and doors close and footsteps come and go, and all I could think was that the nightmare was closing in on all sides of me, that Mary had died after she had revealed to everyone, not merely to Axel, how she had seen Rodric alive after his presumed death in the Marsh last Christmas Eve.

At three o'clock Axel ordered me to bed to snatch some sleep before dawn, but sleep was impossible. Even when Axel came to bed himself half an hour later and fell into an uneasy sleep beside me I still found it impossible to relax my limbs and drift into unconsciousness. At four o'clock I rose from the bed, put on a thick woolen wrap to ward off the cold and went next door into the sitting room. It was pitch dark, but finally I managed to light a candle and sat down, teeth chattering, at the secretaire to write to Alexander.

"If you have not already left Harrow," I wrote, "please leave now. I know not what to think of events taking place here, and am very frightened indeed. Robert Brandson's ward Mary Moore died tonight, and although the doctor diagnosed death due to an inflammation of the lower intestine, I have reason to believe she was poisoned. I think she knew something relating to the deaths of both Robert and Rodric Brandson, something which was apparently so important that she was killed before she could repeat her story enough times to persuade people to take it seriously. If this is so, then Robert Brandson's murderer was not Rodric at all but someone else—and this possibility is not as unlikely as it sounds. Any of them could be guilty, except possibly Ned, the youngest son, who isn't Robert Brandson's son anyway but the result of Esther Brandson's infidelity years ago. All of them had cause. Vere had been involved in smuggling to raise money to pay his debts, and his father had found out and was threatening to tell the Watch at Rye of his activities—this would have been very grave, as apart from the smuggling Vere was dealing with the Frenchman Delancey, and this might constitute treason since we're at war with France. It's generally thought that Rodric was the one who was in league with Delancey in this manner, but a conversation I overheard between Vere and Alice proved that Vere was the guilty one and that Rodric wasn't involved.

"So Rodric really didn't have the motive for murder—unless it was that his father, believing him guilty, had threatened to cut him out of his will; in fact Robert Brandson had already done this in a new will in which he left all to Axel, but this wasn't generally known and I suppose Rodric might have killed his father in the hope of forestalling any change of will. But I don't think Rodric was the kind of man to have done this. To begin with I don't think he would have taken his father's threat seriously. It sounds to me as if Robert Brandson was a man who shouted and roared a great deal in rage but who seldom carried out his worst threats. I don't think Rodric would have believed there was any danger of him being disinherited.

"But if Vere knew that his father believed him guilty of treason and smuggling, that would have been very serious indeed; even if Robert Brandson didn't inform the Watch at Rye (as he threatened to do) he would certainly have eliminated Vere from his will. And that would have been very serious for a man with a wife and three children and neither land nor independent income of any kind.

"Esther Brandson too had cause for murder. She was estranged from her husband and had been for nearly twenty years, since before Ned was born. I'm almost certain she must have hated him and loathed the isolation and rural position of Haraldsdyke. At the time of his death she was having an affair with another man, and it's possible Robert Brandson found out about this or perhaps she thought she would have a new life with this new lover if only her husband were dead. I suppose it's less likely that a woman could have wielded the butt of the gun to club Robert Brandson to death, but Esther is tall and I suspect fairly strong. And if she were enraged she would have even twice her normal strength.

"Axel too had cause for killing his father. He was Esther's lover. He also benefited under his father's new will, a fact which might or might not have been known to him, but if he did know about it, he wouldn't have wanted that new will to be changed; and if his father found out about the affair with Esther the will would naturally have been altered to eliminate Axel as a beneficiary.

"They all had the opportunity. It was generally supposed that Vere was out on the estate till late in the day, but I heard Alice say that he came back to the house much earlier, although no one saw him. Esther apparently discovered the body, but Axel went with her downstairs to the hall, according to Ned who saw them leave Esther's rooms together, and a long time elapsed between their descent to the hall and Esther's screams which marked the discovery of her husband's body.

"But now listen to what happened to Mary. When Axel finally returned to Haraldsdyke later that day with the news that Rodric had apparently drowned in the Marsh Mary was so upset that she went to sit in his, Rodric's, room to meditate among his possessions, and it was here that *she saw* Rodric slip into the room for two seconds to get some money and then slip out again. And Rodric was supposed to be dead! She told Axel, who dismissed the story as a fantasy, and was too timid to go on reiterating the tale although she herself remained convinced she had not imagined the scene. On the day she died she revealed this story to me, and her revelations were ultimately overheard by Esther, Vere, Alice, and Axel, who again dismissed the story in such a way that even I was convinced Mary had been the victim of her imagination. But then she died. I think she was poisoned. Alice keeps poison for the mice somewhere in the kitchens and anyone could have had access to it.

"If Mary really did see Rodric, and I now think she did, does this mean that Rodric is alive today? Whatever it means it seems clear that if she did see him, he didn't drown accidentally in the Marsh as everyone thinks he did. And obviously the murderer wants this story of his accidental death to stand unquestioned so that Rodric can so conveniently take the blame for his father's murder. For instance, if Rodric himself was murdered the authorities would surely look at Robert Brandson's death in a very different light. But if Rodric was murdered, where's his body? And if he's alive, why isn't he here to denounce the true murderer and protest his innocence? Truly I don't know what to think. I don't know for certain that Axel is a murderer, but what's worse, I don't know for certain that he's not. All I know with certainty is that there's a murderer under this roof and I want nothing except to escape.

"Please come. I don't think I've ever needed you more than I do now, and you're all I have."

After I had read the letter through twice I folded it, sealed it, and wrote "ALEXANDER FLEURY, HARROW SCHOOL, HARROW, MIDDLESEX" in large letters on the outside. Then, feeling strangely comforted by having confided my worst fears and most hideous thoughts to paper, I left the sealed letter on the blotter and returned to bed where I fell into an exhausted dreamless sleep almost at once.

I must have slept for a long time for when I awoke the mist was gone, the sun was streaming through the gap in the curtains and I was alone in bed.

I sat up. The clock on the mantelshelf indicated it was eleven o'clock, and as I stared in horrified disbelief at the lateness of the hour I heard the sound of voices in the adjoining room. I slid out of bed, drew on my heavy woolen wrap and crossed the floor to the door. Axel was talking to Esther. I heard first his level tones, and then the sound of her voice raised in anger, and I knew at once that something had happened to upset her considerably.

I opened the door and then froze in amazement, hardly able to believe my eyes at what I saw.

For Esther had in her hands my letter to Alexander, and someone, I saw to my fright and fury, someone had broken the seal.

Anger overcame all fear. Conscious of nothing except that an outrage had been committed I stormed into the room and, shaking with rage, snatched the letter from Esther's fingers before she could even draw breath to speak.

"How dare you!" The words choked in my throat. I could barely see. "How dare you open my letter!"

Bus she took barely five seconds to recover from the shock of my entrance. "And how dare *you!*" she flung back at me. "How dare you write such libelous filth about me in a letter to a schoolboy! I've never been so insulted in all my life!"

"Truth is a defense to libel!" I retorted, "and only a woman who behaved like a deceitful trollop running from lover to lover would stoop to the debasement of opening another's letters—"

"Wait," said Axel icily, and when Esther took no notice, he raised his voice until she fell silent. "Please—no, Esther, listen to me! Listen to me, I say! I think there's no doubt that if my wife behaved badly by gossiping to her brother, you behaved equally badly by opening a sealed letter which was quite clearly addressed to someone else."

"She's always writing to her brother, always so sly and so secretive—I never trusted her! And who is she anyway! The illegitimate daughter of a Lancashire rake and some down-at-heel French emigrée who earned her living as a kept mistress."

"I beg your pardon," said Axel, "but I think such remarks about illegitimacy and immorality fall singularly ill from your lips, madam."

"I—" I began, but he said curtly: "Be quiet." And I was.

". . . pretending she's such a lady," Esther was saying furiously, "always trying to behave as if she's so well-bred."

"And so she is, madam, better-bred than you will ever be, for no one who is not ill-bred would ever dream of opening a letter not addressed to them—no, let me finish! Her father was an English gentleman of much the same class as your husband, and I don't think you ever quarreled with *his* birth or breeding. Her mother was a member of one of the oldest houses in France, an aristocrat, madam, far superior to any of your ancestors in rank—you'll pardon me for being so blunt over such a peculiarly delicate subject as rank, but it was after all you who introduced the subject. And as for her illegitimacy, William the Conqueror was a bastard and he was King of England, and besides, the entire Tudor dynasty was descended from the bastard line of John of Gaunt. So let me hear no more talk of my wife being in any way inferior to you, madam, for in fact the reverse is the truth, and I think you know that all too well."

Something seemed to happen to my mind then, the dark hidden corner which I hid even from myself, the raw wound which never closed, the pain which I would never admit existed. Something happened to the nagging feeling that life had been unjust, to the ache of a pride burdened with the weight of inferiority. And something seemed to happen so that I saw this man for the first time, and he was not a stranger to me at all but the man who would stand by me and speak for me and care for me against the world. And all at once the wound was healed and there were no dark corners of the mind which I was afraid to examine and I had my pride and my self-respect restored to me as strong as they ever had been before I knew what the word legitimacy meant. The cure was so vast and so sudden that there were hot tears in my eyes and I could not speak. And I saw him through my tears, and loved him.

Esther was going. She was white-faced, furious still but her fury repulsed, her abuse shattered. Axel had said to her: "Please leave us now," and she had muttered something and turned abruptly to the door, her footsteps brisk and her head held high. After her the door slammed and we were alone.

"Axel," I said, and burst into tears.

He took me in his arms and I clung to him and wept unashamedly against his breast. His fingers stroked my hair, lingered on the nape of my neck.

"Hush," he said at last. "The incident is hardly so tragic as to deserve such grief! It was a great pity you wrote such a letter but if Esther feels insulted she has only herself to blame. No matter how much she distrusted you or suspected you of writing such foolishness she had no excuse to open the letter."

I could not tell him I was crying for another reason altogether, but perhaps he guessed for he said: "Her words grated on me. If there's one subject I hate discussing with any Englishman or Englishwoman, it's the subject of class and rank. I've too often been slighted and called a foreigner to have any patience with those who try to invoke their own blind prejudices in the name of social degree." He kissed me lightly on the forehead and while I was still unable to speak he took the opened letter which lay on the secretaire where I had let it fall after snatching it from Esther's hands. "I must say, however, that I do find this letter particularly unfortunate."

It was then at last I remembered what I had written in the letter and the horror flooded back into my mind.

"You read it?" I said, hardly able to breathe. "All of it?"

"Under Esther's direction I glanced at the parts where our names were mentioned." He folded the letter up again and not looking at me put it away in his wallet.

All my old fears and anxieties swept over me again. I felt my limbs become taut and aching.

"May I have the letter, please?" I said unsteadily. "I would still like to send it."

He still refused to look at me. It was the first time I had ever seen him embarrassed. "I'm sorry," he said at last, "but I'm afraid I can't possibly consent to you sending it. I've no wish to censor whatever you may want to discuss with Alexander, but in this case I'm afraid I must."

There was a long silence. I felt the color drain from my face. Finally he brought himself to look at me.

"Much of what you say is—unfortunately—true," he said slowly, "but there is also much that is not true. For example, you assume Mary was poisoned with rat poison kept in the kitchens. I can tell you straight away that Alice does *not* keep rat poison in the kitchens. It was kept there for a time but then a servant girl took some to try and poison her lover, and my father promptly ordered that the poison be made when we needed it and not stored. Also, there's absolutely no evidence that Mary was poisoned. It's true that you can think of a reason why it might have become necessary to murder her, but that's not proof of murder and never will be. Similarly, this is true of all your statements; you say that any of us could have killed my father and that all of us had cause and opportunity, and to some extent this is true, but you have no proof which of us killed him—you haven't even proof that Rodric didn't kill him, and before you can begin to accuse anyone else, I think you should first prove Rodric to be innocent. The only evidence that exists all points to the fact that Rodric killed him, and as for Mary saying she saw Rodric alive after he drowned in the Marsh, I'm afraid I'm still convinced the episode was a figment of her imagination. Anyway, if it's anyone's responsibility to discover who killed my father, it's certainly not yours and I would strongly insist that you go no further with your extremely dangerous inquiries. If Mary was poisoned—and I don't for one moment admit that she was—and there's a murderer in this house, then you yourself would be in danger if you persisted in your foolhardy inquiries. I must insist that you leave the matter alone."

I said nothing. I was too uneasy, too nervous, too full of doubts.

"If you send this letter to Alexander," he said, "you stir up the whole affair anew. He's only a seventeen-year-old schoolboy and young for his years, and God knows what trouble he would cause if he panicked and acted foolishly on the receipt of this letter. Besides, there's absolutely no reason for him to leave school early. He'll be home in three weeks' time for Christmas and you'll see him then."

"Four weeks," I said.

"Three—four weeks—what difference does it make? Things will be better by then. I've no doubt Mary's death has been a considerable shock to you, but by Christmas you'll be feeling much less depressed and will have forgotten this involvement which you mistakenly think you have in my father and Rodric and the manner in which they met their deaths."

I was again silent. Then suddenly I burst out impulsively: "Need Esther stay at Haraldsdyke?"

"I'll discuss the matter with her."

The silence was uncomfortable. He reached out uncertainly, touched my arm with his fingers. "I'm sorry," he said, "I'm sorry you had to find out about my past relationship with her. I had hoped you would never have to know."

I turned my head aside sharply so he would not see into my eyes.

"It was very brief," he said. "A moment of madness and foolishness for which I've paid very heavily. I had fancied she would now be as ashamed of the memory as I am but apparently she feels no shame at all. I'll see that she doesn't stay a moment longer under this roof than is necessary, but it's possible she may protest or cause difficulties to spite me, so you must be patient if you have to wait a few weeks yet."

"I see," I said.

His fingers pressed against my cheek and turned my face to his. "Whatever I felt for her in the past is quite finished now," he said. "I hope your realize that."

I nodded, not looking at him. "That's why you're so harsh on Ned, isn't it," I said suddenly. "Because he's the only one who knows you and Esther were ever close, and you're ashamed that he knows."

Axel gave a short mirthless laugh. "Ned's a young rogue," he said. "It's probably not his fault, but that doesn't make any difference. There's a certain element of truth in what you say, but I still hold that he's a rascal who needs discipline." He turned aside. "I must go," he said abruptly. "I have to see the rector to make arrangements for the funeral. Vere has gone into Rye to see the undertaker. I'll see you at dinner, my dear, and meanwhile please no more melodramatic letters to Alexander."

He was gone.

Presently I went back very slowly to the bedroom and stood for a moment by the window as I watched the winter sunlight cast a dappled light on the green expanse of the Marsh. Rye and Winchelsea on their twin hillocks seemed deceptively near.

I wanted so much to believe him. I wanted more than anything else now to believe every word he said and not to be tormented so continuously by all my doubts and anxieties. But he had not explained why such a time had elapsed between the descent to the hall to see his father and Esther's screams when she had discovered the body. He had not let me send the letter to Alexander. And he had refused to admit the possibility that Mary had been murdered . . .

I summoned Marie-Claire, put on a black gown and fidgeted while she dressed my hair. When I was ready at last I went downstairs to the kitchens.

But Axel had been telling the truth about the poison. The cook confirmed the story that no poison had been kept on the premises since the incident with the serving girl.

I went back upstairs to my rooms.

Either Axel was right and Mary had not been murdered at all, or else she had been poisoned. But if she had been poisoned how had the murderer obtained the poison?

I thought of Dame Joan the witch, dismissed the thought and then recalled it, wondering. Dame Joan would know how to prepare a poison. Axel had been in the village that afternoon—he had seen me enter the church . . . He had gone to the village in the hope of finding me, he had said, and had then seen me enter the church. But supposing he had come to the village to get the poison? I had been a long time in the church while I had wrestled with my conscience. Supposing he had seen me go into the church and had then walked past me to Dame Joan's cottage . . .

But I did not really believe Axel was a murderer. It was Axel who understood me. How could I love someone who might be a murderer? But there was no logic any more, only the turbulence of confusion and the agony of doubt. I only knew that love and fear now ran shoulder to shoulder, and that my dilemma seemed even worse than before.

Sitting down once more at the secretaire, I wrote a brief note to Alexander in which without explaining my reasons I begged him to leave Harrow without delay and journey at once to Haraldsdyke.

Ned was in an outhouse by the stables, a gun in his hands. It appeared that he was about to go shooting.

"Will you walk as far as Rye?" I said.

His narrow black eyes looked at me speculatively. He smiled with an air of appraisal. "For you," he said, "I would walk anywhere in England."

"Fiddle-de-dee," I retorted. "I'm not interested in the entire country. I'm only interested in the road from Haraldsdyke to Rye."

"If you're interested in it, then I am too."

"Could you take a letter to Rye for me and see that it goes on the coach to London? You would have to pay for it to be transferred in London to the coach to Harrow in Middlesex. It's for my brother."

"Have you the money?"

I gave him a coin. "This should be enough."

He pocketed it deftly and stowed the letter into the breast of his shirt.

"It's a secret," I said threateningly.

He smiled again. "All right."

"You'll do it for me?"

"I'd never refuse a request from you," he said, and he spoke ironically so that I could not tell how serious he was. "If you ever want anything from me, you know you have only to ask . . ."

The day slipped away. Vere returned from Rye after arranging for the coffin to be made, and Axel returned to the house with the rector who expected to be provided with refreshment. Esther was busy writing to all Mary's distant relatives, and Alice was in conference with the cook to decide on a suitably sombre menu for dinner. It was left to me to interview poor Mary's governess and tell her she could stay at Haraldsdyke for a further month, if necessary, until she found a new position.

This made me remember how nearly I had been forced to be a governess and I spent a long time wondering what would have happened if I had refused Axel's proposal. Perhaps Mary would even be alive . . . but those were useless, abortive thoughts and I did not dwell on them. I did not really want to dwell on any of my thoughts very much, least of all the memory of how I had written again to Alexander against Axel's wishes and had entrusted the letter to Ned.

So I busied myself as much as possible and tried to keep myself fully occupied, and soon it was dark and time for bed.

The next day, Tuesday, followed much the same pattern; several people called to express sympathy and I was busy receiving them courteously and creating a correct impression. The undertakers brought the coffin and Mary was laid out in it amidst the stifling odor of flowers in the small yellow morning room which was normally never used. I went to view the body out of mere respect for convention but I have such a horror of death that I could not bring myself to look in the coffin, and escaped from the room as soon as possible.

The funeral was set for the next day and I retired early to bed to get a good night's rest. I knew in advance that I would find the funeral an ordeal.

In the middle of the night, I woke up suddenly, not knowing what had awakened me, and sat up just in time to see the bedroom door closing as someone slipped out of the room. A glance at the pillows beside me told me that Axel had left. I waited, wondering where he had gone, and then when the minutes passed and there was no sign of him returning I slipped out of bed and donned my woolen wrap.

He was not in the adjoining room. Very cautiously I went out into the passage but it yawned black and empty before me. I nearly went back for a candle, but I thought better of it. I did not want Axel to see me as soon as he came back into sight.

On reaching the landing I glanced down into the hall, but there was no one there either and I was just deciding to go back to bed when I heard the muffled sound of horse's hooves far away. I stood motionless, thinking that I must surely be mistaken, and then I went to the window at the other end of the landing, parted the curtain and peered out into the night.

There was no moon. The night was dark as pitch. Yet I could almost be certain that I heard those muffled hooves again as a horse was ridden away from the house. The minutes passed as I still stood listening by the window, but finally I turned and found my way back to the room. I was amazed. Unless I was much mistaken, Axel had dressed hurriedly, saddled a horse and ridden off into the night.

I lay awake for a long time, but he did not come back. I was just slipping into a drowsy half-consciousness shortly before dawn when I heard the horse's hooves sound faintly again in the distance. I waited, too sleepy to make a second venture down the dark passage to the landing, and at last many minutes later, Axel slipped back into the bedroom and padded through to his dressing room to undress.

When he came to bed he slept straight away as if he were exhausted. His limbs were cold but soon became warmer, as if the night air had chilled him yet the riding had exercised him enough to keep severe cold at bay. I lay awake then, all sleepiness vanished, and wondered where he had been for so long at the dead of night and whether I would ever find out what he had done.

He was very tired the next morning. I saw what an effort it was for him to rise from the bed, and when he was dressed and shaved I noticed the shadows beneath his eyes and the tired set to his mouth. But perhaps the tell-tale signs of weariness were only clear to me who knew how little sleep he had had, for certainly no one else seemed to notice. Everyone was, in any event, much too preoccupied with the funeral.

Mary was buried that morning in Haraldsford churchyard. Rain was falling. I loathed every moment of the ceremony which reminded me horribly of my parents' death, and the emotional strain together with the fact that I myself had had very little sleep the previous night combined to make me feel exhausted.

But there was no respite, even after the return to Haraldsdyke. Several mourners had to be entertained at a formal dinner, and I had to summon all my reserves of strength to be polite and courteous to some distant cousins of Mary who had traveled from Hastings to be present at the funeral. To my horror they decided to stay the night, and I had to give orders for bedrooms to be cleaned, beds to be aired, fresh linen to be taken from the cupboards.

Before I knew it, it was time for tea to be served and there was no escaping that either. Finally after half an hour of dreariness over the tea cups I managed to retire early to my room where I collapsed before the hearth of the sitting room fire and prayed I would never have to attend another funeral for as long as I lived.

I was still feeling too weary even to make the supreme effort to go to bed, when the door opened and Axel came into the room.

"Aren't you in bed yet?" he said, and there was an edge to his voice as if he found my behavior annoying. "I thought you excused yourself on account of weariness."

"I'm almost too tired to undress," I said, but he wasn't listening and I heard him go through into the other room.

A moment later he reappeared.

"Incidentally," he said, his voice abrupt, "what's this?"

I turned. In his hand was the jar containing Dame Joan's potion which I had hidden so carefully behind the tallboy. As I rose to my feet, the color rushing to my face, I saw the expression in his eyes and realized that he knew exactly what the potion was and what it was for.

We stood there looking at each other, he waiting ironically for me to try to tell lies in explanation, I hating that dreadful day which now seemed to be about to culminate in some appalling scene, and as we stood there I heard the footsteps in the corridor, the light hurried footsteps which I knew and loved, and heard that familiar, much-loved voice shouting my name.

It was as if a miracle had happened. Without a word I ran to the door, flung it open and hurled myself headlong into my brother's arms.

Seven

IT SEEMED THAT Alexander had left Harrow after receiving my first letter hinting that something was wrong, and had not even received my last letter which Ned had taken to Rye for me. He had traveled south as quickly as possible, left his bags in Rye itself and walked from there to Haraldsdyke where Vere had received him in the hall. Vere had been in the process of seeking us in our room to tell me of my brother's arrival when Alexander had pushed past him impulsively, and calling my name had run down the passage as if he feared some mishap had already overtaken me.

"How wonderful to see you again!" I said, tears in my eyes. "How wonderful of you to come!"

Axel was furious. Alexander did not seem to notice that he was not welcomed with enthusiasm by his brother-in-law but I knew the signs all too well, the extreme coolness of voice, the deliberately stilted courteousness of manner, the withdrawn opaque expression in his eyes.

"Please Axel," I said politely, trying not to sound as nervous as I felt, "please don't feel obliged to stay up to receive Alexander. I know how tired you must be."

"On the contrary," he said in a voice so icy I was surprised Alexander did not notice it, "I'm no more tired than you are. Let me order refreshment for you, Alexander. You must be cold and hungry after your travels."

I saw at once that he had no intention of leaving us alone together. Frustration mingled with anger overcame me, but Alexander was saying agreeably: "No, actually I feel warm after walking, but I'd like some tea all the same, if that's possible. I'm very partial to tea, particularly in the early morning when it helps me wake up, but I often drink it in the evening too."

We drank tea. Conversation, smothered by Axel's presence, drew to a halt. Alexander eventually began to fidget in the realization that the atmosphere was not as relaxed as it should have been.

"Perhaps you could show me to my room," he said uneasily to me at last.

"I'll show you," said Axel. "Your sister's had a long, exhausting day and should have been in bed an hour ago."

"No, please—"

"But I insist! I'm sorry the room is not particularly pleasing, but owing to these people staying here overnight all the best guest rooms are already in use. My dear," he added to me, "I suggest you ring for your maid and retire at once."

I did not dare protest. On realizing that it was going to be impossible for me to see Alexander alone that night, I made up my mind to wait until the morning; Axel could not keep us both under constant surveillance for an indefinite period of time.

Having resigned myself to this, I did not even wait to summon Marie-Claire but hurried to bed as fast as I could so that I could pretend to be sound asleep when Axel returned; I had just closed my eyes when the door of the room opened and he came into the room.

"We'll discuss this further in the morning," he said, ignoring my efforts to appear asleep. "I think it's sufficient to say now that I'm extremely displeased and intend to send Alexander straight back to school to complete his term—if the authorities at Harrow have not already ordered his expulsion for absenting himself without leave."

"But he told us he had permission!" I half-sat up, then lay back again. "He told the housemaster I was ill . . ."

"I have no intention of involving myself in his lies. He leaves Haraldsdyke tomorrow and I shall pay his travel expenses back to Harrow where he must stay for the remainder of the term."

"He won't go!"

"I think he will, my dear. It's I who hold the purse-strings. If he wants to complete his studies at Harrow and then go up to Oxford he will do exactly as I say."

"But I so want to see him—" My voice broke; I was much too tired and upset to keep back my tears.

"And so you will," he said, "at Christmas when he comes here for the holidays."

"I—"

"There's nothing more to be said. Now please go to sleep and rest yourself without prolonging the conversation further."

At least he made no further mention of the potion.

I tried to stay awake so that I might slip out and warn Alexander and talk to him alone, but presently I realized that Axel was waiting till I slept before sleeping himself and I gave up fighting my weariness. Sleep, absolute and dreamless, overcame me and when I awoke the clock hands pointed to eight o'clock and the rain was dashing itself against the pane.

I was alone.

Seizing the opportunity to see Alexander, I did not even pause to dress but merely snatched my wrap as I ran out of the room. Within seconds I was breathlessly opening the door of the smallest guest room which I knew had been assigned to him.

"Alexander," I said. "Alexander!"

He was apparently deeply asleep, sprawled on his stomach on the bed, the right side of his face pressing against the pillow, one arm drooping towards the floor. Beside him was an empty cup of tea. Axel remembered, I thought, surprised and gratified. He remembered Alexander likes tea in the early morning.

"Alexander!" I said, shaking him. "Wake up!"

But he did not. I shook him in disbelief but he only breathed noisily and remained as inert as before. My disbelief sharpened into horror and the horror into panic.

"Alexander!" I cried. "Alexander, Alexander—"

But he would not wake. My arm knocked the tea cup and when I put out a hand to steady it, I found the china was still warm. Someone had brought Alexander a cup of tea as an early morning token of refreshment—and Alexander had awakened and taken the drink.

But now I was unable to wake him.

I was terrified.

I ran sobbing from the room and stumbled back to my apartments in a haze of shock. Finally, in my bedroom once more I pulled myself together with an enormous effort and quickly dressed as best as I could on my own. There was no time to dress my hair. I twisted it up into a knot at the back of my head so as not to appear too disreputable, and then covered my head with a shawl before slipping out of the house by the back stairs to the stables.

But Ned wasn't there. I saw one of the stable-lads.

"Find Mr. Edwin," I ordered him at once. "He may be in the kitchens. Tell him I want to see him."

The boy mumbled a startled "Yes m'm" and scuttled out of sight.

Five long minutes later the back door opened and Ned crossed the yard to the stables. He moved easily with an unhurried gait, oblivious to the squalling rain and the blustery wind of the November morning.

"Good day to you," he said lightly as he came into the stables, and then he saw my expression and his manner changed. "What's the matter?"

"My brother arrived last night," I said unsteadily. "Something's happened to him. He won't wake up and his breathing is odd. Please take me to Rye to fetch a doctor, please—straightway!"

His eyes were wide and dark. "Have you told anyone?"

"I'm too frightened. I must go and get a doctor—please, don't ask any more questions."

"Dr. Salter lives at Winchelsea."

"I don't want the family doctor. Is there a doctor at Rye?"

"There's Dr. Farrell . . . I'm not sure where he lives. Up past St. Mary's, I think . . . let me saddle a horse." And he moved past me swiftly to the stalls.

I leaned back against the wall in relief.

"Someone may well see us," he said when he had finished. "We'll have to ride out down the drive and hope for the best. Will you be able to ride behind me? I'd advise you to ride astride, unless you really object. It'll be safer in case I have to put the horse to the gallop."

"Very well."

He scrambled into the saddle and then almost lifted me up beside him. He was very strong.

"Are you all right?"

"Yes."

We set off. No one appeared to see us. As we went out on to the Marsh road the rain seemed to lessen and the sky seemed lighter in the west. By the time we reached the towering town walls of Rye it had stopped raining and the sun was shining palely on the wet cobbled streets and the dripping eaves of the alleys.

"Listen," said Ned. "I'm not certain where this doctor lives. Let me leave you in the parlor of the George Inn while I go looking for him. I think he lives in the street opposite St. Mary's church, but I'm not sure."

"Very well."

He took me to the George, left the horse with an ostler and ushered me into a room off the parlor. No one was there. We were alone.

"I have money if you need it," I said and gave it to him.

He took the coins and then closed his hand on mine so that I looked up startled.

"There are other ways of repayment than by coin," he said.

I looked at him, not understanding, my whole mind absorbed with my anxiety, and his face was blurred to me so that I did not even notice the expression in his eyes.

"I'd look after you if you left George," I heard him say. "I'd find work and earn to keep you. I always fancied myself in George's shoes, ever since he brought you home and I saw how young and pretty you were." And suddenly he had pressed strong arms around my waist and was stooping to kiss my mouth and chin and neck. I tried to draw back but his hand took advantage of my movement and slipped from my waist to my breast with an adroitness born of practice.

I twisted with a sharp cry but found myself powerless in the grip of the arm which lingered at my waist. He laughed, his teeth white, his black eyes bright with excitement, and suddenly his greed and his skill and his clever tongue reminded me of his mother Esther and I hated him.

"Bastard!" I spat at him, childish in my helpless fury.

He threw back his head and roared with laughter. "The pot calls the kettle black!" he exclaimed, and drew me all the closer so that he could force his wet mouth on mine and make his ham-fisted fingers familiar in places where they did not belong.

I froze in revulsion.

The next thing I knew was the draft of an open door, a gasp rasping in Ned's throat as his muscles jerked in shock, the sudden removal of all offense. I opened my eyes.

Axel was on the threshold. His face was white and dead and without expression, but the opaque quality was gone from his eyes and so was all hint of their withdrawn look which I knew so well. His eyes blazed. His hands were tight white fists at his sides. He was breathing very rapidly.

"So I was not quite in time," he said.

Ned was backing away against the wall. "George, she asked me to take her to Rye to find a doctor—"

"Get out."

"—her brother's ill—"

"Get out before I kill you."

Ned moved unsteadily towards the door without another word. I could see Axel trying to restrain himself from hitting him and the effort was so immense that the sweat stood out on his forehead. And then as Ned tried to shuffle past him, Axel seemed to find self-control impossible. I saw him seize Ned by the shoulders, shake him and then hit him twice with the palm of his hand before slinging him out into the corridor.

The door closed.

We were alone. I suddenly found I was trembling so violently that I had to sit down.

All he said was: "I told you not to come to Rye with Ned."

And when I did not reply he said: "I think you're too young to have any idea of the power you have to rouse a man's deeper feelings. I suppose you have no idea that Ned wanted you from the moment he set eyes on you. You were too young, your eyes were blind. Your eyes are probably even blind now as you look at me. You're far too young, you're incapable of understanding."

I dimly realized he was trying to excuse my behavior. I managed to stammer: "I only thought of Alexander . . . I knew Ned would take me to Rye—"

"Alexander," he said, "is not in danger. One of the stable-lads has gone to Winchelsea for Dr. Salter."

"I wanted another doctor—"

"Dr. Salter is perfectly reputable."

"But Alexander—"

"Alexander," said Axel, "appears to have taken a non-fatal dose of laudanum. Are you ready to go?"

"Yes, but—"

"Then I suggest we leave without delay."

I followed him mutely to the courtyard where he had left his horse.

"But how—" I stammered, but he would not let me finish.

"I don't propose to discuss the matter here," he said curtly. "We can discuss it later."

But even when we arrived back at Haraldsdyke he still refused to discuss the matter.

"I'm taking you to your room," he said to me, "and you will stay there for the rest of the day. I am becoming tired of watching you to make sure you do nothing foolish, and your behavior has been so far from exemplary that I don't think you can say I'm not justified in insisting you remain in your room today."

"But Alexander—"

"Alexander will get better without any help from you. He can stay on a few more days here and then you can talk to him as much as you like, but you may not talk to him today."

"But—" I began and then Vere came to meet us and I had to stop.

"My wife has been very upset by her brother's illness," said Axel abruptly to Vere. "She wants only to rest all day. Please ask Alice to make arrangements with the servants not to disturb her—she'll be sleeping in our room and I shall move into Rodric's old room so that she may have the maximum amount of peace and rest without interruption."

I was too embarrassed by this open reference to the fact that we were to have separate rooms, to take notice of Vere's reply.

Upstairs I moved towards the corridor which led to our rooms, but he put his hand on my arm and guided me instead down another corridor.

"I've changed my mind," he said quietly. "You shall stay in Rodric's room. I'll bring you anything you may need."

I looked at him in amazement. "But why can't I stay in our rooms?"

"I've changed my mind," was all he said. "I'm sorry."

"But—"

"Please!" he said, and I saw he was becoming angry. "You've flouted my wishes so often recently that I must insist that you don't attempt to disobey me now." He opened the door of Rodric's room and gestured that I should enter. "I'll come and see you every few hours to see you have everything you need," he said abruptly. "Meanwhile I advise you to lie down and rest. And if anyone comes to the door, don't on any account answer them. Do you understand?"

"Yes, Axel."

"Very well, then. I'll return to you in about an hour's time." And closing the door without further delay I heard him turn the key in the lock before walking away swiftly down the echoing corridor.

The mist rolled over the Marsh and smothered the house with soft smooth fingers. The silence seemed to intensify as the hours passed, and it seemed at last to me as I waited in Rodric's room and watched the dusk fall that the silence was so absolute that it was almost audible. Axel had come twice to the room to see if there was anything I had needed, but he had not stayed long and by the time the dusk began to blur with the mist it was a long time since I had last seen him. I stood up restlessly and went over to the window to stare out into the mist, my fingers touching the carving on Rodric's huge desk, and I thought of Mary again, remembering how she had admired Rodric and how we had spoken of him in this room.

The hours crawled by until I could no longer estimate what time it was. The increasing boredom of the enforced confinement made me irritated, and I was just wondering in a fever of impatience how late it was when I heard footsteps outside in the corridor and Axel came in with a tray of food.

"How are you?" he asked peremptorily, and added: "I'm sorry I was so long delayed in bringing you some food. I intended to bring it earlier."

"It doesn't matter—I haven't felt hungry." I wanted to ask a multitude of questions, but I guessed instinctively that he would refuse to answer them. "Axel—"

"Yes?" He paused on his way out of the room, his fingers on the door handle.

"When may I leave this room?"

"Tomorrow," he said, "but not before then."

"And Alexander—"

"He's still drowsy and is resting in his room. He'll be well enough tomorrow. You needn't worry about him."

The door closed; his footsteps receded. I sat down on the edge of the bed again without touching the food and drink on the tray, and tried to be patient and resigned, but I found the inactivity hard to endure and after a while began to rearrange the contents of the desk drawers in an agony of restlessness.

I heard the footsteps much later, when I was contemplating undressing and trying to sleep. The floorboard creaked above me and made me look up. Presently it creaked again. After listening intently I thought I could distinguish the muffled tread of footsteps as if someone was pacing up and down the room above my head.

But there was nothing above this room except the attics and no one slept there any more.

I took the candle and went to the door but the lock was firm and there was no breaking it. I looked around in despair, and then for the third time searched the drawers of the desk, but there was no duplicate key conveniently waiting to be discovered. My glance fell on the knife which lay on my dinner tray. Seizing it I went back to the door, inserted the blade between the door and the frame and scraped at the lock.

Nothing happened.

I stepped back a pace and stared at the door in frustration. Then I took the candle, and holding it at an advantageous angle I peered into the eye of the lock. It was difficult to be certain, but I thought the key was on the other side and that Axel had not troubled to remove it altogether.

Going back to the desk I took two sheets of notepaper from the drawer and inserted then under the door side by side with one another. Then I took the fork and poked it into the keyhole.

The key fell to the ground without much trouble. Holding my breath I stooped and carefully pulled the sheets of paper back through the gap between the floor and the bottom of the door, and soon I saw that the key had fortunately not bounced off the paper on falling to the floor; it came gently towards me on the notepaper, and a second later I was turning the lock to set myself free.

As I opened the door it occurred to me that the footsteps overhead had stopped some minutes before, but I did not pause to question why this had happened. I tip-toed very quietly down the passage, my hand on the wall to guide me, the candle snuffed and abandoned in the room I had just left so that I was in darkness.

The house seemed still enough, but as I neared the landing I could see the light shining from the hall and heard the soft murmur of voices from the drawing room nearby. I hesitated, fearful that someone should come out of the drawing room as I was passing the door, but I knew no other way to the back stairs, so at last I took a deep breath and tip-toed quickly across the landing to another passage at the far end.

Nobody saw me. I paused, heart beating fast, and listened. Everywhere was quiet. Moving into the shadows once more I found the back stairs to the attics and cautiously began to mount them one by one.

I was convinced that the footsteps I had overheard above Rodric's room had been Alexander's, and had immediately suspected Axel of imprisoning him in the attics for some reason. Who else would be pacing up and down there as if he were a caged animal? And into my memory flashed the picture of the diamond-cut inscription of Rodric's on the attic window pane, the reference to his own imprisonment there as a boy. That room at least had been used as a prison before, and if my guess of the house was correct, tonight it was being used as a prison again.

I reached the top of the stairs, and paused to get my bearings. Nervousness and excitement made me clumsy. With my next step forward my ankle turned and I stumbled against the wall with a loud thud. I waited, my heart in my mouth, my ears straining to hear the slightest sound, and once I did think that I heard a door opening and closing far away, but nothing further happened and in the end I judged the noise to be my imagination.

It was pitch dark. I wished desperately that I had brought my candle, for I wasn't even sure of the way to Rodric's attic. At last, moving very quietly, I felt my way down the passage until I reached the point where the passage turned at right angles to run into another wing. I was just beginning to be unnerved by the total blackness when I turned a corner and saw a thin strip of light below the door at the far end of the corridor. I edged towards it, the palms of my hands slipping against the cool walls, my breathing shaky and uneven.

The silence was immense. The prisoner had evidently not resumed his pacing up and down. Some quality in the silence unnerved me. Would Alexander ever have submitted so silently to imprisonment? I visualized him breaking down the door in his rage or shouting to be released, not merely sitting and waiting in passive resignation.

I started to remember ghost stories. My scalp prickled. Panic edged stealthily down my spine, but I pulled myself together and stepped out firmly towards the light which was now not more than a few paces away. It would never do to let my nerve weaken now.

I was just stretching out my arm to guide me alongside the wall when my fingers encountered a human hand.

I tried to scream. My lungs shrieked for air, the terror clutched at my throat, but no sound came. And then a hand was pressed against my mouth and a voice whispered in my ear: "Not a sound, whoever you are" and the next moment the door nearby was pushed open and I was bundled into the dim candlelight beyond.

The door closed. I swung around, trembling from head to toe, and then gaped in disbelief.

My captor gaped too but presently managed to say weakly: "Mrs. Brandson! Why, I do beg your pardon—"

It was young Mr. Charles Sherman, the bachelor brother of James Sherman, the lawyer of Rye.

"Good heavens!" I said still staring at him, and sat down abruptly on a disused stool nearby.

"Good heavens indeed," said Mr. Charles, smiling at me uncertainly as we recovered from our mutual shock. "I wonder if you are more surprised than I or if I am more surprised than you?"

"You could not possibly be more surprised than I," I retorted. "Forgive me if I sound inhospitable, but may I ask what on earth you're doing hiding in the attic of Haraldsdyke at the dead of night, sir?"

"Dear me," said Mr. Charles, torn between his obvious desire to explain his presence and his equally obvious air of conspiratorial secrecy. "Dear me." He scratched his head anxiously and looked puzzled.

This was not very informative. "I suppose it's some sort of plot," I said, since it clearly took a plot to explain Mr. Charles' encampment in the attic. "Did my husband bring you here? What are you waiting for? How long do you intend to remain?"

Mr. Charles cleared his throat, took out a handsome watch from his waistcoat pocket and glanced at it hopefully. "Your husband should be here in a few minutes, Mrs. Brandson. If you would be so obliging as to wait until he arrives, I'm sure he will be able to explain the entire situation very easily."

I was quite sure Axel would do nothing of the kind. He would be too angry that I had escaped from Rodric's room to indulge me with long explanations of his mysterious activities.

"Mr. Sherman," I said persuasively, "could you not at least give me a little hint about why you should be pacing the floor of this attic tonight and waiting for my husband? Please! I know a woman's curiosity is her worst and most disagreeable feature, but—"

"Ah, come, come, Mrs. Brandson!"

"There! I can tell how you despise me for it, but—"

"Not in the least, I—"

"—but I'm so worried about my husband, and if you could just help to put my mind at rest—oh, Mr. Sherman, I would be so grateful to you—"

I had fluttered my eyelashes enough. Mr. Charles' natural kind-heartedness and fondness for flaunted femininity had made him decide to capitulate.

"Let me explain from the beginning, Mrs. Brandson," he said graciously, and sat down on the edge of a table opposite me for all the world as if we were pausing in some drawing room to pass the time of day. "I am, as you so rightly assumed, here at your husband's bidding in an attempt to prove once and for all beyond all reasonable doubt who killed Robert Brandson last Christmas Eve. Your husband has known from the beginning that Rodric could not have killed his father, but for reasons of his own he was reluctant to speak out at the time. For various reasons of delicacy I cannot elaborate further on this except to say that your husband saw Robert Brandson alive and well *after* Rodric had quarreled with his father and ridden off over the Marsh. Therefore he knew Rodric could not have been responsible for Robert Brandson's subsequent murder . . ."

Esther, I was thinking, Esther. Robert Brandson must have caught Axel with her in her rooms. After the quarrel with Rodric he must have gone upstairs to talk to his wife and found Axel with her—in her bedroom . . .

" . . . let me explain what happened: according to your husband, on the day of the murder," Charles Sherman was saying, "your husband took Rodric out shooting on the Marsh since Rodric and Vere had come to blows and George thought it would be best to separate them for a while. When they came back Robert Brandson called to Rodric from the library and summoned him inside to see him."

"Because he suspected Rodric of being involved in smuggling and in league with Delancey."

"Precisely. Rodric told your husband afterwards—"

"But they didn't see each other afterwards!"

"Oh yes, they did, Mrs. Brandson! Patience, and I shall explain it all to you. Rodric told your husband afterwards that this accusation was untrue but that when he had tried to deny it to his father and cast the blame on Vere, the conversation had abruptly degenerated into a quarrel. Rodric walked out and rode off on to the Marsh and Robert Brandson, in a great rage no doubt, stormed upstairs to discuss the matter with—"

Esther, I thought.

"—your husband George—"

Esther, I thought again, and Axel was there. Robert Brandson wanted to ask his wife if she knew which of their two sons was guilty of smuggling and conspiring with Delancey.

"—but George could not help him. However, shortly afterwards he decided to go down to the library to discuss the matter further with his father—"

To talk his way out of a compromising situation, I thought, and to beg his father's forgiveness.

"—and it was then," said Charles Sherman gravely, "that he found Robert Brandson dead. His immediate reaction—after the natural grief and shock, that is—was one of horror in case he himself, or indeed someone else whom he knew to be innocent—"

Esther.

"—was suspected of the crime. He hesitated for some minutes, trying to decide what to do, and then Esther—pardon my informality, I mean Mrs. Brandson—arrived on the scene—"

Liar, I thought. She was with Axel all along, conferring with him, trying to decide what to do.

"—and her screams roused the servants and the other occupants of the house. Rodric was naturally suspected, but Esther refused to believe it, since Rodric was her favorite son, and to pacify her George rode off after Rodric with the idea of warning him and sending him into hiding until there was proof of the murderer's true identity. As I've already said, George himself thought Rodric must be innocent but was prevented from saying why for reasons of delicacy."

"Quite," I said.

Mr. Charles looked at me uneasily and then quickly looked away. "Well," he said, clearing his throat again, "your husband did in fact catch up with Rodric and tell him that someone had killed Robert Brandson and that all the evidence pointed to the fact that Rodric had murdered him. Rodric was all for returning to Haraldsdyke and confronting the person he suspected of murder, but George begged him to be more prudent and eventually Rodric appeared to acquiesce and agree to go into hiding. George suggested they should make a faked death for Rodric for two reasons. First because Rodric would find it easier to flee the country if everyone thought him beneath the Marsh, and second because his mother wouldn't have the same compulsion to clear his name—and thus perhaps jeopardize her own safety—as she would if he were alive and in exile. George said he knew it was a cruel thing to do, but he reasoned he was doing it as much for her own good as for Rodric's; Mrs. Brandson had long been estranged from her husband, you know, and this would have given her a motive of sorts for his murder; if suspicion were diverted from Rodric it might well have fallen upon her.

"George told Rodric to travel to Vienna and go to his house there for food and lodging. George said he would return to Vienna and meet him there as soon as the inquest was over, and in fact he did leave Haraldsdyke as soon as decency permitted and hurried overseas once more, even though Haraldsdyke was now officially his, subject to the one contingency he later fulfilled by marrying you. Robert Brandson, suspecting Rodric of being in league with Delancey and Vere of being incompetent in handling money, had evidently decided to entrust his wealth to your husband.

"Now when George returned to Vienna, Rodric wasn't there.

He searched high and low for him, had inquiries made and so on, but he couldn't gather together any evidence that Rodric had even left England. Naturally this made George very suspicious—especially when he remembered how Mary Moore, poor child, had come to him before he had left England with a wild story of seeing Rodric at Haraldsdyke after Rodric's official *death* in the Marsh. George had dismissed the story at the time, but now he began to wonder. Supposing Rodric had changed his mind after they had parted, walked back to Haraldsdyke leaving his horse and hat by the mere as evidence of his death, slipped into the house by the back stairs and gone to the rooms of the person he suspected of murder in order to confront that person with the truth. And supposing that person had managed to kill him, hide the body and later bury it in secret so as not to disturb the convenient story of Rodric's accidental death in the Marsh as he was guiltily fleeing from the scene of the crime—"

"But Mr. Sherman," I said, interrupting, "who is this person whom Rodric—and now my husband—suspect of Robert Brandson's murder?"

He looked at me as if surprised I had not already guessed, and made a gesture with his hands. "Who else but your brother-in-law Vere?"

The candle flickered in the dark as a draft breathed from the casement frame, but the silence was absolute. I stared at Charles Sherman.

"George suspected Vere from the beginning," he was saying. "As soon as he returned to England he began to search for evidence and two days ago he found it and rode that same night to Rye to ask for my help. We agreed Vere must be guilty, and worked on a plan to trap him once and for all. We reasoned that Vere had cause enough to kill his father—since his father was threatening to go to the Watch at Rye, Vere's whole future and livelihood were at stake. It was vital to him that his father should be silenced. Also Vere had the means and the opportunity to poison Mary, he knows about poisons which kill weeds in the soil and improve the agricultural qualities of the land, he probably has a stock of such poison somewhere on the estate. He could have tampered with the tea Mary drank—George tells me it was Vere who carried the tray upstairs from the hall."

"True . . . So you and my husband are planning . . ."

"What we hope will be a successful trap. We arranged that I should ride over here at dusk today and Axel would meet me at the gate and smuggle me up the back stairs to this attic where he would show me the evidence he had uncovered. We realized we would have to wait till after the funeral before putting our plan into action, as everyone would be too busy on the day of the funeral itself, but then at last when the funeral was over, who should arrive at Haraldsdyke but your brother Alexander! It at once seemed as if everything was doomed to failure, for George knew that if Alexander were once to speak to you alone, you would tell him every detail of the suspicions you had outlined in your long ill-fated letter which was never posted. Then Alexander would be sure to create havoc by making some unpleasant scene. George knew that he himself only needed another twenty-four hours grace, and he was quite determined that no one should interfere with his plans at that late stage. It was easy enough to keep you apart till morning, but when morning came George knew he had to act. In desperation he took some of Mrs. Brandson's laudanum, went down to the kitchens and ordered tea. When it was ready he took the cup from the kitchens, put in the laudanum and gave it to the footman to take to your brother's room."

"And then I panicked," I said dryly. "And not without cause."

"No indeed," Mr. Charles agreed. "Not without cause . . . But before George followed you to Rye he left that same ill-fated letter of yours to your brother in the library where he knew that Vere would be sure to find it; apparently Vere usually goes to the library to write any correspondence connected with the estate or else to read the newspaper in the hour before dinner. When

George brought you home, he told me he was careful to tell Vere to inform Alice that you would be sleeping alone in your apartments tonight. Then after putting you for your own safety in Rodric's old room, he returned to the library—and found the letter had been moved slightly and the hair he had placed on it had fallen to the floor. So it was plain Vere had seen it. We were almost sure that on reading the letter Vere would decide that you knew too much for his peace of mind; in particular you knew about Vere's past involvement with Delancey, and this you remember, was *not* common knowledge. It was supposed that Rodric, not Vere, was the smuggler and the traitor. We thought Vere would try and kill you and put the blame on your husband. According to George himself, one of the servants saw you ride off with young Ned to Rye this morning—it would soon be common knowledge within minutes, and everyone knows Ned's reputation. Later they would think your husband had killed you in a rage."

My eyes widened. "You mean—"

"But of course," said Mr. Charles. "You're not sleeping alone in your room, as Vere supposes. You're safe here in the attic with me, even though your husband intended that you should be safely behind the door of Rodric's room."

But I was not listening. There were footsteps in the corridor, light muffled footsteps, and the next moment the door was opening and Axel himself was entering the room.

I stood up, covered with confusion, and sought feverishly in my mind for an explanation. Axel saw me, turned pale with shock and then white with rage, but before he could speak Charles Sherman intervened on my behalf.

"George, I regret to say I'm to blame for this for your wife heard me and came upstairs to investigate. I thought it best to tell her a little about the situation so that she could assist us by being as discreet and silent as possible. I feared that if I kept her in ignorance she would have had a perfect right to complain very loudly indeed at my somewhat clandestine presence in her household."

Axel was much too adroit to ask me angry questions or to censure me in the presence of a stranger. I saw his face assume a tight controlled expression before he glanced away and pushed back his hair as if such a slight gesture could release some of his pent-up fury.

"I apologize for leaving the room, Axel," I said nervously, "but I thought the footsteps I overheard belonged to Alexander and I decided—wrongly, I know—to try to talk to him."

"It's unfortunate," he said without looking at me, "but now you're here there's little I can do to alter or amend the situation." He turned to Charles Sherman. "Everything is ready and everyone has gone to their rooms. We should take up our positions without delay."

"Which positions do you suggest?"

"If you will, I'd like you to go to my apartments. You can hide yourself in the dressing room on the other side of the bedroom beyond the bed. I'll be at the head of the stairs and will follow him into the bedroom and block his exit into the sitting room should he try to escape. We'll have him on both sides then."

"By God, George, I hope your plan succeeds. Supposing he didn't in fact read the letter? Or supposing he read it and decided not to act upon it in the way we anticipate?"

"He must," said Axel bluntly. "He's killed three times, twice to protect the original crime from being attributed to him. He won't stop now. Let's waste no more time."

"No indeed, we'd better go at once."

Axel turned to me. "It seems I dare not trust you out of my sight," he said dryly. "You'd better come with me."

In the doorway Mr. Charles stopped, appalled. "Surely, George," he began, but was interrupted.

"I would rather have my wife where I can see her," said Axel, still refusing to look at me, "than to run the risk of her wandering about the house on her own and spoiling all our careful plans."

I said nothing. I was much too humiliated to argue, and I knew his lack of trust was justified.

"And remember," he said quietly to me as Mr. Charles went out into the corridor, "you must be absolutely silent and do exactly as I say. I don't know how much Charles told you, but—"

"Everything, within the limits of what he termed 'delicacy.'"

"Then you'll understand how vital it is that nothing should interfere with our attempts to set a trap. I presume I may trust you not to scream no matter what happens."

I promised meekly to make no noise under any circumstances.

We set off down the passage then, and as Axel carried a single candle, its light shaded with his hand, I was able to see the way without trouble. At the top of the back stairs, however, he extinguished the flame and put down the candlestick on the floor.

"Follow me closely," he whispered. "We're going to the landing. If you're frightened of not being able to keep up with me or losing me in the dark, hold the tails of my coat and don't let go."

I smiled, but of course he could not see my smile for we were in total darkness. We started off down the stairs, my left hand on the bannisters, my right holding one of his coattails as he had suggested, and presently we stood in the passage below. When we reached the landing a moment later it seemed lighter, probably because there were more windows in the hall than up in the attics, and I was able to make out dim shapes and corners. Axel led me to the long window on one side of the landing and we stepped behind the immense drawn curtains.

We waited there a long time. I felt myself begin to sway slightly on my feet.

Beside me Axel stiffened. "Are you going to faint?"

I looked coldly through the darkness to the oval blur of his face. "I never faint."

In truth I was shivering and swaying from excitement, nervousness and dread rather than from the arduousness of standing still for so long. I leaned back against the window to attempt to regain my composure, and then just as I was standing up straight at last I again felt Axel stiffen beside me. Following his glance I peered through the small gap in the curtains before us.

My limbs seemed to freeze.

A shape, muffled in some long pale garment, had emerged noiselessly from the dark passage and was crossing the landing to the stairs. Presently it reached the hall and disappeared. From far away came the faint click of a door opening and closing.

I wondered where it had gone, but dared not speak for fear of breaking that immense silence. We went on waiting. And then at last the door opened far away and closed again and the next moment the pale shape emerged into the hall and came silently up the stairs towards us.

I might have been carved out of stone. My limbs were quite still and the only moving organ in my body was my heart which seemed to be banging against my lungs with an alarming intensity. I was aware only of thinking: this is a murderer walking to meet his victim. And; I am the person he intends to kill.

The figure reached the landing. There was nothing then except the shallowness of our breaths as we waited motionless by the slightly parted curtains. A moment later the shape had passed us and had begun to move down the corridor towards our rooms. It carried a gun, one of the guns used for shooting game, a gun such as the one which had killed Robert Brandson.

"Follow me," Axel's order was hardly louder than an unspoken thought. "But not a sound."

He moved forward noiselessly.

The door of our apartments was open. I saw a flicker of white enter the bedroom and for a moment to obscure the light of the single lamp burning by the window. Someone seemed to be asleep in the bed, but the light was uncertain, a mere dim glow from the table several feet away. And then as I watched, the figure in white raised the butt of the gun and began to bludgeon the shapeless form in the bed.

My hand flew to my mouth, but even as I stood still in horror I saw the door of the dressing room open slowly, and as Axel reached the threshold Charles Sherman stepped out to stand opposite him across the room.

The white figure with the gun ceased the bludgeoning, having no doubt realized as suddenly as I did that the figure in the bed was an illusion, a clever trap.

There was a moment when time ceased and the scene became a tableau. Then at last:

"So it was you who killed my father, Alice," said Axel, appalled.

She did not scream.

All I remember now is the great stillness, the silence as if the whole house were suffocated by the shrouds of the mist outside. Even when Alice dropped the gun and began to move, she made no noise but seemed rather to glide across the floor, her white robe floating with an eerie grace so that it seemed for one bizarre moment that she was a ghost, a mere evil spirit seen on Hallowe'en. The gun fell softly onto the bed and made no sound.

Both men stepped forward simultaneously, but Alice was too quick for them; as I watched I saw her hand flash out towards the dresser, grasp a small phial which stood forgotten among the ornaments and wrench off the cap with a quick twist of her strong fingers before raising the phial to her lips.

It was the potion Dame Joan had given me, the potion overlooked by both Axel and myself in the distraction of Alexander's arrival the night before.

Alice drank every drop. Even as Axel shouted her name and sprang forward to stop her she had flung the empty phial in the grate, and after that there was nothing any of us could do except stare at her in shocked disbelief as she smiled back into our eyes, then the poison gripped her like a vice and she fell screaming towards the death which she had first intended for me. I had never heard a human being give such screams or twist her body into such contorted shapes. I stood watching, transfixed with horror, unable to move; and then suddenly all the world heeled over into a bottomless chasm and I did not have to watch her any more.

For the first time in my life I fainted.

Eight

"She substituted that potion, of course," said Axel. "Dame Joan wouldn't have given you poison without Alice egging her on, and Alice did not even know you intended to see her mother that day. But later when her mother told her about the potion Alice must have seen a chance to dispose of you and so she substituted a jar of poison. Then when you apparently ignored the potion and remained alive she must have decided to club you to death by force—especially after she had heard the contents of the confiscated letter you wrote to Alexander and knew you believed Mary and were convinced Rodric was innocent of the crime. You were a great danger—not so much to her, but to Vere who was a more obvious suspect. So you had to be killed, quickly, before you could make any further attempts to display your suspicions to the world."

It was on the afternoon of the next day. We were in our own private sitting room and outside beyond the window a pale November sun was shining across the sweeping expanse of the Marsh. Downstairs Alice was laid out in the horrible yellow morning room where Mary had lain before her burial, and Vere was still shut in the room with his wife as if his poor grieving presence could somehow bring her back to him from beyond the grave.

"I ought to have realized that Alice, not Vere, was the murderer," I said. "If your father was killed because he was threatening to expose Vere's association with Delancey's smuggling,

Vere could hardly have killed him because he didn't know his father had found out the truth. When I overheard that conversation between Vere and Alice it was Alice, not Vere, who knew that Rodric had denied being involved with Delancey and had accused Vere of being the guilty one, and Alice who knew that Mr. Brandson more than half believed Rodric despite his earlier conviction that Rodric was guilty. I suppose that after Alice dragged Mary out of the saloon and pretended to go to the nursery to see the children, she must have slipped back to the saloon to eavesdrop on the entire quarrel. Then she would have realized that to save Vere from serious trouble she would have to kill Mr. Brandson before he could act on his suspicions, and then would have to try to make a scapegoat of Rodric."

"She succeeded very well in some respects," Axel observed wryly. "Rodric had left his gun in the library after the quarrel; the weapon—the perfect weapon for involving Rodric—was waiting for her as soon as she herself entered the library. When Rodric left, my father went upstairs to talk to Esther to discover how much she knew, and while he was gone Alice must have entered the library from the saloon, picked up the gun and waited for him to return. Perhaps she waited behind the door and struck him as he came into the room . . . I suppose it was this use of force that made me think of the act as a man's crime. I never stopped to consider that Alice with her broad shoulders and strong arms was physically quite capable of committing the murder."

I was piecing together the remaining fragments of information in my mind. "Ned must have come into the hall from the stables soon after that," I reflected. "He told me he knocked on the library door and received no reply. By that time Mary would already have returned to the drawing room after running after Rodric to the stables . . . Esther was upstairs in her apartments, and—" I stopped, blushed, looked away.

"—and my father found me with her when he stormed upstairs

to see her after his quarrel with Rodric." I sensed he too was looking away. He was standing very still, as if absorbed with the pain
of memory. "I've never felt so ashamed in all my life," he said
after a pause. "It certainly served to bring me to my senses with
a jolt, but then even before I could begin to apologize to my
father and beg his forgiveness he was murdered."

The bitterness and regret in his voice was unmistakable. In
an effort to turn to some other aspect of the situation I said in a
rush: "Axel, what *did* happen to Rodric? I suppose Alice really
must have killed him?"

"Yes, of course she did. I would assume he returned to the
house—strictly against my advice, of course, but then he always
was reckless—to confront Vere, whom he suspected, and try to
force the truth out of him. He probably went to Vere's apartments
but found not Vere, as he had hoped, but Alice, who was unable
to resist the temptation to kill him to preserve the fiction that
Rodric was a murderer who had met his just end in the Marsh.
After all, how much more convenient to have a corpse for a
scapegoat than a live protesting innocent man! I presume she
caught him unawares and stunned him; he did not suspect her,
remember, and so wouldn't have been anticipating such a thing."

"But what did she do with his body?"

"I wondered about that for a long time. In the end I made a
thorough search of the attics and found a leather bag which I had
often seen Alice use to take presents from Haraldsford to her
mother. I wondered why Alice no longer used it, and then on
examining it I saw that the interior was bloodstained. After
searching the attic further I found an old meat cleaver from the
kitchens under a loose board in the floor and I began to grasp
what had happened. Even then I still didn't think that Alice had
dismembered the body and taken it piece by piece to be buried
in her mother's patch of land at Haraldsford; I suppose I didn't
think a woman could be capable of such a gruesome task. I
merely thought Vere had found the discarded bag in the attic

and used it to convey the dismembered body to some remote section of the Marsh. When I showed the cleaver and bag to Charles Sherman yesterday it didn't occur to him either that anyone but Vere could have been responsible. But we underestimated Alice."

"So Rodric's body . . ." I recoiled from the idea.

"It may not be buried in Dame Joan's herb patch, but I shall most certainly suggest to the authorities that they look there before assuming the body to be buried in the Marsh. No matter how many journeys Alice made to her mother's cottage, her visits would never have given rise to suspicion. What more natural than that she should call on her mother? It would have been the easiest way for her."

I shuddered.

"Of course Alice was also responsible for Mary's death, I think there can be no doubt of that. It seems reasonable to assume that she obtained a phial of poison from her mother whom she visited with the child after church that morning, and then later put the contents of the phial in Mary's cup of tea. I should have remembered that it was Alice who suggested having tea after dinner, and it was Alice who left the room in person to order the tea, ostensibly to spare the servants on a Sunday but in reality no doubt to get the phial from her room. And I should have remembered too that it was Alice who poured out the tea when it arrived. But I didn't remember. I was too busy suspecting Vere."

"I wonder if Vere read my letter which you left in the library to trap him," I said. "I suppose he did read it and then went straight to tell Alice and to ask what he should do."

"He must have done," Axel agreed, "for Alice was a country girl—she could barely read and could only write the most elementary words which she needed in maintaining the household accounts."

"Then perhaps Vere did realize that she was guilty—perhaps they agreed together that I should be killed."

"No, I'm certain Vere wasn't involved to that extent. I've talked to him, and I'm convinced of his innocence. Alice never made him an accomplice because she was too busy trying to protect him: from my father, from Rodric, from Mary, and finally from you." He stood up and moved over to the window to stare out over the Marsh before adding abruptly: "I didn't think you'd be in any danger at all when I brought you to Haraldsdyke." He was facing me again, moving back towards me. "I still think you wouldn't have been in any danger if you had been accustomed to behaving as a conventional young girl might be expected to behave, but since you have this remarkable talent for seeking all possible danger and running headlong towards it—"

I laughed at this. "No, Axel, that's not fair! I was only puzzled and curious."

"You were also a constant source of anxiety to me, my dear," he retorted. "However, be that as it may . . . by the way, how exactly did you manage to escape from that locked room? When I found you in the attic with Charles Sherman, I very nearly killed you myself out of sheer exasperation!"

I described my escape meekly.

"You amaze me," he said, and he was not angry any more, I noticed to my relief, only amused. "I can see I shall never be able to place you safely under lock and key again."

"I hope," I said, "that the need to do so will never arise."

He laughed, caressed my cheek with his finger and leaned forward to brush my lips with his own.

"Am I forgiven for my multitude of deceptions and evasions and, I very much fear, for frightening you on more than one occasion?"

"You leave me no alternative," I said demurely, determined to make him endure the pangs of conscience for as long as possible. "Besides, why didn't you trust me?"

"Did you trust me?" he said, and he was serious now, the amusement gone. "Wasn't I merely a stranger to you? Didn't you consider yourself merely bound to me by ties born of conven- ience? Can you honestly tell me you loved me enough to merit a confidence of such magnitude?"

I could not look at him. I fingered his hand which rested on mine and stared down at the carpet. "Did you expect me to love you straight away?" I said painfully. "You didn't love me. I was a mere child to you. And still seem so, no doubt."

His hand covered mine now and closed upon it. "Your only childishness lies in your lack of perception," he said. "If you were older you would have perceived all too clearly that from the beginning I found you exceedingly attractive. However, I tried to hold myself apart from you as often as possible because I sensed from your questions before our marriage that you dis- liked the idea of extreme intimacy. It was, after all, a marriage of convenience, and although you were benefiting to a certain ex- tent by consenting to it, I was certainly benefiting just as much from your consent and I wanted to make things as pleasant for you as possible, at least for a time."

I remembered my tears at Claybury Park, my loneliness and distress.

"I merely thought you didn't care."

"I cared more than I would ever have dreamed possible," he said, "and soon came to care even more than that. When I found you with Ned at Rye, I knew I cared more than I had ever cared for anyone in my life before. The bitter part—the ironic part—was that having for the first time in my life experienced this depth of emotion, I found it increasingly evident that you were not at- tracted to me. I seemed to fancy you looked too long and often at Ned, and then there was that business of the potion—"

I was consumed with shame. My cheeks seemed to be afire. "Did you see me leave Dame Joan's cottage?"

"Yes, and knew at once why you had gone there."

I stared miserably down at his hand clasped tightly in mine.

"My dear, if you really feel—"

"I feel nothing," I said rapidly, wanting only to repair the harm

I had done. "It's all past now—I never want to see another potion again."

He was silent, wondering, I suppose, if this meant that I cared a little or was merely recoiling from the sordidness of the incident and my narrow escape from death by poisoning.

"It was only because I was frightened," I said. "Frightened of you, frightened of the unknown, frightened of the world. But that's all gone now. I'm not frightened any more."

He was silent still, but his hand relaxed a little. I looked up and saw his withdrawn expression and longed to smooth it from his eyes.

"I wish we could go away," I said impulsively. "I wish we didn't have to stay here. I'm sure I shall never sleep soundly in our bedroom again for fear of seeing Alice's ghost. And the house is so gloomy and oppressive when winter closes in and the mist thickens over the Marsh. I hate it."

"I hate it too," he said frankly to my astonishment. "I always did. I never intended to stay here long—the only reason for my return was to clear Rodric's name and bring my father's murderer to justice. After that I intended to give up the estate by deed of gift to Vere's son Stephen and appoint Vere and the Sherman brothers trustees until the boy comes of age. That will mean Vere can live and work on the estate he loves while the Shermans can curb his more extravagant tendencies. And Vere will be happy in the knowledge that the estate will belong to his son and heir outright. I thought that was the best solution."

"Oh yes indeed!" I tried not to sound too pleased. Stifling my immense relief at the prospect of escape from Haraldsdyke and life in the country I added hesitantly: "But where will we ourselves go? What is to happen to us?"

He smiled at me and I saw he knew what I was thinking. "I've come to the conclusion," he said softly, "that you're much too beautiful to be incarcerated in the depths of the country where no one can see you. I think I'll take you to my town house in Vienna, my dear, to the city I love best in all the world, and you shall make a sparkling, glittering entrance into Viennese grand society."

"Well, that's all very well," said Alexander plaintively when I told him the news later, "but what about me? I shan't be able to come and visit you in the holidays."

"You'll only be at school for a little longer," I pointed out, "and after that you shall come and visit us in Vienna."

"But Vienna . . . well, I mean, it's rather foreign territory, isn't it? Are you sure you'll be all right?"

"But we're as foreign as Axel!" I reminded him crossly. "You always forget that half our inheritance comes from across the Channel. Besides, if Axel wanted to go to America, I would go with him. I would travel around the world with him, if he decided to go."

Alexander looked at me wonderingly. "You're so strange," he said with a sigh. "I shall never be able to keep up with you. You'll be telling me next that you're in love with him . . ."

Vere was grateful to Axel for granting Haraldsdyke to Stephen, but he remained numbed by his loss for a long time, and for at least ten years after Alice's death our rare visits to Haraldsdyke were gloomy, depressing occasions indeed. However, he did eventually remarry when he was about thirty-five years old, and after that the atmosphere at Haraldsdyke became more normal and welcoming to the casual visitor. His second wife was a nice woman, a widow a few years his senior whose first husband had been a clerk in some legal firm in Winchelsea; Vere evidently preferred women of an inferior rank to himself, although his second wife was socially far superior to Alice. Of Vere's three children, Stephen lived to marry and perpetuate the family name, but his younger brother died of diphtheria in childhood, and his sister, although living long enough to marry, died in childbirth a year after her wedding. On the whole I thought that branch of the family more inclined to misfortune than any of the others.

As for Ned, he went to America, became immensely rich, but never married. We heard news of him from Vere to whom he wrote regularly, and twice he came back to England for a visit, but of course we were in Vienna and never saw him.

Esther married that most eligible bachelor Charles Sherman and thereafter lived at Rye, which presumably suited her better than her life as Robert Brandson's estranged wife at Haraldsdyke. But I suspect not much better. Esther was not the kind of woman born to be contented.

Rodric's bones were exhumed from Dame Joan's herb patch and given a proper Christian burial at Haraldsford church. Dame Joan herself denied all knowledge of Rodric's death, but naturally no one believed her. I suppose it might have been possible to charge her with being an accessory after the fact of murder, but I was superstitiously reluctant to meddle with her and so, I discovered, was everyone else. The villagers of Haraldsford summoned the courage to mass before her door and threaten to burn down her cottage, but she disbursed them with a wave of her broomstick; they all turned tail and fled for fear of being cursed and irrevocably doomed. Shortly after that incident Vere sent out a warning that anyone who did not leave her well alone would have to answer to the justices of the peace for his conduct, and Dame Joan was abandoned with much relief to her customary solitude.

My one sorrow during the years that followed my arrival in Vienna was that although he wrote often enough Alexander never visited us; he had decided to pursue a political career, and as it did not pay in the English political arena to have foreign connections, my brother spent much time concealing his French blood and Austrian relatives. However, in the end this availed him little, for the English have no more love for bastards without respectable pedigrees than they have for foreigners, and Alexander's background ultimately told against him. After that, much disillusioned, he went out to the colonies and settled in Jamaica where he managed to involve himself profitably in the spice trade. I thought of him sometimes, far away in a home I had never seen, but on the whole as the years passed I did not think of him too often. I was too absorbed in my own family, my own life.

After we had been in Vienna several years, Axel inherited both a title and more property there from a distant cousin, and the acquisition of the title opened for us all the doors into every section of Austrian society, even those saloons which had previously been beyond our reach. Vienna was ours; and what now can be written about the Vienna of today, the most glittering city in all Europe, which has not already been written? Vienna spiraled to a brilliant zenith of romantic grandeur, and I was there when those sweeping beautiful tunes with their hidden sadness and sensuous nostalgia first enchanted the world. For the waltzes more than anything else seemed to symbolize the new era unfolding in that ancient unique city, and the new era was my era and I was there when it began.

But still sometimes when I sleep I dream not of the brilliant ballrooms of Vienna but of another land of long ago, the land of the green Marsh and of the cobbled alleys of Rye, and suddenly I am on the road to Haraldsdyke again and dreading the moment when I must set foot once more within those oppressive walls. But even as I finally catch a glimpse of the house in my dreams, the mist creeps in across the Marsh with its long white fingers, and I know then that I shall never again reach the Haraldsdyke of my memories, and that it has disappeared forever behind the shrouded walls of time.

The Dark Shore

PROLOGUE

Jon was alone. Outside in the night the city teemed and
throbbed and roared but in the room there was only the quiet
impersonal silence of the hotel room, softly-lit and thick-
carpeted. He went over to the window. Six floors below him to
the left a bus crawled north up Berkeley Street, a noiseless fleck
of red against the dark surface of the road, while immediately
below him the swarms of taxis cruised past the hotel entrance
before turning south towards Piccadilly. The sense of isolation
was accentuated by the stillness in the room. The polish on the
furniture gleamed; the white pillowcases on the bed were spot-
lessly smooth; the suitcases stood martialed along the wall in
faultless formation. He was alone in a vast city, a stranger returning to a forgotten land, and it seemed to him as he stood by
the window and stared out at the world beyond that he had been
foolish to hope that he could establish any contact with the past
by coming back to the city where he had been born.

He spent ten minutes unpacking the basic items from his
luggage and then paused to light a cigarette. Below him on the
bed lay the evening paper, his own photograph still smiling up
at him from the gossip column, and as he picked up the paper
again in contempt he was conscious of a stab of unreality, as if the
photograph was of someone else and the lines beneath described
a man he did not know. They called him a Canadian, of course,
and said he was a millionaire. There was a line mentioning his
mother too and her connection with pre-war London society,

a final sentence adding that he was to remarry shortly and that his fiancée was English. And then the columnist passed on to other topics, confident that he had fully exploited the snob value of this particular visitor to London.

Jon tore the newspaper to shreds and thought of his mother. She would have read it an hour, perhaps two hours ago, when the evening paper was delivered to the spacious house off Halkin Street. So she would know. He wondered if she had any desire to see him, any shred of interest in meeting him again after ten years. He had never written to her. When he had told Sarah that he and his mother no longer kept in touch with each other she had been so shocked that he had felt embarrassed, but justification had been easy and he had thought no more about it. Sarah simply did not understand. She had grown up in a happy sheltered home, and any deviation from the pattern of life which she had always known only emphasized how vulnerable she was when separated from that narrow comfortable little backwater her parents had created for her. One of the reasons why he wanted to marry Sarah was because she was untouched and unspoiled by the world he lived and worked in every day. When they were married, he thought, he would work all day in an atmosphere of boardrooms and balance sheets, and then at last he would be home away from it all and Sarah would be waiting for him. . . . He could see it all so clearly. Sarah would talk of the things he loved and after dinner he would play the piano, and there would be a still cool peace as night fell. And afterwards when they were in bed he would let her know how grateful he was to her for that wonderful peace, and Sarah would love him because he was her shield from the harshest flares of life and she needed him even more than he needed her.

It would all be so different from the past.

He thought of Sophia then, the memory flashing through his brain in the split second before he shut his mind against it. He mustn't think of Sophia. He would not, could not think of her. . . . But he was. While he was in London he would meet Justin and as soon as he saw Justin he would think of Sophia. . . . Nonsense. Justin was a young Englishman nineteen years old with the conventional English background of public school and perhaps a first job in the city. He would think of sports cars and parties and pretty girls and cricket in summer. Justin would be as utterly remote from Sophia as London was from Toronto, and on meeting him again there would be no cruel memories of the past, no dreadful searing pain.

The telephone rang.

The jangling bell was obscene, blasting aside the still silence of the room and making Jon start. Slumping onto the bed he reached for the receiver and leaned back against the pillows.

"Yes?"

"Call for you, Mr. Towers."

"Thank you."

There was a click, and then a silence except for the humming of the wire.

"Hullo?" He was tense suddenly, taut with nervousness.

Another pause. Someone far away at the other end of the wire took a small shallow breath.

"Hullo?" Jon said again. "Who's this?" There was ice suddenly, ice on his forehead, at the nape of his neck, at the base of his spine, although he didn't know why he was afraid.

And then very softly the anonymous voice from the past whispered into the receiver, "Welcome home, Mr. Towers. Does your fiancée know how you killed your first wife ten years ago?"

I

One

JUSTIN TOWERS very nearly didn't buy an evening paper. When he left the office at half-past five his eyes were tired after hours spent poring over figures and the prospect of his return journey on the underground filled him with a violent revulsion. He hated the rush hour tubes, hated being crammed into the long sweating corridors, hated the endless stream of faceless people who jostled past him in the subterranean nightmare. He thought for a long aching moment of his childhood, of the days beneath blue skies by a swaying sea, of the yellow walls and white shutters of Clougy, and then the moment was past and he was standing irresolutely by one of the innumerable entrances to the underground at Bank while the diesel fumes choked his lungs and the traffic roared in his ears. Across the road a number nine bus crawled on its way to Ludgate Circus. Justin made up his mind quickly; as the traffic lights changed he crossed Poultry and Queen Victoria Street and boarded the bus as it wedged itself deep in a line of stationary cars.

By the time the bus reached Green Park he was so sick of the constant waiting and the frustration of the traffic jams that he got out and walked towards the tube without hesitation. He felt desperately tired, and in an attempt to stave off the tedium of the last stretch of the journey he stopped by the newsvendor's stall and bought an evening paper.

He opened it on the platform, glanced at the stock exchange prices and then folded it up again as a train drew in. On finding a small corner at one end of the compartment he glanced at the front page, but he was conscious of his hatred of the crowded train once more and he was thinking not of the paper in his hand but of Clougy on those bright summer afternoons long ago. The scene etched itself clearly in his mind. Flip would be lying on his back, his long tail waving gracefully and the lawn would be soft and green and smooth. From the open windows of the house would come the sound of a piano being touched softly on light keys, and on the wrought-iron white swing-seat across the lawn a woman would be lying relaxed with a bowl of cherries on the wrought-iron table nearby. If he were to venture towards her and ask for a cherry the woman would yawn a wide, rich yawn and smile a warm, luxurious smile and say indulgently in her strange English, "But you'll get so fat, Justin!" And then she would pull him closer to her so that she could kiss him and afterwards she would let him have as many cherries as he wanted.

The hunger of those days was one of the things he remembered best. He had always been hungry, and the days had been full of Cornish cream and Cornish pasties until one evening the man, who would spend so many hours of a beautiful day indoors with a piano, said to him that it was time they both had some exercise before Justin became too fat to move. After that they had fallen into the habit of walking down to the cove together after tea. Further along the cliff path that curled away from the cove were the Flat Rocks by the water's edge, and they would go down there together, the man helping the child over the steeper parts of the cliff. It was a stiff climb. The shore was scored with vast boulders and gigantic slabs of granite, and after the scramble to the water's edge they would lie in the sun for a while and watch the endless motion of the sea as it sucked and spat at the rocky shelves beneath them. Sometimes the man would talk. Justin loved it when he talked. The man would paint pictures in words for him, and suddenly the world would be rich and exciting and full of bright colors. Sometimes the man wouldn't talk at all, which was disappointing, but the excitement was still there because the man was exciting in himself and whenever Justin was with him it seemed that even a walk to the cove and the Flat Rocks could be transformed into a taut racing adventure pounding with life and danger and anticipation. The man seemed to enjoy the walks too. Even when they had people staying at Clougy there would come times when he would want to get away from them all and then Justin had been his only companion, the chosen confidant to share the hours of seclusion.

Justin, immensely proud of his position, would have followed him to the ends of the earth.

And then had come that other weekend, creeping stealthily out of a cloudless future and suddenly the world was gray and streaked with pain and bewilderment and grief. . . .

Afterwards, all he could remember was his grandmother, looking very smart and elegant in a light blue suit. "You're going to come and live with me now, darling—won't that be nice? So much nicer for you to live in London instead of some dreary little place at the back of beyond . . . What? But didn't your father explain it to you? No, of course you can't go abroad with him! He wants you to grow up in England and have a proper education, and anyway he doesn't want a nine-year-old child with him wherever he goes. Surely you can see that. . . . Why hasn't he written? Well, darling, because he simply never writes a letter—gracious me, I should know that better than anyone! But he'll send you something at Christmas and on your birthday, I expect. Unless he forgets. That's more than likely, of course. He was always forgetting my birthday when he was away at school. . . ."

And he had forgotten. That was the terrible thing. He had forgotten and Justin had never heard from him again.

The train thundered along the dark tunnel and suddenly he was in the present again with his collar damp against the back of his neck and the newspaper crumpling in his hot hands. Useless to think back. The past was over, closed, forgotten, and he had long ago schooled himself not to waste time feeling bitter. He would never see his father again and now he had no wish to.

Any attachment that had ever existed between them had been
severed long ago.

The train careered into Hyde Park Station, and as several pas-
sengers moved out on to the platform, Justin folded the paper
down the center and started to turn each half-page mechanically.
The photograph caught his eye less than five seconds later.

"John Towers, the Canadian property millionaire . . ."

The shock was like a white light exploding behind his eyes.

When he got out of the train at Knightsbridge he felt sick and
ill as if he had just vomited and he had to sit down for a moment
at one of the benches on the platform before fighting his way to
the surface. Someone stopped to ask him if he was all right. Outside in the open air he paused for a moment among the swirling
crowds on the pavement and then very slowly he threw the
evening paper in a litter-bin and started the walk home to his
grandmother's house in Consett Mews.

II

In the house in Consett Mews, Camilla opened the top drawer
of her dressing-table, took out a small bottle and tipped two
white pills into the palm of her hand. It was wrong to take two,
of course, but it wouldn't matter once in a while. Doctors were
always over-cautious. After she had taken the tablets she returned to the dressing-table and re-applied her make-up carefully, taking especial care with the eyes and with the lines about
the mouth, but it seemed to her as she stared into the mirror that
the shock still showed in her expression in spite of all the pains
she had taken with the cosmetics.

She started to think of Jon again.

If only it were possible to keep it from Justin. . . . Jon was
obviously only in England on account of his English fiancée or
possibly because of some business reason, and did not intend to
see any of his family. It would only hurt Justin to know that his

father was in London and would be making no attempts to contact him.

The anger was suddenly a constriction in her throat, an ache behind her eyes. It was monstrous of Jon, she thought, to disown his family casually to the extent of returning to England after ten years without even letting his own mother know he was in the country. "It's not that I want to see him," she said aloud, "I don't give a damn whether he comes to see me or not while he's in London. It's merely the principle of the thing."

The tears were scorching her cheeks again, scarring the new make-up irrevocably, and in an involuntary movement she stood up and moved blindly over to the window.

Supposing Justin heard his father was in London. Supposing he went to see Jon and was drawn inevitably towards him until he was completely under his father's influence. . . . It was all very well to say that Justin was grown up, a levelheaded sensible young man of nineteen who would hardly be easily influenced by anyone, let alone by a father who had treated him so disgracefully, but Jon was so accustomed to influencing everyone within his reach. . . . If he should want to take Justin away from her—but he wouldn't, of course. What had Jon ever done for Justin? It was she who had brought Justin up. Jon couldn't have cared less. Justin belonged to her, not to Jon, and Jon would realize that as clearly as she did.

She thought of Jon again for one long moment, the memory a hot pain behind her eyes.

He was always the same, she thought. Always. Right from the beginning. All those nursemaids—and none of them could do anything with him. He would never listen to me. He was always struggling to impose his will on everyone else's and do exactly as he liked when he liked how he liked.

She thought of the time when she had sent him to boarding school a year early because she had felt unable to cope with him any longer. He hadn't missed her, she remembered sardonically, but had reveled instead in his independence; there had been new fields to conquer, other boys of his own age to sway or bully, masters to impress or mock as the mood suited him. And then had come the piano.

"My God!" she said aloud to the silent room. "That dreadful piano!" He had seen one when he was five years old, tried to play it and failed. That had been enough. He had never rested after that until he had mastered the instrument completely, and even now she could remember his ceaseless practice and the noise which had constantly set her nerves on edge. And then after the piano, later on in his life, there had been the girls. Every girl had been a challenge; a whole new world of conquest had suddenly materialized before his eyes as he had grown old enough to see it around him. She remembered worrying in case he entangled himself in some impossible scrape, remembered threatening that he would have to go to his father for help if he got into trouble, remembered how much it had hurt when he had laughed, mocking her anger. She could still hear his laugh even now. He hadn't cared! And then when he had only been nineteen there had come the episode with the little Greek bitch in a backstreet restaurant in Soho, the foolhardy marriage, the casual abandonment of all his prospects in the City. . . . Looking back, she wondered bitterly who had been the angrier, her first husband or herself. Not that Jon had cared how angry they had been. He had merely laughed and turned his back as if his parents had meant even less to him than the future he had so casually discarded, and after that she had hardly ever seen him.

The memories flickered restlessly through her brain: her refusal to accept his wife, Jon's retaliation by moving to the other end of England; after his marriage he had only contacted his mother when it suited him.

When Sophia was dead, for example. He had contacted her then soon enough. "I'm going abroad," he had said. "You'll look after Justin, won't you?"

Just like that. You'll look after Justin, won't you? As if she were some domestic servant being given a casual order.

She had often asked herself why she had said yes. She hadn't intended to. She had wanted to say "Find someone else to do your dirty work for you!" but had instead merely agreed to do as he wished, and then all at once Justin was with her and Jon was in Canada. . . . And he had never once written to her.

She hadn't believed it would be possible for Jon to ignore her so completely. She had not expected to hear from him regularly, but since she had taken charge of his son for him she had expected him to keep in touch with her. And he had never written her a single letter. She had refused to believe it at first. She had thought, There'll be a letter by the next post; he must surely write this week. But he had never written.

The tears were scalding her cheeks, and she turned swiftly back to the dressing-table again in irritation to repair the make-up.

"It's because I'm so angry," she said to herself as if it were necessary to vindicate herself from any accusation of weakness. "It's because it makes me so angry." It wasn't because she was upset or hurt or anything foolish. It merely made her so angry to think that after all she had done to help him he had never even bothered to write to thank her.

She glanced at her watch. Justin would be home soon. With unsteady, impatient movements she obliterated the tears with a paper tissue and reached for the jar of powder. Speed was very important now. Justin must never see her like this. . . .

As she concentrated once more upon the task of make-up she found herself wondering if anyone had ever heard from Jon once he had gone to Canada. Perhaps he had written to Marijohn. She had heard nothing more of Marijohn since the divorce with Michael. She had not even seen Michael himself since the previous Christmas when they had met unexpectedly at one of the drearier cocktail parties someone had given at that time. . . . She had always been so fond of Michael. Jon had never cared for him, of course, always preferring that dreadful man—what had his name been? She frowned, annoyed at the failure of memory. She could remember so well seeing his name mentioned in the gossip columns of the lower type of daily paper. . . . Alexander, she thought suddenly. That was it. Max Alexander.

From somewhere far away, the latch on the front door clicked and someone stepped into the hall.

He was back.

She put the finishing touches to her make-up, stood up and went out on to the landing.

"Justin?"

"Hullo," he called from the livingroom. He sounded calm and untroubled. "Where are you?"

"Just coming." He doesn't know, she thought. He hasn't seen the paper. It's going to be all right.

She reached the hall and moved into the livingroom. There was a cool draught of air, and over by the long windows the curtains swayed softly in the mellow light.

"Ah, there you are," said Justin.

"How are you, darling? Nice day?"

"Hm-hm."

She gave him a kiss and stood looking at him for a moment. "You don't sound too certain!"

He glanced away, moving over to the fireplace, and picked up a package of cigarettes for a moment before putting them down again and moving towards the long windows.

"Your plants are doing well, aren't they?" he said absently, looking out into the patio, and then suddenly he was swinging round, catching her unawares when she was off her guard, and the tension was in every line of her face and body.

"Justin—?"

"Yes," he said placidly. "I've seen the paper." He strolled over to the sofa, sat down and picked up the *Times*. "The photograph didn't look much like him, did it? I wonder why he's in London." When no reply was forthcoming, he started to glance down the personal column but soon abandoned it for the center pages. The room was filled with the rustle of the newspaper being turned inside out, and then he added, "What's for dinner, G.? Is it steak tonight?"

"Justin darling—" Camilla was moving swiftly over to the sofa, her hands agitated, her voice strained and high. "I know just how you must be feeling—"

"I don't see how you can, G., because to be perfectly honest, I don't feel anything. It means nothing to me at all."

She stared at him. He stared back tranquilly and then glanced back at the *Times*.

"I see," said Camilla, turning away abruptly. "Of course you won't be contacting him."

"Of course not. Will you?" He carefully turned the paper back again and stood up. "I'll be going out after dinner, G.," he said presently, going over to the door. "Back about eleven, I expect. I'll try not to make too much noise when I come in."

"I see," she said slowly. "Yes. Yes, that's all right, Justin."

The door closed gently and she was alone in the silent room. She felt relieved that he seemed to have taken such a sensible view of the situation, but she could not rid herself of her anxiety, and amidst all her confused worries she found herself comparing her grandson's total self-sufficiency with Jon's constant assertion of his independence. . . .

III

Eve never bought an evening paper because there was usually never any time to read it. The journey from her office in Piccadilly to her flat in Davies Street was too brief to allow time for reading and as soon as she was home, there was nearly always the usual rush to have a bath, change and go out. Or if she wasn't going out, there was even more of a rush to have a bath, change and start cooking for a dinner-party. Newspapers played a very small, insignificant part in her life, and none more so than the ones which came on sale in the evening.

On that particular evening, she had just finished changing and was embarking on the intricate task of make-up when an unexpected caller drifted into the flat and upset all her carefully-planned schedules.

"Just thought I'd drop in and see you. . . . Hope you don't mind. I say, I'm not in the way, am I?"

It had taken at least ten minutes to get rid of him, and even then he had wandered off leaving his tatty unwanted rag of an evening paper behind as if he had deliberately intended to leave his hall-mark on the room where he had wasted so much of her valuable time. Eve shoved the paper under the nearest cushion, whipped the empty glasses into the kitchen out of sight and sped back to add the final touches to her appearances.

And after all that, the man had to be late. All that panic and rush for nothing.

In the end she had time to spare; she took the evening paper from under the cushion and went into the kitchen absently to put it in the rubbish bin, but presently she hesitated. The paper would be useful to wrap up the bacon which had been slowly going bad since last weekend. Better do it now while she had a moment to spare or otherwise by the time next weekend came . . .

She opened the paper carelessly on the table and turned away towards the refrigerator.

A second later, the bacon forgotten, she turned back towards the table.

"Jon Towers, the Canadian property millionaire . . ."

Towers. Like . . . No, it couldn't be. It was impossible. She scrabbled to pick up the page, allowing the rest of the paper to slide on to the floor, not caring that her carefully-painted nails should graze against the surface of the table and scratch the varnish.

Jon without an H. Jon Towers. It was the same man.

A Canadian property millionaire . . . No, it couldn't be the same. But Jon had gone abroad following the aftermath of that weekend at Clougy. . . . Clougy! How funny that she should still remember the name. She could see it so clearly, too, the yellow house with white shutters which faced the sea, the green lawn of the garden, the hillside sloping down to the cove on either side of the house. The back of beyond, she had thought when she had first seen it, four miles from the nearest town, two miles from the main road, at the end of a track which led to nowhere. But at least she had never had to go there again. She had been there only once and that once had certainly been enough to last her a lifetime.

". . . staying in London. . . . English fiancée . . ."

Staying in London. One of the more well-known hotels, probably. It would be very simple to find out which one. . . .

If she wanted to find out. Which, of course, she didn't.

Or did she?

Jon Towers, she was thinking as she stood there motionless, staring down at the blurred uncertain photograph. Jon Towers. Those eyes. You looked at those eyes and suddenly you forgot the pain in your back or the draught from the open door or a thousand and one other tiresome things which might be bothering you at that particular moment. You might loathe the piano and find all music tedious but as soon as he touched those piano keys you had to listen. He moved or laughed or made some trivial gesture with his hands and you had to watch him. A womanizer, she had decided when she had first met him, but then afterwards in their room that evening Max had said with that casual amused laugh, "Jon? Good God, didn't you notice? My dear girl, he's in love with his wife. Quaint, isn't it?"

His wife.

Eve put down the paper, and stooped to pick up the discarded pages. Her limbs were stiff and aching as if she had taken part in some violent exercise, and she felt cold for no apparent reason. After putting the paper automatically in the rubbish bin, she moved out of the kitchen and found herself re-entering the still, silent livingroom again.

So Jon Towers was back in London. He must have the hell of a nerve.

Perhaps, she thought idly, fingering the edge of the curtain as she stared out of the window, perhaps it would have been rather amusing to have met Jon again. Too bad he had probably forgotten she had ever existed and was now about to marry some girl she had never met. But it would have been interesting to see if those eyes and that powerful body could still infect her with that strange unnerving excitement even now after ten years, or whether this time she would have been able to look upon him with detachment. If the attraction were wholly sexual, it was possible she would not have been so impressed a second time . . . but there had been something else besides. She could remember trying to explain to Max and yet not being sure what she was trying to explain. "It's not just sex, Max. It's something else. It's not just sex."

And Max had smiled his favorite tired cynical smile and said, "No? Are you quite sure?"

Max Alexander.

Turning away from the window she went over to the telephone and after a moment's hesitation knelt down to take out a volume of the London telephone directory.

IV

Max Alexander was in bed. There was only one other place which he preferred to bed and that was behind the wheel of his racing car, but his doctors had advised him against racing that season and so he had more time to spend in bed. On that particular evening he had just awakened from a brief doze and was reaching out for a cigarette when the telephone bell rang far away on the other side of the mattress.

He picked up the receiver out of idle curiosity.

"Max Alexander speaking."

"Hullo, Max," said an unfamiliar woman's voice at the other end of the wire. "How are you?"

He hesitated, aware of a shaft of annoyance. Hell to these women with their ridiculous air of mystery and cool would-be call-girl voices which wouldn't even fool a two-year-old child. . . .

"This is Flaxman nine-eight-double-one," he said dryly. "I think you have the wrong number."

"You've got a short memory, Max," said the voice at the other end of the line. "It wasn't really so long ago since Clougy, was it?"

After a long moment he managed to say politely into the white ivory receiver, "Since *when?*"

"Clougy, Max. Clougy. You surely haven't forgotten your friend Jon Towers, have you?"

The absurd thing was that he simply couldn't remember her name. He had a feeling it was biblical. Ruth, perhaps? Or Esther? Hell, there must be more female names in the Scriptures than that, but for the life of him he couldn't think of any more. It was nearly a quarter of a century since he had last opened a copy of the Bible.

"Oh, it's you," he said for lack of anything better to say. "How's the world treating you these days?"

What the devil was she telephoning for? After the affair at Clougy he had seen no more of her and they had gone their separate ways. Anyway, that was ten years ago. Ten years was an extremely long time.

". . . I've been living in a flat in Davies Street for the past two years," she was saying. "I'm working for a Piccadilly firm now. Diamond merchants. I work for the managing director."

As if he cared.

"You've seen the news about Jon, of course," she said carelessly before he could speak. "Today's evening paper."

"Jon?"

"You haven't seen the paper? He's back in London."

There was a silence. The world was suddenly reduced to a white ivory telephone receiver and a sickness below his heart which hurt his lungs.

"He's staying here for a few days. I gather he's here on some kind of business trip. I just wondered if you knew. Didn't he write and tell you he was coming?"

"We lost touch with each other when he went abroad," said Alexander abruptly and replaced the receiver without waiting for her next comment.

He was sweating, he noticed with surprise, and his lungs were still pumping the blood around his heart in a way which would have worried his doctors. Lying back on the pillows he tried to breathe more evenly and concentrate on the ceiling above him.

Really, women were quite extraordinary, always falling over themselves to be the first bearers of unexpected news. He supposed it gave them some peculiar thrill, some spurious touch of pleasure. This woman had obviously been reveling in her role of self-appointed newscaster.

"Jon Towers," he said aloud. "Jon Towers." It helped him to recall the past little by little, he decided. It was soothing and restful and helped him to view the situation from a disinterested, dispassionate point of view. He hadn't thought of Jon for a long time. How had he got on in Canada? And why should he have come back now after all those years? It had always seemed so obvious that he would never under any circumstances come back after his wife died. . . .

Alexander stiffened as he thought of Sophia's death. That had been a terrible business; even now he could remember the inquest, the doctors, the talks with the police as if it were yesterday. The jury had returned a verdict of accident in the end, although the possibility of suicide had also been discussed, and Jon had left the house after that, sold his business in Penzance and had been in Canada within two months.

Alexander shook a cigarette out of the packet by his bed and lit it slowly, watching the tip burn and smoulder as he pushed it into the orange flame. But his thoughts were quickening, gathering speed and clarity as the memories slipped back into his mind. Jon and he had been at school together. To begin with they hadn't had much in common, but then Jon had become interested in motor-racing and they had started seeing each other in the holidays and staying at one another's houses. Jon had had an odd sort of home life. His mother had been an ex-debutante type, very snobbish, and he had spent most of his time quarreling with her. His parents had been divorced when he was seven. His father, who had apparently been very rich and extremely eccentric, had lived abroad after that and had spent most of his life making expeditions to remote islands in search of botanical phenomena, so that Jon had never seen him at all. There had been various other relations on the mother's side, but the only relation of his that Alexander had ever met had come from old Towers' side of the family. She had been a year younger than Jon and Alexander himself, and her name had been Marijohn.

He wasn't in the room at all now. He was far away in another world and there was sun sparkling on blue waters from a cloudless sky. Marijohn, he thought, and remembered how they had even called her that too. It had never been shortened to Mary. It had always been Marijohn, the first and last syllable both stressed exactly the same. Marijohn Towers.

When he had been older he had tried taking her out for a while as she was rather good-looking, but he might just as well have saved his energy because he had never got anywhere. There had been too many other men all with the same aim in view, and anyway she had seemed to prefer men much older than herself. Not that Alexander had minded; he had never even begun to understand what she was thinking, and although he could tolerate mysterious women in small doses he always became irritated if the air of mystery was completely impenetrable. . . . She had married a solicitor in the end. Nobody had known why. He had been a very ordinary sort of fellow, rather dull and desperately conventional. Michael, he had been called. Michael something-or-other.

But they were divorced now anyway and Alexander didn't know what had happened to either of them since then.

But before Marijohn had married Michael, Jon had married Sophia. . . .

The cigarette smoke was hurting his lungs and suddenly he didn't want to think about the past any more. Sophia, astonishingly enough, had been a Greek waitress in a Soho café. Jon had been nineteen when he had met her and they had married soon afterwards—much to the disgust of his mother, naturally, and to the fury of his father who had immediately abandoned his latest expedition to fly back to England. There had been appalling rows on all sides and in the end the old man had cut Jon out of his will and returned to rejoin his expedition. Alexander gave a wry smile. Jon hadn't given a damn! He had borrowed a few thousand pounds from his mother, gone to the opposite end of England and had started up an estate agent's business down in Penzance, Cornwall. He had paid her back, of course. He had made a practice of buying up cottages in favorable parts of Cornwall, converting them and selling them at a profit. Cornwall had been at its height of popularity then, and it was easy enough for a man like Jon who had had capital and a head for money to earn enough to pay his way in the world. Anyway he hadn't been interested in big money at that particular time—all he had wanted had been his wife, a beautiful home in peaceful surroundings and his grand piano. He had got all three, of course. Jon had always got what he wanted.

The memories darkened suddenly, twisting and turning in his mind like revolving knives. Yes, he thought, Jon had always got what he wanted. He wanted a woman and he had only to crook his little finger; he wanted money and it flowed gently into his bank account; he wanted you to be a friend for some reason and you became a friend. . . . Or did you? When he was no longer there, it was as if a spell had been lifted and you started to wonder why you had ever been friends with him. . . .

He thought of Jon's marriage again. There had only been one

child, and he had been fat and rather plain and hadn't looked much like either of his parents. Alexander felt the memories quicken in his mind again; he was recalling the weekend parties at Clougy throughout the summer when the Towers' friends would drive down on Friday, sometimes doing the journey in a day, sometimes stopping Friday night en route and arriving on Saturday for lunch. It had been a long drive, but Jon and Sophia had entertained well and anyway the place had been a perfect retreat for any long weekend. . . . In a way it had been too much of a retreat, especially for Sophia who had lived all her life in busy crowded cities. There was no doubt that she had soon tired of that beautiful secluded house by the sea that Jon had loved so much, and towards the end of her life she had become very restless.

He thought of Sophia then, the voluptuous indolence, the languid movements, the dreadful stifled boredom never far below the lush surface. Poor Sophia. It would have been better by far if she had stayed in her cosmopolitan restaurant instead of exchanging the teeming life of Soho for the remote serenity of that house by the sea.

He went on thinking, watching his cigarette burn, remembering the rocks beneath the cove where she had fallen. It would have been easy enough to fall, he had thought at the time. There had been a path, steps cut out of the cliff, but it had been sandy and insecure after rain and although the cliff hadn't been very steep or very big the rocks below had been like a lot of jagged teeth before they had flattened out in terraces to the water's edge.

He stubbed out his cigarette, grinding the butt of ashes. It had been a beautiful spot below those cliffs. Jon had often walked out there with the child.

He could see it all so clearly now, that weekend he had been at Clougy for one of the gay parties which Sophia had loved so much. He had come down with Eve, and Michael had come down with Marijohn. There had been no one else, just the four of them with Jon, Sophia and the child. Jon had invited another couple as well but they hadn't been able to come at the last minute so there had only been four visitors at Clougy that weekend.

He saw Clougy then in his mind's eye, the old farmhouse that Jon had converted, a couple of hundred yards from the sea. There had been yellow walls and white shutters. It had been an unusual, striking place. Afterwards when it was all over, he had thought Jon would sell his home, but he had not. Jon had sold his business in Penzance, but he had never sold Clougy. He had given it all to Marijohn.

V

As soon as Michael Rivers reached his home that evening he took his car from the garage and started on the long journey south from his flat in Westminster to the remote house forty miles away in Surrey. At Guildford he paused to eat a snack supper at one of the pubs, and then he set off again towards Hindhead and the Devil's Punchbowl. It was just after seven o'clock when he reached Anselm's Cross, and the July sun was flaming in the sky beyond the pine trees of the surrounding hills.

He was received with surprise, doubt and more than a hint of disapproval. Visitors were not allowed on Tuesday as a general rule; the Mother Superior was very particular about it. However, if it was urgent, it was always possible for an exception to be made.

"You are expected, of course?"

"No," said Rivers, "but I think she'll see me."

"One moment, please," said the woman abruptly and left the room in a swirl of black skirts and black veil.

He waited about a quarter of an hour in that bare little room until he thought his patience must surely snap and then at last the woman returned, her lips thin with disapproval. "This way, please."

He followed her down long corridors, the familiar silence suffocating him. For a moment he tried to imagine what it would be like to live in such a place, cut off from the world, imprisoned with one's thoughts for hours on end, but his mind only recoiled from the thought and the sweat of horror started to prickle beneath his skin. To counteract the nightmarish twists of his imagination he forced himself to think of his life as it was at that moment, the weekdays crammed with his work at the office, his evenings spent at his club playing bridge or perhaps entertaining clients, the weekends filled with golf and the long hours in the open air. There was never any time to sit and think. It was better that way. Once long ago he had enjoyed solitude from time to time, but now he longed only for his mind to be absorbed with other people and activities which would keep any possibility of solitude far beyond his reach.

The nun opened a door. When he passed across the threshold, she closed the door again behind him and he heard the soft purposeful tread of her shoes as she walked briskly away again down the corridor.

"Michael!" said Marijohn with a smile. "What a lovely surprise!"

She stood up, moving across the floor towards him, and as she reached him the sun slanted through the window on to her beautiful hair. There was a tightness in his throat suddenly, an ache behind the eyes, and he stood helplessly before her, unable to speak, unable to move, almost unable to see.

"Dear Michael," he heard her say gently. "Come and sit down and tell me what it's all about. Is it bad news? You would hardly have driven all the way down here after a hard day's work otherwise."

She had sensed his distress, but not the reason for it. He managed to tighten his self-control as she turned to lead the way over to the two chairs, one on either side of the table, and the next moment he was sitting down opposite her and fumbling for his cigarette case.

"Mind if I smoke?" he mumbled, his eyes on the table.

"Not a bit. Can you spare one for me?"

He looked up in surprise, and she smiled at his expression. "I'm not a nun," she reminded him. "I'm not even a novice. I'm merely 'in retreat'."

"Of course," he said clumsily. "I always seem to forget that." He offered her a cigarette. She still wore the wedding ring, he noticed, and her fingers as she accepted the cigarette were long and slim, just as he remembered.

"Your hair's grayer, Michael," she said. "I suppose you're still working too hard at the office." And then, as she inhaled from the cigarette a moment later: "How strange it tastes! Most odd. Like some rare poison bringing a slow soporific death. . . . How long is it since you last came, Michael? Six months?"

"Seven. I came last Christmas."

"Of course! I remember now. Have you still got the same flat? Westminster, wasn't it? It's funny but I simply can't picture you in Westminster at all. You ought to marry again, Michael, and live in some splendid suburb like—like Richmond or Roehampton or somewhere." She blew smoke reflectively at the ceiling. "How are all your friends? Have you seen Camilla again? I remember you said you'd met her at some party last Christmas."

His self-possession was returning at last. He felt a shaft of gratitude towards her for talking until he felt better and then for giving him the precise opening he needed. It was almost as if she had known. . . . But no, that was impossible. She couldn't possibly have known.

"No," he said. "I haven't seen Camilla again."

"Or Justin?"

She must know. His scalp started to prickle because the knowledge was so uncanny.

"No, you wouldn't have seen Justin," she said answering her own question before he could reply. She spoke more slowly, he noticed, and her eyes were turned towards the window, focused on some remote object which he could not see. "I think I understand," she said at last. "You must have come to talk to me about Jon."

The still silence was all around them now, a huge tide of noise-lessness which engulfed them completely. He tried to imagine that he was in his office and she was merely another client with whom he had to discuss business, but although he tried to speak the words refused to come.

"He's come back."

She was looking at him directly for the first time, and her eyes were very steady, willing him to speak.

"Yes?"

Another long motionless silence. She was looking at her hands now, and the long lashes seemed to shadow her face and give it the strange veiled look he had come to dread once long ago.

"Where is he?"

"In London."

"With Camilla?"

"No, at the Mayfair Hotel." The simple routine of question and answer reminded him of countless interviews with clients, and suddenly it seemed easier to talk. "It was in the evening paper," he said. "They called him a Canadian property millionaire, which seemed rather unlikely, but it was definitely Jon because there was a photograph and of course, being the society page, the writer had to mention Camilla. The name of the hotel wasn't stated but I rang up the major hotels until I found the right one—it didn't take very long, less than ten minutes. I didn't think he would be staying with Camilla because when I last met her she said she had completely lost touch with him and didn't even know his Canadian address."

"I see." A pause. "Did the paper say anything else?"

"Yes," he said, "it did. It said he was engaged to an English girl and planned to marry shortly."

She looked out of the window at the evening light and the clear blue sky far away. Presently she smiled. "I'm glad," she said, glancing back at him so that she was smiling straight into his eyes. "That's wonderful news. I hope he'll be very happy."

He was the first to look away, and as he stared down at the

hard, plain, wooden surface of the table he had a sudden longing to escape from this appalling silence and race back through the twilight to the garish noise of London. "Would you like me to—" he heard himself mumbling but she interrupted him.

"No," she said, "there's no need for you to see him on my behalf. It was kind of you to come all this way to see me tonight, but there's nothing more you can do now."

"If—if ever you need anything—want any help . . ."

"I know," she said. "I'm very grateful, Michael."

He made his escape soon after that. She held out her hand to him as he said good-bye but that would have made the parting too formal and remote so he pretended not to see it. And then, minutes later, he was switching on the engine of his car and turning the knob of the little radio up to the maximum volume before setting off on his return journey to London.

VI

After he had gone, Marijohn sat for a long while at the wooden table and watched the night fall. When it was quite dark, she knelt down by the bed and prayed.

At eleven o'clock she undressed to go to bed, but an hour later she was still awake and the moonlight was beginning to slant through the little window and cast long, elegant shadows on the bare walls.

She sat up, listening. Her mind was opening again, a trick she thought she had forgotten long ago, and after a while she went over to the window and opened it as if the cool night air would help her struggle to interpret and understand. Outside was the quiet closed courtyard, even more quiet and closed than her room, but now instead of soothing her with its peace the effect reversed itself stealthily so that she felt her head seem to expand and the breath choke in her throat, making her want to scream. She ran to the door and opened it, her lungs gasping, the sweat breaking out all over her body, but outside was merely the quiet, closed corridor, suffocating her with its peace. She started to run, her bare feet making no sound on the stone floor, and suddenly she was running along the cliffs by the blue sparkling Cornish sea, running and running towards a house with yellow walls and white shutters, and the open air was all around her and she was free.

The scene blurred in her mind. She was in the garden of the old house in Surrey and there was a rose growing in a bed nearby. She plucked it out, tearing the petals to shreds, and then suddenly her mind was opening again and she was frightened. Nobody, she thought, nobody who hasn't this other sense can ever understand how frightening it is. They could never conceive what it means. They can imagine their bodies being scarred or hurt by some ordinary physical force but they can never imagine the pain in the mind, the dark struggles to understand, the knowledge that your mind doesn't belong to yourself alone. . . .

She knelt down, trying to pray, but her prayer was lost in the storm and she could only kneel and listen to her mind.

And when the dawn came at last she went to the Mother Superior to tell her that she would be leaving the house that day and did not know when she would ever return.

Two

I

THE HOTEL staff at the reception desk were unable to trace the anonymous call.

"But you must," said Jon. "It's very important. You must."

The man behind the desk said courteously that he regretted that it was quite impossible. It was a local call made from a public telephone booth but the automatic dialing system precluded any possibility of finding out any further information.

"Was it a man or a woman?"

"I'm afraid I don't remember, sir."

"But you must!" said Jon. "Surely you remember. The call only came through a minute ago."

"But sir—" The man felt himself stammering. "You see—"

"What did he say? Was it a deep voice? Did he have any accent?"

"No, sir. At least it was difficult to tell because—"

"Why?"

"Well, it was little more than a whisper, sir. Very faint. He just asked for you. 'Mr. Towers please,' he said and I said, 'Mr. Jon Towers?' and when he didn't answer I said, 'One moment, please' and connected the lines." He stopped.

Jon said nothing. Then after a moment, he shrugged his shoulders abruptly and turned aside, crossing the hall and reception lounge to the bar, while the man behind the desk wiped his forehead, muttered something to his companion and sat down automatically on the nearest available chair.

In the bar Jon ordered a double Scotch on the rocks. There was a sprinkling of people in the room but it was easy enough to find a seat at a comfortable distance from the nearest group, and when he sat down he lit a cigarette before starting his drink. After a while he became conscious of one definite need dominating the mass of confused thoughts in his mind, and on finishing his drink he stubbed out his cigarette and returned to his room to make a phone call.

A stranger's voice answered.

Hell, thought Jon in a blaze of frustration, she's moved or remarried or both and I'll have to waste time being a bloody private detective trying to discover where she is.

"Mrs. Rivington, please," he said abruptly to the unknown voice at the other end of the wire.

"I think you have the wrong number. This is—"

"Is that Forty-one Halkin Street?"

"Yes, but—"

"Then she's moved," said Jon wearily and added, "Thank you," before slamming down the receiver.

He sat and thought for a moment. Lawrence, the family lawyer, would probably know where she was. Lawrence wouldn't have moved in ten years either; he would be seventy-five now, firmly embedded in his little Georgian house at Richmond with his crusty housekeeper who probably still wore starched collars and cuffs.

Ten minutes later he was speaking to a deep mellifluous voice which pronounced each syllable with meticulous care.

"Lawrence, I'm trying to get in touch with my mother. Can you give me her address? I've just rung Halkin Street but I gather she's moved from there and it occurred to me that you would probably be able to tell me what's been happening while I've been abroad."

Lawrence talked for thirty seconds until Jon could stand it no longer.

"You mean she moved about five years ago after her second husband died and is now living at Five, Consett Mews?"

"Precisely. In fact—"

"I see. Now Lawrence, there's just one other thing. I'm extremely anxious to trace my cousin Marijohn—I was planning to phone my mother and ask her, but I suppose I may as well ask you now I'm speaking to you. Have you any idea where she is?"

The old man pondered over the question.

"You mean," said Jon after ten seconds, "you don't know."

"Well, in actual fact, to be completely honest, no I don't. Couldn't say. Rivers could tell you, of course. Nice chap, young Rivers. Sorry their marriage wasn't a success. . . . You knew about the divorce, I suppose?"

There was a silence in the softly-lit room. Beyond the window far-away traffic crawled up Berkeley Street, clockwork toys moving slowly through a model town.

"The divorce was—let me see . . . six years ago? Five? My memory's not so accurate as it used to be. . . . Rivers was awfully cut up about it—met him at the Law Society just about the time the divorce was coming up for hearing and he looked damn ill, poor fellow. No trouble with the divorce, though. Simple undefended desertion—took about ten minutes and the judge was pretty decent about it. Marijohn wasn't in court, of course. No need for her to be there when she wasn't defending the petition. . . . Are you still there, Jon?"

"Yes," said Jon, "I'm still here." And in his mind his voice was saying Marijohn, Marijohn, Marijohn over and over again, and the room was suddenly dark with grief.

Lawrence wandered on inconsequentially, reviewing the past ten years with the reminiscing nostalgia of the very old. He seemed surprised when Jon suddenly terminated the conversation, but managed to collect himself sufficiently to invite Jon to his home for dinner later that week.

"I'm sorry, Lawrence, but I'm afraid that won't be possible at the moment. I'll phone you later, if I may, and perhaps we can arrange something then."

After he had replaced the receiver he slumped on to the bed and buried his face in the pillow for a moment. The white linen was cool against his cheek, and he remembered how he had loved the touch of linen years ago when they had first used the sheets and pillowcases which had been given to them as wedding presents. In a sudden twist of memory he could see the double bed in their room at Clougy, the white sheets crisp and inviting, Sophia's dark hair tumbling over the pillows, her naked body full and rich and warm. . . .

He sat up, moved into the bathroom and then walked back into the bedroom to the window in a restless fever of movement. Find Marijohn, said the voice at the back of his brain. You have to find Marijohn. You can't go to Michael Rivers so you must go to your mother instead. Best to call Consett Mews, and then maybe you can see Justin at the same time and arrange to have a talk with him. You must see Justin.

But that phone call. I have to find out who made that phone call. And most important of all, I must find Marijohn. . . .

He went out, hailing a taxi at the curb, and giving his mother's address to the driver before slumping on to the back seat. The journey didn't take long. Jon sat and watched the dark trees of the park flash into the brilliant vortex of Knightsbridge, and then the cab turned off beyond Harrods before twisting into Consett Mews two minutes later. He got out, gave the man a ten shilling note and decided not to bother to wait for change. It was dark in the mews; the only light came from an old-fashioned lamp set on a corner some yards away, and there was no light on over the door marked Five. Very slowly he crossed the cobbles and pushed the bell hard and long with the index finger of his right hand.

Perhaps Justin will come to the door, he thought. For the hundredth time he tried to imagine what Justin would look like, but he could only see the little boy with the short fat legs and plump body, and suddenly he was back in the past again with the small trusting hand tightly clasping his own throughout the walks along the cliff path to Clougy. . . .

The door opened. Facing him on the threshold was a woman in a maid's uniform whose face he did not know.

"Good evening," said Jon. "Is Mrs. Rivington in?"

The maid hesitated uncertainly. And then a woman's voice said, "Who is it?" and the next moment as Jon stepped across the threshold, Camilla came out into the hall.

There was a tightness in Jon's chest suddenly, an ache of love in his throat, but the past rose up in a great smothering mist and he was left only with his familiar detachment. She had never cared. She had always been too occupied in finding lovers and husbands, too busy trekking the weary social rounds of cocktail parties and grand occasions, too intent on hiring nursemaids to do her work for her or making arrangements to send him off to boarding school a year early so that he would no longer be in the way. He accepted her attitude and had adjusted himself to it. There was no longer any pain now, least of all after ten years away from her.

"Hullo," he said, hoping she wouldn't cry or make some emotional scene to demonstrate a depth of love which did not exist. "I thought I'd just call in and see you. No doubt you saw in the paper that I was in London."

"Jon . . ." She took him in her arms, and as he kissed her on the cheek he knew she was crying.

So there was to be the familiar emotional scene after all. It would be like the time she had sent him to boarding school at the age of seven and had then cried when the time had come for him to go. He had never forgiven her for crying, for the hypocrisy of assuming a grief which she could not possibly have felt in the circumstances, and now it seemed that the hypocrisy was about to begin all over again.

He stepped backwards away from her and smiled into her

eyes. "Why," he said slowly, "I don't believe you've changed at all. . . . Where's Justin? Is he here?"

Her expression changed almost imperceptibly; she turned to lead the way back into the drawing-room. "No, he's not. He went out after dinner, and said he wouldn't be in until about eleven. . . . Why didn't you phone and let us know you intended to see us? I didn't expect a letter, of course—that would have been too much to hope for—but if you'd phoned—"

"I didn't know whether I was going to have time to come to-night."

They were in the drawing-room. He recognized the familiar pictures, the oak cabinet, the pale willow-pattern china.

"How long are you here for?" she said quickly. "Is it a business trip?"

"In a way," said Jon abruptly. "I'm also here to get married. My fiancée is traveling over from Toronto in ten days' time and we're getting married quietly as soon as possible."

"Oh?" she said, and he heard the hard edge to her voice and knew the expression in her eyes would be hard too. "Am I invited to the wedding? Or is it to be such a quiet affair that not even the bridegroom's mother is invited?"

"You may come if you wish." He took a cigarette from the box on the table and lit it with his own lighter. "But we want it to be quiet. Sarah's parents had the idea of throwing a big society wedding in Canada, but that was more than I could stand and certainly the last thing Sarah wanted, so we decided to have the wedding in London. Her parents will fly over from Canada and there'll be one or two of her friends there as well, but no one else."

"I see," said his mother. "How interesting. And have you told her all about your marriage to Sophia?"

There was a pause. He looked at her hard and had the satisfaction of seeing the color suffuse her neck and creep upwards into her face. After a moment he said to her carefully, "Did you phone the Mayfair Hotel this evening?"

"Did I—" She was puzzled. He saw her eyes cloud in bewilderment. "No, I didn't know you were staying at the Mayfair," she said at last. "I made no attempt to phone you. . . . Why do you ask?"

"Nothing." He inhaled from his cigarette, and glanced at a new china figurine on the dresser. "How are Michael and Marijohn these days?" he asked casually after a moment.

"They're divorced."

"Really?" His voice was vaguely surprised. "Why was that?"

"She wouldn't live with him any more. I've no doubt there were various affairs too. He divorced her for desertion in the end."

He gave a slight shrug of the shoulders as if in comment, and knew, without looking at her, that she wanted to say something spiteful. Before she could speak he asked, "Where's Marijohn now?"

A pause.

"Why?"

He looked at her directly. "Why not? I want to see her."

"I see," she said. "That was why you came to England I suppose. And why you called here tonight. I'm sure you wouldn't have bothered otherwise."

Oh God, thought Jon wearily. More histrionic scenes.

"Well, you've wasted your time coming here in that case," she said tightly. "I've no idea where she is, and I don't give a damn either. Michael's the only one who keeps in touch with her."

"Where does he live now?"

"Westminster," said Camilla, her voice clear and hard. "Sixteen, Grays Court. You surely don't want to go and see Michael, do you, darling?"

Jon leant forward, flicked ash into a tray and stood up with the cigarette still burning between his fingers.

"You're not going, are you, for heaven's sake? You've only just arrived!"

"I'll come again some time. I'm very rushed at the moment." He was already moving out into the hall, but as she followed him he paused with one hand on the front door latch and turned to face her.

She stopped.

He smiled.

"Jon," she said suddenly, all anger gone. "Jon darling—"

"Ask Justin to phone me when he comes in, would you?" he said, kissing her good-bye and holding her close to him for a moment. "Don't forget. I want to have a word with him tonight."

She moved away from him and he withdrew his arms and opened the front door.

"You don't want to see him, do you?" he heard her say, and he mistook the fear in her voice for sarcasm. "I didn't think you would be sufficiently interested."

He turned abruptly and stepped out into the dark street. "Of course I want to see him," he said over his shoulder. "Didn't you guess? Justin was the main reason why I decided to come back."

II

Michael Rivers was out. Jon rang the bell of the flat three times and then rattled the door handle in frustration, but as he turned to walk away down the stairs he was conscious of a feeling of relief. He had not wanted to see Rivers again.

He turned the corner of the stairs and began to walk slowly down the last flight into the main entrance hall, but just as he reached the last step the front door swung open. The next moment a man had crossed the threshold and was pausing to close the door again behind him.

It was dark in the hall. Jon was in shadow, motionless, almost holding his breath, and then as the man turned, one hand still on the latch, he knew that the man was Michael Rivers.

"Who's that?" said the man sharply.

"Jon Towers." He had decided on the journey to Westminster that it would be futile to waste time making polite conversation or pretending that ten years had made any difference to the situation. "Forgive me for calling on you like this," he said directly, moving out of the shadows into the dim evening dusk. "But I wanted your help. I have to trace Marijohn urgently and no one except you seems to know where she is."

He was nearer Rivers now, but he still could not see him properly. The man had not moved at all, and the odd half-light was such that Jon could not see the expression in his eyes. He was aware of a sharp pang of uneasiness, a violent twist of memory which was so vivid that it hurt, and then an inexplicable wave of compassion.

"I'm sorry things didn't work out," he said suddenly. "It must have been hard."

The fingers on the latch slowly loosened their grip; Rivers turned away from the door and paused by the table to examine the second post which lay waiting there for the occupants of the house.

"I'm afraid I can't tell you where she is."

"But you must," said Jon. "I have to see her. You must."

The man's back was to him, his figure still and implacable.

"Please," said Jon, who loathed having to beg from anyone. "It's very important. Please tell me."

The man picked up an envelope and started to open it.

"Is she in London?"

It was a bill. He put it back neatly in the envelope and turned towards the stairs.

"Look, Michael—"

"Go to hell."

"Where is she?"

"Get out of my—"

"You've got to tell me. Don't be so bloody stupid! This is urgent. You must tell me."

The man wrenched himself free of Jon's grip and started up the stairs. When Jon moved swiftly after him he swung round and for the first time Jon saw the expression in his eyes.

"You've caused too much trouble in your life, Jon Towers, and you've caused more than enough trouble for Marijohn. If you think I'm fool enough to tell you where she is, you're crazy. You've come to the very last person on Earth who would ever tell you, and it so happens—fortunately for Marijohn—that I'm the only person who knows where she is. Now get the hell out of here before I lose my temper and call the police."

The words were still and soft, the voice almost a whisper in the silent hall. Jon stepped back and paused.

"So it was you who called me this evening."

Rivers stared at him. "Called you?"

"Called me on the phone. I had an anonymous phone call welcoming me back to England and the welcome wasn't particularly warm. I thought it might be you."

Rivers still stared. Then he turned away as if in disgust. "I don't know what you're talking about," Jon heard him say as he started to mount the stairs again. "I'm a solicitor, not a crank who makes anonymous phone calls."

The stairs creaked; he turned the corner and Jon was alone suddenly with his thoughts in the dim silent hall.

He went out, finding his way to Parliament Square and walking past Big Ben to the Embankment. Traffic roared in his ears, lights blazed, diesel oil choked his lungs. He walked rapidly, trying to expel all the fury and frustration and fear from his body by a burst of physical energy, and then suddenly he knew no physical movement was going to soothe the turmoil in his mind and he stopped in exhaustion, leaning against the parapet to stare down into the dark waters of the Thames.

Marijohn, said his brain over and over again, each thought pattern harsh with anxiety and jagged with distress. Marijohn, Marijohn, Marijohn . . .

If only he could find out who had made the phone call. Even though he had for a moment suspected his mother he was certain she wasn't responsible. The person who had made that call must have been at Clougy during that last terrible weekend, and although his mother might have guessed what had happened with the help of her own special knowledge she would never think that he . . .

Better not to put it into words. Words were irrevocable forms of expression, terrible in their finality.

So it wasn't his mother. And he was almost certain it wasn't Michael Rivers. Almost . . . And of course it wasn't Marijohn. So that left Max and the girl Max had brought down from London that weekend, the tall, rather disdainful blonde called Eve. Poor Max, getting himself in such a muddle, trying to fool himself that he knew everything there was to know about women, constantly striving to be a second-rate Don Juan, when the only person he ever fooled was himself. . . . It was painfully obvious that the only reason why women found him attractive was because he led the social life of the motor racing set and had enough money to lead it in lavish style.

Jon went into Charing Cross Underground Station and shut himself in a phone booth.

It would be Eve, of course. Women often made anonymous phone calls. But what did she know and how much? Perhaps it was her idea of a practical joke and she knew nothing at all. Perhaps it was merely the first step in some plan to blackmail him, and in that case . . .

His thoughts spun round dizzily as he found the number in the book and picked up the receiver to dial.

He glanced at his watch as the line began to purr. It was getting late. Whatever happened he mustn't forget to phone Sarah at midnight. . . . Midnight in London, six o'clock in Toronto. Sarah would be playing the piano when the call came through and when the bell rang she would push the lock of dark hair from her forehead and run from the music room to the telephone. . . .

The line clicked. "Flaxman nine-eight-double-one," said a man's voice abruptly at the other end.

The picture of Sarah died.

"Max?"

A pause. Then! "Speaking."

He suddenly found it difficult to go on. In the end he merely said, "This is Jon, Max. Thanks for the welcoming phone call this evening—how did you know I was in town?"

The silence that followed was embarrassingly long. Then: "I'm sorry," said Max Alexander. "I hope I don't sound too dense but I'm completely at sea. John—"

"Towers."

"Jon Towers! Good God, what a sensation! I thought it must be you but as I know about two dozen people called John I thought I'd better make quite sure who I was talking to. . . . What's all this about a welcoming phone call?"

"Didn't you ring me up at the hotel earlier this evening and welcome me home?"

"My dear chap, I didn't even know you were in London until somebody rang up and told me you'd been mentioned in the evening paper—"

"Who?"

"What?"

"Who rang you up?"

"Well, curiously enough it was that girl I brought down to Clougy with me the weekend when—"

"Eve?"

"Eve! Why, of course! Eve Robertson. I'd forgotten her name for a moment, but you're quite right. It was Eve."

"Where does she live now?"

"Well, as a matter of fact, I think she said she was living in Davies Street. She said she worked in Piccadilly for a firm of diamond merchants. Why on earth do you want to know? I lost touch with her years ago, almost immediately after that weekend at Clougy."

"Then why the hell did she phone you this evening?"

"God knows . . . Look, Jon, what's all this about? What are you trying to—"

"It's nothing," said Jon. "Never mind, Max—forget it; it doesn't matter. Look, perhaps I can see you sometime within the next few days? It's a long while since we last met and ten years is time enough to be able to bury whatever happened between us. Have dinner with me tomorrow night at the Hawaii at nine and tell me all you've been doing with yourself during the last ten years. . . . Are you married, by the way? Or are you still fighting for your independence?"

"No," said Alexander slowly. "I've never married."

"Then let's have dinner by ourselves tomorrow. No women. My days of being a widower are numbered and I'm beginning to appreciate stag-parties again. Did you see my engagement mentioned in the paper tonight, by the way? I met an English girl in Toronto earlier this year and decided I was sick of house-keepers, paid and unpaid, and tired of all American and Canadian women. . . . You must meet Sarah when she comes to England."

"Yes," said Alexander. "I should like to." And then his voice added idly without warning: "Is she like Sophia?"

The telephone booth was a tight constricting cell clouded with a white mist of rage. "Yes," said Jon rapidly. "Physically she's very like her indeed. If you want to alter the dinner arrangements for tomorrow night, Max, phone me at the hotel tomorrow and if I'm not there, you can leave a message."

When he put the receiver back into the cradle he leant against the door for a moment and pressed his cheek against the glass pane. He felt drained of energy suddenly, emotionally exhausted.

And still he was no nearer finding Marijohn. . . .

But at least it seemed probable that Eve was responsible for the anonymous phone call. And at least he now knew where she lived and what her surname was.

Wrenching the receiver from the hook again he started dialing to contact the operator in charge of Directory Inquiries.

III

Eve was furious. It was a long time since she had been let down by someone who had promised to give her an entertaining evening, and an even longer time since she had made a date with a man who had simply failed to turn up as he had promised. To add to her feeling of frustration and anger, the phone call to Max Alexander, which should have been so amusing, had been a failure, and after Alexander had slammed down the receiver in the middle of their conversation she had been left only with a great sense of anticlimax and depression.

Hell to Max Alexander. Hell to all men everywhere. Hell to everyone and everything.

The phone call came just as she was toying with her third drink and wondering whom she could ring up next in order to stave off the boredom of the long, empty evening ahead of her.

She picked up the receiver quickly, almost spilling the liquid from her glass.

"Hullo?"

"Eve?"

A man's voice, hard and taut. She sat up a little, the glass forgotten.

"Speaking," she said with interest. "Who's this?"

There was a pause. And then after a moment the hard voice said abruptly, "Eve, this is Jon Towers."

The glass tipped, jerked off balance by the reflex of her wrist and hand. It toppled on to the carpet, the liquid splashing in a dark pool upon the floor and all she could do was sit on the edge of the chair and watch the stain as it widened and deepened before her eyes.

"Why, hullo, Jon," she heard herself say, her voice absurdly cool and even. "I saw you were back in London. How did you know where I was?"

"I've just been talking to Max Alexander."

Thoughts were flickering back and forth across her mind in confused uncertain patterns. As she waited, baffled and intrigued, for him to make the next move she was again aware of the old memory of his personal magnetism and was conscious that his voice made the memory unexpectedly vivid.

"Are you busy?" he said suddenly. "Can I see you?"

"That would be nice," she said as soon as she was capable of speech. "Thank you very much."

"Tonight?"

"Yes . . . Yes, I could manage tonight."

"Could you meet me at the Mayfair Hotel in quarter of an hour?"

"Easily. It's just round the corner from where I live."

"I'll meet you in the lobby," he said. "Don't bother to ask for me at the reception desk." And then the next moment he was gone and the dead line was merely a dull expressionless murmur in her ear.

IV

After he had replaced the receiver, Jon left the station, walked up to Trafalgar Square and on towards Piccadilly. As he walked he started to worry about Sarah. Perhaps he could clear up this trouble with Eve during the ten days before Sarah arrived, but if not he would seriously have to consider inventing some reason for asking Sarah to delay her arrival. Whatever happened, Sarah must never discover the events which had taken place at Clougy ten years ago. He thought of Sarah for a moment, remembering her clear unsophisticated view of life and the naïve trust which he loved so much. She would never, never be able to understand, and in failing to understand she would be destroyed; the knowledge would tear away the foundations of her secure, stable world and once her world had collapsed she would be exposed to the great flaming beacon of reality with nothing to shield her from the flames.

He walked down Piccadilly to Berkeley Street, and still the traffic roared in his ears and pedestrians thronged the pavements. He was conscious of loneliness again, and the bleakness of the emotion was at once accentuated by his worries. It would have been different in Canada. There he could have absorbed himself in his work or played the piano until the mood passed, but here there was nothing except the conventional ways of finding comfort in a foreign city. And he hated the adolescent futility of getting drunk and would have despised himself for having a woman within days of his coming marriage. It would have meant nothing, of course, but he would still have felt ashamed afterwards, full of guilt because he had done something which would hurt Sarah if she knew. Sarah wouldn't understand that the act with an unknown woman meant nothing and less than nothing, and if she ever found out, her eyes would be full of grief and bewilderment and pain. . . .

He couldn't bear the thought of hurting Sarah.

But the loneliness was hard to bear too.

If only he could find Marijohn. There must be some way of finding her. He would advertise. Surely someone knew where she was. . . .

His thoughts swam and veered in steep sharp patterns, and then he had reached the Ritz and was turning off into Berkeley Street. Ten yards down the road he paused listening, but there was nothing, only a sense of unrest and distress which was too vague to be identified. He walked on slowly, and two minutes later was entering the lobby of the hotel.

As he crossed the floor to the desk to ask for his key, he was conscious of someone watching him. With the key in his hand a moment later he swung round to look at the occupants of the open lounge directly behind him, and as he moved, the tall blonde with the faintly disdainful expression stubbed out her cigarette and looked across at him with a slight, cool smile.

He recognized her at once. He had never had any difficulty in remembering faces, and suddenly he was back at Clougy long ago and listening to Sophia say languidly, "I wonder who on earth Max will turn up with this time?"

And Max had arrived an hour later in a hot-rod open Bentley with this elegant, very fastidious blonde on the front seat beside him.

Jon slipped the key of his room into his pocket and crossed the lobby towards her.

"Well, well," she said wryly when he was near enough. "It's been a long time."

"A very long time." He stood before her casually, his hands in his pockets, the fingers of his right hand playing with the key to his room. Presently he said, "After I'd spoken to Max on the phone this evening, I realized I should get in touch with you."

She raised her eyebrows a fraction, almost as if she didn't understand him. It was cleverly done, he thought. "Just because I phone Max out of interest and tell him you're back in town," she said, "and just because Max later tells you that I phoned him, why does it automatically follow that you should get in touch with me?"

The lobby was sprinkled with people; there was one group only a few feet away from them seated on the leather chairs of the open lounge.

"If we're going to talk," he said, "you'd better come upstairs. There's not enough privacy here."

She still looked slightly bewildered, but now the bewilderment was mingled with a cautious tinge of pleasure, as if events had taken an unexpected but not unwelcome turn. "Fine," she said, her smile still wary but slightly less cool as she rose to her feet to stand beside him. "Lead the way."

They crossed the wide lobby to the elevator, the girl walking with a quick smooth grace which she had acquired since he had last seen her. Her mouth was slim beneath pale lipstick, the lashes of her beautiful eyes too long and dark to be entirely natural, her fair hair swept upwards simply in a soft, full curve.

On entering the elevator he was able to look at her more closely, but as he glanced across towards her he knew she was aware of his scrutiny and he turned aside abruptly.

"Six," he said to the elevator operator.

"Yes, sir."

The lift drifted upwards lazily. Canned music was playing softly from some small, insidious loudspeaker concealed beneath the control panel. Jon was reminded of Canada suddenly; ceaseless background music was one of the transatlantic traits which he had found most difficult to endure when he had arrived from England long ago, and even now after ten years he still noticed it with a sense of irritation.

"Six, sir," said the man as the doors opened.

Jon led the way down the corridor to his room, unlocked the door and walked in.

The girl shrugged off her coat.

"Cigarette?" said Jon shortly, turning away to take a fresh packet of cigarettes from a drawer by the bed.

"Thanks." He could feel her watching him. While he was giving her the cigarette and offering her a light he tried to analyze her expression, but it was difficult. There was a hint of curiosity in her eyes, a glimpse of ironic amusement in the slight curve of her smile, a trace of tension in her stillness as if her composure were not as effortless as it appeared to be. Some element in her manner puzzled him, and in an instinctive attempt to prolong the opening conversation and give himself more time to decide upon the best method of handling the situation, he said idly, "You don't seem to have changed much since that weekend at Clougy."

"No?" she said wryly. "I hope I have. I was very young when I went to Clougy, and very stupid."

"I don't see what was so young and stupid about wanting to marry Max. Most women would prefer to marry rich men, and there's always a certain glamor attached to anyone in the motor racing set."

"I was young and stupid not to realize that Max—and a hell of a lot of other men—just aren't the marrying kind."

"Why go to the altar when you can get exactly what you want by a lie in a hotel register?" He flung himself into a chair opposite her and gestured to her to sit down. "Some women have so little to offer on a long-term basis."

"And most men aren't interested in long-term planning."

He smiled suddenly, standing up in a quick, lithe movement and moving over to the window, his hands deep in his pockets. "Marriage is on a long-term basis," he said. "Until the parties decide to get divorced." He flung himself down in the chair again with a laugh, and as he felt her eyes watching him in fascination he wondered for the hundredth time in his life why women found his restlessness attractive.

"I should like to meet your new fiancée," she said unexpectedly, "just out of interest."

"You wouldn't like her."

"Why? Is she like Sophia?"

"Utterly different." He started to caress the arm of the chair idly, smoothing the material with strong movements of his fingers. "You must have hated Sophia that weekend," he said at last, not looking at her. "If I hadn't been so involved in my own troubles I might have found the time to feel sorry for you." He paused. Then: "Max did you a bad turn by taking you down to Clougy."

She shrugged. "It's all in the past now."

"Is it?"

A silence. "What do you mean?"

"When you called me on the phone this evening it seemed you wanted to revive the past."

She stared at him.

"Didn't you call me this evening?"

She still stared. He leaned forward, stubbed out his cigarette and was beside her on the bed before she had time to draw breath.

"Give me your cigarette."

She handed it to him without a word and he crushed the butt to ashes.

"Now," he said, not touching her but close enough to show her he would and could if she were obstinate. "Just what the hell do you think you're playing at?"

She smiled uncertainly, a faint fleeting smile, and pushed back a strand of hair from her forehead as if she were trying to decide what to say and finding it difficult. He felt his irritation grow, his patience fade, and he had to hold himself tightly in control to stem the rising tide of anger within him.

Something in his eyes must have given him away; she stopped, her fingers still touching her hair, her body motionless, and as she looked at him he was suddenly seized with a violent longing to shake her by the shoulders and wrench the truth from behind the cool, composed expression.

"Damn you," he said quietly to the woman. "Damn you."

There was a noise. He stopped. The noise was a bell, hideous and insistent, a jet of ice across the fire of his anger. Pushing the woman aside, he leant across and reached for the cold black receiver of the telephone.

"Jon—" she said.

"It's my son." He picked up the receiver. "Jon Towers speaking."

"Call for you, Mr. Towers. Personal from Toronto from a Miss Sarah—"

"Just a minute." He thrust the receiver into the pillow, muffling it. "Go into the bathroom," he said to the woman. "It's a private call for me. Wait in the bathroom till I've finished."

"But—"

"Get out!"

She went without a word. The bathroom door closed softly behind her and he was alone.

"Thank you," he said into the receiver. "I'll take the call now."

The line clicked and hummed. A voice said, "I have Mr. Towers for you," and then Sarah's voice, very clear and gentle, said, "Jon?" rather doubtfully as if she found it hard to believe she could really be talking to him across the entire length of the Atlantic Ocean.

"Sarah," he said, and suddenly there were hot tears pricking his eyes and an ache in his throat. "I was going to phone you."

"Yes, I know," she said happily, "but I simply couldn't wait to tell you so I thought I'd ring first. Jonny, Aunt Mildred has come back to London a week early from her cruise—she got off at Tangier or something stupid because she didn't like the food—and so I've now got a fully qualified chaperone earlier than I expected! Is it all right if I fly over to London the day after tomorrow?"

Three

AFTER JON had replaced the receiver he sat motionless on the edge of the bed for a long moment. Presently the woman came out of the bathroom and paused by the door, leaning her back against the panels as she waited for him to look up and notice her.

"You'd better go," he said at last, not looking at her. "I'm sorry."

She hesitated, and then picked up her coat and slipped it quietly over her dress without replying straight away. But after a moment she said, "How long will you be in London?"

"I'm not sure."

She hesitated again, toying with the clasp of her handbag as if she could not make up her mind what to say. "Maybe I'll see you again if there's time," she said suddenly. "You've got my phone number, haven't you?"

He stood up then, looking her straight in the eyes, and she knew instinctively she had said the wrong thing. She felt her cheeks burn, a trick she thought she had outgrown years ago, and suddenly she was furious with him, furious at his casual invitation to his hotel, furious at the casual way he was dismissing her, furious because his casual manner was an enigma which she found as fascinating as it was infuriating.

"Have a lovely wedding, won't you," she said acidly in her softest, sweetest voice as she swept over to the door. "I hope your fiancée realizes the kind of man she's marrying."

She had the satisfaction of seeing the color drain from his face, and then the next moment she was gone, slamming the door behind her, and Jon was again alone with his thoughts in his room on the sixth floor.

II

After a long while it occurred to him to glance at his watch. It was late, well after midnight, and Justin should have phoned an hour ago. Jon sat still for a moment, his thoughts swiftly recalling the evening's events. Perhaps Camilla had forgotten to ask Justin to phone the hotel. Or maybe she hadn't forgotten but had deliberately withheld the message out of malice. Perhaps she also knew where Marijohn was and had lied when she had told him otherwise. . . . But no, Rivers had said he was the only one who had any form of contact with Marijohn, so Camilla had been telling the truth.

Michael Rivers.

Jon leaned over on the bed, propping himself up on one elbow, and picked up the telephone receiver.

"Yes, sir?" said a helpful voice a moment later.

"I want to call number five, Consett Mews, W.8. I don't know the number."

"Thank you, sir. If you would like to replace the receiver we'll ring you when we've put through your call."

The minutes passed noiselessly. The room was still and peaceful. After a while Jon idly began to tidy the bed, straightening the counterpane and smoothing the pillows in an attempt to smother his impatience by physical movement, and then the bell rang and he picked up the receiver again.

"Your number is ringing for you, Mr. Towers."

"Thank you."

The line purred steadily. No one answered. They're in bed, thought Jon, half-asleep and cursing the noise of the bell.

He waited, listening to the relentless ringing at the other end of the wire. Ten . . . Eleven . . . Twelve . . .

"Knightsbridge five-seven-eight-one."

This was an unknown voice. It was quiet, very distinct and even self-possessed.

"I want," said Jon, "to speak to Justin Towers."

"Speaking."

There was a silence. God Almighty, thought Jon suddenly. To his astonishment he noticed that his free hand was a clenched fist, and felt his heart hurting his lungs as he drew a deep breath to speak. And then the words wouldn't come and he could only sit and listen to the silence at the other end of the wire and the stillness in the room around him.

He tried to pull himself together. "Justin."

"Yes, I'm still here."

"Did your grandmother tell you I'd called at the Mews this evening?"

"Yes, she did."

"Then why didn't you phone when you arrived back? Didn't she tell you that I wanted you to phone me?"

"Yes, she did."

Silence. There was something very uncommunicative about the quiet voice and the lack of hesitation. Perhaps he was shy.

"Look, Justin, I want to see you very much—there's a lot I have to discuss with you. Can you come round to the hotel, as soon as possible tomorrow morning? What time can you manage?"

"I'm afraid I can't manage tomorrow," said the quiet voice. "I'm going out for the day."

Jon felt as though someone had just thrown an ice-cold towel in his face. He gripped the receiver tightly and sat forward a little further on the edge of the bed.

"Justin, do you know why I've come to Europe?"

"My grandmother said you were here to get married."

"I could have married in Toronto. I came to England especially to see you."

No reply. Perhaps the nightmare was a reality and he simply wasn't interested.

"I have a business proposition to make you," said Jon, fumbling for an approach which would appeal to this impersonal voice a mile away from him in Knightsbridge. "I'm very anxious to discuss it with you as soon as possible. Can't you put off your engagement tomorrow?"

"All right," said the voice indifferently after a pause. "I suppose so."

"Can you have breakfast with me?"

"I'm afraid I'm very bad at getting up on Saturday mornings."

"Lunch?"

"I'm—not sure."

"Well, come as soon after breakfast as you can and then we can talk for a while and maybe you can have lunch with me afterwards."

"All right."

"Fine," said Jon. "Don't forget to come, will you? I'll see you tomorrow."

After he had replaced the receiver he sat for ten seconds on the edge of the bed and stared at the silent telephone. Presently when he went into the bathroom, he saw that there was sweat on his forehead and his hands as he raised them to flick the sweat away were trembling with tension. This is my mother's fault, he thought; she's turned the boy against me just as she tried to turn me against my father. When I meet Justin tomorrow he'll be a stranger and the fault will be hers.

He felt desolate suddenly, as if he had taken years of accumulated savings to the bank only to have them stolen from him as he approached the counter to hand over the money. He undressed and had a shower, but the desolation was with him even as he slid into bed, and he knew he would never be able to sleep. He switched out the light. It was after one o'clock, but the night yawned effortlessly ahead of him, hours of restless worry and anxiety, a steady deepening of the pain behind his eyes and the ache of tension in his body. The thoughts whirled and throbbed in his brain, sometimes mere patterns of consciousness, sometimes forming themselves into definite words and sentences.

Sarah would be coming to London in two days' time. Supposing Eve made trouble . . . He could pay her off for a time, but in the end something would have to be done. If only he could find Marijohn . . . but no one knew where she was, no one at all except Michael Rivers. Hell to Michael Rivers. How could one make a man like Michael talk? No good offering him money. No good urging or pleading or cajoling. Nothing was any good with a man like that. . . . But something would have to be done. Why did no one know where Marijohn was? The statement seemed to imply she was completely withdrawn from circulation. Perhaps she was abroad. Perhaps there was some man. She wouldn't live with Michael any more, Camilla had said; no doubt there were affairs too.

But that was all wrong. There would have been no real affairs. No real affairs.

But no one knew where Marijohn was and something would have to be done. Perhaps Justin would know. Justin . . .

The desolation nagged at him again, stabbing his consciousness with pain. Better not to think of Justin. And then without warning he was thinking of Clougy, aching for the soft breeze from the sea, pining for the white shutters and yellow walls and the warm mellow sense of peace. . . . Yet that was all gone, destroyed with Sophia's death. The sadness of it made him twist over in bed and bury his face deep in the pillow. He had forgotten until that moment how much he had loved his house in Cornwall.

He sat up in bed, throwing back the bedclothes and going over to the window. "I want to talk about Clougy," he thought to himself, staring out into the night. "I want to talk about Sophia and why our marriage went so wrong when I loved her so much I could hardly bear to spend a single night away from her. I want to talk about Max and why our friendship was so completely destroyed that we were relieved to go our separate ways and walk out of each other's lives without a backward glance. I want to talk about Michael who never liked me because I conformed to no rules and was like no other man he had ever had to deal with in his narrow little legal world in London. I want to talk about Justin whom I loved because he was always cheerful and happy and comfortable in his plumpness, and because like me he enjoyed being alive and found all life exciting. And most of all I want to talk to Marijohn because I can discuss Clougy with no one except her. . . ."

He went back to bed, his longing sharp and jagged in his mind, and tossed and turned restlessly for another hour. And then just before dawn there was suddenly a great inexplicable peace soothing his brain and he knew that at last he would be able to sleep.

III

After he had breakfasted the next morning, he went into the open lounge in the hotel lobby and sat down with a newspaper to wait for Justin to arrive. There was a constant stream of people crossing the lobby and entering or leaving the hotel, and at length he put the paper aside and concentrated on watching each person who walked through the swinging doors a few feet away from him.

Ten o'clock came. Then half-past. Perhaps he had changed his mind and decided not to come. If he wasn't going to come he should have phoned. But of course he would come. Why shouldn't he? He had agreed to it. He wouldn't back out now. . . .

A family of Americans arrived with a formidable collection of white suitcases. A young man who might easily have been Justin drifted in and then walked up to a girl who was sitting reading near Jon in the lounge. There was an affectionate reunion and they left together. A couple of foreign business men came in speaking a language that was either Danish or Swedish, and just behind them was another foreigner, dark and not very tall, who looked as though he came from Southern Europe. Italy, perhaps, or Spain. The two Scandinavian business men moved slowly over towards one of the other lounges, their heads bent in earnest conversation, their hands behind their backs like a couple of naval officers. The young Italian made no attempt to follow them. He walked slowly over to the reception desk instead, and asked for Mr. Jon Towers.

"I think, sir," said the uniformed attendant to him, "that Mr. Towers is sitting in one of the armchairs behind you to your left."

The young man turned.

His dark eyes were serious and watchful, his features impassive. His face was plain but unusual. Jon recognized the small snub nose and the high cheekbones but not the gravity in the wide mouth nor the leanness about his jaw.

He walked across, very unhurried and calm. Jon stood up, knocking the ash-tray off the table and showering ashes all over the carpet.

"Hullo," said Justin, holding out his hand politely. "How are you?"

Jon took the hand in his, not knowing what to do with it, and then let it go. If only it had been ten years ago, he thought. There would have been no awkwardness, no constraint, no polite empty phrases and courteous gestures.

He smiled uncertainly at the young man beside him. "But you're so thin, Justin!" was all he could manage to say. "You're so slim and streamlined!"

The young man smiled faintly, gave a shrug of the shoulders which reminded Jon instantly and sickeningly of Sophia, and glanced down at the spilt ashes on the floor.

There was silence.

"Let's sit down," said Jon. "No point in standing. Do you smoke?"

"No, thank you."

They both sat down. Jon lit a cigarette.

"What are you doing now? Are you working?"

"Yes. Insurance in the city."

"Do you like it?"

"Yes."

"How did you get on at school? Where were you sent in the end?"

Justin told him.

"Did you like it?"

"Yes."

There seemed suddenly so little to say. Jon felt sick and ill and lost. "I expect you'd like me to come to the point," he said abruptly. "I came over here to ask you if you'd be interested in working in Canada with a view eventually to controlling a branch of my business based in London. I haven't opened this branch yet, but I intend to do so within the next three years. Ultimately, of course, if you made a success of the opportunity I would transfer the entire business to you when I retire. My business is property. It's a multi-million dollar concern."

He stopped. The lounge hummed with other people's steady conversation. People were still coming back and forth through the swing-doors into the hotel.

"I don't think," said Justin, "I should like to work in Canada."

A man and woman near them got up laughing. The woman had on a ridiculous yellow hat with a purple feather in it. The stupid things one noticed.

"Any particular reason?"

"Well . . ." Another vague shrug of the shoulders. "I'm quite happy in England. My grandmother's very good to me and I've got plenty of friends and so on. I like working in London and I've got a good opening in the City."

He was reddening slowly as he spoke, Jon noticed. His eyes were still watching the spilt ashes on the floor.

Jon said nothing.

"There's another reason too," said the boy, as if he sensed his other reasons hadn't been good enough. "There's a girl—someone I know. . . . I don't want to go away and leave her just yet."

"Marry her and come to Canada together."

Justin looked up startled, and Jon knew then that he had been lying. "But I can't—"

"Why not? I married when I was your age. You're old enough to know your own mind."

"It's not a question of marriage. We're not even engaged."

"Then she can't be so important to you that you would ignore a million-dollar opening in Canada to be with her. Okay, so you've got friends in England—you'd find plenty more in Canada. Okay, so your grandmother's been good to you—fine, but what if she has? You're not going to remain shackled to her all your life, are you? And what if you have got a good opening in the City? So have dozens of young men. I'm offering you the opportunity of a lifetime, something unique and dynamic and exciting. Don't you want to be your own master of your own business? Haven't you got the drive and ambition to want to take up a challenge and emerge the winner? What do you want of life? The nine-till-five stagnation of the city and years of comfortable boredom or the twenty-four hour excitement of juggling with millions of dollars? All right, so you're fond of London! I'm offering you the opportunity to come back here in three years' time, and when you come back you'll be twenty times richer than any of the friends you said good-bye to when you left for Canada. Hasn't the prospect any appeal to you at all? I felt so sure from all my memories of you that you wouldn't say no to an opportunity like this."

But the dark eyes were still expressionless, his face immobile. "I don't think property is really my line at all."

"Do you know anything about it?"

Justin was silent.

"Look, Justin—"

"I don't want to," said the boy rapidly. "I expect you could find someone else. I don't see why it has to be me."

"For Christ's sake!" Jon was almost beside himself with anger and despair. "What is it, Justin? What's happened? Don't you understand what I'm trying to say? I've been away from you for ten whole years and now I want to give you all I can to try and make amends. I want you to come into business with me so we'll never be separated again for long and so that I can get to know you and try to catch up on all the lost years. Don't you understand? Don't you see?"

"Yes," said Justin woodenly, "but I'm afraid I can't help you."

"Has your grandmother been talking to you? Has she? Has she been trying to turn you against me? What has she said?"

"She's never mentioned you."

"She must have!"

The boy shook his head and glanced down at his watch. "I'm afraid—"

"No," said Jon. "No, you're not going yet. Not till I've got to the bottom of all this."

"I'm sorry, but—"

"Sit down." He grasped the boy's arm and pulled him back into his chair. Justin wrenched himself away. "There's one question I'm going to ask you whether you like it or not, and you're not leaving till you've given me a proper answer."

He paused. The boy made no move but merely stared sullenly into his eyes.

"Justin, why did you never answer my letters?"

The boy still stared but his eyes were different. The sullenness had been replaced by a flash of bewilderment and suspicion which Jon did not understand.

"Letters?"

"You remember when I said good-bye to you after I took you away from Clougy?"

The suspicion was gone. Only the bewilderment remained. "Yes."

"You remember how I explained that I couldn't take you with me, as I would have no home and no one to help look after you, and you had to go to an English school? You remember how I promised to write, and how I made you promise you would answer my letters and tell me all you'd been doing?"

The boy didn't speak this time. He merely nodded.

"Then why didn't you write? You promised you would. I wrote you six letters including a birthday present, but I never had a word from you. Why was it, Justin? Was it because you resented me not taking you to Canada? I only did it for your own good. I would have come back to see you, but I got caught up in my business interests, so involved that it was hard even to get away for the odd weekend. But I wanted to see you and hear from you all the time, yet nothing ever came. In the end I stopped writing because I thought that in some strange way the letters must be hurting you, and at Christmas and on your birthday I merely sent over money to be paid into your trust fund at your grandmother's bank. . . . What happened, Justin? Was it something to do with that last time at Clougy when—"

"I have to go," said the boy, and he was stammering, his composure shattered. "I—I'm sorry, but I must go. Please." He was standing up, stumbling towards the swinging doors, not seeing nor caring where he went.

The doors opened and swung in a flash of bright metal, and then Jon was alone once more in his hotel and the failure was a throbbing, aching pain across his heart.

IV

It was eleven o'clock when Justin arrived back at Consett Mews. His grandmother, who was writing letters in the drawing room, looked up, startled by his abrupt entrance.

"Justin—" He saw her expression change almost imperceptibly as she saw his face. "Darling, what's happened? What did he say? Did he—"

He stood still, looking at her. She stopped.

"What happened," he said, "to the letters my father sent me from Canada ten years ago?"

He saw her blush, an ugly red stain beneath the careful make-up, and in a sudden sickening moment he thought, It's true. He did write. She lied to me all the time.

"Letters?" she said. "From Canada?"

"He wrote me six letters. And sent a birthday present."

"Is that what he said?" But it was only a halfhearted attempt at defense. She took a step towards him, making an impulsive gesture with her hands. "I only did it for your own good, darling. I thought it would only upset you to read letters from him when he had left you behind and gone to Canada without you."

"Did you read the letters?"

"No," she said at once. "No, I—"

"You let six letters come to me from my father and you destroyed them to make me think he had forgotten me entirely?"

"Justin, no, Justin, you don't understand—"

"You never had any letters from him so you didn't want me to have letters from him either!"

"No," she said, "no, it wasn't like that—"

"You lied and deceived and cheated me year after year, day after day—"

"It was for your own good, Justin, your own good . . ."

She sat down again as if he had exhausted all her strength, and suddenly she was old to him, a woman with a lined, tear-stained face and bent shoulders and trembling hands. "Your father cares nothing for anyone except himself," he heard her whisper at last. "He takes people and uses them for his own ends, so that although you care for him your love is wasted because he never cares for you. I've been useful to him at various times, providing him with a home when he was young, looking after you when he was older—but he's never cared. You'll be useful to him now to help him with his business in Canada. Oh, don't think I can't guess why he wanted to see you! But he'll never care for you yourself, only for your usefulness to him—"

"You're wrong," said Justin. "He does care. You don't understand."

"Understand! I understand all too well!"

"I don't believe you understood him any better than you understood me."

"Justin—"

"I'm going to Canada with him."

There was a moment of utter silence.

"You can't," she said at last. "Please, Justin. Be sensible. You're talking of altering your whole career, damaging all your prospects in London, just because of a ten-minute meeting this morning with a man you hardly know. Please, please be sensible and don't talk like this."

"I've made up my mind."

Camilla looked at him, the years blurring before her eyes, and suddenly the boy before her was Jon saying in that some level, obstinate voice which she had come to dread so much: "I've made up my mind. I'm going to marry her."

"You're a fool, Justin," she said, her voice suddenly harsh and clear. "You've no idea what you're doing. You know nothing about your father at all."

He turned aside and moved towards the door. "I'm not listening to this."

"Of course," said Camilla, "you're too young to remember what happened at Clougy."

"Shut up!" he shouted, whirling to face her. "Shut up, shut up!"

"I wasn't there, but I can guess what happened. He drove your mother to death, you do realize that, don't you? The jury said the death was accidental, but I always knew it was suicide. The marriage was finished, and once that was gone there was nothing else left for her. Of course anyone could have foreseen the marriage wouldn't last! Her attraction for him was entirely sexual and after several years of marriage it was only natural that he should become bored with her. It was the same old story—she cared for him, but basically he never cared for her, only for the pleasure she could give him in bed. And once the pleasure had been replaced by boredom she meant nothing to him at all. So he started to look round for some other woman. It had to be some woman who was quite different, preferably someone rather aloof and unobtainable, because that made the task of conquest so much more interesting and exciting. And during the weekend that your mother died, just such a woman happened to be staying at Clougy. Of course you never knew that he and Marijohn—"

Justin's hands were over his ears, shutting her voice from his mind as he stumbled into the hall and banged the door shut behind him. Then, after running up the stairs two at a time, he reached his room, found a suitcase and started to pack his belongings.

V

It was noon. On the sixth floor of the Mayfair Hotel, Jon was sitting in his room working out an advertisement for the personal column of the *Times* and wondering whether there would be any point in trying to see Michael Rivers again. Before him on the table lay his penciled note of Eve's telephone number, and as he worried over the problem he picked up the slip of paper idly and bent it between his fingers. He would have to get in touch with the woman to get to the bottom of this business of the anonymous phone call, but if only he could find Marijohn first it would be easier to know which line to adopt. . . . He was just tossing the scrap of paper aside and concentrating on his message for the *Times* when the phone rang.

He picked up the receiver. "Yes?"

"There's a lady here to see you, Mr. Towers."

"Does she give her name?"

"No, sir."

It would be Eve ready to lay her cards on the table. "All right, I'll come down."

He replaced the receiver, checked the money in his wallet and went out. Canned music was still playing in the lift. On the ground floor he walked out into the lobby and crossed over to the leather chairs of the open lounge below the reception desk.

His mind saw her the instant before his eyes did. He had a moment of searing relief mingled with a burst of blazing joy, and then he was moving forward again towards her and Marijohn was smiling into his eyes.

II

One

I

SARAH SPENT the journey across the Atlantic alternating between a volume of John Clare's poetry and the latest mystery by a well-known crime writer. Occasionally it occurred to her that she hadn't understood a word she was reading and that it would be much more sensible to put both books away, but still she kept them on her lap and watched the written page from time to time. And then at last, the lights of London lay beneath the plane, stretching as far as the eye could see, and she felt the old familiar feeling of nervousness tighten beneath her heart as she thought of Jon.

She loved Jon and knew perfectly well that she wanted to marry him, but he remained an enigma to her at times and it was this strange unknown quality which made her nervous. She called it the Distant Mood. She could understand Jon when he was gay, excited, nervous, musical, sad, disappointed or merely obstinate, but Jon in the Distant Mood was something which frightened her because she knew neither the cause of the mood nor the correct response to it. Her nervousness usually reduced her to silence, and her silence led to a sense of failure, hard to explain. Perhaps, she had thought, it would be different in England; he would be far from the worries and troubles of his work, and perhaps when he was in an easier, less complex frame of mind she would be able to say to him: "Jon, why is it that sometimes you're so far away that I don't know how to reach out to communicate with you? Why is it that sometimes you're so abrupt

I feel I mustn't talk for fear of making you lose your temper and quarrel? Is the fault mine? Is it that I don't understand something in you or that I do something to displease you? If it's my fault, tell me what I'm doing wrong so that I can put it right, because I can't bear it when you're so far away and remote and indifferent to the world."

He had been in the Distant Mood when she had telephoned him in London two nights ago. She had recognized it at once, and although she had done her best to sound gay and cheerful, she had cried when she had replaced the receiver. That had led to the inevitable scene with her parents.

"Sarah dear, if there's any doubt in your mind, don't . . ."

"Far better to be sorry now than be sorry after you're married."

"I mean, darling, I know you're very lucky to be marrying Jon. In many ways your father and I both like him very much, but all the same, he's many years older than you and of course, it *is* difficult when you marry out of your generation. . . ."

And Sarah had very stupidly lost her temper in the face of these platitudes and had locked herself in her room to face a sleepless night on her own.

The next day had been spent in packing and preparing for the journey to London on the following day. He would phone that night, she had thought. He would be certain to phone that night, and when he talked he would sound quite different and everything would be all right again.

But the phone call never came.

Her mother had decided Sarah's distress was due to pre-marital nerves and had talked embarrassingly for five whole minutes littered with awkward pauses on the intimate side of marriage. In the end, Sarah had gone out to the nearest cinema to escape and had seen an incredibly bad epic film on a wide screen which had given her a headache. It had been almost a relief to board the plane for London the following day and take a definite course of action at last after so much restless waiting and anxiety.

The plane drifted lower and lower over the mass of lights until

Sarah could see the landing lights of the runway rising from the ground to meet them, and then there were the soft thumps of landing and the long cruise to a halt on English soil. Outside the plane, the air was damp and cool. The trek through customs came next, her nerves tightening steadily as the minutes passed, until at last she was moving into the great central lobby and straining her eyes for a glimpse of Jon.

Something had gone wrong. He wasn't there. He was going to break off the engagement. He had had an accident, was injured, dying, dead. . . .

"God Almighty," said Jon's voice just behind her. "I thought you were a white sheet at first! Who's been frightening the life out of you?"

The relief was a great cascading warmth making her limbs relax and the tears spring to her eyes.

"Oh Jon, Jon."

There was no Distant Mood this time. He was smiling, his eyes brilliantly alive, his arms very strong, and when he kissed her it seemed ridiculous that she should ever have had any worries at all.

"You look," he said, "quite frighteningly sophisticated. What's all this green eye-shadow and mud on your eyelashes?"

"Oh Jon, I spent hours—" She laughed suddenly in a surge of happiness and he laughed too, kissing her again and then sliding his arm round her waist.

"Am I covered in Canada's most soigné lipstick?"

He was. She produced a handkerchief and carefully wiped it off.

"Right," he said briskly, when she had finished. "Let's go. There's dinner waiting for us at the Hilton and endless things to be discussed before I take you to your Aunt Mildred's, so we've no time to waste. . . . Is this all your luggage or has Cleopatra got another gold barge full of suitcases sailing up the customs' conveyor belt?"

There was a taxi waiting and then came the journey into the

heart of London, through the Middlesex suburbs to Kensington, Knightsbridge and the Park. The warmth of London hummed around them, the roar of engines revved in their ears, and Sarah, her hand clasped tightly in Jon's, thought how exciting it was to come home at last to her favorite city and to travel through the brightly-lit streets to the resplendent glamor of a lush, expensive world.

"How's Cleopatra feeling now?"

"Thinking how much nicer than Mark Antony you are and how much better than Alexandria London is."

He laughed. She was happy. When they reached the Hilton she had a moment's thrill as she crossed the threshold into the luxury which was still new to her, and then they were in the diningroom and she was trying hard to pretend she was quite accustomed to dining in the world's most famous restaurants.

Jon ordered the meal, chose the wines and tossed both menu and wine-list on one side.

"Sarah, there are a lot of things I have to discuss with you."

Of course, she thought. The wedding and honeymoon. Exciting, breath-taking plans.

"First of all, I want to apologize for not phoning you last night. I became very involved with my family and there were various difficulties. I hope you'll forgive me and understand."

She smiled thankfully, eager to forgive. "Of course, Jonny. I thought something like that must have happened."

"Secondly I have to apologize for my manner on the phone the other night. I'm afraid I must have sounded very odd indeed but again I was heavily involved with other things and I wasn't expecting you to call. I hope you didn't think I wasn't pleased that you were going to come over to England earlier than expected. It was a wonderful surprise."

"You—did sound a little strange."

"I know." He picked up the wine-list and put it down again restlessly. "Let me try and explain what's been happening. I arrived here to find my mother had left her house in Halkin Street, so naturally I had to spend time tracing her before I could go and see her. That all took time, and then I managed to meet Justin and have a talk with him—"

"You did?" She had heard all about Justin, and Jon's plans to invite him to Canada. "Is it all right? What did he say?"

"He's coming to Canada. He hesitated at first, but now he's made up his mind, so that's all settled, thank God." He unfolded the table napkin absentmindedly and fingered the soft linen. "Then there were various other people I had to see—Max Alexander, an old friend of mine, for instance . . . and various others. I haven't had much time to spare since I arrived."

"No, you must have been very busy." She watched his restless fingers. "What about the wedding, Jonny, and the honeymoon? Or haven't you had much chance to make any more definite arrangements yet?"

"That," said Jon, "is what I want to talk to you about."

The first course arrived with the first wine. Waiters flitted around the table and then withdrew in a whirl of white coats.

"What do you mean, darling?"

He took a mouthful of hors d'oeuvres and she had to wait a moment for his reply. Then: "I want to get married right away," he said suddenly, looking straight into her eyes. "I can get a special license and we can be married just as soon as possible. Then maybe a honeymoon in Spain, Italy, Paris—wherever you like, and a few days in England before we fly back to Canada with Justin."

She stared at him, the thoughts whirling dizzily in her brain. "But Jon, Mummy and Daddy aren't here. I—I haven't bought all the trousseau. . . . I was waiting till Mummy was here before I bought the last few things—"

"Hell to the trousseau. I don't care if you come away with me dressed in a sack. And why can't you go shopping without your mother? I'm sure your taste is just as good if not better than hers."

"But Jon—"

"Do you really feel you can't get married without your parents being here?"

She swallowed, feeling as if she was on a tightrope struggling to keep her balance. "I—I just want to be fair to them, and—and I know . . . Yes, I do want them to be here, Jon, I really do. . . . But if—I just don't understand. Why are you in such a hurry to get married all of a sudden?"

He looked at her. She felt herself blush without knowing why, and suddenly she was afraid, afraid of the Distant Mood, afraid of hurting her parents, afraid of the wedding and the first night of the honeymoon.

"Jon, I—"

"I'm sorry," he said, his hand closing on hers across the table. "That was wrong of me. Of course you shall have your parents here. I was just being selfish and impatient."

"Perhaps I'm the one who's being selfish," she said ashamed. "I did say I wanted a quiet wedding—"

"But not as quiet as the one I've just suggested." He wasn't angry. "It's all right—I understand. We'll keep it the way you want it. After all, the actual wedding will be much more important to you than to me. That's only natural."

"I suppose so," she said, struggling to understand. "The wedding's the bride's day, isn't it? And then, of course, you've been married before so—"

"So I'm blasé about it!" he teased, and she smiled.

They concentrated on the hors d'oeuvres for a few minutes.

"Sarah."

Something else was coming. She could sense her nerves tightening and her heart thudding a shade quicker as she waited.

"No matter when we get married, I would like to talk to you a little about Sophia."

She took a sip of wine steadily, trying to ignore the growing tension in her limbs. "You needn't talk about her if you don't want to, Jon. I understand."

"I don't want you to get one of these dreadful first-wife complexes," he said, laying down his knife and fork and slumping back in his chair. "Don't for God's sake, start imagining Sophia to be something so exotic that you can hardly bear to tip-toe in her footsteps. She was a very ordinary girl with a lot of sex-appeal. I married her because I was young enough to confuse lust with love. It's quite a common mistake, I believe." He drained his glass and toyed idly with the stem as his eyes glanced round the room. "For awhile we were very happy, and then she became bored and I found I could no longer love her or confide in her as I had when I married her. We quarreled a lot. And then, just as I was thinking of the idea of divorce, she had the accident and died. It was complete and utter hell for me and for everyone else who was staying at Clougy at the time, especially as the inquest had a lot of publicity in the local papers and all sorts of rumors started to circulate. One rumor even said that I'd killed her. No doubt some vicious-minded crank had heard we weren't on the best of terms and had drawn his own melodramatic conclusions when he heard that Sophia had fallen down the cliff path and broken her neck on the rocks below. . . . But it was an accident. The jury said it could have been suicide because she wasn't happy at Clougy, but that was ridiculous. They didn't know Sophia and how much she loved life—even if life merely consisted of living at Clougy far from the glamor of London. Her death was an accident. There's no other explanation."

She nodded. Waiters came and went. Another course was laid before her.

"And anyway," said Jon, "why would I have wanted to kill her? Divorce is the civilized method of discarding an unwanted spouse, and I had no reason to prefer murder to divorce." He started to eat. "However, I'm wandering from the point. I just wanted to tell you that you needn't ever worry that you're inadequate compared to Sophia, because there simply is no comparison. I love you in many different ways and Sophia I only loved in one way—and even that way turned sour in the end. . . . You understand, don't you? You follow what I'm saying?"

"Yes, Jon," she said. "I understand." But her thoughts, the most private of her thoughts which she would never have disclosed to anyone, whispered: She must have been very good in bed. Supposing . . . And then, even her private thoughts subsided into a mass of blurred fears and worries which she automatically pushed to the furthest reaches of her mind.

Jon was smiling at her across the table, the special message of laughter and love in his eyes. "You still want to marry me?"

She smiled back, and suddenly she loved him so much that nothing mattered in all the world except her desire to be with him and make him happy. "Yes," she said impulsively. "I do. But don't let's wait for my parents, Jonny—I've changed my mind. Let's get married right away after all. . . ."

II

At half-past eleven that night, Jon dialed a London telephone number.

"Everything's fine," he said into the receiver presently. "We're marrying this week, honeymoon in Paris for ten days, a pause for a day or two in London to collect Justin, and then we all go back to Canada—and well away from the anonymous phone caller and any danger of Sarah finding out anything. It's best for her not to know."

A pause.

"Yes, I did. No trouble at all. She didn't even ask any questions about Sophia. I concentrated on the angle you suggested."

Another pause. The night deepened. Then: "How will I explain to her? It'll look pretty damned odd if I go back there, especially in view of my conversation with her tonight about Sophia. . . . Why yes, of course! Yes, that's reasonable enough . . . All right, I'll see you in about a fortnight's time, then. Goodbye, darling . . . and think of me."

III

The hotel in Paris was very large and grand and comfortable, and Sarah beneath her gay smile and excited eyes felt very small and lost and nervous. Later in the evening at the famous restaurant she tried to do justice to the food that was placed before her, but the nervousness and tension only increased until she could not eat any more. And then at last they returned to the hotel, said goodnight to the team on duty at the reception desk and travelled up in the elevator to their suite on the first floor.

Jon wandered into the bathroom. As Sarah undressed slowly she heard the hiss of the shower, and knew that she would have a few minutes to herself. She tried not to think of Sophia. What would Sophia have done on her wedding night? She wouldn't have sat trembling through an exotic dinner or spent precious minutes fumbling to undress herself with leaden fingers. . . . Perhaps Jon had lived with Sophia before he had married her. He had never asked Sarah to do such a thing, but then of course she was different, and Sophia had been so very attractive—and foreign. . . . Being foreign probably made a difference. Or did it?

She sat down at the dressing-table in her nightdress and fidgeted uncertainly with her hair. I wonder what Sophia looked like, she thought. I've never asked Jon. But she must have been dark like Justin, and probably slim and supple. Darker and slimmer than I am, I expect. And more attractive, of course. Oh God, how angry Jon would be if he could hear me! I must stop thinking of Sophia.

Jon came back from the bathroom and threw his clothes carelessly into an armchair. He was naked.

"Perhaps I'll have a bath," said Sarah to her fingernails. "Would it matter, do you think?"

"Not in the least," said Jon, "except that we'll both be rather hot in bed."

The bathroom was a reassuring prison of steam and warmth. The bath took a long time to run, almost as long as it took her to wash. She lingered, drying herself and then paused to sit on the stool as the tears started to prick her eyes. She tried to fight them back, and then suddenly she was caught in a violent wave of homesickness and the tears refused to be checked. The room swam, the sobs twisted and hurt her throat as she fought against them, and she was just wondering how she would ever have the strength to return to the bedroom when Jon tried the handle of the locked door.

"Sarah?"

She wept soundlessly, not answering.

"Can you let me in?"

She tried to speak but could not.

"Please."

Dashing away her tears she stumbled to the door and unlocked it. As she returned blindly to the stool and the mirror she heard Jon come in. She waited, dreading his mood, praying he wouldn't be too angry.

"Sarah," she heard him say. "Darling Sarah." And suddenly he had taken her gently in his arms as if she had been very small, and was pressing her tightly to him in a clumsy comforting gesture which she found unexpectedly moving. She had never before thought him capable of great tenderness. "You're thinking of Sophia," he whispered in her ear. "I wish you wouldn't. Please, Sarah, don't think of Sophia any more."

The fears ebbed from her mind; when he stooped his head to kiss her on the mouth at last she was conscious first and foremost of the peace in her heart before her world quickened and whirled into the fire.

IV

When they arrived back in London ten days later, Jon spent two hours making involved transatlantic telephone calls and dealing with various urgent business commitments; his right-hand man, whom Sarah had met in Canada, had flown to Europe for some reason connected with the business, and the first night in town was spent in dining with him at a well-known restaurant. On the following day they had lunch with Camilla in Knightsbridge. When they were travelling back to their hotel afterwards, Sarah turned to Jon with a puzzled expression in her eyes.

"Where was Justin? He was never mentioned, so I didn't like to ask."

"There was a slight awkwardness when he decided he was going to Canada to work for me. After he had given in his notice and finished his work in the City I gave him some money and told him to go on holiday until I was ready to go back to Canada, and in fact he's gone down to Cornwall to stay with a cousin of mine."

"Oh, I see."

The taxi cruised gently out of the Hyde Park underpass and accelerated into Piccadilly. On the right lay the green trees of the park and the warmth of the summer sun on the short grass. It was hot.

"As a matter of fact," said Jon idly, glancing out of the window, "I'd rather like you to meet this cousin of mine. I thought maybe we might hire a car and drive down to Cornwall this weekend and spend a few days in the country before flying straight back to Canada."

Sarah glanced up at the cloudless sky and thought longingly of golden sands and waves breaking and curling towards the shore. "That sounds lovely, Jonny. I'd like to stay just a little longer in England, especially as the weather's so good now."

"You'd like to go?"

"Very much. Whereabouts does your cousin live?"

"Well . . ." He paused. The taxi approached the Ritz and had to wait at the traffic lights. "As it happens," he said at last, "she's now living at Clougy."

The lights flashed red and amber; a dozen engines throbbed in anticipation.

"When I left ten years ago," Jon said, "I never wanted to see the place again. I nearly sold it so that I could wash my hands of it once and for all, but at the last minute I changed my mind and gave it to my cousin instead. It was such a beautiful place, and so unique. I loved it better than any other place in the world at one time, and I suppose even after everything that had happened I was still too fond of the house to sell it to a stranger. My cousin goes back there once or twice a year and lets it for periods during the summer. I saw her briefly in London before you arrived, and when she talked of Clougy and how peaceful it was I found I had a sudden longing to go back just to see if I could ever find it peaceful again. I think perhaps I could now after ten years. I know I could never live there permanently again, but when my cousin suggested we go down to stay with her for a few days I felt so tempted to go back for a visit. . . . Can you understand? Or perhaps you would rather not go."

"No," she said automatically, "I don't mind at all. It won't have any memories for me. If you're willing to go back, Jon, then that's all that matters." But simultaneously she thought: How could he even think of going back? And her mind was confused and bewildered as she struggled to understand.

"It's mainly because of my cousin," he said, as if sensing her difficulties. "I'd love to have the chance to see her again and I know she's anxious to meet you."

"You've never mentioned her to me before," was all she could say. "Or is she one of the cousins on your mother's side of the family, the ones you said you wouldn't trouble to invite to the wedding?"

"No, Marijohn is my only relation on my father's side of the family. We spent a lot of time together until I was seven, and then after my parents' divorce my father took her away from the house where I lived with my mother and sent her to a convent. He was her guardian. I didn't see much of her after that until I was about fifteen, and my father returned to England for good to live in London and remove Marijohn from the convent. I saw a great deal of her then until I married and went down to Cornwall to live. I was very fond of her."

"Why didn't you invite her to the wedding?"

"I did mention it to her, but she couldn't come."

"Oh."

"I don't know why I didn't mention her to you before," he said vaguely as the taxi drew up outside the hotel. "I lost touch with her when I went to Canada and I didn't honestly expect to see her again when I returned. However, she heard I was in London and we had a brief meeting. . . . So much happened in those two days before you arrived, and then, of course, when you did arrive I forgot everything except the plans for the wedding and the honeymoon. But when I woke this morning and saw the sunshine and the blue sky I remembered her invitation to Clougy and started wondering about a visit to Cornwall. . . . You're sure you'd like to come? If you'd rather stay in London don't be afraid to say so."

"No, Jon," she said. "I'd like to spend a few days by the sea." And as she spoke she thought: There's still so much about Jon that I don't understand and yet he understands me through and through. Or does he? Perhaps if he really understood me he'd know I don't want to go to the house where he lived with his first wife. . . . But maybe I'm being unnecessarily sensitive. If he had an ancestral home I would go back there to live with him no matter how many times he'd been previously married, and wouldn't think it in the least strange. And Jon has no intention of living at Clougy again anyway; he's merely suggesting a short visit to see his cousin. I'm being absurd, working up a Sophia complex again. I must pull myself together.

"Tell me more about your cousin, Jon," she said as they got out of the taxi. "What did you say her name was?"

But when they went into the hall Jon's Canadian business associate crossed the lobby to meet them, and Marijohn wasn't mentioned again till later in the afternoon when Jon went up to their room to make two telephone calls, one to his cousin in

Cornwall and the other to inquire about hiring a car to take them to St. Just. When he came back he was smiling and her uneasiness faded as she saw he was happy.

"We can have a car tomorrow," he said. "If we leave early we can easily do the journey in a day. We'll be a long way ahead of the weekend holiday traffic, and the roads shouldn't be too bad."

"And your cousin? Is she pleased?"

"Yes," said Jon, pushing back his hair in a luxurious, joyous gesture of comfort. "Very pleased indeed."

V

The sun was a burst of red above the sea by the time they reached the airport at St. Just, and as Jon swung the car off on to the road that led to Clougy, his frame seemed to vibrate with some fierce excitement which Sarah sensed but could not share. She glanced back over her shoulder at the soothing security of the little airport with its small plane waiting motionless on the runway, and then stared at the arid, sterile beauty of the Cornish moors.

"Isn't it wonderful?" said John to her, his hands gripping the wheel, his eyes blazing with joy. "Isn't it beautiful?"

And suddenly she was infected by his excitement so that the landscape no longer seemed repellant in its bleakness but fascinating in its austerity.

The car began to purr downhill; after a moment Sarah could no longer see the small huddle of the airport buildings with their hint of contact with the civilized world far away, and soon the car was travelling into a green valley dotted with isolated farms and squares of pasture bordered by gray stone walls. The road was single-track only now; the gradient was becoming steeper, and the sea was temporarily hidden from them by sloping hills. Soon they were passing the gates of a farm, and the next moment the car was grating from the smooth tarmac on to the rough uneven stones of a cart-track. As they passed the wall by the farm gate, Sarah was just able to catch a glimpse of a notice with an arrow pointing down the track, and above the arrow someone had painted the words "To Clougy."

The car crawled on, trickling downhill stealthily over the rough track. On either side the long grass waved gracefully in the soft breeze from the sea, and above them the sky was blue and cloudless.

"There's the water wheel," said Jon, and his voice was scarcely louder than an unspoken thought, his hands tightening again on the wheel in his excitement. "And there's Clougy."

The car drifted on to smoother ground and then turned into a small driveway. As the engine died Sarah heard for the first time the rushing water of the stream as it passed the disused water wheel on the other side of the track and tumbled down towards the sea.

"How quiet it is," she said automatically. "How peaceful after London."

Jon was already out of the car and walking toward the house. Opening her own door she stepped on to the gravel of the drive and stood still for a moment, glancing around her. There was a green lawn, not very big, with a white swing-seat at one end. The small garden was surrounded by clumps of rhododendron and other shrubs and there were trees, bent backwards into strange contorted shapes by the prevailing wind from the sea. She was standing at one side of the house but slightly in front of it so that from her angle she could glimpse the yellow walls and white shutters as they basked in the summer sun. A bird sang, a cricket chirped and then there was silence, except for the rushing stream and, far away, the distant murmur of the tide on the pebbled beach.

"Sarah!" called Jon.

"Coming!" She stepped forward, still feeling mesmerized by the sense of peace, and as she moved she saw that he was in the shade of the porch waiting for her.

She drew closer, feeling absurdly vulnerable as she crossed the sunlit drive while he watched her from the shadows, and then she saw that he was not alone and the odd feeling of defenselessness increased. It must be a form of self-consciousness, she thought. She felt exactly as if she were some show exhibit being scrutinized and examined by a row of very critical judges. Ridiculous.

And then she saw the woman. There was a dull gleam of golden hair, the wide slant of remote eyes, the slight curve of a beautiful mouth, and as Sarah paused uncertainly, waiting for Jon to make the introductions, she became aware of an extreme stillness as if the landscape around them was tensed and waiting for something beyond her understanding.

Jon smiled at the woman. He made no effort to speak, but for some odd reason his silence didn't matter, and it suddenly occurred to Sarah that she had not heard one word exchanged between the two of them even though she had been well within earshot when they had met. She was just wondering if Jon had kissed his cousin, and was on the point of thinking that it was most unlikely that they would have embraced without some form of greeting, when the woman stepped from the shadows into the sunlight.

"Hullo, Sarah," she said. "I'm so glad you could come. Welcome to Clougy, my dear, and I hope you'll be very happy here."

Two

THEIR BEDROOM was filled with the afternoon sun, and as Sarah crossed to the window she saw the sea shimmering before her in the cove, framed by the twin hillsides on either side of the house. She caught her breath, just as she always did when she saw something very beautiful, and suddenly she was glad they had come and ashamed of all her misgivings.

"Have you got everything you want here?" said Marijohn, glancing round the room with the eye of a careful hostess. "Let me know if I've forgotten anything. Dinner will be in about half an hour, and the water's hot if you should want a bath."

"Thank you," said Sarah, turning to face her with a smile. "Thank you very much."

Jon was walking along the corridor just as Marijohn left the room. Sarah heard his footsteps pause.

"When's dinner? In about half an hour?"

Marijohn must have made some gesture of assent which she didn't say aloud. "I'll be in the kitchen for a while."

"We'll come down when we're ready, and have a drink." He walked into the room, closed the door behind him and yawned luxuriously, stretching every muscle with slow precision. "Well?" he inquired presently.

"Well?" She smiled at him.

"Do you like it?"

"Yes," she said. "It's very beautiful, Jon."

He kicked off his shoes, pulled off his shirt and waded out of his trousers. Before she turned back uneasily towards the window to watch the sun sparkling on the sea she saw him pull back the covers from the bed and then fling himself down on the smooth white linen.

"What shall I wear for dinner?" she said hesitantly. "Will Marijohn change?"

He didn't reply.

"Jon?"

"Yes?"

She repeated the question.

"I don't know," he said. "Does it matter?" His fingers were smoothing the linen restlessly, and his eyes were watching his fingers.

She said nothing, every nerve in her body slowly tightening as the silence became prolonged. She had almost forgotten how frightened she was of his Distant Mood.

"Come here a moment," he said abruptly, and then, as she gave a nervous start of surprise: "Good God, you nearly jumped out of your skin! What's the matter with you?"

"Nothing, Jon," she said, moving towards him. "Nothing at all."

He pulled her down on to the sheets beside him and kissed her several times on the mouth, throat and breasts. His hands started to hurt her. She was just wondering how she could escape from making love while he was in his present mood, when he rolled away from her and stood up lazily in one long fluent movement of his body. He still didn't speak. She watched him open a suitcase, empty the entire contents on to the floor and then survey the muddle without interest.

"What are you looking for, darling?"

He shrugged. Presently he found a shirt and there was a silence while he put it on. Then: "You must be tired after the journey," he said at last.

"A little." She felt ashamed, inadequate, tongue-tied.

For a moment she thought he wasn't going to say anything else but she was mistaken.

"Sex still doesn't interest you much, does it?"

"Yes, it does," she said in a low voice, the unwanted tears pricking at the back of her eyes. "It's just that it's still rather new to me and I'm not much good when you're rough and start to hurt."

He didn't answer. She saw him step into another pair of trousers and then, as he moved over to the basin to wash, everything became blurred and she could no longer see. Presently she found a dress amongst the luggage and started to change from her blouse and skirt, her movements automatic, her fingers stiff and clumsy as she fumbled with zip fasteners and buttonholes.

"Are you ready?" he said at last.

"Yes, almost." She didn't dare stop to re-apply her lipstick. There was just time to brush her hair lightly into position and then they were going out into the corridor and moving downstairs to the drawing-room, the silence a thick invisible wall between them.

Marijohn was already there but Justin had apparently disappeared to his room. Sarah sat down, her limbs aching with tension, the lump of misery still hurting her throat.

"What would you like to drink, Sarah?" said Marijohn.

"I—I don't mind. . . . Sherry or—or a martini—"

"I've some dry sherry. Would that do? What about you, Jon?"

Jon shrugged his shoulders again, not bothering to reply. Oh God, thought Sarah, how will she cope? Should I try to cover up for him? Oh Jon, Jon . . .

But Marijohn was pouring out a whisky and soda without waiting for him to answer. "I've enjoyed having Justin here," she said tranquilly, handing him his glass. "It's been fascinating getting to know him again. You remember how we used to puzzle over him, trying to decide who he resembled? It seems so strange now that there could ever have been any doubt."

Jon turned suddenly to face her. "Why?"

"He's like you, Jon. There's such a strong resemblance. It's quite uncanny sometimes."

"He doesn't look like me."

"What on Earth have looks got to do with it? Sarah, have a cocktail biscuit. Justin went specially to Penzance to buy some, so I suppose we'd better try and eat a few of them. . . . Jon darling, do sit down and stop being so restless—you make me feel quite exhausted, just sitting watching you. . . . That's better. Isn't the light unusual this evening? I have a feeling Justin has sneaked off somewhere to paint one of his secret watercolors. . . . You must persuade him to show you some of them, Jon, because they're very good—or at least, they seem good to me, but then I know nothing about painting. . . . You paint, don't you, Sarah?"

"Yes," said Jon, before Sarah could reply, and suddenly his hand was on hers again and she knew in a hot rush of relief that the mood had passed. "She also happens to be an authority on the Impressionists and the Renaissance painters and the—"

"Jon, don't exaggerate!"

And the golden light of the evening seemed to deepen as they laughed and relaxed.

After dinner Jon took Sarah down to the cove to watch the sunset. The cove was small and rocky, its beach strewn with huge boulders and smooth pebbles, and as Jon found a suitable vantage point Sarah saw the fins of the Atlantic sharks coasting offshore and moving slowly towards Cape Cornwall.

"I'm sorry," said Jon suddenly from beside her.

She nodded, trying to tell him without words that she understood, and then they sat down together and he put his arm round her shoulders, drawing her closer to him.

"What do you think of Marijohn?"

She thought for a moment, her eyes watching the light change on the sea, her ears full of the roar of the surf and the cry of the gulls. "She's very—" the words eluded her. Then: "—unusual," she said lamely at last, for lack of anything better to say.

"Yes," he said. "She is." He sounded tranquil and happy, and they sat for a while in silence as the sun began to sink into the sea.

"Jon."

"Yes?"

"Where—" She hesitated and then plunged on, reassured by his complete change of mood. "Where did Sophia—"

"Not here," he said at once. "It was farther along the cliff going south to Sennen. The cliff is shallow and sandy in parts and during the last war they cut steps to link the path with the flat rocks below for some reason. I won't take you out there, don't worry."

The sun disappeared beyond the rim of the world and the twilight began to gather beneath the red afterglow of the sky. They lingered for a while, both reluctant to leave the restless fascination of the sea, but in the end Jon led the way up the path back to the house. As they entered the driveway Marijohn came out to meet them, and Sarah wondered if she had been watching them from some vantage point upstairs as they walked up from the beach.

"Max phoned, Jon. He said you'd mentioned something about inviting him to Clougy for a day or two."

"God, so I did! When I dined with him in London he said he would have to go down to Cornwall to visit a maiden aunt at Bude or Newquay or one of those huge tourist towns up the coast, and I told him there was a remote possibility that I might be revisiting Clougy at about this time . . . What a bloody nuisance! I don't want Max breezing up in his latest sports car with some goddamned woman on the seat beside him. Did he leave his phone number?"

"Yes, he was speaking from Bude."

"Hell . . . I'd better invite him to dinner or something. No, that's not really very sociable—I suppose he'll have to stay the night. . . . No, damn it, why should he turn up here and use Clougy as a base for fornication? I had enough of that in the past."

"He may be alone."

"What, Max? Alone? Don't be ridiculous! Max wouldn't know what to do with himself unless he had some woman with him all the time!"

"He didn't mention a woman."

Jon stared. "Do you want him here?"

"You made the gesture of having dinner with him in London and renewing the friendship. He's obviously content to forget. If you made a semi-invitation to him to visit Clougy, then I don't see how you can turn round now and tell him to go to hell."

"I can do what I damn well like," said Jon. He turned to Sarah. "I've told you about Max, haven't I? Would you be cross if he came to dinner tomorrow and spent the night?"

"No, darling, of course not. I'd like to meet him."

"All right, then. So be it." He turned aside and then glanced at her. "You go up to bed if you're tired. I won't be long. I'd better phone Max now while I still feel in a hospitable mood."

"All right," she said, glad of the excuse to go to bed, for she was by now feeling sleepy after the long journey followed by the long hours of sea air. "I'll go on up. Goodnight, Marijohn."

"Goodnight." The mouth smiled faintly. When Sarah paused at the top of the stairs to glance back into the hall, she saw that the woman was still watching her, but even as she stopped abruptly on the landing, Marijohn merely smiled again and moved into the livingroom to join Jon.

The door closed softly behind her.

Sarah still stood motionless at the top of the stairs. Two minutes elapsed, then a third. Suddenly, without knowing the reason but moving through instinct, she padded softly back downstairs and tiptoed across the hall until she was standing outside the door of the drawing-room.

Jon wasn't on the phone.

"There's only one thing that puzzles me," she heard him say, and her cheeks were hot with shame as she stood eavesdropping on their conversation. "And that's the anonymous phone call I had on my arrival in London, the call saying I'd killed Sophia.

I still don't understand who it could have been. It must have been either Michael or Max or Eve, but why didn't they follow it up with something definite such as blackmail? It doesn't make sense."

There was a long pause. And then Jon said sharply: "What do you mean?"

"I tried to tell you before dinner when we were all having drinks."

Another silence. Then: "No," said Jon. "I don't believe it. It couldn't have been. You don't mean—"

"Yes," said Marijohn quietly from far away. "It was Justin."

II

The sound of the piano drifted from the house and floated up the cliff path which led north to Cape Cornwall and Zennor Head. Justin's knowledge of classical music was adequate but not exceptional; he could not name the title of the Mozart composition.

He was just gathering his painting gear together and stowing it neatly in his canvas bag when below him he heard the music stop and then far away the distant click of a latch as the French windows into the garden opened. He paused, straining his eyes in the gathering dusk, and saw a figure leave the shadow of the rhododendrons and stop to scan the hillside.

Automatically, without hesitation, Justin stepped behind a rock.

Footsteps sounded faintly, growing louder with every second. Justin scowled at his painting gear, shoved it behind a boulder and sat down waiting, his eyes watching the night darken the sea. He didn't have to wait very long.

"Ah, there you are," said Jon easily, stepping out of the darkness. "I thought you might be up here. Have you been painting?"

"No, I went for a walk." He stared out to sea, as his father sat down beside him on the long rock and took out a cigarette case.

"Justin, if I ask you an honest question will you try and give me an honest answer?"

The sea was a dark motionless pool, the surf distant flecks of gray. "Of course," said Justin politely, and felt the sweat begin to moisten his palms.

"Does this place remind you too much of your mother?"

"My mother?" His voice was untroubled, vaguely surprised, but his eyes didn't see the view before him any more, only the bowl of cherries long ago and the woman's voice saying indulgently, "But you'll get so *fat*, Justin!" He cleared his throat. "Yes, it does remind me of her from time to time. But not enough to matter. I'm glad I came back because it was like coming home after a long time abroad."

"You were very fond of your mother, weren't you?"

Justin said nothing.

"I didn't realize," said Jon, "that you blamed me for her death."

Horror ebbed through Justin in dark suffocating waves. Putting his hands palm downwards on either side of his thighs, he clasped the ridge of rock and stared blindly down at the dusty path beneath his feet.

"What happened, Justin?" said his father's voice gently. "Why did you think I'd murdered her? Did you overhear something? Did you see us quarrel once when we didn't know you were there?"

He managed to shake his head.

"Then why?"

"I—" He shrugged his shoulders, glad of the darkness which hid his tears. "I—I don't know."

"But there must be some reason. You wouldn't have made the phone call unless there was some reason."

"I hated you because I thought you hadn't written and because I thought you were going to pass through London without bothering to contact me. It—it doesn't matter now." He took a deep breath, filling his lungs with the sea air. "I'm sorry," he whispered, the apology little more than a sigh. "I didn't mean it."

The man was silent, thinking.

"How did you know about the call?" said Justin suddenly. "How did you know it was me?"

"Marijohn guessed."

"But how did she know?"

"She says you are very like me and so she finds it easy to understand you."

"I don't see how she can possibly understand." He clasped the ridge of rock a little tighter. "And I'm not like you at all."

There was silence.

"When I was ten," said Jon, "my father paid one of his rare visits to London. The news of his arrival was in the evening paper because the expedition had received a certain amount of publicity, and my mother spent the entire evening saying she was quite sure he wouldn't bother to come and see me. So, just out of interest, I sent a telegram to his hotel saying I was dead, and sat back to watch the results. I expect you can imagine what happened—complete chaos. My mother wept all over the house saying she couldn't think who could have been so cruel as to play such a dreadful practical joke, and my father without hesitation took me by the scruff of the neck and nearly belted the life out of me. I never forgave him for that beating; if he hadn't neglected me for years at a time I wouldn't have sent the telegram, so in effect he was punishing me for his own sins."

Justin swallowed unevenly. "But you didn't neglect me."

"I did when you didn't answer my letters." He leaned back, slumping against another rock and drew heavily on his cigarette so that the glowing tip wavered in the darkness. "Justin, I have to know. Why did you think I'd killed your mother?"

"I—I knew she wasn't faithful to you." He leaned forward, closing his eyes for a moment in a supreme effort to explain his emotions of ten years ago. "I knew you quarreled, and it gradually became impossible for me to love you both any more. It was like a war in which one was forced to choose sides. And I chose your side because you always had time for me and you were strong and kind and I admired you more than anyone else in the world. So when she died, I—I didn't blame you, I only knew it was just and right, and so I never said a word to anyone, not even to you because I thought it was the best way of showing my—my loyalty—that I was on your side. And then when you went away to Canada and I never heard from you again, I began to think I'd made the wrong judgment and gradually I grew to hate you enough to make that phone call when you came back to London." He stopped. Far away below them, the surf thudded dully on the shingle and the waves burst against the black cliffs.

"But Justin," said Jon, "I didn't kill your mother. It was an accident. You must believe that, because it's the truth."

Justin turned his head slowly to face him. There was a long silence.

"Why did you think I'd killed her, Justin?"

The night was still, the two men motionless beneath the dark skies. For a moment Justin had a long searing desire to tell the truth, and then the ingrained convictions of ten years made him cautious and he shrugged his shoulders vaguely before turning away to stare out to sea.

"I suppose," he said vaguely, "because I knew you were always quarreling and I felt you hated her enough to have pushed her to death. I was only a child, muddled and confused. I didn't really know anything at all."

Was it Justin's imagination or did his father seem to relax almost imperceptibly in relief? Justin's senses sharpened, his mind torn by doubts. In the midst of all his uncertainties he was aware of his brain saying very clearly: I must know. I can't let it rest now. I must find out the truth before I go away to Canada. Aloud he said: "Shall we go back to the house? I'm getting rather cold as I forgot to bring a sweater and Marijohn and Sarah will be wondering where we are . . ."

III

It was late when Jon came to the bedroom, and Sarah opening her eyes in the darkness, saw that the luminous hands of her clock pointed to half-past eleven. She waited, pretending to be asleep, and presently he slid into bed beside her and she felt his body brush lightly against her own. He sighed, sounding unexpectedly weary, and she longed to take him in her arms and say, "Jonny, why didn't you tell me about the anonymous phone call? You told me about the dreadful rumors which circulated after Sophia's death, so why not tell me about the call? And after Marijohn had said the caller was Justin, why did you go through to the other room to the piano and start playing that empty stilted rondo of Mozart's which I know perfectly well you dislike? And why did you say nothing else to Marijohn and she say nothing to you? The conversation should have begun then, not ended. It was all so strange and so puzzling, and I want so much to understand and help . . ."

But she said nothing, not liking to confess that she had eavesdropped on their conversation by creeping back downstairs and listening at the closed door, and presently Jon was breathing evenly beside her and the chance to talk to him was gone.

When she awoke the piano was playing again far away downstairs and the sun was slanting sideways through the curtains into the room. She sat up. It was after nine. As she went down the corridor she heard the sound of the piano more clearly and she realized with a shaft of uneasiness that he was again playing Mozart. After a quick bath she dressed in a pair of slacks and a shirt and went tentatively downstairs to the music room.

He was playing the minuet from the thirty-ninth symphony, lingering over the full pompous chords and the mincing quavers so that the arrangement bore the faint air of a burlesque.

"Hullo," she said lightly, moving into the room. "I thought you didn't like Mozart? You never played his music at home." She stopped to kiss the top of his head. "Why have you suddenly gone Mozart-mad?" And then she suddenly glanced over her shoulder and saw that Marijohn was watching them from the window-seat.

Jon yawned, decided to abandon classical music altogether and began to play the Floyd Cramer arrangement of Hank Williams' "You Win Again." "Breakfast is ready and waiting for you, darling," he said leisurely. "Justin's in the diningroom and he'll show you where everything is."

"I see." She went out of the room slowly and made her way towards the diningroom; she felt baffled and ill-at-ease for a reason she could not define, and her uneasiness seemed to cast a shadow over the morning so that she started to feel depressed. She opened the diningroom door and decided that she didn't want much breakfast.

"Good morning," said Justin. "Did you sleep well?"

"Yes," she lied. "Very well."

"Cereal?"

"No, thank you. Just toast." She sat down, watching him pour out her coffee, and suddenly she remembered the conversation she had overheard the previous night and recalled that for some unknown reason Justin had anonymously accused Jon of murdering Sophia.

"Are you sure you wouldn't like a cooked breakfast?" he asked politely. "There are sausages and eggs on the hot plate."

"No, thank you."

The piano started to play again in the distance, abandoning the American country music and reverting to classical territory with a Chopin prelude.

"Are you going painting this morning, Justin?" she asked, her voice drowning the noise of the piano.

"Perhaps. I'm not sure." He glanced at her warily over the *Times* and then stirred his coffee with nonchalance. "Why?"

"I thought I might try some painting myself," she said, helping herself to marmalade. "I was going to consult you about the best views for a landscape watercolor."

"Oh, I see." He hesitated, uncertain. "What about my father?"

"It rather sounds as if he's going to have a musical morning."

"Yes," he said. "I suppose it does."

"Does Marijohn play the piano?"

"No, I don't think so."

"Oh . . . the piano seems very well-tuned."

"Yes," said Justin. "But then she knew he was coming."

"She didn't know for certain till yesterday afternoon!"

He stared at her. "Oh no, she knew a long while before that. She had a man up from Penzance to tune the piano last week."

The shaft of uneasiness was so intense that it hurt. Sarah took a large sip of her coffee to steady her nerves and then started to spread the marmalade over the buttered toast.

From somewhere far away the piano stopped. Footsteps echoed in the corridor and the next moment Jon was walking into the room.

"How are you this morning, darling?" he said, kissing her with a smile and then moving over to the window to glance out into the garden. "You hardly gave me a chance to ask just now. . . . What do you want to do today? Anything special?"

"Well, I thought I might paint this morning, but—"

"Fine," he said. "Get Justin to take you somewhere nice. Marijohn has shopping to do in Penzance and I've promised to drive her over in the car. You don't want to come to Penzance, do you? It'll be crammed with tourists at this time of year and much too noisy. You stay here and do just what you like." He swung round to face her again, still smiling. "All right?"

"Yes . . . all right, Jon."

"Good! Look after her, Justin, and be on your best behavior." He moved to the door. "Marijohn?"

There was an answering call from the kitchen and he closed the door noisily behind him before moving off down the corridor to the back of the house.

Justin cleared his throat. "More coffee, Sarah?"

"No," she said. "No, thank you."

He stood up, easing back his chair delicately across the floor. "If you'll excuse me, I'll just go and assemble my painting gear. I won't be long. What time would you like to leave?"

"Oh . . . any time. Whenever you like."

"I'll let you know when I'm ready, then," he said and padded out of the room towards the hall.

She lingered a long time over the breakfast table before going upstairs to extract her paintbox and board from one of her suitcases. Jon called her from the hall just as she was pausing to tidy her hair.

"We're just off now, darling—sure you'll be all right?"

"Yes, I'm almost ready myself."

"Have a good time!"

She sat listening to the closing doors, the quick roar of the engine bursting into life, the crunch of the tires on the gravel, and then the sound of the car faded in the distance and she was alone. She went downstairs. In the drawing-room she found Justin waiting, studiously reading the *Times,* scrupulously dressed in the best English tailored casual clothes, but still managing to look like a foreigner.

"I don't know which way you'd like to go," he said. "We could take Marijohn's car and drive south to Sennen and Land's End, or north to Kenidjack Castle and Cape Cornwall. The views from the cliff out over the ruined mines of Kenidjack are good to paint." He paused, waiting for her comment, and when she nodded he said politely, "Would you care to go that way?"

"Yes, that sounds fine."

They set off, not speaking much, and drove north along the main road to the crossroads beyond St. Just where the left fork took them towards the sea to the mine workings of Kenidjack. At the end of the road high up on the cliffs they parked the car and started walking and scrambling over the hillside to the best view of the surrounding scenery. Below them the sea was a rich blue, shot with green patches near the off-shore rocks, and there was no horizon. As the cliff path wound steeply above the rocks the great cliffs of Kenidjack and the withered stones of the old mine workings rose ahead of them, and Sarah saw that the light was perfect. When she sat down at last, gasping after the climb, she felt the excitement quicken within her as she gazed over the shimmering view before her eyes.

"I've brought some lemonade and some biscuits," said Justin, modestly demonstrating his presence of mind. "It's hot walking."

They sat down and drank some lemonade in silence.

"It would be nice for a dog up here," said Sarah after a while. "All the space in the world to run and chase rabbits."

"We used to have a dog. It was a sheepdog called Flip, short for Philip, after the Duke of Edinburgh. My mother, like many foreigners, loved all the royal family."

"Oh." She broke off a semi-circle of biscuit and looked at it with unseeing eyes. "And what happened to Flip?"

"My mother had him put to sleep because he tore one of her best cocktail dresses to shreds. I cried all night. There was a row, I think, when my father came home." He reached for his canvas bag and took out his painting book absentmindedly. "I don't feel much like doing watercolors this morning. Perhaps I'll do a char-coal sketch and then work up a picture in oils later when I get home."

"Can I see some of your paintings?"

He paused, staring at a blank page. "You won't like them."

"Why not?"

"They're rather peculiar. I've never dared show them to any-one except Marijohn, and of course she's quite different."

"Why?" said Sarah. "I mean, why is Marijohn different?"

"Well, she is, isn't she? She's not like other people. . . . This is a watercolor of the cove—you probably won't recognize it. And this—"

Sarah drew in her breath sharply. He stopped, his face sud-denly scarlet, and stared down at his toes.

The painting was a mass of greens and grays, the sky torn by stormclouds, the rocks dark and jagged, like some monstrous animal in a nightmare. The composition was jumbled and unskilled, but the savage power and sense of beauty were unmistakable. Sarah thought of Jon playing Rachmaninoff. If Jon could paint, she thought, this is the type of picture he would produce.

"It's very good, Justin," she said honestly. "I'm not sure that I like it, but it's unusual and striking. Can you show me some more?"

He showed her three more, talking in a low, hesitant voice, the tips of his ears pink with pleasure.

"When did you first start painting?"

"Oh, long ago . . . when I went to public school, I suppose. But it's just a hobby. Figures are my real interest."

"Figures?"

"Math—calculations—odds. Anything involving figures. That's why I started with an insurance firm in the City, but it was pretty boring and I hated the routine of nine till five."

"I see," she said, and thought of Jon talking of his own first job in the city, Jon saying, "God, it was boring! Christ, the routine!"

Justin was fidgeting with a stick of charcoal, edging a black square on the cover of his paint book. Even his restlessness reminded her of Jon.

"You're not a bit as I imagined you would be," he said unexpectedly without looking up. "You're very different from the sort of people who used to come down here to Clougy."

"And very different from your mother too, I expect," she said levelly, watching him.

"Oh yes," he said, completely matter-of-fact. "Of course." He found a clean page in his book and drew a line with his stick of charcoal. "My mother had no interests or hobbies, like painting or music. She used to get so bored, and the weekend parties were her main interest in life. My father didn't really want them. Sometimes he and I used to walk down to the Flat Rocks just to get away from all the people—but she used to revel in entertaining guests, dreaming up exotic menus and planning midnight swimming parties in the cove."

"There were guests staying here when she died, weren't there?"

"Yes, that's right." He drew another charcoal line. "But no one special. Uncle Max drove down from London and arrived on Friday evening. He had a new car which he enjoyed showing off and boasting about as soon as he arrived, but it really was a lovely thing. He took me for a ride in it, I remember. . . . Have you met Uncle Max yet?"

"No, not yet."

"He was fun," said Justin. "He and my father used to laugh a lot together. But my mother thought he was rather boring. She was never interested in any man unless he was good-looking and was always bitchy to any woman who didn't look like the back end of a bus. . . . Uncle Max was very ugly. Not that it mattered. He always had plenty of girlfriends. My parents used to play a game whenever they knew he was coming down—it was called the Who-Will-Max-Produce-This-Time, and they used to try to guess what she would look like. The girl was always different each time, of course. . . . During that last weekend they played the game on the morning before Max arrived and bet each other he would turn up with a petite redhead with limpid blue eyes. They were so cross when he turned up with a statuesque blonde, very slim and tall and elegant. She was called Eve. I didn't like her at all because she never took any notice of me the entire weekend."

He closed the paint book, produced a pair of sunglasses and leaned back against the grassy turf to watch the blue sky far above. "Then Uncle Michael came down with Marijohn. They'd been in Cornwall on business, I think, and they arrived together at Clougy just in time for dinner. Uncle Michael was Marijohn's husband. I always called him Uncle, although I never called her Aunt . . . I don't know why. He was nice, too, but utterly different from Uncle Max. He was the sort of person you see on suburban trains in the rush-hour reading the law report in the *Times*. Sometimes he used to play French cricket with me on the lawn after tea. . . . And then there was Marijohn." He paused. "To be honest, I never liked her much when I was small, probably because I always felt she was never very interested in me. It's different now, of course—she's been so kind to me during the past fortnight, and I've become very fond of her. But ten years ago . . . I think she was really only interested in my father at the time. Nobody else liked her except him, you see. Uncle Max always seemed to want to avoid being alone with her, Eve the statuesque blonde, never seemed to find a word to say to her, and my mother naturally resented her because Marijohn was much more beautiful than she was. And Uncle Michael . . . no, I'd forgotten Uncle Michael. It was obvious he loved her. He kissed her in public and gave her special smiles—oh God, you know! The sort of thing you notice and squirm at when you're a small boy. . . . So there they all were at Clougy on Friday evening, and twenty-four hours later my mother was dead."

The sea murmured far away; gulls soared, borne aloft by the warm breeze.

"Was it a successful party?" Sarah heard herself say tentatively at last.

"Successful?" said Justin, propping himself upon one elbow to stare at her. "Successful? It was dreadful! Everything went wrong from start to finish. Uncle Max quarreled with the statuesque blonde—they had an awful row after breakfast on Saturday and she went and locked herself in her room. I've no idea what the row was about. Then when Uncle Max went to his car to work off his anger by driving, my mother wanted him to take her to St. Ives to get some fresh shellfish for dinner; but my father didn't want her to go so there was another row. In the end my father went off to the Flat Rocks and took me with him. It was terrible. He didn't speak a word the entire time. After a while Marijohn came and my father sent me back to the house to find out when lunch would be ready. We had a maid help at Clougy in those days to do the mid-day cooking when there were guests. When I got back to the house I found Uncle Michael looking for Marijohn so I told him to go down to the Flat Rocks. After I'd found out about the lunch and stopped for elevenses I started off back again, but I met my father on his own coming back from the cliff path and he took me back to the house and started to play the piano. He played for a long time. In the end I got bored and slipped back to the kitchen to inquire about lunch again. I was always hungry in those days. . . . And then Uncle Michael and Marijohn came back and shut themselves in the drawing-room. I tried listening at the key-hole but I couldn't hear anything, and anyway my father found me listening and was cross enough to slap me very hard across the seat of my trousers so I scuttled down to the cove out of the way after that. My mother and Uncle Max didn't come back for lunch and Eve stayed in her room. I had to take a tray up to her and leave it outside the door, but when I came to collect it an hour later it hadn't been touched so I sat down at the top of the stairs and ate it myself. I didn't think anyone would mind. . . .

"My mother and Uncle Max came back in time for tea. I was rather frightened, I think, because for some reason I expected my father to have the most almighty row with her, but—" He stopped pulling up grass with his fingers, his eyes staring out to sea.

"But what?"

"But nothing happened," said Justin slowly. "It was most odd. I can't quite describe how odd it was. My father was playing the piano and Marijohn was with him, I remember. Uncle Michael had gone fishing. And absolutely nothing happened. . . . After tea Uncle Max and my mother went down to the cove for a bathe, and still nothing happened. I followed them down to the beach but my mother told me to go away, so I walked along the shore till I found Uncle Michael fishing. We talked for a while. Then I went back and snatched some supper from the larder as I wasn't sure whether I'd be dining with the grown-ups or not. As it happened I was, but I didn't want to be hungry. Then Eve came downstairs, asking for Uncle Max and when I told her he'd gone swimming with my mother she walked off towards the cove.

"Dinner was at eight. It was delicious, one of my mother's best fish-dishes, fillet of sole garnished with lobster and crab and shrimps. . . . I had three helpings. I particularly remember because no one else ate at all. Eve had gone back to her room again, I believe, so that just left Max, Michael, Marijohn and my parents. My mother made most of the conversation but after a while she seemed bewildered and didn't talk so much. And then—" He stopped again, quite motionless, the palms of his hands flat against the springy turf.

"Yes?"

"And then Marijohn and my father started to talk. They talked about music mostly. I didn't understand a word of what they were saying and I don't think anyone else did either. At last my mother told me to go to bed and I said I'd help with the washing-up—my usual dodge for avoiding bed, as I used to walk into the kitchen and straight out of the back door—but she wouldn't hear of it. In the end it was Uncle Michael who took me upstairs, and when we stood up from the dinner table, everyone else rose as well and began to filter away. The last thing I remember as I climbed the stairs and looked back into the hall was my father putting on a red sweater as if he was going out. Uncle Michael said to me: 'What are you looking at?' and I couldn't tell him that I was wondering if my father was going out for a walk to the Flat Rocks and whether I could slip out and join him when everyone thought I was in bed. . . . But Uncle Michael was with me too long, and I never had the chance. He read me a chapter of *Treasure Island* which I thought was rather nice of him. However, when I was alone, I lay awake for a long time, wondering what was going on, and listening to the gramophone in the music room below. It was an orchestral record, a symphony, I think. After a while it stopped. I thought: maybe he's going down now to the Flat Rocks. So I got out of bed and pulled on a pair of shorts and pullover and my sand shoes. When I glanced out of the window, I saw a shadow move out of the driveway and so I slipped out to follow him.

"It was rather spooky in the moonlight. I remember being frightened, especially when I saw someone coming up the path from the beach towards me and I had to hide behind a rock. It was Eve. She was breathing hard as if she'd been running and her face was streaked with tears. She didn't see me."

He was silent, fingering the short grass, and after a while he took off his sunglasses and she saw his dark eyes had a remote, withdrawn expression.

"I went up the cliff path a long way, but he was always too far ahead for me to catch him up and the sea would have drowned my voice if I'd called out. In the end I had to pause to get my breath, and when I looked back I saw someone was following me. I was really scared then. I dived into a sea of bracken and buried myself as deep as I could. Presently the other person went by."

A pause. Around them lay the tranquillity of the summer morning, the calm sea, the still sky, the quiet cliffs.

"Who was it?" said Sarah at last.

Another pause. The scene was effortlessly beautiful. Then: "My mother," said Justin. "I never saw her again."

Three

I

WHEN THEY ARRIVED back at Clougy they found the car standing in the drive but the house was empty and still. In the kitchen something was cooking in the oven and two saucepans simmered gently on the stove; on the table was a square of paper covered with a clear printed writing.

"Justin!" called Sarah.

He was upstairs putting his painting gear away. "Hullo?"

"Marijohn wants you to go up to the farm to get some milk." She replaced the note absently beneath the rolling pin and wandered out into the hall just as he came downstairs to join her. "I wonder where they are," she said to him as he stopped to check how much money he had in his pockets. "Do you think they've gone down to the beach for a stroll before lunch?"

"Probably." He apparently decided he had enough money to buy the milk, and moved over to the front door. "Do you want to come up to the farm?"

"No, I'll go down to the beach to meet them and tell them we're back."

He nodded and stepped out into the sunshine of the drive. The gravel crunched beneath his feet as he walked away out of the gate and up the track to the farm.

After he had gone, Sarah followed him to the gate and took the path which led down into the cove, but presently she stopped to listen. It was very still. Far away behind her she could still hear the faint rush of the stream as it tumbled past the disused waterwheel. But apart from that there was nothing, only the calm of a summer morning and the bare rock-strewn hills on either side of her. London seemed a thousand miles away.

Presently the path forked, one turning leading up on to the cliffs, the other descending into the cove. She walked on slowly downhill, and suddenly the sound of the sea was in her ears and a solitary gull was swooping overhead with a desolate empty cry, and the loneliness seemed to increase for no apparent reason. At the head of the beach she paused to scan the rocks but there was no sign of either Jon or his cousin and presently she started to climb uphill to meet the cliff path in order to gain a better view of the cove.

The tide was out; the rocks stretched far into the sea. She moved further along the path round the side of the hill until presently, almost before she had realized it, the cove was hidden from her and the path was threading its way through the heather along the shallow cliff.

And below were the rocks. Hundreds of thousands of rocks. Vast boulders, gigantic slabs, small blocks of stone all tumbled at the base of the cliff and frozen in a jagged pattern as if halted by some invisible hand on their race into the sea.

The path forked again, one branch leading straight on along the same level, the other sloping downhill to the cliff's edge.

Sarah stopped.

Below her the rocks formed a different pattern. They were larger, smoother, flatter, descending in a series of levels to the waves far below. There were little inlets, all reflecting the blue sky, and the waves of the outgoing tide were gentle and calm as they washed effortlessly over the rocky shelves and through the seaweed lagoons.

It was then that she saw Jon's red shirt. It lay stretched out on a rock to dry beneath the hot sunshine, and as she strained her eyes to make sure she was not mistaken, she could see the pebbles weighting the sleeves to prevent the soft breeze from blowing it back into the water.

She moved on down the path to the cliff's edge. The cliff was neither very steep nor very high but she had to pause all the same to consider how she was going to scramble down. She saw the rough steps, but one was missing and another seemed to be loose; the sand around them bore no trace of footmarks to indicate that it would be easy enough to find another way down. She stood among the heather, her glance searching the cliff's edge, and suddenly she realized she was frightened and angry and puzzled. This was where Sophia had died. The steps were the ones leading down the cliff and the rocks below were the Flat Rocks. And Jon had come back. He had come back deliberately to the very spot where his wife had been killed. Marijohn had taken him. It was her fault. If he had not wanted to see her again he wouldn't have dreamed of returning to Clougy. He had talked of how fond he was of the place and how much he wanted to see it again in spite of all that had happened, but it had been a lie. He had come back to see Marijohn, not for any other reason.

She sat down suddenly in the heather, her cheeks burning, the scene blurring before her eyes. But why, her brain kept saying, trying to be sensible and reasonable. Why? Why am I crying? Why do I feel sick and miserable? Why am I suddenly so convinced that Jon came back here not because he loved Clougy but solely because of his cousin? And why should it matter even if he did? Why shouldn't he be fond of his cousin? Am I jealous? Why am I so upset? Why, why, why?

Because Jon lied to me. He had planned this trip before he ever mentioned it to me—and Marijohn had the piano tuned because she knew he was coming.

Because he talks to Marijohn of things which he has never mentioned to me.

Because this morning he preferred Marijohn's company to mine . . .

She dashed away her tears, pressing her lips together in a determined effort to pull herself together. She was being absurd, worse than an adolescent. Trust was a basic element of marriage, and she trusted Jon. Everything was perfectly all right and she was imagining all kinds of dreadful possibilities without a grain of proof. She would go down to the rocks to meet them because there was no reason why she should be afraid of what she might find and because it was utterly ridiculous to sit on top of a cliff weeping. She would go right away.

She found a way to the first shelf after a few minutes and started to scramble over towards the red shirt. In spite of herself she found she was thinking about Marijohn again. Marijohn wasn't like other people, Justin had said. Marijohn could talk to Jon when he was in the Distant Mood. She could cope with him when Sarah did not even begin to know how to deal with the situation. Marijohn . . .

The scramble over the rocks was more difficult than it had appeared from the cliff path above. She found herself making wide detours and after a time she had lost sight of the red shirt and realized she had been forced to move too far over to the left.

It was then that she heard Jon laugh.

She stopped, her heart thumping from the exertion of the scramble and from something else which she refused to acknowledge. Then, very slowly, despising herself for the subterfuge, she moved forward quietly, taking great care that she should see them before they should see her.

She suddenly realized she was very frightened indeed.

There was a large white rock ahead, its surface worn smooth by centuries of wind and rain. It was cold beneath her hot hands. She moved forward, still gripping the rock, and edged herself sideways until she could see round it to the rocks beyond.

Relief rushed through her in great warm overwhelming waves.

Beyond her was a small lagoon, similar to the ones she had seen from the cliff-path, and a flat ledge of rock sloped gently to the water's edge. Marijohn was lying on her back on the rocks enjoying the sunshine. She wore a white bathing costume and dark glasses which were tilted to the edge of her nose and as she gazed up at the blue sky far above her, her arms were behind her head, the palms of her hands pillowing her hair.

Jon, in black bathing trunks, was sitting by the water's edge some distance away from her and was paddling his feet idly in the still water of the lagoon.

Sarah was just about to call out to him and move out from behind the rock when Jon laughed again and splashed one foot lazily in the water.

Marijohn sat up slowly, propping herself on one elbow and took off her sunglasses. Sarah couldn't see her face, only the back of her shining hair and the smooth tanned skin above the edge of her bathing costume.

"Why?" she said. She said nothing else at all, only the one monosyllable, and Sarah wondered what she meant and what she was querying.

Jon swiveled round, and Sarah instinctively withdrew behind the white boulder so that he would not see her.

"I don't know," she heard him say uneasily. "There's no reason why I should feel so happy."

"I know."

There was a silence. When Sarah had the courage to look at them again she saw that Jon was standing up, looking out to sea and that although Marijohn was also standing up she was still several paces away from him.

They were motionless.

The sea lapped insistently at the rocks beyond the lagoon; a wave broke into the pool and the spray began to fly as the tide turned. Nothing else happened. There was no reason at all why suddenly Sarah should feel aware of panic. And as she stood rigid with fear, hardly able to breathe, she heard Jon say quietly to his cousin, "Why don't you come to Canada?"

There was a pause. Everything seemed to cease except the sea. Then: "My dear Jon, what on earth would be the point of that?"

"I don't know," he said, and he sounded strangely lost and baffled. "I don't know."

"We've been into all this before, Jon."

"Yes," he said emptily. "We've been into all this before."

"After your wife was dead and my marriage was in ruins we went into it in detail right here at Clougy."

"For God's sake!" he shouted suddenly. "For God's sake don't talk of that scene with Sophia again! Christ Almighty—"

"Jon, darling."

And still they stood apart from one another, he slumped against a rock, his hands tight, white fists at his sides, she motionless by the water's edge, the sun shining full on her hair.

"Marijohn," he said, "I know we've never, never mentioned this in words either now after I met you again or ten years ago after it all happened, but—"

"There's no need to mention it," she said swiftly. "I understand. There's no need to talk about it."

"But . . . oh God, why? Why, Marijohn? Why, why, why?"

She stared at him, still motionless, but somehow that strange stillness was lost as if a spell had been broken and the mystery of the quiet scene was shattered.

She doesn't understand him, thought Sarah suddenly. She's going to have to ask him what he means.

And somehow the knowledge was a victory which she could neither understand nor explain.

"Yes," said Jon. "Why? Why did you have to kill Sophia?"

A wave thudded against the rocks and exploded in a cloud of spray so that the lagoon was no longer still and peaceful but a turmoil of boiling surf. And after the roar of the undertow had receded came a faint shout from the cliff high above them, and Sarah saw Justin standing on the top of the cliffs waving to attract their attention.

She drew further out of sight at once so that he wouldn't see her, and began to scramble back over the rocks to find a hiding-place before the others started to retrace their steps to the cliff path. When she eventually sank down to rest behind a pile of boulders her breath was coming in gasps which hurt her lungs, and her whole body was trembling with the shock. She sat there numbly for a while, and then the tide began to surge across the rocks towards her as it ate its way greedily inland to the cliffs, and she knew she would have to go back.

Moving very slowly, she stood up and began to stumble blindly back towards the cliff path to Clougy.

II

When Justin returned from the farm with the milk he met the postman pushing his bicycle up the track from Clougy and they paused for a moment to talk to one another.

"Only two letters today," said the Cornishman placidly, extracting a large handkerchief to mop his forehead. "One for Mrs. Rivers, t'other for yourself. Lor' it's hot today, ain't it! Makes a change, I say. Too much rain lately."

Justin agreed politely.

Presently when he reached the house he put the milk down on the hall table and stopped to examine the mail. The letter to Marijohn was postmarked London, the address typewritten. Perhaps it was from Michael Rivers' office. Rivers, Justin knew, still handled Marijohn's legal affairs.

The other envelope was white and square and covered by a large level handwriting which he did not recognize, *J. Towers, Esq.*, the writer had scrawled, *Clougy, St. Just, Penzance, Cornwall*. The post-mark was also London.

Justin fumbled with the flap of the envelope, wondering who could be writing to him. The sensation of puzzled interest was pleasant and when he pulled the single sheet of white paper from the close-fitting envelope he sat down on the stairs before opening the folded slip of paper to see the signature.

The signature was very short. Only three letters. Someone had merely written *Eve* in that same large level handwriting, but even as he realized with a jolt that the letter wasn't meant for him his glance travelled to the top of the paper automatically.

Dear Jon, Eve had written. *Had dinner with Max in London last week. He wanted to know why you had asked him where I lived and why you had sounded so interested in me. We ended up by having a long talk about that time ten years ago, and in the end he told me you were back at Clougy and that he had decided to come down and see you. Just thought I'd drop you a line to warn you to be pretty damn careful, as he knows more than you think. If you're interested in hearing more about this, why don't you come and see me any time from Saturday onwards—address and phone number above. I'm staying in St. Ives for a few days and won't be going back to town till Tuesday. Eve.*

Justin read the letter three times. Then, very carefully, he replaced the sheet of notepaper in its neat white envelope and tucked the letter deep into the privacy of his wallet.

III

When Sarah reached the house at last there was a silver-gray Rolls Royce in the driveway and the sound of laughter floated from the open windows of the drawing-room towards her on the still air. She slipped into the house by the sidedoor and managed to creep up to her room without being seen. Sitting down in front of the dressing-table she stared into the mirror for one long moment before fumbling with the jars of make-up, and then she stood up blindly and moved into the bathroom to wash the tear-stains from her face. When she came back to the dressing-table Jon was on the lawn below and calling something over his shoulder.

". . . imagine what can have happened to her," she heard him say. "Are you sure she said she was going down to the cove, Justin?"

She could not hear Justin's reply. She stood by the window shielded by the curtain and watched Jon as he began to move forward again across the lawn.

". . . better go and find her in case she's got lost . . ." His voice tailed away and presently she found her view of him was blurring before her eyes until she could scarcely see.

She sat down again at the dressing-table.

"Of course she's not lost," Marijohn's voice said clearly from the lawn below, sounding surprisingly close at hand. "She's probably gone for a walk before lunch."

"Another walk?" said a man's unfamiliar drawl, sounding amused. "God, she must be an Amazon! No normal woman would spend the morning toiling up the cliffs at Kenidjack and then toiling over some more cliffs around Clougy for a pre-prandial stroll! Jon never told me he'd married one of these keen outdoor types."

"He hasn't," said Marijohn briefly. "She's not."

"Thank God for that! I had a sudden hideous vision of a hearty female with muscular shoulders and tombstone teeth. . . . What's she like? Is she pretty? Jon said that physically she was just like Sophia."

"Justin," said Marijohn to the room behind her. "Would you—"

"He's gone. He slipped out a second ago when I was making my anti-Amazon speech. Well, tell me about Sarah, Marijohn. Is she—"

"You'll meet her soon enough."

"Is Jon very much in love with her?"

"He married her."

"Yes, I know. I was very surprised. She must be damn good."

"Good?"

"In bed. Can I have another drink?"

"Of course."

There was a pause, the stillness of a hot summer morning.

"And you," said Max Alexander. "You. I'm surprised you never married again. What happened after the divorce? Did you go abroad? I never saw you in London."

"I worked in Paris for a while."

"God, that sounds glamorous!"

"It was extremely boring. I could only endure it for a year."

"And then?"

"I came back. Do you want some ice in your drink?"

"No, no, I can't bear this American fetish of loading every drink with ice. . . . Thanks . . . I see. And what did you do when you returned?"

"Nothing special."

"Did you come back here?"

"Not straight away."

"Lord, it's strange coming back! Didn't it seem strange to you?"

"No, why should it?"

"Why should it?"

"Yes, why should it? Clougy has many happy memories for me."

"You're not serious, of course."

"Perfectly. Why shouldn't I be?"

"Oh."

Another pause. A gull drifted far overhead, its wings outstretched, its neck craning towards the sun.

"I must say," said Max Alexander, "I never thought Jon would come back here, least of all with his new wife. Does he ever speak of Sophia?"

"Never."

"He's closed the door, as it were, on that part of his past?"

"Why do you suppose he asked you down here?"

"I was hoping," said Alexander, "that you could tell me."

"I'm not sure I quite understand you."

"No? Hell, Jon was crazy about Sophia, wasn't he? Any husband would have been. With a woman like that—"

"Sophia no longer exists. Jon's made a new life for himself and Sophia's memory is nothing to him now. Nothing at all."

"Yet he's married someone who physically and sexually—"

"Men often prefer one type of looks in a woman. It means nothing at all. Besides there's more to love than merely a sexual relationship or a physical attraction."

"That *is* the common delusion, I believe."

"You think any relationship between a man and a woman is basically sexual?"

"Of course it is! It's impossible for a man and a woman to have an intimate relationship with no sex in it whatsoever!"

"I think," said Marijohn, "we've somehow succeeded in wandering from the point."

"But don't you agree with me?"

"Agree with you? What am I supposed to be agreeing with?"

"That it's impossible for a man and a woman to have an intimate relationship with no sex in it whatsoever."

"That would depend upon the man and woman."

"On the contrary I'd say it depended entirely on their sexual capacity! Take Jon for instance. He's married twice and had a lot of women but no woman's going to interest him unless she attracts him physically."

"Why shouldn't Jon have his share of sex? Most men need it and get it so why shouldn't he? And why should his 'sexual capacity,' as you call it, affect any other relationship he might have? And what's so special about sex anyway? It often has nothing whatsoever to do with real intimacy. Why talk of it as if it were the beginning and end of everything? Sex is so often nothing but pointless futility."

Alexander hesitated slightly before he laughed. The hesitation made the laughter sound a little uncertain.

"For pointless futility it certainly seems to be doing very well!" And when she didn't answer he said easily, "That sounds very much a woman's point of view, Marijohn."

"Perhaps," she said flatly, not arguing, her footsteps moving into the house. "I must go and see how burnt the lunch is getting. Excuse me."

"Of course."

There was silence. Sarah found she was still clutching the edge of the dressing-table stool. She glanced into the mirror. Her dark eyes stared back at her, her dark hair straggling untidily from its position, her mouth unsmiling, devoid of make-up. She reached automatically for her lipstick.

I want to go, she thought; please, Jon, let's go—let's go anywhere so long as it's somewhere far from this place. Let's go now. If only I could go. . . .

She started to re-apply her powder.

I don't want to meet Max. I don't care if he was your friend once, Jon; I don't want to meet him because I can't bear men who talk of women and sex in bored amused voices as if they've seen all there is to see and know all there is to know. I want to go, Jon, now, this minute. If only we could go. . . .

She undid her hair and let it fall to her shoulders before brushing it upwards again and picking up her comb.

And most of all, Jon, I want to go away from your cousin because she doesn't like me, Jon, I know she doesn't, and I hate her, no matter how hard I try to pretend I don't. . . . I hate her and I'm afraid of her although I don't know why, and Jon, can't we go soon, Jon, because I want to escape. . . . It's not just because she dislikes me—in fact "dislike" is the wrong word. She despises me. You won't believe she despises me, Jon, because she's always been so kind to me ever since we set foot in this house, but she does, I know she does, because I can feel it. She despises me just as she despised Sophia.

She put down her comb and examined the little jar of liquid eye-shadow.

Better not to think of Sophia.

But all those lies. Jon, all those lies. And you swore to me her death was an accident. You lied and lied and lied for Marijohn. . . .

Oh, God, I want to go, I want to get away. Please Jon, take

me away from this place because I'm frightened and I want to escape. . . .

She went out into the corridor. It was cool there, and the bannister was smooth against her hot palm. She walked downstairs, crossed the hall and entered the drawing-room.

The man turned as she came in. He turned to face her and she saw all that she had not seen when she had listened to his conversation earlier—the humorous mouth, the wide blue eyes that for some reason seemed very honest and trusting, the broken nose, the traces of plastic surgery which stretched from his left temple to the jawbone. There were lines about the mouth. They were deep lines which would get deeper with time, but apart from this there was no other indication that he had suffered and known pain. He looked older than Jon, but not much older. The suffering hadn't aged him, as it would have aged some men, nor had it given him the worn, tired appearance of exhaustion.

She stood staring, suddenly at a loss for words. It was some seconds before she realized that he too was experiencing difficulty in choosing his opening remarks.

"Good Lord!" he said at last, and his blue eyes were wide with honest surprise. "But you're young! I thought you were Jon's age. No one ever told me you were young."

She smiled awkwardly. "Not as young as all that!"

He smiled too, not saying anything, his eyes still faintly astonished, and she wondered what he was thinking and whether she was as like Sophia, as he had imagined she would be. "Where's Jon?" she said, for lack of anything else to say.

"He went out to look for you, as a matter of fact."

"Did he? I must have just missed him." She helped herself to a cigarette and he gave her a light. "When did you arrive?"

"About half an hour ago. Justin was the only one at home so he went down to the cove to tell everyone I'd arrived. Apparently I wasn't expected to lunch. . . . Jon tells me you're both going over to see some old friends of his in Penzance this afternoon?"

"Are we? I mean—" She blushed and laughed. "I haven't seen

Jon since breakfast. He and Marijohn went into Penzance this morning to do some shopping—"

"Ah, he must have arranged something when he was over there. . . . I was just wondering what I could do with myself while you're out. Marijohn says uncompromisingly that she has 'things to do' and Justin is taking her car to go over to St. Ives for some reason, so I'll be on my own. Maybe I'll have a swim or a paddle, depending on how Spartan I feel. I never usually bathe except in the Mediterranean. . . . Ah, here's Jon! He must have decided you hadn't lost yourself after all. . . . Jon!" He moved out through the open French windows on to the lawn beyond, his arm raised in greeting, and when he next spoke she heard the hard careless edge return to his voice. "Jon, why didn't you tell me how young and pretty your new wife is?"

IV

"I don't want to go," she said to Jon. "Would it matter awfully if I didn't come? I feel so tired."

The bedroom was quiet, shadowed by the Venetian blinds.

"Just as you like," said Jon. "I happened to meet this fellow when I was in Penzance this morning—I used to do a certain amount of business with him in the old days. When he invited us over this afternoon for a spin in his motor-boat, I thought it would be the sort of invitation you'd enjoy."

"I—I'm sorry, Jon."

"Of course you must rest if you're tired. Don't worry." He stooped to kiss her on the forehead. "Perhaps Marijohn will come," he said presently. "I'll ask her."

"She told Max she was going to be very busy this afternoon."

"That was probably merely a polite way of excusing herself from entertaining him. I'll see what she says." He turned to go.

"Jon, if you don't want to go alone, I'll—"

"No, no," he said. "You lie down and rest. That's much the

most important thing. But I'll have to go over and see this fellow and his new motor-boat—I've committed myself. If Marijohn doesn't want to come I'll go alone."

So she waited upstairs in misery as he went down to talk with Marijohn, but when he came back she heard that Marijohn had decided against going with him.

"I'll be back around six," he said, kissing her again before he left the room. "Sleep well."

But she did not sleep. Presently she dressed, putting on slacks and a shirt and went downstairs. Justin had gone off to St. Ives and Marijohn was relaxing on the swing-seat in the garden with some unanswered correspondence and a pen. Alexander was nowhere to be seen.

In order that Marijohn would not see her, Sarah left the house by the back door and moved through the back gate on to the hillside behind the house. Five minutes later she was by the beach of the cove.

Alexander wasn't paddling. He had taken off his shirt to bask in the heat and eased off his shoes but he was sitting on one of the rocks facing the sea, a book in his hands, a pair of sunglasses perched insecurely on the bridge of his nose. As she moved forward and began to scramble towards him he caught sight of her and waved.

"Hullo," he said when she was in earshot. "I thought you were resting."

"I decided I didn't want to waste such a lovely afternoon." She ignored his outstretched hand and climbed up on to the rock beside him. The tide was still rising and before them the surf thundered among the boulders and reefs in great white clouds of spray.

"I see," said Alexander. His skin was already tanned, she noticed. He had probably been abroad that summer. His chest and shoulders were muscular but were beginning to run to fat. She thought of Jon's body suddenly, remembered the powerful lines and hard flesh and strong muscles, and suddenly she wondered how often Max Alexander had been compared with his friend in the past and how often the comparison had been unfavorable.

"Tell me about yourself," Alexander said sociably, closing the book and fumbling for a cigarette. "How on Earth did you come to be in a god-forsaken country like Canada?"

She started to talk. It was difficult at first, for she was shy, but gradually she began to relax and speech came more easily. He helped her by being relaxed himself.

"I've been mixed up in motor racing most of my adult life," he said casually when she asked him a question about his hobbies. "It's a hell of a thing to get mixed up in. It's all right if you want to play chess with death and have half your face burnt off and get kicks out of a fast car and the smell of scorched rubber, but otherwise it's not much fun. I've more or less had enough."

"What are you going to do now, then?"

"Depends on how long I live," he said laconically. "I have heart trouble. I'll probably go on doing damn all and paying my taxes until I drop dead, I should think."

She wasn't sure how she should reply. Perhaps she was beginning to sense that he wasn't nearly as relaxed and casual as he appeared to be.

"It must be strange for you to come back here," she said suddenly after a pause. "Are you glad you came?"

He swiveled his body slightly to face her, and the sun shone straight into the lenses of his dark glasses so that she could not see his expression.

"It's nice to see Jon again," he said at last. "We'd drifted right apart. I was rather surprised when he rang up and said he wanted to bury the hatchet. . . . There was a hatchet, you know. Or did you?"

"Yes," she said, lying without hesitation. "Jon told me."

"Did he? Yes, I suppose he would have." He fidgeted idly with the corner of his book. "When I knew he was going back to Clougy, I—well, quite frankly I was astonished. So astonished that I couldn't resist coming down here when the opportunity arose to find out why he'd come back." There was a little tear in the dust-jacket of his book, and he tore the paper off at right-angles so that he had a small yellow triangle of paper in his hand. "I didn't know Marijohn was living here."

"Jon was very anxious to see her before he returned to Canada."

"Yes," said Alexander. "I dare say he was."

"Jon told me all about it."

He looked at her sharply again. "About what?"

"About himself and Marijohn."

"I didn't know," said Alexander, "that there was anything to tell."

"Well . . ." She was nonplussed suddenly, at a loss for words. "He said how fond of her he was as they'd spent some of their childhood together."

"Oh, I see." He sat up a little and yawned unconcernedly. "Yes, they're very fond of each other." For a moment she thought he wasn't going to say any more and then without warning he said abruptly: "What do you think of Marijohn?"

"I—"

"Sophia hated her; did Jon tell you that as well? To begin with, of course, it didn't matter because Jon worshipped the ground Sophia walked on and for Sophia the world was her oyster. She could say, do, want anything she wished. A pleasant position for a woman to be in, wouldn't you think? Unfortunately Sophia didn't know how lucky she was—she had to abuse her position until one day she discovered she hadn't any position left and her worshipping husband was a complete stranger to her." He drew on his cigarette for a moment and watched the surf pound upon the rocks a few yards away before being sucked back into the ocean with the roar of the undertow. "But of course —I was forgetting. Jon's told you all about that."

The waves were eating greedily across the shingle again swirling round the rocks.

"I felt sorry for Sophia," said Alexander after a while. "I think I was the only person who did. Marijohn despised her; Jon became totally indifferent to her; Michael—well, God, a conventional pillar of society such as Michael would always look down his nose at a sexy little foreign girl like Sophia who had no more moral sense than a kitten! But I felt sorry for her. It was terrible at the end, you know. She couldn't understand it—she didn't know what to do. I mean, Christ, what was there to do? There was nothing there, you see, nothing at all. It wasn't as if she'd caught Jon in bed with someone else. It wasn't as if he'd thrashed her with a horsewhip twice a day. There was nothing tangible, nothing you could pinpoint, nothing you could grasp and say, 'Look, this is what's wrong! Stop it at once!' She discovered quite suddenly that her loving husband didn't give a damn about her, and she didn't even know how it had happened."

"Maybe she deserved it. If she was constantly unfaithful to Jon—"

"Oh God, it wasn't like that! She behaved like a spoiled child and grumbled and sulked and complained, but she wasn't unfaithful. She flirted at her weekend parties and made Jon go through hell, time and again with her tantrums and whims, but she wasn't unfaithful. What chance did she have to be unfaithful stuck down here at the back of beyond? And anyway underneath her complaints and sulks she probably found Jon attractive enough and it was pleasant to be adored and worshipped all the time. It was only when she realized that she'd lost him that she was unfaithful in an attempt to win him back."

Sarah stared at him.

"And he didn't give a damn. She flaunted her infidelity and he was indifferent. She was sexy as hell in an attempt to seduce him back to her bed and he was still indifferent. It was a terrible thing for a woman like Sophia whose only weapons were her sex and her femininity. When she found both were worthless she had nothing—she'd reached the end of the road. And still he didn't care."

"He—" The words stuck in Sarah's throat. "He must have cared a little. If he'd loved her so much—"

"He didn't give a damn." He threw away his cigarette and the glowing tip hissed as it touched the seaweed pool below. "I'll tell you exactly what happened so that you can see for yourself.

"I came down to Clougy that weekend with a friend called Eve. We were having an affair, as I'm sure Jon has told you, but at that particular stage the affair was wearing rather thin. We arrived on Friday evening, spent an unsatisfactory night together and quarreled violently after breakfast the next morning. Not a very bright start to a long weekend by the sea! After the quarrel she locked herself in her room or something equally dramatic, and I went out to my car with the idea of going for a spin along the coast road to St. Ives or over the hills to Penzance. I find driving soothing after unpleasant scenes.

"I was just getting into the car when Sophia came out. God, I can see her now! She wore skin-tight black slacks and what Americans would call a 'halter'—some kind of flimsy arrangement which left her midriff bare, and exposed an indecent amount of cleavage. Her hair was loose, waving round her face and falling over her shoulders in the style which Brigitte Bardot made so famous. 'Ah Max!' she said, smiling brilliantly, 'are you going into St. Ives? Take me with you!' She made it sound so exactly like an invitation to bed that I just stood and gaped, and then as I started to stammer 'Of course' or something mundane, Jon came out of the front door and called out to her, but she took no notice, merely slidng into the passenger seat and wriggling into a comfortable position.

"'Sophia', he said again, coming over to the car. 'I want to talk to you.'

"She just shrugged idly and said she was going into St. Ives with me to buy shellfish for dinner that night. Then Jon turned on me. 'Did you invite her,' he said furiously, 'or did she invite herself?'

"'Jon darling,' said Sophia before I could reply, 'you're making *su-uch* an exhibition of yourself.' She had the habit of drawing out some syllables and thickening her foreign accent sometimes when she was annoyed.

"Jon was shaking with rage. I could only stand and watch him helplessly. '*You're* the one who's making an exhibition of yourself!' he shouted at her. 'Do you think I didn't notice how you did your damnedest to flirt with Max last night? Do you think Eve didn't notice? Why do you think she and Max quarreled this morning? I'll not have my wife behaving like a whore whenever we have guests down here. Either you get out of that car and stop acting the part of a prostitute or I'll put a stop to your week-end parties once and for all.'

"'Look, Jon—' I tried to say, but he wouldn't listen to me. I did my best to pour oil on troubled waters, but I was wasting my breath.

"'That's ridiculous!' cried Sophia, and she was as furious as hell too. 'Your stupid jealousy! I want to get some shellfish for dinner and Max is going to St. Ives—why shouldn't he give me a lift there? Why shouldn't he?'

"Well, of course, put like that it did make it seem as if Jon was making a fuss about nothing. But there she sat in the front seat of my car, her hair tumbling over her shoulders, her breasts all but spilling out of that scanty halter, her mouth sulky—Christ, any husband would have had the excuse for thinking or suspecting or fearing all kinds of things! 'You'd better stay, Sophia,' I said. 'I'll get your shellfish for you. Tell me what you want.'

"'No,' she said. 'I'm coming with you.'

"It was extremely embarrassing. I didn't know what to do. She was looking at Jon and he was looking at her, and I was just trying to work out how I could tactfully make my escape when there was the sneeze from the porch. Jon and I swung round. It was the child. He'd been standing listening, I suppose, poor little bastard, and wondering what the hell was going on.

After he sneezed, he turned to sidle indoors again but Jon called out to him and he came sheepishly out into the sunlight.

"'Come on, Justin,' Jon said, taking him by the hand. 'We're going down to the Flat Rocks.'

"He didn't say anything else. He took the child's hand in his and the child looked up at him trustingly, and the next moment they were walking across the lawn away from us and we were alone.

"So we went to St. Ives. It was a hot day, rather like this one, and after we'd bought the shellfish we paused at one of the coves down the coast to bathe. I've forgotten what the cove was called. It was very small and you could only reach it when the tide was out a certain distance. No one else was there.

"I don't make excuses for what happened. I made love with my best friend's wife, and there can be no excuse for that—no valid excuse. Of course it was Sophia who suggested the swim, and Sophia who knew the cove, and Sophia who took off her clothes first and Sophia who made the first physical contact with her hands, but what if it was? I suppose if I'd had half an ounce of decency I could have said no all along the line, but I didn't. I suppose I'm not really a particularly decent person. And there were other reasons . . . Jon had often taken things of mine, you see. I'd had girls and then as soon as they saw Jon they weren't interested in me any more. He was interested in motor-racing for a while, and when I introduced him to the right contacts it turned out that he could drive better than I could and the contacts became more interested in him than in me. Oh, there were other situations too, other memories. . . . It wasn't Jon's fault. It was just the way he was made. But I built up quite a store of resentment all the same, a long list of grudges which I barely acknowledged even to myself. When his wife was mine for the taking, I never even hesitated.

"We arrived back at Clougy at about four o'clock in the afternoon. Everyone was very still. At first we thought everyone must be out, and then we heard the piano.

"'He's crazy,' said Sophia indolently. 'Imagine playing the piano indoors on a beautiful afternoon like this!' And she walked down the corridor and opened the door of the music room. 'Jon—' she began and then stopped. I walked down to see why she had stopped, and then I saw that Jon wasn't alone in the music room. Marijohn was with him.

"I can't describe how strange it was. There was no reason why it should be strange at all. Marijohn was sitting on the window-seat, very relaxed and happy, and Jon was on the piano-stool, casual and at ease. They weren't even within six feet of each other.

"'Hullo,' said Marijohn to Sophia, and her eyes were very blue and clear and steady. 'Did you manage to get the shellfish in St. Ives?' I'll always remember the way she said that because I saw then for the first time how much she despised Sophia. 'Did you manage to get the shellfish in St. Ives?'

"And Sophia said, 'Where's Michael?'

"Marijohn said she had no idea. And Jon said, 'Didn't he go fishing?' And they laughed together and Jon started to play again.

"We might as well not have existed.

"'I'm going down to the cove with Max,' said Sophia suddenly.

"'Oh yes?' Jon said, turning a page of music with one hand.

"'Don't get too sunburnt,' said Marijohn. 'The sun's hot to-day, isn't it, Jon?'

"'Very,' said Jon, and went on playing without looking up.

"So we went out. Sophia was furious although she said nothing. And then when we arrived at the beach we found the child was following us, and she vented her temper on him, telling him to go away. Poor little bastard! He looked so lost and worried. He wandered off along the shore and was soon lost from sight amongst the rocks.

"We had a swim and after that Sophia started to talk. She talked about Marijohn, and in the end she started to cry. 'I hate it when she comes here,' she said. 'I hate it. Nothing ever goes right when she comes.' And when I asked what Marijohn did, she couldn't explain and only cried all the more. There was nothing, you see, that was what was so baffling. There was nothing there to explain. . . .

"I was just trying to console her and take her in my arms when the worst thing possible happened—Eve had heard I was back from St. Ives and had come down from her room to look for me. Of course she found me in what I believe is generally termed a 'compromising' position, so there was another row and she went back to the house. She didn't come down to dinner that evening.

"Dinner was very unnerving. Sophia had been supervising the cooking in the kitchen so we didn't come into the diningroom together, but it was obvious she had decided to act the part of the good hostess and be bright and talkative, pretending nothing had happened at all. I responded as best as I could and Michael joined in from time to time, I remember. But Marijohn and Jon never said a word. Gradually, after a while, their silence became oppressive. It's very difficult to describe. One was so conscious somehow of their joint silence. If one had been silent and the other talkative it wouldn't have mattered, but it was their joint silence which was so uncanny. In the end Sophia fell silent too, and I could think of nothing more to say, and Michael was quiet. And it was then, when the whole room was silent, that Marijohn started to speak.

"She talked exclusively to Jon. They discussed music, I remember, a topic which was open to no one but themselves because no one else knew much about it. They talked to one another for ten minutes, and then suddenly they were silent again and I was so taut with uneasiness I could scarcely move my knife and fork. Presently Sophia told the child to go to bed. He made rather a fuss, I remember, and didn't want to go, but in the end Michael took him upstairs. I remember having the strong impression that Michael wanted to escape. . . . We all stood up from the table then and Jon went out into the hall. He put on a red sweater and Sophia said: 'You're not going out, are you?' and he said, 'Marijohn and I are going for a stroll down to the cove.'

"So they went out. They weren't gone too long, only ten minutes or so and then they came back and went to the music room. Presently Michael came downstairs and went into the music room to join them. I was in the kitchen with Sophia helping her wash up, but when they came back she went to the door to listen. The gramophone was playing. She said, 'I'm going in to see what's happening,' and I said, 'Leave them alone—come out with me for a while. Michael's with them anyway.' And she said, 'Yes, I want to hear what he says.' I told her there was no reason why he should say anything at all, but she said she still wanted to see what was happening.

"We were in the hall by then. She said she would meet me later in the evening—'somewhere where we can be alone,' she said, 'somewhere where we can talk and not be overheard. I'll meet you down by the Flat Rocks at ten o'clock.' When I agreed, she went into the music room and I was alone in the hall. I can remember the scene so clearly. The gramophone stopped a moment later. There was no light in the hall, just the dusk from the twilight outside, and Jon's discarded red sweater lay across the oak chest by the door like a pool of blood.

"I went out soon after that. I walked down to the cove and watched the sea for a while, and then I walked back to the house to get a sweater as it was rather colder than I'd anticipated. After that I went out again, taking the cliff path which led out to the Flat Rocks, and about quarter of an hour later I was waiting by the water's edge."

He stopped. The tide roared over the shingle.

"I waited some time," he said, "but of course Sophia never came. I heard the scream just as I was wondering what could have happened to her, but although I moved as fast as I could she was dead when I reached her."

He stopped again. Presently he took off his sunglasses and she saw the expression in his eyes for the first time.

"Poor Sophia," he said slowly; "it was a terrible thing to happen. I always felt so sorry for Sophia. . . ."

Four

I

JUSTIN WAS in St. Ives by the time the church clock near the harbor was tolling three that afternoon. Holiday-makers thronged the streets, spilling over the pavements to make driving hazardous. The pedestrians ruled St. Ives, dictating to the cars that crawled through the narrow streets, and Justin was relieved when he reached the freedom of the car park at last and was able to switch off the engine. He got out of the car. The air was salt and fresh, the sun deliciously warm. As he walked up the steps along by the town wall the gulls wheeled around the fishing boats in the harbor and the houses clustered on the rising ground of the peninsula were white-walled and strangely foreign beneath that hot southern sky.

Justin reached the harbor, turned up Fish Street and then turned again. There was an alley consisting of stone steps leading to a higher level, and at the top was another narrow cobbled lane slanting uphill. The door marked Five was pale blue and a climbing plant trailed from the corner of the windows to meet above the porch.

He rang the bell.

A woman answered the door. She had a London accent and London clothes and a paint smear across the back of her left hand.

"Is Eve in?" said Justin hesitantly, suddenly nervous.

"Ah yes, you're expected, aren't you? Come on in. She's upstairs—second door on the right."

"Thank you." The hall was a mass of brass and copper ornaments. His hand gripped the hand rail of the stairs tightly and
then he was walking quietly up the steps, neither pausing nor
looking back. The woman was watching him. He could feel her
eyes looking him up and down, wondering who he was and what
connection he could possibly have with the woman waiting upstairs, but he didn't stop and the next moment he was on the
landing and pausing to regain his breath. It suddenly seemed
very hot.

The second door on the right was facing him. Presently he
took a pace forward and raised his hand to knock.

"Come in," called the woman's voice from beyond as his
knuckles touched the wood, and suddenly he was back in the
past again, a little boy catching sight of the untasted supper tray
outside the closed door and knocking on the panels to inquire if
he could eat the food which she had ignored.

He stood rigid, not moving, the memories taut in his mind.

"Come in!" called the woman again, and even as he moved to
turn the handle on the door she was opening the door for him so
that a second later they were facing each other across the
threshold.

No hint of recognition showed in her face. He caught a glimpse
of disappointment, then of irritation, and he felt his ears burn
scarlet in a sudden rush of embarrassment.

"You must want one of the other lodgers," he heard her say
shortly. "Who are you looking for?"

He swallowed, all his careful words of introduction forgotten,
and wondered vaguely in the midst of all his panic how on Earth
he had had the nerve to come. He stared down at her toes. She
wore white sandals, cool and elegant, and in spite of his confusion he was aware of thinking that her smart, casual clothes were
much too chic and well-tailored for that little holiday resort far
from London.

"Wait a minute," she said. "I know you."

He cleared his throat. Presently he had enough confidence to glance up into her eyes. She looked bewildered but not hostile, and he began to feel better.

"You're Justin," she said suddenly.

He nodded.

For a moment she made no move, and then she was opening the door wider and turning back into the room.

"You'd better come in," she said over her shoulder.

He followed her. The room beyond was small with a view from the window of rooftops and a distant glimpse of the sun sparkling on blue sea.

"You're not much like either of your parents, are you?" she said absently, sitting down on the stool of the crowded dressing-table and flicking ash into a souvenir ashtray. "I hardly recognized you. You've lost such a lot of weight."

He smiled warily, easing himself on to the edge of the bed.

"Well," she said at last when the silence threatened to become prolonged. "Why have you come? Have you got a message from your father?"

"No," he said, "he doesn't know you're here. Your note reached me by mistake and I didn't show it to him. I didn't see why you should bother my father when he's still more or less on his honeymoon."

She was annoyed. As she swiveled round to face him, he could see the anger in her eyes. "Just what the hell do you think you're playing at?" she demanded coldly.

He had forgotten his panic and shyness now. He stared back at her defiantly. "You wanted to talk about what happened at Clougy ten years ago," he said. "You wanted to talk about Max."

"To your father. Not to you."

"I know more than you think I do."

She smiled, looking skeptical. "How can you?" she said. "You were just a child at the time. You couldn't have understood what was happening so how can you know anything about it?"

"Because I saw my mother's death," he said, and even as he

spoke he saw her eyes widen and her expression change. "I saw it all, don't you see? I followed the murderer up on the cliffs that night and saw him push my mother down the cliff-path to her death. . . ."

II

Sarah left the beach soon after five and walked up to the house to see if Jon had returned from his visit to Penzance. Alexander stayed behind in the cove. When she reached the drive she saw that a blue Hillman was parked behind Max's silver-gray Rolls Royce and she wondered who the visitors were and whether they had been there long.

The hall was cool and shadowed after the shimmering brilliance of the early evening, and she paused for a moment before the mirror to adjust her hair before crossing the hall and opening the drawing-room door.

Marijohn was sitting at the desk by the window. There was a pen in her hand. Behind her, slightly to her left so that he could look over her shoulder was a tall man, unobtrusively good-looking, with quiet eyes and a strong mouth. Both he and Marijohn looked up with a start as Sarah came into the room.

"Oh, it's only you." Marijohn put down the pen for a moment. "Michael dear, this is Sarah. . . . Sarah—Michael Rivers."

"How do you do," said Rivers, giving her a pleasant smile while looking at her with lawyer's eyes. And then as she echoed the greeting, the lawyer's cautious scrutiny faded into a more formal appraisal and there was warmth in his eyes and kindness in the set of his mouth. "May I offer my congratulations on your marriage? I expect belated congratulations are better than none at all."

"Thank you," she said shyly. "Thank you very much."

There was a pause. She said awkwardly, as if to explain her presence, "I—I just wondered if Jon was back yet? He didn't say what time he would be returning from Penzance, but I thought perhaps—"

"No," said Marijohn, "he's not here yet." She turned to Michael. "Darling, how many more of these do I have to sign?"

"Just the transfer here . . ." He bent over her again and something in the way he moved made Sarah stop to watch them. Phrases of Justin's sprang back to her mind. "It was obvious he loved her. He kissed her in public and gave her special smiles—oh God, you know! The sort of thing you notice and squirm at when you're a small boy. . . ."

It seemed strange to know they were divorced.

"Fine," said Rivers, gathering up the papers as Marijohn put down her pen. "I'll take these back with me to London tomorrow."

"Are you staying near here?"

"With the Hawkins over at Mullion."

"The Hawkins! Of course! Do they still live in that funny little cottage by the harbor?"

"No, they—" He stopped, listening.

Marijohn was listening, too.

Sarah felt her heart begin to thump faster as she too turned to face the door.

From far away came the sound of footsteps crunching on the gravel of the drive.

"That'll be Jon," said Rivers. "Well, I must be going. I'll phone you about the outcome of those transfers and contact Mathieson in the city about the gilt-edged question."

But Marijohn was still listening. The footsteps echoed in the porch and then moved through the open front door into the hall.

There was an inexplicable pause—the footsteps halted.

"Jon!" called Marijohn suddenly.

The latch clicked; the door swung wide.

"Hullo," said Jon, unsurprised and unperturbed. "How are you, Michael? Hullo, Sarah darling—feeling better now?" And as the others watched he stooped to give her a kiss.

"Much better," she said, clasping his hand tightly as he kissed her and releasing it only when he moved away towards the desk.

Jon turned to Rivers. "Why didn't you ring up to tell us you were coming, Michael? Are you staying to dinner?"

"No," said Rivers. "I'm spending a couple of days with friends at Mullion, and just called in to discuss one or two business matters with Marijohn."

"Phone your friends and say you're dining out tonight. They wouldn't mind, would they? Stay and have dinner with us!"

"I'm afraid that's not possible," said Rivers pleasantly. "But thank you all the same."

"Marijohn!" said Jon to his cousin, his eyes bright, his frame taut and vibrant with life. "You'd like Michael to stay for dinner, wouldn't you? Persuade him to stay!"

Marijohn's eyes were very clear. She turned to Rivers. "Won't you, Michael?" was all she said. "Please."

He shrugged, making a helpless gesture with his hands, and then she gave him a warm, brilliant, unexpected smile and he was lost. "When did you last have dinner with me?"

He shrugged again, not replying, but Sarah saw him bend his head slowly in acquiescence and knew that he had agreed to stay against his better judgment.

"Where's Max, Sarah?" said Jon to her, making her jump.

"He—he's still down by the cove, sunbathing."

"And Justin?"

"Still in St. Ives presumably," said Marijohn, moving over to the French windows. "Michael, come out and sit on the swing-seat and forget all those dreary legal documents for a while. I expect Jon wants to be alone with Sarah."

That was said for effect, thought Sarah instantly and unreasonably. All this is for effect to make some definite impression on Michael. This is all for Michael. And Jon is playing the same game; he's set the key for the evening and she's responding note for note. The key involved inviting Michael to dinner, giving the impression that the past is buried and forgotten, and now they want to show him that everything is normal and that there's nothing to hide.

Her thoughts raced on and on, no matter how hard she tried to stem her rising feeling of panic. How could Jon and Marijohn be working in conjunction with one another when Jon hadn't even known Michael was calling in that evening? But he had known. He had walked into the room and said "Hullo, Michael" although he could not have known before he opened the door that Michael would be there. . . . Perhaps he had recognized Michael's car. But the car wasn't ten years old! Jon could never have seen the car before. And yet he had known, he had known before he had opened the door that he would find Michael with Marijohn in the room . . .

"Come upstairs and talk to me, darling," said Jon, putting his arm round her waist. "I want to shower and change my clothes. Come and tell me what you've been doing."

So she went upstairs and sat on the edge of the bath as he had a shower and then rubbed himself vigorously with the rough towel. He told her about his friend in Penzance and described the motor-boat and the afternoon spin on the sea in detail. Finally as he returned to the bedroom to dress he paused to smile at her.

"Now tell me what you've been doing! You've hardly said a word to me all day! Do you still love me?"

There was a lump in her throat suddenly, a deep unreasoning ache that only deepened against her will. "Oh Jon," was all she could say, and then the next moment she was in his arms and pressing her face against his chest and he was crushing the sobs from her body and kissing her eyes to stop her tears.

"Sarah," he said, upset. "Sarah, darling Sarah, what is it? What's the matter? What have I said?"

"I—" She summoned together all her strength and managed to look straight into his eyes. "Jon," she said. "Jon, I want something very badly. Could you—"

"Tell me what it is," he said instantly, "and you shall have it. Just tell me what it is."

She took a deep breath, checked her tears. "I—I want to go back to Canada, Jon—I don't want to stay here. I just want to go home. Please, Jon, let's go. I don't want to stay here. I'm terribly sorry, but I—"

"I don't understand," he said. "Why don't you want to stay? I was planning to stay for another week."

She couldn't cry now. She could only stare into his face and think: It's all true. There *is* something. Max wasn't lying. There's something intangible, something impossible to describe, just as he said there was. It's all true.

"I thought you liked it here," he said. "What's wrong? What is it?"

She shook her head dumbly. "Marijohn—"

"What about Marijohn?" he said. He spoke much too quickly, and afterwards looked annoyed with himself for betraying his feelings.

"She doesn't like me."

"Rubbish. She thinks you're very pretty and just right for me and she's very glad I've married someone so nice."

She twisted away from him, but he held her tightly and wouldn't let her go. "Come here."

The towel slipped from his waist. He pulled her down on the bed and suddenly she clung to him in a rush of passion and desire which was terrible to her because she was so afraid it would strike no response in him.

"Sarah . . ." He sounded surprised, taken aback but not indifferent. And suddenly his passion was flowing into her own, and the more she poured out her love to him in movement and gesture the more he took her love and transformed it with his own.

When they parted at last the sweat was blinding her eyes and there were tears on her cheeks and her body felt bruised and aching.

"I love you," she said. "I love you."

He was still trying to find his breath, still trembling, his fists clenched with his tension and his eyes tight shut for a second as if in pain. He can't relax, she thought, and neither can I. There's no peace. We should be able to sleep now for a while but we won't. There's no peace here, no rest.

"Jon," she said. "Jon darling, take me away from here. Let's go tomorrow. Please. Let's go back to London, back to Canada, anywhere, but don't let's stay here anymore."

His fists were clenched so tightly that the skin was white across the knuckles. "Why?" he said indistinctly into the pillow, his voice truculent and hostile. "Why? Give me one good reason."

And when she was silent he reached out and pulled her towards him in a violent gesture of love. "Give me another couple of days," he said. "Please. If you love me, give me that. I can't go just yet."

She tried to frame the word "why" but it refused to come. She got up, went into the bathroom and washed, but when she returned from the bathroom she found that he was still lying in the same position. She started to dress.

Time passed.

At last, sitting down in front of the mirror, she began to do her hair but still she made no attempt to speak, and the silence between them remained unbroken.

"Sarah," Jon said at last in distress. "Sarah, please."

She swiveled round to face him. "Is Marijohn your mistress?"

There was utter silence. He stared at her, his eyes dark and opaque.

"No," he said at last. "Of course not. Sarah—"

"Has she ever been your mistress?"

"No!" he said with sudden violent resentment. "Never!"

"Were you having an affair with her when Sophia was killed?"

"No!" he shouted, springing off the bed and coming across the room towards her. "No, no, no!" He took her by the shoulders and started to shake her. "No, no, no—"

"Jon," she said gently. "Shhh, Jon . . ."

He sank down beside her on the stool. "If that's why you want to leave, you can forget it," he said tightly. "There's nothing like that between us. She—" He stopped.

"She?"

"She detests any form of physical love," he said. "Didn't you guess? She can't even bear being touched however casually by a man. Did you never notice how I've always avoided touching her? Did you never notice how I didn't kiss her when we met? Didn't you notice any of those things?"

She stared at him. He stared back, his hands trembling.

"I see," she said, at last.

He relaxed, and she knew in a flash that he had not understood. He thought she understood only the key to Marijohn's remoteness, and he never knew that all she understood was the despair in his eyes and the physical frustration in every line of his tense, taut frame.

III

When Sarah went downstairs the hall was dim and quiet and she decided the others must still be in the garden. There was no sign of Max Alexander. After pausing by the open front door to glance up the hillside and listen to the rushing water beyond the gateway she crossed the hall and opened the drawing-room door.

She had been wrong. Rivers and Marijohn were no longer in the garden. As she entered the room, Rivers swung round abruptly to face the door and Marijohn glanced up from her position on the sofa.

"I—I'm sorry," stammered Sarah. "I thought—"

"That's all right," Rivers said easily, lulling her feeling of embarrassment. "Come on in. We were just wondering whether Max has been washed away by the tide down in the cove."

Marijohn stood up. She wore a plain linen dress, narrow and simple, without sleeves. It was a beautiful color. She wore no makeup and no jewelry, and Sarah noticed for the first time that she had even removed her wedding-ring.

"Where are you going?" said Rivers sharply.

"Just to see about dinner." She moved over to the door, not hurrying, her eyes not watching either of them, and went out into the hall.

There was a silence.

"Drink, Sarah?" said Rivers at last.

"No, thank you." She sat down, twisting the material of her dress into tight ridges across her thighs and wondering what Rivers had been saying before she had interrupted him. She was just trying to think of some remark which might begin a polite conversation and ease the silence in the room when Rivers said, "Is Jon upstairs?"

"Yes—yes, he is."

"I see." He was by the sideboard, his hand on the decanter. "Sure you won't join me in a drink?"

She shook her head again and watched him as he mixed himself a whisky and soda.

"How long," he said presently, "are you staying here?"

"I don't know."

He turned to face her abruptly and as she looked at him she saw that he knew.

"You want to go, don't you?"

"No," she said, lying out of pride. "No, I like it here."

"I shouldn't stay here too long if I were you."

She shrugged, assuming indifference. "Jon wants to stay here for a day or two longer."

"I'm sure he does." He took a gulp of his drink and she saw his fingers tighten on the stem of his glass. "I didn't realize you would both be coming down here," he said evenly at last. "I didn't think he would be seeing Marijohn again. She had made up her mind not to see him again, I know. I suppose he persuaded her to change her mind."

She stared at him blankly. From somewhere far away she heard the clatter of a saucepan in the kitchen.

"He wanted to see her again—I know that because he came to me in an attempt to find out where she was. Naturally I didn't tell him. I knew she had made up her mind that it would be much better for her not to see him again, and I knew too that it would be disastrous if—"

He stopped.

There were footsteps on the stairs, Jon whistling the old American country song *You Win Again.*

"Listen," said Rivers suddenly. "I must talk to you further about this. It's in both our interests, don't you understand? I must talk to you."

"But I don't see. Why should—"

"You have to get Jon away from here. I can't persuade Marijohn to leave—we're not even married any more. But you can persuade Jon. God, you're all but on your honeymoon, aren't you? Get him away from here, right away. Back to Canada, anywhere —but get him away from this place."

"From this place?"

"From Marijohn."

The whistling stopped; the door opened.

"Sarah? Ah, there you are! Come on down to the cove with me and rescue Max!"

"I think," said Rivers, "that he's just walking up to the gateway."

"Well, so he is!" Jon moved out on to the lawn. "Max!" he shouted his hand raised in welcome. "Where've you been, you bastard? We thought you'd drowned yourself!"

Rivers was already beside her even as she stood up to follow Jon out on to the lawn.

"Come for a walk with me after supper and I'll explain."

"I—"

"You must," he interrupted. "I don't think you understand the danger you're in."

She felt the color drain from her face as she stared into his eyes. And then Jon was blazing across the silence, bursting back into the room to mix a round of drinks, and Alexander was crossing the threshold of the French windows with a lazy, indolent smile on his face.

"Why, Michael! Fancy that! Just like old times! How are you these days? Still soliciting?"

There was brittle, empty conversation for a few minutes. Max started to expound the virtues of his latest car. Jon, moving across to Sarah, kissed her on the mouth with his back to the others and sat down beside her on the sofa.

"All right?"

When she nodded he put his hand over hers and kept it there. She stared blindly down at his fingers, not hearing Max Alexander's voice, aware of nothing except that Jon was a stranger to her whom she could not trust. It occurred to her dully to wonder if she had ever imagined unhappiness to be like this; it's not the raw nagging edge of desolation, she thought, but the tight darkness of fear. The pain is convex and opaque and absolute.

Marijohn returned to the room fifteen minutes later.

"I suppose Justin's coming back for dinner, Jon?"

He shrugged. "I've no idea. I imagine so."

"Can I get you a drink, Marijohn?"

"No . . . no thanks. I think I'll go out for a while. Dinner will be in about another half hour."

On the sofa Sarah felt Jon stir restlessly.

"Another drink, Jon?" offered Max Alexander from the sideboard.

Jon didn't answer.

"Jon," said Sarah, pressing against him instinctively. "Jon."

"Do you want to come, Michael?" said Marijohn. "I don't want to walk far, just down to the cove and back."

"No," said Rivers. "I'm in the middle of a perfectly good whisky and soda and I want to finish it and have another one to follow."

"Don't look at me, Marijohn," advised Max Alexander. "I've

staggered down to the cove and back already this afternoon. I've had my share of exercise today."

Jon stood up, hesitated and then reached for the cigarette box to help himself to a cigarette.

"Do you want to go, Jon?" said Rivers pleasantly.

"Not particularly." He lit the cigarette, wandered over to the fireplace and started to straighten the ornaments on the mantelshelf.

Marijohn walked away across the lawn. She walked very slowly, as if savoring each step. Jon glanced after her once and then abruptly turned his back on the window and flung himself down in the nearest armchair.

"Why don't you go, Jon?" said Rivers. "Don't feel you have to stay here and entertain us—I'm sure Sarah would make an admirable hostess. Why don't you go with Marijohn?"

Jon inhaled from his cigarette and watched the blue smoke curl upwards from between his fingers. "We've been down to the sea already today."

"Oh, I see. . . . Not to the Flat Rocks, by any chance?"

"I say," said Alexander suddenly, "what the hell's Justin doing in St.—"

"No," said Jon to Rivers. "Just down to the cove."

"How strange. Marijohn told me she hadn't been down to the cove today."

"Sarah," said Max. "Do you know what Justin's doing in St. Ives?"

"Do you often come down here?" said Jon idly to Rivers. "It must take up a lot of your time if you have to visit Marijohn personally whenever it's necessary to discuss some business problem with her. Or do you like to have a good excuse to visit her as often as possible?"

"At least," said Rivers, "my excuse for coming here is a damned sight better than yours."

"Look," said Max, spilling his drink slightly on the carpet, "for Christ's sake, why doesn't one of you go down to the cove with

Marijohn now? Michael, she asked you—why the hell don't you go if you've come down here to see her?"

Jon flung his cigarette into the fireplace and stood up. "Come on, Sarah, we'll go down together."

There was a silence. They were all looking at her.

"No," she said too loudly, "no, I don't want to come. I'd rather stay here."

Jon shrugged his shoulders. "Just as you like," he said shortly, sounding as if he couldn't have cared less, and walked through the open French windows across the lawn without even a hint of a backward glance.

IV

In St. Ives the white houses were basking in the golden glow of evening and the sea was still and calm. In the little house in one of the back-alleys near Fish Street, Justin was holding a mug of steaming coffee in his hands and wondering what had possessed him to tell this woman the story of his life. It was her fault. If she had not questioned him so closely about the aftermath of that terrible weekend at Clougy he would not have needed to explain anything about his grandmother and the parting from his father, but for some reason he had wanted to explain. At first he had been guarded and cautious, but when she had seemed to understand he had lost some of his reserve. She hadn't laughed at him. As the afternoon slid gently away from them, he began to trust her sufficiently to be able to talk more freely.

"And you never told anyone what you saw that night?" she said at last. "You said nothing?"

"I didn't think it would help my father."

"But you're sure now that he didn't kill her."

"He told me he didn't. Someone else must have killed her. I have to find out who it was."

She thought about it for a long moment, and the smoke from

her cigarette curled lazily upwards until it was caught in the slanting rays of sunlight and transformed into a golden haze.

"I thought at the time that Jon had probably killed her," she said at last. "But it was a mere suspicion backed up by the knowledge that he had more than enough provocation that weekend. . . . And then last week Max phoned me and asked me out to dinner. As soon as I saw him I realized he was itching to discuss his meeting with Jon earlier and speculate on why Jon should return to Clougy. We talked for hours, recalling all our memories, and in the end he said Jon had half-invited him down to Clougy and he had a good mind to accept in order to have the chance of finding out what was going on. He was convinced that Jon had killed Sophia and he thought it curious, to say the least, that Jon should take his new wife back there ten years later. I'd planned to take a few days' holiday anyway at around this time, and I suddenly thought it might be rather interesting to come down here so that I would be close at hand if Max should discover anything. . . . But the more I thought about Jon and his connection with Sophia's death, the more I felt—" She stopped.

"Felt?"

"I—I felt that it was better to let sleeping dogs lie. . . . After all, it was ten years ago, and Jon's married again now. I suddenly disliked the thought of Max deliberately going down to Clougy with the idea of probing a past which was better buried and forgotten."

"So you wrote to my father to warn him."

"Yes, I thought he should know Max's motives in returning to Clougy." She leant forward and stubbed out her cigarette. "Odd how convinced Max was that she had been murdered. . . . After all, murder was never mentioned at the time, was it? And the jury at the inquest decided it was an accident. But maybe we all knew she'd been murdered although we were too frightened to say so. That's ironic, isn't it! We all had a motive, you see, each one of us. We all had a reason for killing her, so we all kept silent and accepted the verdict of accident because we were afraid of

The Dark Shore

casting suspicion on ourselves by speaking our suspicions aloud to the police. . . . What's the matter? Didn't you guess I might have had a motive for wishing your mother dead?"

He shook his head wordlessly, watching her.

"I was an outsider from the first," she said, lighting another cigarette and shaking out the match as she spoke. "They all belonged to a different world—all of them except Sophia, and even her world of Soho cafés wasn't exactly mine. I was only eighteen then; I hadn't been working in London for very long. I met Max by accident at some party which I and a few friends had gate-crashed and I didn't know the kind of man he was. I just knew he was rich and moved in an expensive, exciting world, and I didn't find it difficult to fall in love and start to imagine all kinds of exotic, romantic pictures. It's so easy when one's only eighteen to live with one's head in the clouds, isn't it? Anyway, we had an affair, and eventually he took me to Clougy for that weekend.

"I was still in love with him then, still dreaming my romantic little daydreams.

"I think I hated Clougy from the first moment that I saw it. As for the other people, I didn't understand them at all—God, how baffling they seemed at the time! I found Jon interesting but he scarcely seemed to notice I existed—he was entirely engrossed with his wife and his cousin, and cared for nothing else. As for his cousin—well, I had nothing to say to her; we simply didn't even begin to talk the same language. The solicitor-husband was nice but too polite to be friendly, and anyway he too seemed to be almost entirely wrapped up in his personal problems. I disliked Sophia straight away, but it wasn't a very active dislike. I remember thinking that she just seemed rather common and vulgar.

"She started to flirt with Max about an hour after we'd arrived. I didn't take her seriously at first because I thought she surely couldn't flirt with one of her guests under her husband's nose, but that was my mistake. She meant it all right. The next morning Max and I quarreled violently and he went off with Sophia to St. Ives on a—quote 'shopping expedition,' unquote. I don't think

I've ever been so unhappy either before or since. I stayed in my room all morning and until the early evening when I heard them come back from St. Ives. After a while I went to look for Max and you told me—do you remember?—that he'd gone down to the cove with your mother for a swim. So I went out, taking the path down to the beach.

"I heard them talking before I saw them. She was saying in that ugly foreign voice of hers that she had a wonderful scheme all planned. She was sick to death of Clougy and wanted to get away from Jon and go back to London, and Max was to be her savior. She had it all worked out—a cosy little ménage à deux with just the right-sized luxury flat in Mayfair and maybe a cosy little divorce at the end of the rainbow. It sounded wonderful. God, how I hated her! I can't describe how much I hated her at that moment. And then I realized that Max wasn't exactly enthralled with all these beautiful schemes and I suddenly wanted to laugh out loud. He tried to put it tactfully at first but when she refused to understand, he spoke more frankly. He didn't want a ménage à deux in Mayfair or the scandal and publicity of being corespondent in his best friend's divorce suit! The last thing he wanted was to have Sophia permanently on his hands in London! He didn't really want an affair with the woman at all and the thought of her shouting from the rooftops that she was his mistress was enough to make his blood run cold. 'Look,' he said to her. 'I can't and won't play your game the way you want it played. You'd better find yourself another lover.' And then just as I was closing my eyes in sheer relief I heard the woman say, 'I have to get away from here—you don't understand. I'll go mad if I have to stay here any longer. If you don't take me to London and give me money and somewhere to live I'll make you the most famous corespondent in town and blow your friendship with Jon to smithereens.'

"And Max said with a laugh, 'You wouldn't have a hope in heaven of doing either of those things!'

"'Wouldn't I?' she said. 'Wouldn't I? Just you try and see!'

"And after a moment Max said, 'I'd better have time to think about this and then I'll have to talk to you again. I'll meet you out at the Flat Rocks after dinner this evening and we can discuss the situation in detail.'

"I moved then. I came round the rocks towards them and Max saw straight away that I'd heard what they'd been saying. When he lost his temper with me and asked me what the hell I thought I was doing spying on him, I turned on Sophia and called her all the names I could think of. I blamed her for everything—Max's changed attitude towards me, my own misery, his violent loss of temper which upset me more than anything else in the world. And she just laughed. I stormed and raged and poured out abuse and all she did was laugh.

"I found my way back to the house somehow. I went to my room and stayed there while I shed enough tears to fill the Atlantic Ocean. I knew then that everything was finished as far as Max and I were concerned, and that I meant no more to him than Sophia—or any other woman—did. I'd been deceiving myself for weeks that he cared for me, and I knew then that I'd been both incredibly blind and incredibly stupid. But I was only eighteen . . . It's so easy to make mistakes at eighteen, isn't it?

"I knew what time he was going to meet Sophia. I thought that if I could see him for a few minutes alone, if I could meet him by the Flat Rocks before Sophia arrived, I could perhaps persuade him not to listen to her, to call her bluff, and perhaps I could show him how much I still loved him. But I didn't know where the Flat Rocks were or how one reached them. In the end on an impulse I went out of my room and moved downstairs. It was late. There was a hell of a row going on in the music room, but I didn't stop to listen. I went outside to the gate to see if there was any sign of Max leaving for the Flat Rocks, and just as I reached the gate I saw him; he was walking down towards the beach. At the head of the cove he paused to watch the sea for a few minutes, and then he turned to retrace his steps and he saw me straight away. When

I asked him where he was going he shrugged and said he was going back to the house.

"'I thought you'd gone to keep your rendezvous with Sophia,' I said. 'Why have you come back?'

"'It's colder than I thought,' he said. 'I've come back for a sweater.'

"I tried to talk with him then, pleading with him to ignore Sophia and begging him to take me back to London straight away, but it was no good. He wouldn't listen, and just told me not to try to organize his life for him as he was perfectly capable of organizing it himself. When we reached the house again, he left me while he went inside to fetch his sweater, and I waited in the bushes by the gate, meaning to follow him when he came out again.

"He came out again almost at once.

"I followed him a little way, but he must have seen me for he lay in wait and stepped out in front of me as I reached the point where the path forked to go up to the cliffs. We had one final bitter useless row there and then he went on out towards the Flat Rocks while I sat down on a rock near the fork in the path and tried to pull myself together.

"When I finally went back to the house there was a light on in the music room where I had heard them all quarreling earlier, but the door was open now and no one was there. I was just standing in the hall and wondering where they all were when Jon came down the stairs. 'Marijohn' he called, seeing my shadow on the wall and thinking I was his cousin, and then he saw it was me. 'Where's Marijohn?' he said. 'Where's she gone?' I shook my head. He was very white. 'I have to find her. I have to find Marijohn.' He kept saying it over and over again. 'Where is everyone?' he said at last. 'Where's Max?' I told him then, and he went straight away to the front door, stopping for a moment by the chest as if he were pausing to look for something, but there was nothing there. The next moment he was in the drive and I was alone again in the hall."

She shook ashes from her cigarette onto the carpet. "I didn't kill your mother," she said at last. "I could have done it, but I didn't. I went up to my room again and stayed there until Max came up to tell me the news."

There was a silence in the room. When she next glanced at him she saw to her surprise that he was leaning forward and his eyes were dark with concentration.

"My father was at the house when you returned to it from the cove?"

"Why, yes," she said. "I told you."

"What was he wearing?"

"What was he wearing? God, I haven't the faintest idea! I wasn't in a mood for noticing clothes that night. Why?"

"Was he wearing a red sweater?"

"I don't think so—no, I'm sure he wasn't. When I saw him he was wearing only a shirt and a pair of trousers—I remember noticing that his shirt was open at the neck and I could see the sweat glistening on the skin at his throat. God, he did look shaken! He was white as a sheet and all he could do was ask for Marijohn. . . ."

Five

I

As soon as it was dark that evening Sarah made an excuse to go up to her room, and then slipped outside into the cool night air to wait in the shadows by the gate. She didn't have to wait long. As she plucked a leaf from the rhododendron bush nearby and tore it to shreds in her fingers she saw the front door open noiselessly and the next moment Rivers was crossing the drive towards her.

"Sarah?"

"Yes," she said. "I'm here."

"Good." He drew closer to her and she was conscious of his air of authority. He could cope with the situation, she thought with a rush of relief. He's spent his life dealing with other people's problems and her own problem was something which probably he alone was fully able to understand. "The first thing to do," he said, "is to walk away from the house. I don't want to run the risk of anyone overhearing our conversation."

"Shall we go down to the cove?"

"No," he said, "that would be the first place they'd look for us. We'll go up on to the cliffs."

They set off along the path, Rivers leading the way, and the night was dark and clouded, muffling the roar of the sea.

"Don't let's go too far," said Sarah suddenly.

"We'll stop around the next corner."

It was much too dark. Sarah found her feet catching in the heather and jarring on the uneven ground.

"Michael—"

"All right," he said. "We'll stop here."

There was an outcrop of rocks below the path and he helped her down the hillside until they could sit side by side on a rocky ledge and watch the dark mass of the sea straight in front of them. Far below them the surf was a fleck of whiteness on the reefs and lagoons of the shore.

"Cigarette?" said Rivers.

"No, thank you."

"Mind if I do?"

"No, not at all." How polite we are, she thought. We should be in a stately London drawing-room instead of on Cornish cliffs at night far from the formalities of civilization.

"How did you meet Jon?" he said suddenly, jolting her away from her thoughts.

She tried to concentrate on the effort of conversation.

"We met through a friend of mine," she said. "Frank's business was connected with Jon's, and one night we all had dinner together—Frank and I, Jon and some girl whom I didn't know. It never occurred to me at the time that Jon was the slightest bit interested in me, but the next day he phoned and asked to take me out to a concert. I went. I shouldn't have because of Frank, but then . . . well, Frank and I weren't engaged, and I—I wanted to see Jon again."

"I see." The cigarette tip glowed red in the darkness and flickered as he inhaled. "Yes, that sounds like Jon."

She said nothing, waiting for him to go on, and, after a moment, he said, "I met both Jon and Marijohn when old Towers died. I was then the assistant solicitor in the firm which had looked after his legal affairs and I was helping the senior partner in the task of proving the will and winding up the estate. Marijohn was eighteen. I'll never forget when I first saw her."

The cigarette tip glowed again.

"I managed to take her out once or twice, but there were about ten other men all wanting to take her out and there are only seven evenings in a week. They had more money and were older and more sophisticated than I was. She always chose the older men; the ones that mattered were all over thirty-five, but I was still fool enough to go on trying and hoping . . . until I went to the party and heard people talking about her. It was then for the first time that I realized she was completely and utterly promiscuous and slept with any man who would give her the best time.

"I left her alone for a while after that, but then I met her again and it was impossible to put her out of my mind. I had to keep phoning her, finding out who she was living with, going through a self-induced hell every day and night. And it was all for nothing, of course. She didn't give a damn.

"Then, quite suddenly, everything changed. One of her affairs went very, very wrong and she had to have an abortion. She had no money and was very ill. And she came to me. It was I who helped her, I who put up the money, arranged the abortion, paid off the necessary doctors—I, a solicitor, committing a criminal offense! But nobody ever found out. Gradually she got better and I took her away to a quiet corner in Sussex for a while to convalesce, but she wasn't fit enough to sleep with me even if she'd wanted to, and after a week she left me and went back to London.

"I followed her back and found she was planning to go down to Cornwall. 'I want to see Jon,' she said to me. I can see her now, standing there, her eyes very blue and clear. She was wearing a dark blue dress which was too big for her because she'd lost so much weight. 'I don't want you to come,' she said. 'I want to be alone with Jon for a while and then when I come back perhaps I'll live with you and you can look after me.' When I said—for the hundredth time—that I wanted to marry her she said that she didn't even know if she could live with me let alone marry me, and that I would have to wait until she had seen Jon. I said, 'What's Jon got to do with it? How can he help you?' And she turned to me and said: 'You wouldn't understand even if I tried to explain.'

"She came back from Cornwall a month later and said she

would marry me. She was transformed. She looked so much better that I hardly recognized her.

"We had a very quiet wedding. Jon and Sophia didn't come and although I thought at the time that it was strange, the full significance never fully occurred to me. For a while we were very happy—I suppose I had six months of complete happiness, and even now when I look back I would rather have had those six months than none at all. And then Jon came up to town one day from Penzance, and nothing was ever the same again.

"It was a gradual process, the disintegration of our marriage. For the first time I didn't even realize what was happening and then I realized that she was becoming cold, withdrawn. Ironically enough, the colder she became the more I seemed to need her and want her, and the more I wanted her the less she wanted me. In the end she said she wanted a separate bedroom. We quarreled. I asked her if there was some other man, but she just laughed, and when she laughed I shouted out, 'Then why do you see so much of Jon? Why is he always coming up to London? Why do we always get so many invitations to Clougy? Why is it you have to see so much of him?'

"And she turned to me and said, 'Because he's the only man I've ever met who doesn't want to go to bed with me.'

"It was my turn to laugh then. I said, 'He'd want to all right if he wasn't so wrapped up in his wife!'

"And she said, 'You don't understand. There's no question of our going to bed together.'

"It was so strange, the way she said that. I remember feeling that curious sickness one gets in the pit of the stomach the second after experiencing a shock. I said sharply, 'What the hell are you talking about?' And she just said, 'I can't describe how peaceful it is. It's the most perfect thing in all the world.'

"I suppose I knew then that I was frightened. The terrible thing was that I didn't know what I was frightened of. 'You're living with your head in the clouds,' I remember saying to her brutally, trying to shatter my own fear and destroy the barrier between us which she had created. 'You're talking nonsense.' And she said untroubled, as if it were supremely unimportant, 'Think that if you like. I don't care. But no matter what you think, it doesn't alter the fact that sex for me has long since lost all its meaning. It just seems rather ridiculous and unnecessary.' And as if in afterthought she added vaguely, 'I'm so sorry, Michael.' It was funny the way she said that. It had a peculiar air of bathos, and yet it wasn't really bathos at all. 'I'm so sorry, Michael . . .'

"I still couldn't stop loving her. I tried to leave, but I had to go back. I can't even begin to describe what a hell it was. And then we had that final invitation to Clougy, and I resolved that I must talk to Jon and lay my cards on the table. I knew he was absorbed with his wife, and I thought at the time that his relationship with Marijohn would be a much more casual, unimportant thing than her attitude towards him.

"We hadn't been five minutes at Clougy before I realized that Sophia was driving him to the limits of his patience and testing his love beyond all the bounds of endurance. And suddenly, that weekend, his patience snapped and he turned away from her—he'd had enough and could stand no more of her petulance and infidelity. And when he turned away, it was as if he turned to Marijohn.

"It was the most dangerous thing that could have happened; I was beside myself with anxiety, and tried to get Marijohn away, but she refused to go. I tried to talk to Jon but he pretended he hadn't the faintest idea what I was talking about and that there was nothing wrong between him and Marijohn. And then—then of all moments—Sophia had to stumble across what was happening and drag us all towards disaster.

"She'd been having an affair with Max and they'd driven into St. Ives for the afternoon. Jon was in the music room with Marijohn, and rather than make an unwelcome third I went out fishing and tried to think what the hell I was going to do. I didn't come to any conclusion at all. The child came, I remember, and sat talking to me and in some ways I was grateful to him because he took my mind off my troubles. When he went I stayed for a little longer by the shore and then eventually I went back to the house for dinner.

"Sophia and Max were back, and Sophia was looking very uneasy. She talked too much at the start of the meal, and then, when Jon and Marijohn were silent she made no further efforts at conversation. When Jon and Marijohn began to talk to each other at last, ignoring the rest of us entirely, I saw then without a doubt that Sophia had realized what was happening and was going to make trouble.

"The child seemed to sense the tension in the atmosphere for he became very troublesome, and suddenly I felt I had to get out of the room and escape. I took the child upstairs. It was the only excuse I could think of which enabled me to get away, and I stayed upstairs with him for about half an hour, putting him to bed and reading to him. I can't even remember what we read. All I could think of was that Sophia believed Jon intended to be unfaithful to her, and was going to make trouble. My mind was going round and round in circles. Would she divorce Jon? What would she say? How much would come out? How much would it affect Marijohn? Would it succeed in driving Jon and Marijohn more firmly together than ever? What was going to happen? And I went on reading to the child and pretending to him that everything was normal, and inside my heart felt as if it were bursting. . . .

"When I went back downstairs, they were alone in the music room and there was a record playing on the gramophone. Sophia was in the kitchen with Max. I closed the door and said to Jon, 'Sophia knows—you realize that?' And he said, looking me straight in the eyes, 'Knows what?'

"I said there was no sense in pretending any longer and that the time had come to be perfectly frank with each other. Marijohn tried to interrupt, telling me not to make such an exhibition of myself, but I shut my mind to her and refused to listen. 'You may not be technically committing adultery with my wife,' I said to Jon, 'but you're behaving exactly as if you are, and Sophia isn't going to accept all these airy fairy tales about a relationship with no sex in it. She's going to believe the worst and act accordingly, and in many ways she'd be justified. Whatever your relationship with my wife is, it's a dangerous one that should be stopped—and it must be stopped.'

"They looked at each other. They looked at me. And as they were silent, thinking, I knew instinctively what it was that was so wrong. They were sharing each other's minds. Sophia, close as she might have been to Jon as the result of physical intimacy, was as a stranger to him in the face of that uncanny intangible understanding he shared with Marijohn. Sophia was being forced into the position of outsider—but not by any means which she could recognize or label. For because their relationship was so far beyond her grasp—or indeed the grasp of any ordinary person—it was impossible for her to identify the wrongness in the relationship although it was possible to sense that wrongness did exist.

"Jon said, 'Look Michael—' but he got no further. The door opened and Sophia walked into the room."

He stopped. The sea went on murmuring at the base of the cliffs, and there was no light as far as the eye could see. The darkness made Sarah more conscious of her dizziness and of her hot, aching eyes.

"Don't tell me any more," she whispered. "Don't. Please."

But he wasn't listening to her.

"What is it?"

"I thought I heard something." He went on listening but presently he relaxed a little. "There was a terrible scene," he said at last. "I can't begin to tell you what was said. It ended with Jon leaving the room and walking out across the lawn. Marijohn went up to her room, and I was left alone with Sophia. I tried to reason with her but she wouldn't listen and in the end she went upstairs to change her shoes before going out. There was some rendezvous with Max on the Flat Rocks, although I didn't know that at the time. I stayed in the drawing-room until I heard her go, and then

I went up to my room to find Marijohn but she was no longer there. I stayed there thinking for a long while.

"After Sophia's death, I thought for a time that everything was going to work out at last, but I was too optimistic. Marijohn and Jon had a very long talk together. I don't know what was said, but the upshot of it was that they had decided to part for good. I think Sophia's death—or rather, the scene that preceded her death —had shaken them and they realized they couldn't go on as they were. Jon went to Canada, to the other side of the world, and Marijohn returned with me to London, but she didn't stay long and we never lived together as man and wife again. She went to Paris for a while, came back but couldn't settle down in any place with anyone. I wanted to help her as I knew she was desperately unhappy, but there was nothing I could do and the love I offered her was useless. In the end she turned to religion. She was living in a convent when Jon returned to England a few weeks ago."

He threw away his cigarette. The tip glowed briefly and then died in the darkness.

"So you see," he said slowly at last, "it's quite imperative that you get Jon away from here. It's all happening again, can't you realize that? It's all happening again—we're all here at Clougy, all of us except that woman of Max's, and you've been assigned Sophia's role."

Stone grated on stone; there was the click of a powerful torch, a beam of blinding light.

"Just what the hell are you trying to suggest to my wife, Michael Rivers?" said Jon's hard, dangerous voice from the darkness beyond the torch's beam.

II

"Stay and have dinner with me," said Eve to Justin. "I don't know a soul in this town. Take me somewhere interesting where we can have a meal."

"No," he said, "I have to get back to Clougy." And then, realizing his words might have sounded rude and abrupt, he added hastily, "I promised to get back for dinner."

"Call them and tell them you've changed your mind."

"No, I—" He stopped, blushed, shook his head. His fingers fidgeted with the door handle. "I'm sorry, but I have to get back— it's rather important. There's something I have to talk about with my father."

"About your mother's death?" she said sharply. "Was it something I said? You're sure now that he didn't kill her, aren't you?"

"Yes," he said, and added in a rush: "And I think I know who did." He opened the door and paused to look at her.

She smiled. "Come back when you can," was all she said. "Tell me what happens."

He thanked her awkwardly, his shyness returning for a moment, and then left the room to go downstairs to the hall.

Outside, the golden light of evening was soothing to his eyes. He moved quickly back towards Fish Street, and then broke into a run as he reached the harbor walls and ran down the steps towards the car park. The sea on his right was a dark blue mirror reflecting golden lights from the sky and far away the waves broke in white wavering lines of foam on the sand-dunes of Hayle.

He was panting when he reached the car and had to search for his keys. For one sickening moment he thought he had lost his key-ring, but then he discovered the keys in the inside pocket of his jacket and quickly unlocked the car door. He suddenly realized he was sweating and fear was a sharp prickling tension crawling at the base of his spine.

St. Ives was jammed with the summer tourist traffic leaving the town at the end of the day. It took him quarter of an hour to travel from the car park through the town and emerge on the Land's End road.

He had just reached the lonely stretch of the wild coast road between Morvah and Zennor when the engine spluttered, coughed and was still. He stared at the petrol gauge with incredulous eyes for one long moment, and then, wrenching open the car door he started to run down the road back to Zennor with his heart hammering and pounding in his lungs.

III

Rivers stood up. He didn't hurry. "Put out that torch, for God's sake," he said calmly with a slight air of irritability. "I can't see a thing."

The torch clicked. There was darkness.

"Sarah," said Jon.

She didn't move. She tried to, but her limbs made no response.

"Sarah, what's he been saying to you?"

Rivers took a slight step nearer her and she sensed he had moved to reassure her. Her mouth was dry as if she had run a long way with no rest.

"Sarah!" shouted Jon. "Sarah!"

"For God's sake, Jon," said Rivers, still with his calm air of slight irritability. "Pull yourself together. I suggest we all go back to the house instead of conducting arguments and recriminations on the top of a cliff on a particularly dark Cornish night."

"Go—yourself," said Jon between his teeth and tried to push past him, but Rivers stood his ground.

"Let me by."

"Relax," said Rivers, still calm. "Sarah's perfectly all right but she's had a shock."

"Get out of my—"

They were struggling, wrestling with one another, but even as Sarah managed to stand up Michael made no further attempts to hold Jon back, and stepped aside.

"Sarah," said Jon, trying to take her in his arms. "Sarah—"

She twisted away from him. "Let me go."

"It's not true about Marijohn! Whatever he said to you isn't true!"

She didn't answer. He whirled on Rivers. "What did you tell her?"

Rivers laughed.

"What did you tell her?" He had left Sarah and was gripping Rivers' shoulders. "What did you say?"

"I told her enough to persuade her to leave Clougy as soon as possible. Nothing more."

"What the hell do you—"

"I didn't tell her, for instance, that Sophia's death wasn't accidental. Nor did I tell her that she was pushed down the cliff-path to her death by someone who had a very good motive for silencing her—"

"Why, you—" Jon was blind with rage and hatred. Rivers was forced to fight back in self-defense.

"For Christ's sake, Jon!"

"Jon!" cried Sarah suddenly in fear.

He stopped at once, looking back at her, his chest heaving with exertion. "Did he tell you?" he said suddenly in a low voice. "Did he tell you?"

She leaned back against the rock, too exhausted to do more than nod her head, not even sure what she was affirming. From far away as if in another world she heard Rivers laugh at Jon's panic, but she was conscious only of a great uneasiness prickling beneath her skin.

Jon whirled on Rivers. "How could you?" he gasped. "You love Marijohn. We all agreed ten years ago that no one should ever know the truth. You said yourself that it would be best for Marijohn if no one ever knew that she and I were—" He stopped.

"Jon," said Rivers, a hard warning edge to his voice. "Jon—"

"Yes," cried Sarah in sudden passion. "That you and she were what?"

"That she and I were brother and sister," said Jon exhausted, and then instantly in horror: "My God, you didn't know . . . ?"

IV

Justin managed to get a lift to a garage and paid the mechanic for taking him back to his car with a can of petrol.

It was after sunset. The dusk was gathering.

"Should do the trick," said the mechanic, withdrawing his head from the bonnet. "Give 'er a try."

The starter whined; the engine flickered briefly and died.

"Funny," said the mechanic with interest. "Must be trouble in the carburetor. Petrol not feeding properly. Did the gauge say you was dead out of petrol?"

"No," said Justin. "According to the gauge there was still a little in the tank. I just thought the gauge must have gone wrong."

"Funny," said the mechanic again with a deeper interest, and put his head cautiously back under the bonnet. "Well, now, let me see . . ."

V

Sarah was running. The heather was scratching her legs and the darkness was all around her, smothering her lungs as she fought for breath. And then at last she saw the lighted windows of Clougy and knew she would be able at last to escape from the suffocation of the darkness and the isolation of the Cornish hillsides.

Max Alexander came out into the hall as she stumbled through the front door and paused gasping by the stairs, her shoulders leaning against the wall, her eyes closed as the blood swam through her brain.

"Sarah! What's happened? What is it?"

She sank down on the stairs, not caring that he should see her tears, and as the scene tilted crazily before her eyes she felt the sobs rise in her throat and shudder through her body.

"Sarah . . ." He was beside her, his arm round her shoulders almost before he had time to think. "Tell me what it is. . . . If there's anything I can do—"

"Where's Marijohn?"

"In the kitchen, I think, clearing up the aftermath of the meal. Why? Do you—"

"Max, can you—would you—"

"Yes?" he said. "What is it? Tell me what you want me to do."

"I—I want to go away. Could you drive me into St. Ives, or Penzance, anywhere—"

"Now?"

"Yes," she whispered, struggling with her tears. "Now."

"But—"

"I want to be alone to think," she said. "I must be able to think."

"Yes, I see. Yes, of course. All right, I'll go and start the car. You'd better pack a suitcase or something, hadn't you?"

She nodded, still blind with tears, and he helped her to her feet.

"Can you manage?"

"Yes," she said. "Yes, thank you."

He waited until she had reached the landing and then he walked out of the open front door and she heard the crunch of his footsteps on the gravel of the drive.

She went to her room. Her smallest suitcase was on the floor of the cupboard. She was just opening it and trying to think what she should pack when she sensed instinctively that she was no longer alone in the room.

"Max," she said as she swung round, "Max, I—"

It wasn't Max. It was Marijohn.

The silence which followed seemed to go on and on and on.

"What is it?" said Sarah unsteadily at last. "What do you want?"

The door clicked shut. The woman turned the key in the lock

and then leaned back against the panels. Somewhere far away the phone started to ring but no one answered it.

"I heard your conversation with Max just now," she said after a while. "I knew then that I had to talk to you."

There was silence again, a deep absolute silence, and then Marijohn said suddenly, "If you leave Jon now it would be the worst thing you could possibly do. He loves you, and needs you. Nothing which happened in the past can ever change that."

She moved then, walking over to the window and staring out at the dark night towards the sea. She was very still.

"That was Sophia's mistake," she said. "He loved and needed her too but she flung it back in his face. It was an easy mistake for her to make, because she never really loved him or understood him. But you do, don't you. I know you do. You're quite different from Sophia. As soon as I saw you, I knew you were quite different from her."

It was difficult to breathe. Sarah found her lungs were aching with tension and her fingernails were hurting the palms of her hands.

"I want Jon to be happy," Marijohn said. "That's all I want. I thought it would make him happy to come down here with you to stay. I thought that if we were to meet again here of all places nothing would happen between us because the memories would be there all the time, warning us and acting as a barrier. But I was wrong and so was he, and there can never be another occasion like this now. He's leaving tomorrow—did you know that? And when he leaves I know I shall never see him again."

She took the curtain in her hands, fingering its softness delicately, her eyes still watching the darkness beyond the pane.

"I don't know what I shall do," she said. "I haven't allowed myself to think much about it yet. You see . . . how can I best explain? Perhaps it's best to put it in very simple language and not try to wrap it up in careful, meaningless phrases. The truth of the matter is that I can't live without Jon, but he can live perfectly well without me. I've always known that. It's got nothing to do with love at all. It's just something that *is*, that exists. I do love Jon, and he loves me, but that's quite irrelevant. We would have this thing which exists between us even if we hated one another. I can best describe it by calling it color. When he's not there, the world is black and gray and I'm only half-alive and dreadfully alone. And when he is there the world is multicolored and I can live and the concept of loneliness is nothing more than a remote unreal nightmare. That's how it affects me, but Jon I know isn't affected in the same way. When I'm not there, he doesn't live in a twilight black-and-white world as I do. He lives in a different world but the world is merely colored differently and although he may miss me he's still able to live a full, normal life. That's why he's been able to marry and find happiness, whereas I know I can never marry again. I should never even have married Michael. But Jon told me to marry. I was unhappy and he thought it was the answer to all my difficulties. I was always unhappy. . . .

"I can't remember when I first discovered this thing. I suppose it was after Jon's parents were divorced and I was taken away from Jon to live in a convent. I knew then how strange the world seemed without him. . . . Then when I was fourteen his father took me away from the convent and I was able to live at his house in London and Jon came back into my life. We both discovered the thing together then. It was rather exciting, like discovering a new dimension. . . . But then his father misunderstood the situation and, thinking the worst, decided to separate us again for a while. That was when I began to have affairs with as many men as I could—anything to bring color back to my gray, black-and-white world. . . . Jon married Sophia. I was glad he was happy, although it was terrible to lose him. I wouldn't have minded so much if I'd liked her, but she was such a stupid little bitch—I couldn't think what he saw in her. . . . I went on, having affair after affair until one day things went wrong and I had a great revulsion—a hatred of men, of life, and of the whole world. It was Jon who cured me. I went down to Clougy to see him and he brought me back to life and promised he'd keep in touch. I married Michael after that. Poor Michael. He's been very good to me always, and I've never been able to give him anything in return."

She stopped. It was still in the room. There was no sound at all.

"Even Michael never understood properly," she said at last. "Even he tended to think I had some kind of illicit relationship with Jon, but it wasn't true. Jon and I have never even exchanged an embrace which could remotely be described as adulterous. The thing we share is quite apart from all that, and I can't see why it should be considered wrong. But Michael thought it was. And Sophia . . . Sophia simply had no understanding of the situation at all. My God, she was a stupid little fool! If ever a woman drove her husband away from her, that woman was Sophia."

A door banged somewhere in the distance. There were footsteps on the stairs, a voice calling Sarah's name.

Marijohn unlocked the door just as Jon turned the handle and burst into the room. "Sarah—" he began and then stopped short as he found himself face to face with Marijohn.

"I was trying to explain to her," she said quietly. "I was trying to tell her about us."

"She already knows. You're too late."

Marijohn went white. "But how—"

"I told her myself," said Jon, and as he spoke Sarah saw them both turn towards her. "I thought Michael had already told her. I'm sure she must have guessed by now that we both had a first-class motive for murdering Sophia."

VI

It was dark on the road but fortunately the mechanic had a torch and could see what he was doing. Justin, glancing around in an agony of impatience, caught sight of a lighted window of a farm-house a few hundred yards from the road and began to move over towards it.

"I won't be long," he called to the mechanic. "I have to make a phone call."

The track was rough beneath his feet and the farm-yard when he reached it smelled of manure. The woman who answered the door looked faintly offended when he asked her politely if he could use her telephone, but showed him into the hall and left him alone to make the call.

He dialed the St. Just exchange with an unsteady hand. It seemed an eternity before the operator answered.

"St. Just 584, please."

Another endless space of time elapsed, and then he could hear the bell ringing and his fingers gripped the receiver even tighter than before.

It rang and rang and rang.

"Sorry, sir," said the operator at last, cutting in across the ringing bell, "but there seems to be no reply. . . ."

VII

They were still looking at her, their eyes withdrawn and tense, and it seemed to her as she watched them that their mental affinity was never more clearly visible and less intangible than at that moment when they shared identical expressions.

"What did Sophia threaten to do?" she heard herself say at last, and her voice was astonishingly cool and self-possessed in her ears.

"Surely you can guess," said Jon. "She was going to drag Marijohn's name right across her divorce petition. Can't you picture the revenge she planned in her jealousy, the damage she wanted to cause us both? Can't you imagine the longing she had to hurt and smear and destroy?"

"I see." And she did see. She was beginning to feel sick and dizzy again.

"Marijohn is illegitimate," he said, as if in attempt to explain the situation flatly. "We have the same father. Her mother died soon after she was born and my father—in spite of my mother's protests and disgust—brought her to live with us. After the divorce, he naturally took her away—he had to. My mother only had her there on sufferance anyway."

The silence fell again, deepening as the seconds passed.

"Jon," said Sarah at last. "Jon, did you—"

He knew what she wanted to ask, and she sensed that he had wanted her to ask the question which was foremost on her mind.

"No," he said. "I didn't kill Sophia. You must believe that, because I swear it's the truth. And if you ask why I lied to you, why I always told you Sophia's death was an accident, I'll tell you. I thought Marijohn had killed her. Everything I did which may have seemed like an admission of guilt on my part was in order to protect Marijohn—but although I didn't know it at the time, Marijohn thought *I'd* killed her. In spite of all our mutual understanding, we've both been suffering under a delusion about each other for ten years. Ironic, isn't it?"

She stared at him, not answering. After a moment he moved towards her, leaving Marijohn by the door.

"The scene with Sophia came after supper on the night she died," he said. "Michael was there too. After it was over, I went out into the garden to escape and sat on the swing-seat in the darkness for a long while trying to think what I should do. Finally I went back into the house to discuss the situation with Marijohn but she wasn't there. I went upstairs, but she wasn't there either and when I came downstairs again I met Eve in the hall. She told me Sophia had gone out to the Flat Rocks to meet Max, and suddenly I wondered if Marijohn had gone after Sophia to try and reason with her. I dashed out of the house and tore up the cliff path. I heard Sophia shout 'Let me go!' and then she screamed when I was about a hundred yards from the steps leading down to the Flat Rocks, and on running forward I found Marijohn at the cliff's edge staring down the steps. She was panting as if she'd been running—or struggling. She said that she'd been for a walk along the cliffs towards Sennen and was on her way back home when she'd heard the scream. We went down the steps and found Max bending over Sophia's body. He'd been waiting for her on the Flat Rocks below." He paused. "Or so he said."

There was a pause. Sarah turned to Marijohn. "What a coincidence," she said, "that you should be so near the steps at the time. What made you turn back at that particular moment during your walk along the cliffs and arrive at the steps just after Sophia was killed?"

"Sarah—" Jon was white with anger, but Marijohn interrupted him.

"I could feel Jon wanted me," she said simply. "I knew he was looking for me so I turned back."

Sarah scarcely recognized her voice when she next spoke. It was the voice of a stranger, brittle, hard and cold. "How very interesting," she said. "I've never really believed in telepathy."

"What are you suggesting?" said Jon harshly. "That I'm lying? That Marijohn's lying? That we're both lying?"

Sarah moved past him, opening the door clumsily in her desire to escape from their presence.

"One of you must be lying," she said. "That's obvious. Sophia before she fell called out 'Let me go' which means she was struggling with someone who pushed her to her death. Somebody killed her, and either of you—as you tell me yourself—had an ideal motive."

"Sarah—"

"Let her go, Jon. Let her be."

Sarah was in the corridor now, taking great gulps of air as if she had been imprisoned for a long time in a stifling cell. She went downstairs and out into the drive. The night air was deliciously cool, and as she wandered further from the house the freedom was all around her, a vast relief after the confined tension in that upstairs room.

He was waiting for her by the gate. She was so absorbed in her own emotions and her desire to escape that she never even noticed, as she took the cliff path, that she was being followed.

VIII

"It's a funny thing," said the mechanic when Justin reached the car again, "but I can't make her go. T'aint the carburetor. Can't understand it."

Justin thought quickly. He could get a lift to St. Just and a lift out to the airport, but he would have to walk the mile and a half from the airport down into the valley to Clougy. But anything was better than waiting fruitlessly by the roadside at Zennor. He could try another phone call from the square at St. Just.

"All right," he said to the mechanic. "I'll have to try and get a lift home. Can you fix up for someone from your garage to tow away my car tomorrow and find out what's wrong?"

"Do it right now, if you like. It only means—"

"No, I can't wait now. I'll have to go on ahead." He found a suitable tip and gave it to the man who looked a little astonished by this impatience. "Thank you very much for all your trouble. Goodnight."

"Goodnight to you," said the mechanic agreeably enough, pocketing the tip, and climbed into his shooting brake to drive back along the road towards St. Ives.

IX

Sarah first saw the dark figure behind her when she was half a mile from the house. The cliff path had turned round the hillside so that the lighted windows were hidden from her, and she was just pausing in the darkness to listen to the sea far below and regain her breath after the uphill climb when she glanced over her shoulder and saw the man.

Every bone in her body suddenly locked itself into a tight white fear.

You've been assigned Sophia's role. . . .

The terror was suffocating, wave after wave of hot dizziness that went on and on even after she began to stumble forward along the cliff path. She never paused to ask herself why anyone should want her dead. She only knew in that blind, sickening flash that she was in danger and she had to escape.

But there was no cover on the stark hillside, nowhere to shelter.

It was then that she thought of the rocks below. In the jumbled confusion of boulders at the foot of the cliffs there were a thousand hiding places, and perhaps also another route by the sea's edge back to the cove and the house. If she could somehow find the way down the cliff to the Flat Rocks. . . .

The path forked slightly and remembering her exploring earlier that day, she took the downward path and found the steps cut in the cliff which led to the rocks below.

Her limbs were suddenly awkward; the sea was a roar that receded and pounded in her ears, drowning even the noise of her gasps for breath.

She looked back.

The man was running.

In a panic, not even trying to find the alternative route down the cliff, she scrambled down the steps, clinging to the jutting rocks in the sandy face and sliding the last few feet to the rock below. She started to run forward, slipped, fell. The breath was knocked out of her body and as she pulled herself to her feet she looked up and saw him at the head of the steps above her.

She flattened herself against the large rock nearby, not moving, not breathing, praying he hadn't seen her.

"Sarah?" he called.

He sounded anxious, concerned.

She didn't answer.

He cautiously began to descend the steps.

Let him fall, said the single voice in her mind drowning even the noise of the sea. Let him slip and fall. She couldn't move. If she moved he would see her and she would have less chance of escape.

He didn't like the steps at all. She heard him curse under his breath, and a shower of sand and pebbles scattered from the cliff face as he fumbled his way down uncertainly.

He reached the rock below at last and stood still six feet away from her. She could hear his quick breathing as he straightened his frame and stared around, his eyes straining to pierce the darkness.

"Sarah?" he called again, and added as an afterthought: "It's all right, it's only me."

She was pressing back so hard against the rock that her shoulder-blades hurt. Her whole body ached with the strain of complete immobility.

He took a step forward and another and stood listening again.

Close at hand the surf broke on the reefs and ledges of the Flat Rocks and was sucked back into the sea again with the undertow.

He saw her.

He didn't move at all at first, and then he came towards her and she started to scream.

Six

JUSTIN WAS running, the breath choking his lungs. He was running past the farm down the track to Clougy, not knowing why he was afraid, knowing only that his mother's murderer was at the house and that no one knew the truth except Justin himself and the killer. He didn't even know why his mother had been killed. The apparent motivelessness of the crime nagged his mind as he ran, but he had no doubts about the murderer's correct identity. According to Eve it would only be one person. . . .

He could hear the stream now, could see the hulk of the disused waterwheel on one side of the track, and suddenly he was at Clougy at last and stumbling through the open front door into the lighted hall.

"Daddy!" he shouted, and the word which had lain silent in the back of his vocabulary for ten years was then the first word which sprang to the tip of his tongue. "Where are you? Marijohn!"

He burst into the drawing-room but they weren't there. They weren't in the music room either.

"Sarah!" he shouted. "Sarah!"

But Sarah didn't answer.

He had a sudden premonition of disaster, a white warning flash across his brain which was gone in less than a second. Tearing up the stairs, he raced down the corridor and flung open the door to his father's bedroom.

They were there. They were sitting on the window seat together, and he was vaguely conscious that his father looked drawn and unhappy while Marijohn's calm, still face was streaked with tears.

"Justin! What in God's name—"

"Where's Sarah?" was all he could say, each syllable coming unevenly as he gasped for breath. "Where is she?"

There were footsteps in the corridor unexpectedly, a shadow in the doorway.

"She's gone for a walk with Michael," said Max Alexander.

II

"It's all right," Michael Rivers' voice was saying soothingly from far away. "It's all right, Sarah. It's only me. . . . Look, let's find a better place to sit down. It's too dark here."

She was still shuddering, her head swimming with the shock, but she let him lead her further down towards the sea until they were standing on the Flat Rocks by the water's edge.

"Why did you follow me?" she managed to say as they sat down on a long low rock.

"I saw you leave and couldn't think where on Earth you were going or what you wanted to do. I believe I thought you might even be thinking of committing suicide."

"Suicide?" She stared at him. "Why?" And in the midst of her confusion she was conscious of thinking that in spite of all that had happened, the thought of suicide to escape from her unhappiness and shock had never crossed her mind.

"You've been married—how long? Two weeks? Three? And you discover suddenly that your husband has a rather 'unique' relationship with another woman—"

"We're leaving tomorrow," she interrupted. "Marijohn told me. Jon's decided to leave and never see her again."

"He decided that ten years ago. I'm afraid I wouldn't rely too much on statements like that, if I were you. And what do you suppose your marriage is going to be like after this? He'll never fully belong to you now, do you realize that? Part of him will always be with Marijohn. Good God, I of all people should know what I'm talking about! I tried to live with Marijohn after Jon had first disrupted our marriage, but it was utterly impossible. Everything was over and done with, and there was no going back."

"Stop it!" said Sarah with sudden violence. "Stop it!"

"So in the light of the fact that you know your three-week old marriage is finished, I don't see why you shouldn't think of committing suicide. You're young and unbalanced by grief and shock. You come out here to the Flat Rocks to the sea, and the tide is going out and the currents are particularly dangerous—"

She tried to move but he wouldn't let her go.

"I thought of suicide that weekend at Clougy," he said. "Did you guess that? I went fishing that afternoon by the sea and thought and thought about what I could do. I was out of my mind. . . . And then the child came and talked to me and afterwards I went back to the house. Marijohn was in our bedroom. I knew then how much I loved her, and I knew that I could never share her with any man, even if the relationship she had with him was irreproachable and completely above suspicion. I foresaw that I would be forced to have a scene with Jon in an attempt to tell him that I could stand it no longer and that I was taking Marijohn away. . . . So after dinner we had the final scene. And I was winning. . . . It was going to be all right. Jon was shaken —I can see his expression now. . . . And then, oh Christ, Sophia had to come in, threatening divorce proceedings, threatening exposure to anyone who would listen—God, she would have destroyed everything! And Marijohn's name smeared all across the Sunday papers and all my friends and colleagues in town saying, 'Poor old Michael—ghastly business. Who would have thought . . .' and so on and so on. . . . All the gossip and publicity, the destruction of Marijohn, of everything I wanted. . . . Sophia was going to destroy my entire world."

"So you killed her."

He looked at her then, his face oddly distant. "Yes," he said. "I killed her. And Jon went away, saying he would never have any further communication with Marijohn, and I thought that at last I was going to have Marijohn back again and that at last I was going to be happy."

His expression changed. He grimaced for a moment, his expression contorted, and when he next spoke she heard the grief in his voice.

"But she wouldn't come back to me," he said. "I went through all that and committed murder to safeguard her and preserve her from destruction, and all she could do was say how sorry she was but she could never live with me again."

The surf broke over the rocks at their feet; white foam flew for a moment in the darkness and disintegrated.

"Sophia knew they were brother and sister," he said. "Not that it mattered. She would have made trouble anyway. But if she had never known they were brother and sister, the scope of her threats would have been narrower and less frightening in its implications . . . But she knew. Very few people did. The relationship had always been kept secret from the beginning in order to spare Jon's mother embarrassment. Old Towers made out that Marijohn was the child of a deceased younger brother of his. And when they were older they kept it secret to avoid underlining Marijohn's illegitimacy. I always did think it would have been best if Sophia had never known the secret, but Jon told her soon after they were married, so she knew about it from the beginning."

There was another pause. Sarah tried to imagine what would happen if she attempted to break away. Could she reach the cover of the nearby rocks in time? Probably not. Perhaps if she doubled back . . . She turned her head slightly to look behind her, and as she moved, Rivers said,

"And now there's you. You'll divorce Jon eventually. Even if your marriage survives this crisis there'll be others, and then it'll all come out, the relationship with Marijohn, your very natural jealousy—everything. Marijohn's name will be dragged across the petition because like Sophia, you know the truth, and when the time comes for you to want a divorce you'll be embittered enough to use any weapon at your disposal in an attempt to hit back at both of them. And that'll mean danger to Marijohn. Whatever happens I want to avoid that, because of course I still love her and sometimes I can still hope that one day she'll come back. . . . Perhaps she will. I don't know. But whether she comes back or not I still love her just the same. I know that better than anything else in the world."

There was no hope of escape by running behind them across the rock. The way was too jagged and Sarah guessed it would be too easy in the dark to stumble into one of the pools and lagoons beyond the reefs.

"It would be so convenient if you committed suicide," he said. "Perhaps I could even shift the blame on to Jon if murder were suspected. I tried to last time. I planned the death to look like an accident, but I wore a red sweater of Jon's just in case anyone happened to see me go up the cliff path and murder was suspected afterwards. I knew Sophia was meeting Max on the Flat Rocks. I heard Sophia remind him of their rendezvous after supper, and saw Max leave the house later. Then after the scene in the drawing-room when we all went our separate ways, I didn't go up to my bedroom as I told you earlier this evening. Jon went into the garden, Marijohn went to the drawing-room, Sophia went upstairs to change her high-heeled shoes for a pair of canvas beach shoes, and I took Jon's sweater off the chest in the hall and went out ahead of her to the cliffs. I didn't have to wait long before she came out from the house to follow me. . . .

"But they never suspected murder, the slow Cornish police. They talked of accident and suicide, but murder was never mentioned. Nobody knew, you see, of any possible motives. They were all hidden, secret, protected from the outside world. . . ."

"Michael."

He turned to look at her and she was close enough to him to

see in the darkness that his eyes were clouded as if he were seeing only scenes of long ago.

"If I said that I wasn't going to divorce Jon and that the secret was safe with me—"

"You'd be wasting your breath, I'm afraid, my dear. I've confessed to you now that I'm a murderer and that's one secret I could never trust you to keep."

She swung round suddenly to face the cliffs. "What's that?"

He swung round too, swiveling his body instinctively, and even as he moved she was on her feet and running away from him in among the rocks to escape.

He shouted something and then was after her and the rocks were the towering tombstones of a nightmare and the roar of the sea merged with the roaring of the blood in her ears. The granite grazed her hands, tore at her stockings, bruised her feet through the soles of her shoes. She twisted and turned, scrambling amongst the rocks, terrified of coming up against a blank wall of rock or falling into a deep gully. And still he came after her, gaining slowly every minute, and her mind was a blank void of terror depriving her of speech and voice.

When she was at the base of the cliff again she caught her foot in a crevice and the jolt wrenched her ankle and tore off her shoe. She gave a cry of pain, the sound wrenched involuntarily from her body, and as the sound was carried away from her on the still night air she saw the pin-prick of light above her on the cliff-path.

"Jon!" she screamed, thrusting all her energy into that one monosyllable. "Jon! Jon!"

And then Rivers was upon her and she was fighting for her life, scratching, clawing, biting in a frenzy of self-preservation. The scene began to blur before her eyes, the world tilted crazily. She tried to scream again but no sound came, and as the energy ebbed from her body she felt his fingers close on her throat.

There was pain. It was a hot red light suffocating her entire brain. She tried to breathe and could not. Her hands were just slackening their grip on his body when there was a sound far above her, and the pebbles started to rattle down the cliff face, flicking across her face like hail stones.

She heard Rivers gasp something, and then he was gone and she fell back against the rock.

The blackness when it came a second later was a welcome release from the swimming nightmare of terror and fear.

III

When she awoke, there was a man bending over her, and although it seemed that an eternity had passed since Rivers had left her, she learned afterwards that she had been unconscious for less than a minute. The man was frantic. There was sweat on his forehead and fear in his eyes and he kept saying, "Sarah, Sarah, Sarah" as if his mind would not allow him to say anything else.

She put up her hand and touched his lips with her fingers.

"Is she all right?" said another vaguely familiar voice from close at hand. "Where the hell is Rivers?"

The man whose lips she had touched stood up. "Stay here with Sarah, Max. Have you got that? Don't leave her alone for a moment. Stay with her."

"Jon," her voice said. "Jon."

He bent over her again. "I'm going to find him," he said to her gently. "Justin's gone after him already. Max'll look after you."

"He—he killed Sophia, Jon. . . . He told me—"

"I know."

He was gone. One moment he was there and the next moment he had moved out of her sight and she was alone with Alexander. He was breathing very heavily, as if the sudden violent exercise had been too much for him.

"Max—"

"Yes, I'm here." He sat down beside her, still panting with exertion, and as he took her hand comfortingly in his she had the odd instinctive feeling that he cared for her. The feeling was so strange and so illogical that she dismissed it instantly without a second thought, and instead concentrated all her mind on the relief of being alive.

And as they waited together at the base of the cliffs, Jon was sprinting over the Flat Rocks to the water's edge, the beam of the torch in his hand warning him of the gullies and the crevices, the reefs and lagoons.

By the water's edge he paused.

"Justin!"

There was an answering flicker of a torch further away, a muffled shout.

Jon moved forward again, leaping from rock to rock, slithering past seaweed and splashing in diminutive rock pools. It took him two minutes to reach his son.

"Where is he?"

"I don't know." Justin's face was white in the torchlight, his eyes dark and huge and ringed with tiredness.

"You lost sight of him?"

"He was here." He gestured with his torch. They were standing on a squat rock, and six feet below them the sea was sucking and gurgling with the motions of the tide. "I saw him reach this rock and then scramble over it until he was lost from sight."

Jon was silent. Presently he shone his torch up and down the channel below, but there was nothing there except the dark water and the white of the surf.

"Could he—do you think he would have tried to swim round to the cove?"

"Don't be a bloody fool."

The boy hung his head a little, as if regretting the stupidity of his suggestion, and waited wordlessly for the other man to make the next move.

"He couldn't have fallen in the darkness," said Jon after a moment. "When you reach the top of a rock you always stop to look to see what's on the other side. And if he had slipped into this channel he could have clambered out on to the other side—unless he struck his head on the rocky floor, and then we'd be able to see his body."

"Then—"

"Perhaps you're right and he went swimming after all. . . . We'd better search these rocks here just to make sure, I suppose. You take that side and I'll take this side."

But although they searched for a long while in the darkness they found no trace of Michael Rivers, and it was many weeks before his body was finally recovered from the sea.

IV

"What'll happen?" said Justin to his father. "What shall we do?"

They were in the drawing-room at Clougy again. It was after midnight, and the tiredness was aching through Justin's body in great throbbing waves of exhaustion. Even when he sat down the room seemed to waver and recede dizzily before his eyes.

"We'll have to call the police."

"You're mad, of course," said Alexander from the sofa. "You must be. What on Earth are you going to say to the police? That Michael's dead? We don't know for sure that he is. That Michael tried to kill Sarah? The first question the police are going to ask is why the hell should Michael, a perfectly respectable solicitor, a pillar of society, suddenly attempt to murder your wife. My dear Jon, you'll end up by getting so involved that the police will probably think we're all in one enormous conspiracy to pull wool over their eyes. They'll ask you why, if you *knew* your first wife had been murdered, you didn't say so at the time. They'll ask you all sorts of questions about Marijohn and your reasons for wanting to protect her. They'll probe incessantly for motives—"

"For Christ's sake, Max!"

"Well, stop talking such God almighty rubbish."

"Are you scared for your own skin or something?"

"Oh God," said Alexander wearily, and turned to the boy hunched in the armchair. "Justin, explain to your father that if he goes to the police now Sophia—and probably Michael too —have both died in vain. Ask him if he really wants Sarah's name smeared all across the Sunday papers. 'Canadian millionaire in murder mystery. Horror on the Honeymoon.' God, can't you imagine the headlines even now? 'Sensation! Millionaire's first wife *murdered!* Millionaire helping the police in their inquiries.' It would be intolerable for you all, Jon—for Sarah, for Justin, for Marijohn—"

The door opened. He stopped as Marijohn came into the room.

"How is she?" said Jon instantly. "Is she asking for me? Is she all right?"

"She's asleep. I gave her two of my sleeping tablets." She turned away from him and moved over towards the boy in the corner. "Justin darling, you look quite exhausted. Why don't you go to bed? There's nothing more you can do now."

"I—" He faltered, looking at his father. "I was wondering what's going to happen. If you call the police—"

"Police?" said Marijohn blankly. She swung round to face Jon. "Police?"

"Tell him he's crazy, Marijohn."

"Look, Max—"

There they go again, thought Justin numbly. More arguments, more talk. Police or no police, what to tell and what not to tell, Michael's death or disappearance and what to do about it. And I'm so very very tired. . . .

He closed his eyes for a second. The voices became fainter and then suddenly someone was stooping over him and there was an arm round his shoulders and the cold rim of the glass against his lips. He drank, choked and opened his eyes as the liquid burnt his throat.

"Poor Justin," said the voice he had loved so much ten years ago. "Come on, you're going to bed. Drink the rest of the brandy and we'll go upstairs."

There was fire in his throat again. The great heaviness in his limbs seemed to lessen fractionally and with his father's help he managed to stand up and moved over to the door.

"I'm all right now," he heard himself say in the hall. "Sorry to be a nuisance."

"I'll come upstairs with you."

There seemed more stairs than usual, an endless climb to the distant plateau of the landing, but at last they were in the bedroom and the bed was soft and yielding as he sank down on it thankfully.

"I'm all right," he repeated automatically, and then his shirt was eased gently from his body and the next moment the cool pajama jacket brushed his skin.

"I'm afraid I've been very selfish," said his father's voice. "I haven't said a word of thanks to you since you arrived back and all I could do down on the Flat Rocks was to be abrupt and short-tempered."

"It—it doesn't matter. I understand."

"I'll never forget that it was you who saved Sarah. I want you to know that. If Sarah had died tonight—"

"She'll be all right, won't she? She's going to be all right?"

"Yes," said Jon. "She's going to be all right."

The sheets were deliciously white, the pillow sensuously soft and yielding. Justin sank back, pulling the coverlet across his chest and allowing his limbs to relax in a haze of comfort and peace.

He never even heard his father leave the room.

When he awoke it was still dark but someone had opened the door of his room and the light from the landing was shining across the foot of his bed.

"Who's that?" he murmured sleepily, and then Marijohn was stooping over him and he twisted round in bed so that he could see her better. "What's happened?" he said, suddenly very wide awake, his brain miraculously clear and alert. "Have you called the police?"

"No." She sat down on the edge of the bed and for a moment he thought she was going to kiss him but she merely touched his cheek lightly with her fingertips. "I'm sorry I woke you up. I didn't mean to disturb you. Jon's just gone to bed and Max is still downstairs drinking the last of the whisky. We've been talking for nearly three hours."

He sat up a little in bed. "Haven't you decided anything?"

She looked at him and he thought he saw her smile faintly, but the light was behind her and it was difficult for him to see her face.

"You're leaving tomorrow—you and Sarah and Jon," she said and there was a curious dull edge to her voice which he didn't fully understand. "You'll go straight to London and catch the first plane to Canada. Max and I are going to handle the police."

He stared at her blankly. "How?" he said. "What are you going to tell them?"

"Very little. Max is going to drive Michael's car up past the farm and abandon it on the heath near the airport. Then tomorrow or the day after I'm going to phone the police and tell them that I'm worried about Michael and think he may have committed suicide—I'm going to say that Max and I have found Michael's car abandoned on the heath after you all departed for London. Our story is going to be that Michael came down here in the hope of persuading me to go back to him, and when I refused—finally and forever—there was a scene which ended in him leaving the house and driving away. We shall say he threatened suicide before he left. Then the police can search for him as thoroughly as they wish, and when his body is eventually recovered—as I suppose it must be, even on this rocky coast— it'll lend support to our story."

"Supposing Michael isn't dead?"

"He must be. Jon is convinced of it. Michael had nothing left to live for, nothing at all."

"But . . ." He hesitated, trying to phrase what he wanted to say. Then: "Why is it so vital that the police don't know the truth from start to finish?" he blurted out at last. "I mean, I know the scandal would be terrible, but—"

"There are reasons," she said. "Your father will tell you."

"But why did Michael try to kill Sarah? And why did he kill my mother? I don't—"

"He wanted to protect me," she said, her voice suddenly flat and without life. "It was all for me. Your father will explain everything to you later when you're all far away in Canada."

He still stared at her. "I couldn't see why he was the murderer," he repeated at last. "I knew he must have been the murderer but I couldn't see why."

"What did Eve tell you? What did she say that suddenly made you realize Michael was guilty?"

"I—I persuaded her to talk to me about her own memories of that weekend at Clougy, and her memories, when I pieced them together with my own, spelled the real sequence of events." He paused to collect his thoughts, thinking of Eve and the little room in St. Ives above the blue of the bay. "I thought my father had killed my mother because I followed a man with a red sweater up the cliff-path and saw him push my mother to her death in the darkness. . . . As soon as I'd seen her fall I ran away up the hillside and over the hill-top to Clougy. I didn't take the cliff-path back to the house because I was afraid my father would see me, so I never discovered that the man in the red sweater wasn't my father at all. But I think Michael must have returned to the house by a similar route to the one I took, because neither you, coming from Sennen, nor my father, coming from Clougy along the cliff-path, saw either Michael or myself. My father told me tonight that you and he had met by the steps soon after my mother fell.

"When I left the house to follow the man in the red sweater I met Eve—she was coming up the path from the beach just as

I was about to take the fork which led up on the cliffs. I hid from her, and she didn't see me.

"This afternoon she told me what had happened to her that evening. She said that when she reached the house again after I'd seen her she met my father. That proved to me that the man in the red sweater couldn't have been my father, and she also remembered he wasn't wearing a sweater when she saw him and that the red sweater he'd worn earlier in the evening had been removed from the chest in the hall.

"That meant the man had to be either Michael or Max. And according to Eve, it couldn't possibly have been Max because she'd seen him go off along the cliff-path to the Flat Rocks some while before she passed me on her way back to the house. She said they had quarreled at the spot where the path from Clougy forks, one track leading up on to the cliffs and one leading down to the cove, and afterwards he had gone off up the cliff-path to wait for my mother—Eve saw him go. Then she sat down by the fork in the path to try to pull herself together and decide what she should do. She would have seen Max if he had come back from the cliffs, but he didn't come back. And the man in the red sweater, whom I followed had started out *from the house* a few minutes before I saw Eve coming back up the path to Clougy where she was to meet my father. So the man had to be Michael. My father was still at the house and Max had already gone out to the Flat Rocks. There was no one else it could possibly be."

"I see." She was silent for a moment, and he wondered what she was thinking. And then she was standing up, smoothing the skirt of her dress over her hips automatically, and moving towards the door again. "You'd better get some more sleep," she said at last. "I mustn't keep you awake any longer."

She stepped across the threshold, and as she turned to close the door and the light slanted across her face, something in her expression made him call out after her.

But she did not hear him.

V

Max had just finished the whisky when Marijohn went downstairs to lock up and switch off the lights. A half-smoked cigarette was between his fingers and as she came into the room the ash dropped from the glowing tip to the carpet.

"Hullo," he said, and he didn't sound very drunk. "How's my fellow-conspirator?"

She drew the curtains back, not answering, and reached up to fasten the bolt on the French windows.

"You know why I'm doing it, don't you?" he said sardonically. "I'm not doing it for you or for Jon. Between you you've destroyed a good man and were indirectly responsible for Sophia's death. You deserve all you get. So I'm not doing this for you. I'm doing this for the girl because I don't see why she should suffer any more than she's suffered already. Quixotic, isn't it? Rather amusing. But then I've always been a fool over women. . . . Lord, what a fool I was over Sophia! I wanted her dead just as much as everyone else did, did you ever realize that? I told Sarah this afternoon that I felt sorry for Sophia, and so I did—to begin with. But I left several details out of my story to Sarah; I never told her that Sophia was trying to force me into taking her away to London with me, never mentioned that Sophia was threatening me, never hinted that it was I, not Sophia, who suggested the rendezvous on the Flat Rocks so that I could try and make her see reason. . . . And once she was dead, of course, I said nothing, never breathing a word of my suspicions to anyone, because I had a strong motive for wanting her dead and in any police murder inquiry I would naturally be one of the chief suspects. . . . And even now you won't have to worry in case I decide to change my mind and say too much to the police some time in the future, because I know for a fact that I haven't long to live and when I die you'll all be quite safe, you and Jon, Sarah and the boy. . . .

N

The boy will have to know the full story, of course. I can't say I envy Jon having to explain. . . . You're fond of the boy, aren't you? I suppose it's because he reminds you of Jon."

Yes, said a voice in her brain instantly in a sudden flare of grief, and no doubt I shall always have to share him just as I've had to share Jon. Aloud she said, "I've no mental affinity with Justin at all. He doesn't remind me of Jon as much as all that."

There was a pause before Alexander said, "And what will you do? You won't stay here longer than you can help, will you?"

"No," she said. "Jon wants me to sell Clougy. He says he never wants to see the place again."

"Poor old Jon," said Alexander inconsequentially, swallowing the dregs of his whisky. "Who would have thought the day would have come when he would say he never wanted to see Clougy again? He'll be saying next that he never wants to see you again either."

"He doesn't have to say that," said Marijohn, and the tears were like hot needles behind her eyes. "I already know."

VI

When Sarah awoke it was dim and she could see that there was a white mist swirling outside the window beyond the chink in the curtains. She stirred. Memory returned suddenly in sickening flashes of consciousness, and even as she reached for him instinctively, Jon was pulling her close to him and burying his face in her hair as he kissed her.

"How are you feeling?"

She pressed against him, savoring his nearness and her own security. "Jon . . . Jon . . ."

"We're leaving with Justin after breakfast," he said. "Then as soon as we get to London we're flying home to Canada. I'll explain later how Max and Marijohn are going to cope with the police—you don't have to worry about anything at all."

She put her hand to his face and traced the outline of his jaw as she kissed him on the mouth.

"I love you," he said in between her kisses, and his voice was unsteady so that it didn't sound like his voice at all. "Do you hear? I love, love, love you, and you're never never going to have to go through anything like this again."

"Will we come back to England?" she murmured. The question didn't seem very important somehow but she had a feeling it should nevertheless be asked.

"No," he said, his voice firm and positive again. "Never."

"Oh." She sighed, half-wondering why she had no feeling of sadness. "We must find time to say good-bye to your mother before we leave," she said as an afterthought. "I feel sorry for her in some ways. I'm sure she'll miss Justin terribly."

"She'll get over it." His mouth was hardening again. "Like most beautiful women she's egocentric enough to care for no one deeply except herself."

"That's nonsense, Jonny, and you know it!" She felt almost cross. "It's obvious to any outsider that she cares very deeply for you—no, I don't care what you say! I know I'm right! We must invite her out to Canada to visit us. She's got plenty of money so she'll be able to come whenever she likes. And anyway I think Justin should have the opportunity to keep in touch with his grandmother—after all, she brought him up, didn't she? In spite of the row they had when you offered him the job in Canada, I'm sure he must be very fond of her. Before we fly back to Canada we must call on her and arrange something."

Jon's mouth was still a hard stubborn line. "Sarah—"

She slipped her hand behind his head and pressed his face to hers to kiss the stubbornness from his expression. "Please, Jon!"

The victory came in less than five seconds. She felt him relax, saw his eyes soften, felt his mouth curve in a smile, and she knew then for the first time that there would be no more dread of the Distant Mood, no more tension and worry because she did not

understand or could not cope with his changes of humor. When
he bent over her a moment later and she felt the love in every
line of his frame flow into hers, she knew he would never again
belong to anyone else except her.

EPILOGUE

When they had all gone and she was alone in the still quiet house, Marijohn sat down at the desk in the drawing-room and took a clean sheet of notepaper and a pen.

She sat thinking for a long while. It was very peaceful. Outside the sky was blue and the stream rushed past the waterwheel at the end of the drive.

She dipped her pen in the ink.

"My darling Jon," she wrote quickly at last with firm, resolute strokes of the pen. "By the time you read this, you will be home in Canada in the midst of your new life. I know there's so much for you there, more now than ever before, as both Sarah and Justin will be with you and in time Sarah will have children of her own. I want you to know first and foremost how glad I am about this, because almost more than anything else on Earth I want you to be happy and to lead a rich, full, worthwhile life.

"I have decided to go back to the only world I think I could ever live in now, the world of Anselm's Cross—or of any convent anywhere. I did think of avoiding this by traveling abroad, Jon, just as you suggested, but I don't think I would find peace abroad any more than I would find peace here at Clougy.

"When I look back I can see how clearly the fault was mine. In a way, it was I who killed Sophia and I who killed Michael and I who almost killed Sarah. I ruined Michael's life and very nearly yours as well. You could forgive me for both I expect, but I know you'll never really forgive me for what happened to Sarah

that night. Max always said *you* were the one who was the constant source of danger to everyone around you, but he was wrong.
I was the source of danger, not you. Everything I touch seems to
turn into a disaster. If you're honest with yourself you'll see that
as clearly as I see it now.

"You did talk when we parted of perhaps seeing me again in
the very distant future, but Jon darling, I know you so well and
I know when you're lying to save me pain. I shall never see you
again, not because you think it's better for us to be apart or because you owe it to Sarah or for any other noble reason, but because you *don't want* to see me—because you know, just as I
know, that it was through me that Sarah was nearly killed and
your second marriage nearly wrecked as utterly as your first, and
you never want to run the risk of that happening again. I don't
blame you; in a way, the knowledge that I'll never see you again
helps me to see more clearly which course I now have to take.

"I've just three things left to say. Don't pity me, don't blame
yourself, and don't ever try to communicate with me, even out
of kindness, in the years to come.

"All my love, darling, now and always, and all the happiness
you could ever wish for,

"Your own,

"Marijohn"